PRAISE FOR PETER ABRAHAMS

Last of the Dixie Heroes

"There is plenty of suspense . . . It takes a deft touch to be able to mingle the modern world of Atlanta with glimpses of that bloody past which still haunts the South, and Abrahams has that skill."
 —*I Love a Mystery* newsletter

"Spellbinding . . . Fast-paced . . . An exciting psychological thriller."
 —BookBytes.com

"With his diverse settings, quirky characters, and intriguing story lines, Abrahams has set himself up as a master of engrossing, off-the-beaten-track suspense yarns."
 —*Publishers Weekly*

A Perfect Crime

"Abrahams gets the human dimensions just right. . . . Each stage of this perverse puzzle has been constructed with deadly artistry."
 —*The New York Times Book Review*

Crying Wolf

"Great suspense . . . Tightly written and full of unexpected but plausible twists . . . Abrahams is among the best at this game."
 —*The Denver Post*

Also by Peter Abrahams

Published by Ballantine Books

LAST
OF THE
DIXIE
HEROES

Peter Abrahams

FAWCETT BOOKS • NEW YORK

A Fawcett Book
Published by The Ballantine Publishing Group
Copyright © 2001 by Pas de Deux
Excerpt from *The Tutor* copyright © 2002 by Pas de Deux

This book contains an excerpt from the forthcoming hardcover edition of *The Tutor* by Peter Abrahams. This excerpt has been set for this edition only and may not reflect the final content of the forthcoming edition.

www.ballantinebooks.com

ISBN 0-345-43940-6

Manufactured in the United States of America

First Hardcover Edition: June 2001
First Paperback Edition: June 2002

OPM 10 9 8 7 6 5 4 3 2 1

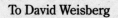

To David Weisberg

Many thanks to F. George Emanuel and the men of D Company, 22nd Massachusetts Volunteer Infantry; Andrew H. Addoms III, 34th Battalion, Virginia Cavalry; Al Aritos; Martha McCullough; Mack Westbrook; Frederick H. Crudder; Skippy White; Mark Tavani; and my wife Diana, who gave me the idea.

The fiery trial through which we pass will light us down, in honor or dishonor, to the last generation.

Abraham Lincoln

ONE

Roy thought he heard his son crying in the night. He got up, went down the hall, opened Rhett's door, smelled the emptiness inside.

And woke up. Must have been asleep until that moment. How else to explain it? Roy didn't turn on the light.

Must have been sleepwalking, or something close to it, and dreaming uneasy dreams, because first, Rhett had never done much crying in the night, not even as a baby, and now he was eleven years old; and second, his empty bedroom had been empty for more than six months—Roy could probably have calculated the exact duration if he'd had a mind to. No need to turn on the light, no need to see last year's posters left behind, outgrown clothes in the closet, how neat everything was. No one had switched off the air conditioner in the window. Cold air followed Roy back to his room.

Roy awoke for good a few hours later, alone in a bed meant for two. There'd been a time in his life, back when he himself was a boy and even after, when he'd awakened every morning with a bubble of happiness in his chest, when he'd actually jumped out of bed. He could remember that feeling; not bring it back, just remember.

Roy found an inch of coffee in the pot, left over from the day before, or maybe the day before that. Heated it up, drank it down. Alone in a bed made for two: a weepy kind of line that could have come straight from a country song, and not even a good one. Roy's mother had loved country, he'd practically been raised on country, but Roy didn't like it

1

anymore. The truth was he'd begun listening to gospel when no one was around, a bit funny maybe, since he didn't believe in God.

Six months, two weeks, seven hours. It was easy to calculate, because Marcia had walked out late on a Sunday night.

"What's the meaning of this?" said Roy, climbing into the passenger seat of Gordo's Altima. They took turns driving each other to work.

"Meaning of what, good buddy?"

Roy's beeper went off; then Gordo's. They checked the numbers.

"Do Mondays suck enough?" said Gordo. 6:09—not light, not dark, not warm, not cold. They pulled away from Roy's house, drove a few quick blocks, hit traffic.

"The stuff in the back," Roy said.

"Oh, that," said Gordo; but he didn't go on.

"Funny look on your face," Roy said.

"Just the teensiest bit hungover."

"Besides that," Roy said. Gordo was the teensiest bit hungover most Monday mornings. "Kind of sheepish," Roy said.

"Sheepish?"

Roy twisted around, had a good look in back.

What Roy saw: a strange-colored jacket, not yellow, not brown, something in between, with wood buttons; heavy gray wool trousers with yellow suspenders; a funny little cap, like the cops wore in those Inspector Clouseau movies Rhett liked, but gray; a belt with a big metal buckle and a black pouch hanging off it; and a long rifle with one of those tamping-down things at the end, Roy couldn't think of the name. With some difficulty—it was much heavier than he'd expected and too long for the car—he wrestled the rifle into the front seat. A kid stared down from the back of a Range Rover. The kid's lips moved. Her mother, talking on a cell phone at the wheel, turned to look down too. The light changed to green and the Range Rover turned up Peachtree; Gordo continued straight ahead.

"It's just a reproduction," Gordo said. "You have no idea what the real ones go for."

"The real what?" said Roy.

"Enfield muskets. That's an exact reproduction of the 1853 fifty-eight caliber. Made in London, Roy. London, England."

"It was?"

"The originals," Gordo said. "This is from Italy."

Roy sniffed the muzzle. "Is it loaded?"

"Course not. We don't fire bullets anyway. Just black powder cartridges."

"Who's we?"

Gordo glanced at him, still sheepish, but smiling now. "Seventh Tennessee Cavalry."

Roy didn't get it.

"CSA."

"CSA?"

"For Christ sake, Roy—the Confederacy."

Roy looked at Gordo: sheepish, hungover, sleepless. Despite all that, he seemed pretty cheerful, which wasn't like Gordo on the morning commute. Cheerful, and unaware of the blood seeping from a shaving cut on his neck, forming a tiny bubble that would soon overflow and stain the white collar of his shirt.

Gordo took the northbound 75/85 ramp, nosed his way into the mass of cars, all poised to move but none moving, like grains of sand in the upper half of a blocked hourglass. Roy checked his watch. It was going to be close. It was always close. The sky was getting lighter, light enough to see there wasn't a cloud in it. Not a cloud in the sky, but it wasn't blue, more like the color of brass, one of those red brass alloys with a high copper content. Roy felt that tightness in his chest and throat, realized he wasn't getting enough air. Headlights blinked out, first two by two, then by the hundreds, thousands. But no one moved. This was the moment Gordo would say Monday sucked again, or work sucked, or life sucked; but he didn't.

"Ever been up to Kennesaw, Roy?"

"Sure. With you—that charity golf thing. It was only last—"

"I mean the battlefield."

Roy thought, Was there a high school trip? He had a clear memory of Mrs. Sangster, the history teacher, asleep on the bus, head back, mouth open, bad teeth; and a vague memory of headstones. Roy himself had good teeth. He brushed twice a day and flossed once. That had been one of his mother's rules: *Don't you go ruinin' that smile on me now*. "Maybe," Roy told Gordo.

"They had a reenactment up there this weekend," Gordo said.

"Reenactment of what?" Roy's mind had wandered: the thought of high school had brought Rhett to mind, Rhett who'd be getting ready for school at that moment. Roy could picture him getting dressed—it still took him a while to tie the laces of his sneakers, and there'd be that little shock of hair standing up at the back of his head no matter what he did.

"Not the real battle," Gordo said. "There weren't any Union men, not this time of year. It was more like educational—drilling, firing the artillery, that kind of thing. Anyway, it being Sunday, with Brenda's ma in town—"

"Meaning church," Roy said.

"Right. So I kind of drove myself on up to Kennesaw. And before you'd know it—boom."

"Boom what?"

"I'm enlisted."

"Enlisted?"

"In the Seventh Tennessee. You're not listening, Roy."

"It's real?"

"The Seventh Tennessee? Fought at Chickamauga—what's realer than that?"

"I meant now."

"Course we're not at 1863 strength, nowhere near, but everything's as close to the same as it can be. Check out that shell jacket—identical down to the thread count. Just there's no bullets and no horses, excepting the colonel's."

"And they gave you all this stuff?"

"Gave? You have to buy it off the sutler."

"What's that?"

"Like a store, but in a tent."

"How much?"

"Eleven hundred."

"Dollars?"

"Plus tax."

"You were carrying that kind of cash?"

"Don't be dumb, Roy. They take Visa."

"The official card of the Civil War?" Roy said; wouldn't ordinarily have said that aloud, but he wasn't dumb.

Gordo looked at him from the corner of his eye, then laughed. "I'll have to pass that on."

"To who?"

"The boys in the unit. They've got a good sense of humor about all this."

"Does Brenda?"

"She doesn't exactly know yet."

Gordo didn't look quite so cheerful anymore. Roy knew Gordo couldn't afford that kind of money for funny-looking clothes and a reproduction musket. No more than he could. They worked the same job, made the same money: $42,975 a year. Roy tried to figure in his head what percentage 1,100 was of 42,975. That kind of thing didn't come naturally to him, but it was good practice. He'd noticed that people who got promoted at work always had a head for figures. Traffic started moving. Gordo picked that moment to honk in frustration, so it must have been at Brenda, or something like that. Roy came up with a figure around four percent, but that didn't seem right.

Their building appeared in the northwest, just off the connector. It was a shiny brass-colored tower, not unlike the color of the sky at that moment, with the word *Chemerica* in red letters at the top. Except this morning, when all it said was: *hem*.

"What's going on?" Gordo said.

"Putting up bigger letters," Roy said.

They parked in the employee lot in sublevel five under the building, got into an elevator containing two execs. "Up five-eighths already and it's only—" one was saying. He stopped when he saw Roy and Gordo. Roy noticed that the execs had their weight on the balls of their feet, like sprinters. The elevator couldn't go fast enough for them.

Roy and Gordo got off at sublevel one. A right turn led to shipping, left to receiving. Roy and Gordo turned right. No actual shipping or receiving took place in the Chemerica building; nothing went in or out but product orders, the weights, volumes, packaging protocols, routes, carriers, tariffs, handling instructions, and state, federal, and internationally mandated warnings, all coded in digital transmissions. Roy and Gordo worked in the Asia/Oceania section, a cluster of a dozen cubicles in the far corner of the floor. A sign overhung their section from one of the strip lights: THE IRREGULARS. The sign had been slung up at a Christmas party several years before by a shipper fired not long after. The name remained.

6:59. Roy entered his cubicle, B27. It had shoulder-high padded walls, a chair, a desk, a monitor, a keyboard, a shelf holding the reg books— tariffs, carriers, customs, rates, routes, safety—and a framed photo of Rhett in his Pop Warner uniform. Next to it was an empty rectangle of unfaded wall padding. Marcia's picture lay in the bottom drawer of Roy's desk.

Roy checked his screen. He had a ton of KOH from Mobile due at their subsidiary in Osaka in a week; calcium carbonate, amount unspecified, to Karachi, P. of O. unspecified, date unspecified; two ounces of radioactive uranyl acetate to the Ministry of Science and Engineering in Singapore; three forty-footers and one twenty-footer of—

"Gentlemen?"

Roy looked up; got up, since you couldn't see over the wall sitting down. Cubicles worked against you coming and going. Curtis was standing in the open area between

Asia/Oceania and Central/South America (except Mexico). The shippers from the two departments, all men, all white, were looking at him over their walls. Curtis wore a wireless headset so he could communicate at all times with whomever he communicated with, a charcoal-gray suit, a navy shirt with white collar and cuffs, a deep crimson tie. He was probably the best-dressed employee in the building, including the ones in seventeenth-floor corner offices. That bothered a lot of the guys, but not Roy. Roy liked Curtis.

"Morning," Curtis said. "There's been a little—"

P.J., B33, two cubicles behind Roy's, came hurrying in late from the elevator, knotting his tie—they all wore ties, a Chemerica rule—saw there was some kind of meeting, slowed down, tried to look inconspicuous, not easy at his size. Roy noticed that P.J. had a shaving cut too, worse than Gordo's.

"—screwup," Curtis continued, not even glancing at P.J. "Email on this was supposed to go out from New York last week, with activation set for next week, but A didn't happen and B seems to be happening ahead of schedule. Like today. Anyone see anything different on the way in?"

No one had.

"No one noticed the company name descending?"

Roy had, of course: he just hadn't known that was what Curtis was after. He'd been too busy listening to the way Curtis talked; long sentences and big words just rolling out of him, like he should have been a preacher.

"Fact is," Curtis said, "as of today, there is no Chemerica."

Roy saw something flash across the computer screens, looked down at his, saw that *Chemerica* had been replaced by *Globax*.

"Welcome, gentlemen, to Globax." Curtis paused, appeared to be listening to something. "A new name, more in tune with the reality of our position in the world economy. Everything else stays the same." He looked around. "Any questions?"

"This mean raises all around?" said DeLoach, B30.

"You won't believe how big," said Curtis.

No one laughed.

"And in the real world," Curtis said, "the stock was up a couple ticks in the overnight."

No one said anything about that. Roy himself owned no shares of Chemerica, Globax, or anything else.

"New ID tags'll be down by three." Curtis turned to go, paused. "And P.J.?"

"Yeah."

"Stop the bleeding."

Curtis walked away toward his office, a big glass-walled room built on a sort of square dais in the center of the vast space. As he did, he spotted something on the wall of Gordo's cubicle. It affected his stride for a moment, as though one leg had gone fleetingly numb. After he was gone, Roy stood up to look. Gordo had stuck a tiny flag on his wall, the red flag with the crossing blue bars and the white stars.

"Stop the bleeding?" said P.J. when they were all back in their cubicles. He spoke in a low voice, but Roy could hear him. "What the hell's that supposed to mean?"

"You've got a shaving cut," Roy said, not looking up from his screen. Three freight cars of ammonium nitrate had gone missing somewhere between Shanghai and Chongqing. He clicked on *Maps*.

Voices rose over the padded walls.

"And your ass is on the line," said DeLoach.

"Fuck you," said P.J. "And that's pretty funny, what with him taking a shot at New York. Curtis is New York's blue-eyed boy."

One weird way of putting it, even if true. There was a long silence. Then Gordo spoke, almost inaudible. "Ain't going to be no jobs for nobody."

"What are you talking about?" said DeLoach.

"Globax," said Gordo. "Can't you see what's happening?"

"It's just a name change," Roy said.

He stared for a moment at the map on the screen. Shanghai, Chongqing, Osaka, Karachi, Singapore: he'd never been to any of those places but he kind of knew their quirks. That was one of the things he liked about the job. What else? He liked the guys. And there was opportunity for promotion—Roy had seen lots of men get promoted from his floor, transferred to jobs all over the world. At Curtis's suggestion, he'd signed up for an industrial management course at Georgia Tech one night a week, to make his chances a little better. As for the negatives: the hours, seven to four-thirty, which always meant five, Monday to Friday; the vacation time—Roy was up to thirteen paid days after eight years with the company; the health plan—

Roy stopped thinking about it. Every job had negatives.

He got back to those three overdue freight cars of ammonium nitrate somewhere between Shanghai and Chongqing. Ammonium nitrate was water reactive: that was the tricky part. Roy wondered whether it was raining in China and whether they'd made sure to use the watertight cars specified in the order. For a moment Roy, picturing what happened on the training films when moisture got into a load of ammonium nitrate, felt that not-getting-enough-air thing. He clicked back to his original order and found that he had indeed specified watertight cars. He took his hand off the inhaler in his pocket.

Roy sent thirty overdue gallons of methane sulfonic acid on a commercial flight to Kuala Lumpur; found himself in a misunderstanding with the Miami office over a container of assorted specialty chemicals and tried without much success to sort it out; sent a twenty-footer of methyl mercaptan to Manila via a freighter out of Oakland; tried again with Miami; failed to find the ammonium nitrate between Shanghai and Chongqing; went down to the cafeteria, came back with a burrito and a Coke—Coke ran free in the cafeteria, one of the perks—ate at his desk. He heard Gordo ripping the tinfoil off his fried chicken from home—didn't have to look, he could smell it—and was thinking of saying something about that flag stuck to the wall of Gordo's cubicle, when his phone rang. He thought: Cesar in Miami. But it wasn't.

"Mr. Hill?" A woman; Roy didn't recognize her voice. Ten years ago he would have said she was from up north, hadn't been raised down here, but now, at least in the city, it was getting harder to tell.

"Yes," said Roy.

"This is—" Ms. Somebody. Roy didn't catch the name—a long one, maybe Jewish; which was odd because he was used to catching all kinds of strange foreign names. "I'm the assistant principal at Buckhead Middle School," the woman said.

Roy caught everything after that. He said stupid things like "But I thought my wi— I thought Marcia—" and "What do you mean, incident?", but he caught it.

He checked the time: 1:37. You didn't leave work at Chemerica—Globax—at 1:37. Not on a Monday, not when things were this busy, not for personal reasons. It wasn't part of the corporate culture. Roy called Marcia's work, was told she wasn't in today, tried the cell and home numbers, got voice mail each time, said nothing. Who else to call? There was no one. Roy rose.

Gordo glanced up at him over the padded wall. "What's up?"

"Something with Rhett."

"Like what?"

"Got to go get him."

"Now? What's wrong?"

Roy left his cubicle, crossed the floor, went up the steps to Curtis's glassed-in office. Curtis had someone in there: a silver-haired guy, the kind who worked on the seventeenth floor. Roy hesitated outside. Curtis waved him in.

"Speak of the devil," Curtis said.

Roy didn't know what to make of that.

"Just talking about you, Roy, Bill and I. Know Bill Pegram?"

Roy didn't know Bill Pegram. They shook hands.

"Mr. Pegram's VP tech personnel." Tech personnel included shipping.

"Curtis's been saying some nice things about you, Roy," said Bill Pegram. "Real nice things."

Roy wasn't taking this in very well. He had to get out of there.

"You're doing a fine job for us, Roy," said Pegram. "How you likin' it?"

"Liking it?"

"Working for the company."

"It's a good job, Mr. Pegram."

Pegram nodded. "I know you've been passed over a few times when it comes to promotions, Roy. Doesn't mean we don't appreciate your good work. The competition is tough. Didn't make you bitter, did it, Roy?"

"Not at all." Where the hell was this going? He fought the urge to check his watch.

"Glad to hear it," said Pegram. "Bitterness is like the snake that bites his own damn tail." He paused, waiting for a response.

Roy nodded, maybe a little too impatiently. The snake idea came from a motivational speaker they'd had last year, or the year before that.

"That's the boy," said Pegram. "If you can keep this under your hat, there may be a few things opening up soon. Nice things, Roy."

Roy got it: he was being considered for promotion at last. He should probably say he was grateful or they wouldn't be disappointed or something like that. He said: "Curtis, can I talk to you a moment?"

Pegram looked puzzled, the way some people do, half lowering one eyelid. Curtis was doing the same thing. "About this?" he said.

"Something's come up," Roy said, moving toward the door, almost taking Curtis by the hand; he didn't know how else to get him alone.

Curtis followed him out. They stood on the other side of the glassed-in office, Pegram watching from within.

"Just don't tell me it's a big bang somewhere," Curtis said. The big bang—an explosion caused by some shipping error—was their worst fear.

Roy told him what it was.

Curtis's eyelid fluttered down again, came back up. He gave Roy a look. "If you can get someone to cover for you," he said in the kind of voice used for someone you don't know well. He went back inside.

Roy started down Curtis's stairs. He tried not to turn back, but couldn't help himself. Curtis was talking to Pegram. Pegram was watching Roy. His face seemed to get narrower.

Gordo covered for him. "And Roy?" Gordo said. "Here's a little present for the boy."

Gordo handed Roy a stained white thing, maybe an inch long, rounded at one end, surprisingly heavy. Lead, probably, oxidized lead. "What's this?"

"A bullet, Roy. A real bullet from Kennesaw. One of ours—you can tell by the two rings."

"You found it?"

"In the souvenir shop," Gordo said. "Seventy-five cents."

Roy put it in his pocket, took the elevator down to employee parking on S5, went to his space, found it empty. Empty. He felt real funny for a moment, like some bad fate was happening, then recalled he'd driven in with Gordo. Therefore—what?

Taxi. Roy went to the elevators, saw they were all at seventeen, hurried up the ramp on foot. He was running by the time he came to the exit booth.

No taxis on the street. Roy hardly ever took taxis. In the movies they were always cruising up and—

"Hey, Roy," said the attendant in the booth. The old guy who always wore a Braves cap, and in fact looked a little like Henry Aaron, as Aaron might have looked if he'd developed a drinking problem.

"I need a taxi."

"Yes, sir," said the old man, picking up his phone.

Roy rode in a taxi. He checked the time: 2:27. One of the side mirrors was tilted up at a useless angle, reflecting the image of the new sign high above. He'd been right about one thing: the letters were bigger. They'd also changed from red to blue. GLOBAX was already in place, except for the big blue *X*, rising on a crane. From the window of the taxi, the whole city seemed unfamiliar, as though Roy had touched down somewhere new. He started getting less air, reached for the inhaler, felt Gordo's bullet instead. It had a nice shape, felt comfortable in his hand. He held on to it like a prayer bead.

TWO

Rhett lay on the couch in the school nurse's office, holding a bloody tissue over his nose. One eye, swollen and purpling, was closed; his open eye stared at the ceiling. The nurse was on the phone, laughing softly at whatever she was being told.

Roy stepped in front of Ms. Steinwasser and walked over to him. The nurse got off the phone.

Roy didn't know what to say. "Hey." That was what he said, the word coming out a little deeper than he'd intended, and a little ragged.

Rhett's good eye moved, found him. Roy saw a lot of emotion in that eye, far more than he wanted to, far more than he could read. "I got in a fight, Dad." Rhett's lower lip trembled and so did his voice, but he didn't cry.

"I can see that," Roy said. Maybe he should have said something else.

Rhett cried then, just one sob before he got a grip.

Roy put his hand on Rhett's shoulder, so bony. "Hey," he said again.

"Take me home, Dad."

That meant Marcia's. "Now you're talking," he said.

The nurse was on her feet. "I'll just check on that nosebleed one last time."

Roy turned to Ms. Steinwasser. "I'm still not clear on what happened exactly."

"As I mentioned, Mr. Hill, there was a fight at recess. The

fields are very well supervised here at Buckhead, but unfortunately the boys got behind the big magnolia by the wall and no one saw them right away."

"How many were in it?" Roy said.

"In it?" said Ms. Steinwasser.

"The fight."

"Just two," said Ms. Steinwasser. "Which was quite enough, as you can see."

As you can see: Roy didn't quite get that part. Was she saying that Rhett's face was convenient proof of some theory of hers? "Where's the other kid?" Roy said.

"We sent him home."

"Who started it?"

Ms. Steinwasser's tone changed slightly, but enough to bring back memories of his own schooling. "We haven't really found it productive to dwell on issues of that sort," she said. "The rule is that fighting for any reason is forbidden."

"Cody started it," Rhett said, raising his head; a tiny drop of blood appeared at the opening of one nostril. Roy's mind made a weird connection to Gordo's and P.J.'s shaving cuts. "He hit me for no reason."

"Better lay back down now," said the nurse.

Rhett lay back down.

"In this case," said Ms. Steinwasser, "both boys claim the other was the instigator. That's not uncommon. The policy mandates a minimum level-two sanction of three after-school detentions. Given that it's a first offense in each case, I'm going to forgo anything more severe, such as suspensions, on this occasion."

It all sounded sensible and crazy at the same time. Roy felt like objecting, but he didn't know where to start. He was back in school, all right. Roy went over to the table. "Let's go, son." He fought an urge to just lift the boy up and carry him away, instead watched Rhett struggle up to a sitting position, swing his legs out, stand up.

"Bleeding's pretty much stopped is one good thing," the nurse said. "Not dizzy, are you, Reed?"

"I'm fine," said Rhett, but the color drained from his face.

"It's Rhett," Roy said. He took the boy's arm and walked him out.

They waited in front of the school for a taxi. Buckhead-type cars went by—Benzes, Audis, Lexuses, big SUVs—but no taxis. Rhett withdrew his arm.

A little farther up the street, a Jaguar convertible pulled over to the curb, top down. A boy jumped off a swing in the play area and trotted to the car; a broad-faced boy about Rhett's age, but a lot bigger. As he was getting into the Jag, the boy noticed Rhett and gave him a big, smirking smile. Rhett recoiled.

"That the one?" Roy said.

Rhett didn't answer. The boy turned to them as the car passed by. Roy got a good look at his face: not a mark on it. The boy made a hitchhiking gesture with his thumb. Then he said something to the driver, who looked like a grown-up version of himself. The driver tousled the boy's hair as they disappeared around the corner. Roy thought he saw a cigar stub spinning through the air.

"I want to punch his fucking face in," Rhett said.

"Shouldn't say fucking," Roy said, and felt like an idiot.

Rhett said no more. He had both hands squeezed into tight fists, little cubes incapable of doing much damage. Roy saw a taxi, good thing, because by now he'd proved even to himself that he had no idea how to make this better with words. He raised his hand.

They sat in the back of the cab, Rhett with his fists on his knees. Roy had to make an effort to keep his own hands relaxed. After five or ten minutes, Rhett's hands relaxed a little too.

Roy tried again. "What was it all about?"

"I already told you. He hit me for no reason."

"Just out of the blue."

"I said I scored a touchdown in Pop Warner last season."

"And then?"

Rhett's voice rose. "I told you—then he punched me in the eye. Are you retarded or something?"

The driver's eyes shifted in the mirror.

Roy tried silence again. They went over a hill. The houses got bigger, brick mansions set farther and farther back from the street. It turned out that living in Buckhead had always been one of Marcia's dreams: the word itself was magic to her. The house she and Roy had bought in Virginia-Highland, a fixer-upper but a house she'd wanted very badly, had been, in her mind, it also turned out, the first step in a series of moves that would end on a street like this; like landing on Boardwalk at last. The street Marcia now lived on wasn't quite as nice as this—the houses not so old, not so big, not set so far back—but it was Buckhead. The driver turned onto it.

Roy glanced at Rhett. He was sitting very still, looking straight ahead. Roy could see only one half of his face, the swollen half. The closed eye was puffier now, more purple; the long lashes hung limp and damp from the rim of the lid. Roy had one more thought.

"I was a skinny kid too," he said.

"I don't care."

Bad idea. Either Rhett hadn't got the part that was meant to be comforting—that Roy had grown up to be big and strong, at least big and strong enough to have suited up on the Bulldog special teams in his freshman, and only, year over in Athens—or it hadn't been comforting, period. Maybe the opposite. Was it possible Rhett didn't see him as big and strong? Roy made third team all-state as a tight end his senior year in high school, even though he hadn't weighed what tight ends should weigh. He caught the reflection of his face in the side window, realized he was closer to tight end level now, the added pounds being of the wrong kind and years too late. The reflection of Rhett's swollen face loomed behind his. Roy had no idea how the boy saw him. The taxi stopped in front of Marcia's house.

*   *   *

Marcia's house, with its three-story central section and two-story wings, wasn't big by neighborhood standards, but it was a lot bigger than the house she'd left behind. Was it as nice? Not in Roy's opinion, but he knew nothing about architecture. And why did he think of it as Marcia's house? It was the boyfriend's house and would be until she married him.

"Where's your mom today?" Roy said.

"At work."

Not true, but Roy didn't say anything. Rhett took out his key and opened the door.

Roy had never been inside the house. The Saturday passing back and forth of Rhett always took place on the front steps. Brenda, Gordo's wife, had once asked Roy what the house was like inside. Gordo had given her a look. Roy didn't know, didn't want to know. He followed Rhett into the house.

First came a big square entrance hall, with a high ceiling and a polished hardwood floor. Roy could see that it was a stylish kind of room, but there was nothing in it except a chandelier tilted against the wall in one corner, some of the crystals loose on the floor. They went through another high-ceilinged empty room, possibly a dining room, and into the kitchen.

The kitchen had built-in appliances, three chairs and a card table piled with unopened mail, and a phone blinking its red message light.

"Hungry?" Roy said.

Rhett was staring out the back window. A pile of dirt lay by a hole in the backyard. Roy opened the fridge.

A big fridge, the biggest he'd ever seen. There was a bottle of Absolut on one shelf, two containers of mocha yogurt on another, and three lemons in the fruit drawer. Roy closed the door.

He went over and stood by Rhett. "What's the hole all about?"

"Who cares?" Rhett said. He left the room.

Roy stood in Marcia's kitchen. He found himself staring

out the window as Rhett had, his gaze on the dirt pile. A strange feeling overcame him, a sense of being cut off from his own life, completely disconnected. At the same time, he started having problems with his air supply. Roy turned from the window, eyed the mail on the table: bills, almost all of it. The disconnected feeling didn't go away. He took a deep breath, or tried to, and went to find Rhett.

Roy walked back through some more rooms—one had a big-screen TV and a futon, the others were empty—and up a broad, winding staircase. At the top was a long corridor with four or five doors off it, all ajar. Roy glanced in the first two rooms, both bare, and then the third.

The third room was furnished. It had a rug, a king-size bed, unmade and rumpled, another big-screen TV, and a desktop computer. A man sat at the computer, his back to the door. The man, who might once have been in shape but wasn't now, was in his underwear. This was Barry. Roy had met him only once, in the course of one of those front steps exchanges. No shaking hands or anything: just a nod back and forth. Barry had been dressed for golf that time, in a silk polo shirt and a big straw hat. Seeing him like this, with his pudgy pale back and a little crack showing above the band of his briefs, was a lot different. Roy rapped his knuckles on the inside of the door.

Barry spun around. "Ever heard of knocking?"

"I knocked."

"Anyway you're late. It was supposed to be ten."

Roy remembered that Barry was from Boston or somewhere. He had a way of talking that Roy didn't like.

"You're the electric guy, right?" said Barry.

Roy put a few things together: Ms. Steinwasser's calls from the school, the blinking message light, Barry here the whole time, not picking up. *Barry says I can call him Daddy too.*

"I'm Rhett's father," Roy said.

Barry squinted at him. "So you are." He hunched forward a

little; his hands crossed over his groin. "What are you doing here, anyway?"

"Where's Marcia?"

"Momentito there, amigo. I asked the first question." He rose, a flabby guy but big, much bigger than Roy, and confident even in his underwear. "Or maybe you're forgetting this is my house you barged into."

"I'm not forgetting anything."

"What's that supposed to mean?" Barry came closer.

Roy said an ugly thing. It just popped out, popped out of some pit of weird and angry confusion inside him. "Your tits are bigger than hers," he said. He regretted it at once. To cheapen Marcia like that, to mix her up with this guy in a physical way, was sickening.

Barry reddened, but just from the neck up. The rest of him went even paler. Roy knew this was crazy, two grown men moving toward violence. He knew that, but deep inside him a voice that sounded like his, but rawer, was saying: Take a swing at me. His lungs suddenly filled with oxygen, rich and potent.

Moving toward violence, with Rhett in the house. Wouldn't there be something very wrong with a father like that? Inside him, the raw voice went silent.

At the same time Barry's computer beeped. "You're going to regret this very much," said Barry. "Trust me. Do I have to tell you what Marcia will say when she gets home from the hospital?"

"Hospital?"

Barry turned back to the computer.

"What's she doing in the hospital?"

On the computer screen, something happened that Barry didn't like. He banged his fist on the desk.

"Is something wrong with her?" Roy said.

"Time's up," said Barry.

"What are you talking about?"

Barry's eyes were on the screen. "Can't you see I've got a play going here?"

"Play?"

Barry shot him a glance, so brief Roy almost missed the strange look on his face, almost triumphant. "I'm shorting Yahoo," he said. "There's a freebie you don't deserve."

Roy backed out of the room. The last thing he saw was the king-size bed. Mixing Marcia with this guy in a physical way: maybe the dumbest thought he'd ever had. How much more mixed could they be? They fucked in that bed every night. *Shouldn't say fucking.* And Barry didn't even bother getting dressed in the morning.

Roy went down the hall, tried the next room. Rhett was inside, lying on the bed, face to the wall, hand between his knees. It was a bigger bedroom than his old one, and had things his old one didn't—a TV, compact stereo system, video game console. The little tuft of hair was sticking up at the back of Rhett's head.

"I thought Barry owned a mortgage company," Roy said.

There was a long silence. Roy heard Barry banging his fist on the desk again. "He did," Rhett said. "Now he trades online."

"Is that a step up?" Roy said.

Rhett laughed, soft and quickly ended, but a laugh.

"Let's go home," Roy said.

Rhett turned over, head at a funny angle to get Roy in view with his good eye. "Home?"

"Just for the night." The counselor had advised that Rhett not sleep in his old bedroom: *We like to smooth the transition.* "I'll get you to school in the morning."

"I'm not going back to school."

"Got to go to school, Rhett."

"Why?"

"If kids don't go, the whole system falls apart. Then where would we be?"

"Is that meant to be funny?"

"Guess not, if you have to ask."

Rhett smiled, not much of one and quickly erased, but a smile. He got off the bed. Roy walked him down the hall.

"We'll be at my place," Roy said as they passed the master bedroom.

Hunched over his computer, Barry made no reply. Roy was getting plenty of air now, his lungs working effortlessly. Maybe the Buckhead atmosphere agreed with him.

THREE

Rhett loved Monopoly. Roy ordered pizza, got out the board. Rhett chose the cannon, Roy the top hat. Pizza came. Rhett picked the pepperoni off his slices and laid them aside. They polished off a family-size Coke. Roy landed on North Carolina with a hotel, rolled snake eyes on his next turn, hitting Pennsylvania, also with a hotel, to end the game. Rhett counted his winnings to the last dollar, brandished the wad of play money, and said, "I'm the man."

After that, they watched a sitcom that Roy had never seen and didn't find funny. It was about a group of people in their twenties sharing an apartment in a big city and putting each other down.

"You like this?"

"It's cool."

Rhett's swollen eye started seeping a little. He got tired, went to bed in his old bedroom. Roy thought of tucking him in, even reading him a story, but did none of that. The boy was going on twelve. " 'Night," he said from in front of the TV; and turned it off the moment Rhett was gone.

Roy called Gordo at home.

"He's out drilling," Brenda said.

"Drilling?"

"With the regiment. It's part of the initiation."

Roy felt the weight of the oxidized lead bullet against his thigh.

"Didn't he tell you about the regiment?" Brenda said.

"He told me."

"Pretty stupid, if you ask me."

"I don't know," Roy said, although he thought it was.

"Do you realize he may even have to pay for some kind of uniform? What army makes you do that? He said it could cost three or four hundred dollars."

Roy said nothing.

"It's even more, isn't it?" Brenda said. Brenda was quick; there were women like that all over the place these days.

"Did he mention anything about a train?" Roy said.

"What's a train got to do with it?"

"Just tell him I called," Roy said.

"A model train? 'The General,' or something like that?"

Roy sat down at the kitchen table. He had a stack of bills, not like Barry's—Barry's and Marcia's—but big for him. A legal bill—divorce was expensive; the counselor's bill; the mortgage, all his now; the home equity line; the car payment—two, in fact, since he'd missed last month; the two credit cards, both near their limits; utilities, phones, property tax. He wrote the checks he could cover, then sorted the remaining bills into immediate and less-immediate categories. *There may be a few things opening up soon. Nice things, Roy.* He considered calling Mr. Pegram at home. *A promotion would sure be nice, Mr. Pegram.* He didn't know how to put that in a businesslike way. Job, salary, payments, money in and out—it was a little like Monopoly, but no fun at all. Roy corrected that thought right away—he wasn't complaining. He liked the job, he liked the house, and his car, an Altima like Gordo's, but a little older, was all right too.

Roy got up, walked around the house—a small house, and a fixer-upper, but solid, and built of brick just like Marcia's, meaning no termites. He hadn't done much fixing up—any, in fact—since Marcia left. There were tools and a workbench in the cellar, his housewarming present from the Irregulars. Roy went downstairs.

He hadn't been in the cellar in months. A box of square

tiles—not marble but something that looked like marble—sat on the workbench. Marcia had wanted him to replace the linoleum in the downstairs bathroom. A long two-by-two was clamped in the vise. It took Roy a moment to recall what he'd been building when he'd left off: shelves for Rhett's room. Measurements were penciled on the two-by-two. Roy plugged in his Black & Decker and started sawing.

There hadn't been any tools in the series of small apartments he'd grown up in with his mother. This was Roy's first set. He liked using them. Sawdust sprayed in gold arcs lit by the hanging overhead bulb. Roy sawed, sanded, drilled, screwed the frame together, then started cutting the shelves from long pine boards. He lost himself in the sound of the saw, the grain patterns in the wood, the smell of cut pine. Especially the smell: it brought back memories, not specific memories, more the feeling, of when he was very young and they—ma, pappy, Roy—were all together, up in Tennessee.

A hand touched his shoulder.

Roy jumped inside his skin, spun around, his finger still on the trigger of the saw, and there was Marcia, the blade buzzing between them. He shut the thing off, got ready for her to be angry about something—the school, Rhett, his visit to her house. But Marcia didn't look angry. Neither did she look sick or hurt; if she'd been in the hospital, it couldn't have been serious. Marcia looked great—was still the best-looking woman he'd ever seen. That was his honest reaction. Roy tried to suppress it stillborn, but it popped to life in his head anyway.

Marcia looked up at him. "Thanks for handling everything today, Roy."

In the silence—a special silence in the aftermath of the sawing and what with being down below street level—Roy heard every subtlety in Marcia's voice, all the tones, all the vibrations, as though he could see the sound being produced by her throat, mouth, tongue. She had a beautiful voice. He started having the air supply problem again, bad enough for the inhaler this time, but he wouldn't reach for it with Marcia there.

"How is he?" she said.

"Sleeping."

"I looked in," Marcia said. "But I didn't want to turn on the light."

"He's got a black eye, is all."

"How did that happen?"

"Some schoolyard thing," Roy said.

They looked at each other. "I guess Barry didn't hear the phone," Marcia said.

"Too busy making money."

"That's a good one."

Roy didn't get that. Wasn't busy or wasn't making money? Couldn't be the latter: Roy had seen the brand-new Benz with the BARRY vanity plate, and more than that, he could tell that Barry was the moneymaking type, just from the way he pointed his chin at you when he was talking.

Marcia was looking at Rhett's shelves, coming together on the workbench. "Roy?"

"Yeah?"

She started to say something, changed her mind. "Got anything to drink?"

"Coke?"

"A grown-up drink, Roy."

"Have to look."

They went upstairs, Marcia leading, Roy trying to keep his eyes off her body. Marcia was in better shape than ever. How amazing that there'd been a time when a woman with a body like that had shared his bed.

Roy opened the fridge. He had a six-pack of Bud, one bottle gone.

"Any Chardonnay?" Marcia said.

"Sorry." Roy wasn't much of a drinker. Not that he didn't like booze: he knew that he liked it a little too much. His father had gone that route.

Roy opened two bottles of Bud, poured one into a glass for Marcia. She drained half of it in one gulp.

"Barry said you were in the hospital."

She nodded.

"You okay?"

"Just having my lips done, Roy."

He didn't understand.

"My lips. It's something I've always wanted."

Roy hadn't known; hadn't known she'd been dissatisfied with her lips, hadn't known what bothered her about them, didn't see anything different now.

"What do you think?" she said, smacking them together, sticking them out at him.

Roy studied her lips.

Marcia laughed. "You're hopeless," she said. "Don't you see how much fuller they are? Not those pencil-thin little miss priss things anymore. Full, Roy. Generous."

"Generous," Roy said. The word seemed strange in the context of lips, but it got him thinking.

Marcia laughed again. "You're something, Roy. You surely are." Meaning something stupid, he thought, ignorant when it came to changing lips, shorting Yahoo, all that. But then her foot touched his under the kitchen table.

Just for a moment.

He took a sip of beer, glanced at her over the bottle. Couldn't tell anything about the lips, but now that he thought about it, her hair seemed a little different, kind of copper-colored in a way that reminded him of the sky on the way to work that morning.

She was looking at him too.

"Did it hurt?" Roy said.

"Hurt?"

"The lip implant."

She laughed, spraying Bud across the table. "Implants are for tits, Roy. This was just an injection."

"Of what?" Roy said.

Marcia shrugged. "Something they shoot in there."

Tits: he remembered the ugly thing he'd said to Barry but the truth was he'd forgotten what Marcia's breasts looked like. Not that he wouldn't recognize them, he just couldn't picture them. Funny thing, though, he could recall the springy feel of them with a precision that made him uncomfortable.

"Another beer?" he said.

"You're not drinking."

"I am." He took a sip, fetched another bottle, refilled Marcia's glass. His forearm happened to brush her shoulder. She didn't shy away; the opposite, if anything.

He sat down.

"How's work?" she said.

"Work?" said Roy. "Not bad." He was tempted to tell her about being in line for a promotion. That awkward moment or two in Curtis's office, the mix-up with the train, none of that would add up to much. The important things were that Rhett was home safe in bed, and here was Marcia sitting around having a beer. "How's yours?" he asked.

She made that contemptuous little upper-lip movement of hers. Roy noticed the change then. "Busy," she said.

Marcia took a big drink, her lips a double crescent on the rim of the glass. Yes, they'd changed: sexy lips, no doubt about it. Her new lips reminded him a little of the lips of Curtis's girlfriend, who worked in the mayor's office and had once been on the cover of *Ebony*; maybe not the kind of thought you were supposed to have.

"I was in your house today," Roy said.

Marcia paused, eyeing him over the glass. "I'm sorry if there was a scene."

"No scene," Roy said, "but it's pretty impressive," and when she didn't reply, added, "your house in Buckhead."

"Buckhead," she said, almost like she now had some problem with it. Was it possible that she'd changed, that she'd come around to thinking that some simpler place was just as good? He took a close look at her, thought he detected changes other than the lips, internal ones.

"You lost some weight, Roy," she said.

He knew that wasn't true.

"Working out some?"

"Not much." Not at all—he'd let his gym membership lapse, was getting soft around the middle, didn't care. Maybe he seemed in shape compared to Bar—

"I'm of a mind to do something pretty crazy right now, Roy," she said, draining her glass.

"Like what?" Roy said. He thought: She's going to give me custody of Rhett.

Marcia reached across the table, laid her hand on his. Roy felt a jolt right through his body. The fact that she wasn't wearing the wedding ring he'd given her, had a big green stone, a real emerald, maybe, in its place, did nothing to lessen his reaction, possibly increased it. He gazed into her eyes, tried to stop, couldn't.

"Remember that time up in Tennessee?" she said.

He did, just from that.

"What was the name of that crick?"

"Crystal."

"Yeah," she said, getting up and coming over to him, standing behind his chair, close. "Crystal. I've been thinking about Crystal Crick lately." She touched him, very light, on the back of the neck, sent another jolt through him, this one with cold tingles at the end.

"What are you doing, Marcia?"

"What I want," she said, her fingers trailing down under his shirt collar. "What you want too, I hope."

He turned and stood up, breaking contact. "I don't understand," he said.

She raised her hand, as though she were about to lay it on his chest, but didn't. "You took over today."

"I'm his father." Roy would have stepped back, but the table was there.

"He's a lucky boy." Marcia's hand came down on his chest, her fingertips twisting around a button.

What was going on? Roy looked in her eyes, learned

nothing. All he knew was that she'd met Barry at a conference seven months ago, left Roy a few weeks later, and their divorce had come through last week. She'd always been decisive, long as he'd known her.

Marcia tilted up her face. "Give me a kiss, Roy."

"Why?" Roy said.

She paused. "Why?" she said. "Don't you want to?"

"But what's it for?" Roy said.

Marcia wrinkled her forehead in a way that was new, made him wonder if confusing things were happening in her life, made him feel a little sorry for her. "What's a kiss for?" she said. "Is that what you're asking?"

"What's this kiss for?" Roy said.

She stepped back. "You don't like me much anymore, do you?"

"It's not that," Roy said. "But what about Barry?" And a hundred other things, but that one came first.

"Do we have to talk about him?" Marcia said.

Roy didn't understand. In this very room, at almost the same time of night, she'd said: *I never dreamed I could feel this way about a person.* Meaning about Barry: that was the night Roy had first heard of him.

"We do," Roy said.

Marcia's eyes filled with tears. She wasn't a crier. "No one can ever make a mistake in your world, is that it?"

A mistake? Had it all been a mistake? "What kind of mistake?"

"Oh, Roy, don't badger me. I'm so tired I can't hardly think right now."

"Does this mean you and Barry aren't getting—"

Marcia started crying, just as he was thinking, She doesn't look tired, she looks great. But then she didn't look great anymore, with the tears, and her face all blotchy.

"I deserve this, you not caring anymore," she said, or something like that, it was hard to distinguish the words.

Roy's arms came up. His hands opened. They curled around her upper arms. He pulled her in.

Marcia cried against Roy's chest. Maybe it would have been all right if they'd left it at that, but one thing led to another.

Something buzzed in the night. Roy woke, turned on the light. Marcia was sitting on the edge of the bed, her back to him, bent over, fumbling through clothes on the floor. She straightened, put her cell phone to her ear. The buzzing stopped.

"Hello?" she said.

She listened. "I don't know any Grant—" she began, stopped. "Oh, I didn't recognize you without the doctor part. Why, yes, thank you, I'm fine." She listened some more, said, "Same to you," clicked off.

Marcia turned to Roy. For a moment her eyes didn't appear to be seeing him at all; then they did, although the look in them seemed a little funny, maybe too thoughtful for the middle of the night.

"Barry?" Roy said.

"Don't be silly, Roy. That was the doctor."

"What doctor?"

"Why, Dr. Nordman, the lip doctor. Doing his post-op check."

"Isn't it a bit late?"

"He just got out of surgery."

They looked at each other. He waited for the return of the expression he'd seen in her eyes before they fell asleep, a look not unlike the one she'd had on that trip down Crystal Creek. It didn't come back.

"Who's Grant?" he said.

"Dr. Nordman's Christian name. That's why I didn't recognize him at first."

She picked up her bra, slipped a strap over her shoulder, shrugged one of her breasts—he'd be able to picture them now—inside.

"You going?" Roy said.

She turned, smiled. "Can't very well stay all night, now can I?" She laughed. "Isn't this the craziest thing?"

"How do you mean?"

"Like an affair, or something." Shrug, and her other breast disappeared from view.

"What happens next?" Roy said.

She leaned forward, patted his arm. He could smell her; she smelled good. "We go from here," she said.

"How, exactly?"

"We'll think of something." She kissed him on the mouth, but quick, and turned off the light on her way out.

Roy thought he heard Rhett crying in the night. He got up, went down the hall, looked in Rhett's room. Rhett was in his bed, crying in the night. Roy lay down beside him.

"Everything's going to be fine," he said. He felt hope inside him, a good feeling, almost like happiness.

The crying stopped soon after.

FOUR

Rhett's eye looked a little better when Roy woke him in the morning, a lighter shade of purple and not so swollen.

"Not going to school," he said.

"Got to," Roy said.

"Why?"

"You're eleven. Going to school's what you do on school days."

"That's the reason?"

"Yeah. What else are you going to do?"

"Hang out."

"And go back to school when?"

Rhett shrugged, one shoulder slipping out of the neck of his T-shirt, those knuckle-shaped bones on top almost sticking through his skin.

"Got to go to school," Roy said.

"You're an inflexible jerk," Rhett said. "Like Barry."

Inflexible was a favorite of Marcia's. Roy probably should have been angry; he even wondered a bit why he was not. "Maybe a jerk," he said. "But not like Barry."

Rhett gave him a long look, then sat up and started getting out of bed.

In the car on the way to school, Rhett said: "How tall are you?"

Roy told him.

"What do you weigh?"

"Haven't weighed myself lately."

33

"How many push-ups can you do?"

"Not many."

"Like what?"

"Twenty, maybe." That seemed reasonable—in his football days, high school and that one year in Athens, he'd been able to do a hundred, winning free beers sometimes at parties. The air supply problems came later.

"That's all? Cody can do thirty-one."

And you? Roy thought. That's what counts. He didn't say it. Rhett was making his tight little fists again.

"I've got something for you," Roy said, reaching into his pocket. "Something you can show the kids." He handed Rhett the oxidized lead bullet.

"What's this?"

"A real bullet from the battle of Kennesaw Mountain."

Rhett gazed without much interest at the bullet resting on his palm. "It doesn't look like a bullet."

"It's old," Roy said. "You know about the battle of Kennesaw Mountain?"

"No."

Roy tried to recall the details of the battle and failed. "They haven't got to the Civil War yet?" he said.

"Mrs. Pullian calls it the War Between the States. That's what she says—'the War Between the States, or as some folks like to say, the Civil War.' "

Roy remembered he'd had one or two teachers like that too. "You like history?" he said.

"What do you mean?"

"Is it one of your favorites?"

"Favorite what?"

"Subjects."

"What are the subjects?" Rhett said.

"Like math, science, reading."

"I hate all the subjects," Rhett said, as Roy pulled up to the school.

"But your last report wasn't too bad."

"So what? They give you a break for self-esteem. I suck at school."

Roy checked the time; he was already an hour late for work. He didn't know what to say, heard himself trying, "But you like football."

"Football's not until the fall."

"Practice starts in August. Be here before you know it." He reached across the front seat, opened Rhett's door. "You're walking home after school, don't forget."

"Where?"

"Home to momma. Get on, now."

Rhett didn't move. "Were there bullies back in your day?"

"They rode up on dinosaurs."

"You're not funny."

"Sure there were bullies."

"But you were big, right?"

"I was built kind of like you."

"You were?"

"Yeah." Roy motioned to the open door.

Rhett didn't move. "Did any of them pick on you?"

"No," Roy said, but then he had a funny memory, a taste memory, the taste of blood in his mouth. His own blood, and the inside of a barn, one of those sagging old barns with the cantilevered additions they have in east Tennessee. "I got into scraps, like any other kid."

"Did you win?"

"They weren't serious."

"But did you beat the shit out of them?"

Kids were streaming into the school. "Git," Roy said.

Rhett was watching the kids. "You saw my touchdown, didn't you, Dad?"

"Sure did."

He turned to Roy. "I picked up that fumble."

"And took it in for six."

"I didn't hot dog."

"Course not. You're a classy kid."

Rhett took a deep breath. He got out of the car.

"See you," Roy said.

"When?"

"Got a second?" Curtis said, popping out of nowhere as Roy hurried across the floor. Gordo was standing in his cubicle, his hand half raised as though he had something to say.

"I know I'm a little late," Roy said, following Curtis into the glass office. "It won't—"

"Take a seat," Curtis said. He was rubbing at some stain on his French cuff with a silk handkerchief, hadn't been listening. "Truth of the matter," Curtis said, folding the handkerchief so it came to a point and sticking it in his breast pocket, "Bill doesn't really think you're ready."

Who was Bill? That confusion tempered Roy's initial disappointment. Then he remembered: *Pegram, VP tech personnel,* and felt its full force. He'd been stupid, let down his guard, forged crazy chain links deep in his mind, like: promotion, money, emeralds, Marcia. Gotten ahead of himself. One of his mother's favorites: *Now, Roy, don't you be gettin' ahead of yourself.* He'd loved that voice of hers, the way the *y* in *Roy* was hardly a sound at all, more like flowing air, a breeze.

"Thanks for thinking of me anyway," Roy said, getting up.

Curtis waved him back down. "Whoa," he said. "Getting a little ahead of yourself." The phrase gave Roy a shock. "Thing is, Roy"—the *y* almost exactly like his mother's, another shock—"Bill doesn't think you're ready, but I do. And since—how can I put it?—questions of maturity have been raised about his preferred candidate, Bill's agreed to go along with my choice."

Roy wasn't following this too well, the meaning of it, but all of a sudden the disappointment was gone. "Have you made it yet?" he said.

"Made what?"

"Your choice."

"Why, it's you, Roy. That's what I'm trying to communicate here. Feeling all right?"

"Yeah," Roy said, already thinking, Promotion, money, emeralds, Marcia.

" 'Cause you're usually a little sharper than this. Don't you even want to know what the job is?"

"Sure."

"Sure?" Curtis smiled. "You crack me up sometimes." Curtis glanced down at some notes on a legal pad, made a check mark. "Know where we're weak, Roy? Where we *were* weak? Chemerica, I'm talking about."

Roy wasn't sure.

"Eastern Europe," said Curtis; Roy remembered hearing something about that. "Dates way back to the Cold War. Now, with Globax, we start shaking that tree. Going to demand a lot of my time. New York's designating a new post, regional supervisor or area manager, name's not set yet, to take some of the pressure off. I'll be spending half my time up on seventeen, so we'll get another desk in here for you."

"Another desk?"

"Meaning you're it, Roy. The new regional supervisor, area manager, whatever."

"I'll be in here?"

"With bells on. Congratulations. Only reason I'm not shaking hands is they've got big eyes down there on the floor, and we're keeping things under wraps until New York makes everything official."

"What's everything?"

"A little reshuffling, no concern of ours." Curtis made another check mark on the pad. "Now, we get to the nitty-gritty."

"What's that?"

"Why, the money, Roy. Any idea what you're going to be making? To start, that is."

Roy shook his head.

"Guess."

Roy thought. "I just don't know."

"Take a shot."

"Fifty-three thousand."

Curtis smiled. "Seventy-two seven, Roy. And that's before bonuses."

Roy was stunned. His first reaction was childish: if only he could tell his mom, just to see the look on her face. Seventy-two seven, before bonuses. Bonuses! He'd never had a job that paid bonuses, unless you counted the case of beer the landscapers sometimes got when they worked late on Saturdays, that first year of scrambling around after he'd left Athens. "Bonuses?" Roy said.

"Never less than ten percent of base, in my experience," Curtis said.

Eighty grand. Roy's lungs filled so full of air he thought he'd rise off the floor.

"I know what you're thinking," Curtis said. " 'What's the catch?' "

That hadn't occurred to Roy.

"No catch, my man. Do good work, get rewarded. Things are straight up more often than people think."

That was what Roy liked about Curtis, right there. *Things are straight up more often than people think.* Roy believed it too, not because of this wonderful break in his life, and not because he'd made a careful study of human behavior and come to that conclusion, but because he just did.

"Thanks," he said. "Whatever you had to do with this, thanks."

Curtis's phone buzzed. "We'll tend to the details in the next week or two," he said, reaching for it. "For now, just enjoy the feeling."

Roy rose, glanced quickly around the glass office, soon part his. Outside, down on the floor, the cubicles shrank row on row into the distance, like a science project demonstrating perspective. Roy's gaze found his own cubicle, empty, and Gordo's right beside. Gordo's face was turned up, very small from where Roy was, but Roy could tell Gordo was watching him.

Questions of maturity have been raised about his candidate. Closing the glass door, Roy looked back at Curtis.

Curtis was talking on the phone, and dabbing again at the stain on the white cuff. Roy walked across the floor. He spotted the little flag sticker on Gordo's wall from a long way off.

"Son of a bitch give you the boot?" Gordo said, leaning over the cubicle wall the moment Roy sat in front of his screen.

"The boot?" Roy said. The cubicles were small: he could smell the sourness of last night's alcohol on Gordo's breath.

"The boot, Roy. Canned, fired, sacked."

"Why would he? That's the first time I ever left early in eight years."

"Not that," Gordo said. "I thought maybe he got wind of what went down after."

Roy lowered his voice. "The nitrate?" he said.

"Fuckin' right the nitrate," said Gordo, much too loud. "Coulda blown a nice little hole in the map of Asia, good buddy."

"How? Watertight's in the specs. I double-checked."

"Over there they say it wasn't. Some scene went down— rain clouds rolling in, train off on a siding, coolies, tarps, the first drops coming out of the sky—you get the picture."

Roy got the picture. It took away his air supply, tinged everything yellow, like he was going to faint. He watched his yellow fingers, as though from far away, tapping on the keys. The ammonium nitrate order popped up on the screen, the letters all yellow. He didn't get it: there it was, beyond doubt, the water-reactive codes in place. Roy read the order three times before he glanced up at the dateline and caught the mistake: BEI. BEI was Beijing. The nitrate was sent from Shanghai—SHA—but his order had gone to Beijing. A mistake, big, undeniable, unaccountable. How had they even cleared the shipment, gotten it on the train? *Just don't tell me it's a big bang somewhere.* Roy dug out the inhaler, squeezed a shot down his throat. In front of Gordo: but he had to. Promotion? Forget the job he had now.

"But hey," said Gordo. "He didn't get wind of it, not to worry. It's all taken care of."

"All taken care of?"

"I'm a pro, Roy. Who taught you the goddamn ropes? And that K. C. Chen guy, subagent in Shanghai? No problems there. He's not even upset. Turns out he's even got a sense of humor. I emailed him that parrot joke."

"What parrot joke?"

"The one about the Viagra Olympics."

"K. C. Chen's a woman," Roy said, starting to feel better.

"A woman, huh?" said Gordo: drinks after work at Sportz. "She emailed me back one of those sideways smiley faces."

"I hate all that Internet shit," said P.J., going to the can.

Roy ordered another round, paid the waitress.

"Wasn't that my turn?" Gordo said.

"Not today."

"Hey," said Gordo. "You'd of done the same for me."

Roy clinked glasses, his beer against Gordo's JD on the rocks. "I owe you."

"No owing," Gordo said, downing half his drink. "I'm having a pretty good week, is all."

"How's that?" said Roy.

"First of all, I save your ass. Second—just between us—I think something good's about to happen careerwise. Can't tell you how I know, so don't ask. Third, Brenda's not so ticked off about the regiment anymore. Fact is, she's spending Saturday night in camp."

"Camp?" said P.J., sitting back down beside Roy. The air in the bench cushion went hissing out.

"With the regiment," Gordo said.

"They have women?" said P.J.

"Civilian reenactors. A whole 'nother thing. The women wear long skirts and bonnets, cook over wood fire pits. But it's authentic—they had wives in the camps, especially at the start of the war."

"Brenda's going to wear a bonnet and cook over a wood fire pit?" P.J. said.

Gordo leaned forward. "One of the guys—an old guy, been married thirty years—told me things get pretty hot in those tents. Like some kind of transformation takes place."

"Any single women?" P.J. said.

"Come and see." Gordo looked at Roy. "The both of you."

"My great-great-great—can't remember how many greats—grandfather fought at Chattanooga," P.J. said.

"So did mine," said Roy.

Gordo paused, drink halfway to his lips. "You never told me that."

Roy shrugged.

"What was his name?"

"Same as mine," Roy said. "Roy Singleton Hill."

"Singleton?" said P.J. "What the hell is that?"

"I don't know," said Roy.

"But you're named after him," Gordo said.

"My old man was too," Roy said. "It's just kind of a family—"

"Tradition," Gordo said.

"Yeah." He'd been about to say *thing*.

Roy drank four beers, more than he'd had at one sitting in years. He felt pretty good on the way home: *Seventy-two seven*. Before bonuses. That crazy emerald idea took hold again, and half an hour later he was in Phipps Plaza, the kind of place he never went, gazing through a jewelry store window. Then he was inside. Then someone was saying, "These are really quite special," and Roy was examining a necklace that didn't even look like emeralds.

"Tumbled emeralds, sir, unfaceted, graduated, really rather special. I assume this is a gift."

"Yes."

"For someone who appreciates quality, I take it?"

"Yes."

"And would take pleasure in wearing something that I might say is a cut or two above?"

"Yes."

Roy put down a deposit—$2,000—maxing out his credit cards. The remaining $6,000 he could cover by topping out the home equity loan in the morning. What did it matter now? Seventy-two seven, plus bonuses.

He went home happy. No one there, of course, too quiet, too lonely, but tonight it didn't bother him. He was on his way down to the cellar to work on Rhett's shelves when the phone rang.

Gordo. "You didn't tell me he was some kind of hero."

"Who?"

"Roy Singleton Hill."

"I don't know much about him."

"The colonel does."

"What colonel?"

"My colonel. In the regiment. He wants to meet you, Roy. He's invited you up for the weekend."

"Up where?"

"We've got the Girl Scout camp, out seventy-eight."

"Saturday's my day with Rhett."

"Sunday, then."

Roy thought about that goddamn ammonium nitrate. The goddamn ammonium nitrate and the job Gordo believed was his. How could he say no?

FIVE

Ma said things like *Don't you go ruinin' that smile on me now* and *Don't you be gettin' ahead of yourself* and *Will you look at that sky, Roy—blue as your eyes and not a cloud in it!* When Roy was three or four, after her marriage broke up, the two of them had come down from Tennessee, staying first with a cousin or acquaintance of some kind—Roy had almost no memories of this period—and then in places of their own. Neither did Roy remember all the jobs his mother had worked—in a Hardee's kitchen, then a bakery in Five Points, a flower shop, receptionist in a doctor's office, assistant manager of another flower shop, a few other things, then back at reception for Dr. Moore again, a good thing because he looked after her care personally when she got sick. First they'd thought it was one thing, then another; it had ended up being a combination.

Roy had expected to bury her back in Tennessee, but in her will she specified Atlanta, didn't matter what cemetery long as it was Atlanta. She lay under a small white stone in the Oakland cemetery, about fifteen minutes from Roy's house. He'd visited once or twice the first few years, but whatever calming spiritual thing that was supposed to happen hadn't happened for him. Saturday, driving north to Buckhead to pick up Rhett, he'd thought of paying another visit. *Seventy-two seven.* To tell her that—not for his pleasure, for hers. He'd say, *Before bonuses, Ma,* and she'd start laughing and repeat it a few times, stressing the different syllables in *bonuses.*

43

Bonuses, Roy. Like it was the most outlandish concept in the world. And the look on her face. Roy actually tried to imagine it. He was able to visualize several different looks: on the breathing machine at the end, scared eyes trying to tell him something, but what?; home after spending all day on her feet at one of the flower shops, sitting on her velveteen couch, trying to keep her eyes open; and years and years earlier, picking up the phone to hear his father on the other end, the only time Roy remembered him calling, and how all sorts of strange lines appeared in her forehead, lines he didn't see again until a few months before the end. Roy could picture all those looks on her face, but how would she have looked when he told her seventy-two seven before bonuses? That he couldn't see at all.

Roy walked up to Marcia's door. A red flower torn from one of the planters lay on the welcome mat, roots and all. Roy bent down to pick it up, and was still straightening when the door opened. He recalled how things had gone with Barry the last time, wished he wasn't holding the flower.

But it was Marcia who looked out, not Barry. Her eyes went to him, the flower, back to him. "Why, Roy," she said.

"Saturday," he said, interpreting the expression on her face as puzzlement. "Collecting Rhett."

"Come on in," Marcia said, turning to call, "Rhett. Your daddy's here."

Roy stepped into the big square entrance hall. It was empty, as before, except for the chandelier still tilted in one corner of the floor, in a little sea of broken crystals. Then he saw something new, a red stain on the creamy wall. Alarming, until he realized it was the purple red of wine, not the bright red of blood.

"What have you got there?" Marcia said.

The flower. An explanation formed in his mind about how he hadn't brought it for her, simply found it on the step, but all he ended up doing was making some kind of sound and handing it over, a tiny clod of earth coming loose from the roots and falling on the polished oak floor. That was when Rhett appeared—at the moment Roy and Marcia were facing each other, both with a hand on the flower—Rhett, walking in through the door that led to the living room, picking his nose.

There was a silence. Roy imagined he could feel all sorts of forces in the room, invisible but physical, tugging here and there. He and Marcia backed a little away from each other; she held on to the flower.

"All set?" Roy said.

Rhett took his finger out of his nose, nodded. His eye looked a lot better, swelling all gone, the discoloration now the muted shades of Easter.

"What are you guys going to do?" Marcia said. She'd never asked that before, seldom even appeared on change-over day. "If I'm not being too nosy," she added.

"I joined this new gym near my— in the Highlands," Roy said. "Thought Rhett and I would have a workout, sit in the whirlpool, then get some lunch, maybe see a movie if it keeps raining like this. How's that sound?"

"Workout?" Rhett said. They'd never had a workout before. Roy'd been thinking a little physical training might help the boy the next time he ran into a bully; he also felt like a workout himself, a feeling he hadn't had in some time.

"Why not?" Roy said.

"Sounds good." Which is what he'd hoped to hear, except it was Marcia saying it, not Rhett.

"Then get your stuff," Roy said. Which is what he would have said to Rhett, except his eyes were on Marcia when he said it.

"Yes, sir," said Marcia, turning and leaving the room. Rhett stood there with his mouth open. His gaze met Roy's. Roy came very close to shooting him a wink.

They got in Roy's car—the Altima, with 103,000 miles on it, dust on the dashboard, empty coffee cups here and there, nothing to be done about it—Roy and Marcia in front, Rhett in the back. Roy turned the key. Music came blasting out of the speakers: *Yes I'm going to walk that milky white way, oh Lord, some of these days.* "Milky White Way," one of Roy's favorites. He snapped it off.

"What was that?" Marcia said.

"Uh," Roy said.

"Sounded like gospel." Marcia popped the CD out of the slot, examined the label. "You going religious on me, Roy?" she said.

"No."

"But?"

"It's music."

"Just music, you mean?"

"Yeah."

"What're you guys talking about?" said Rhett from the backseat.

"Big ears," Marcia said.

Roy laughed. He felt good: loose, natural, at ease. And in his pocket—in his pocket because he'd never owned an object so valuable that didn't come with a steering wheel and he was afraid to leave it behind—was the emerald necklace, like an ace in the hole.

They went to Roy's gym. Roy paid two guest fees. "Depending on how much you all are going to use this, you might consider a family membership," the girl behind the counter told Roy, handing out towels.

They did ten minutes on the stationary bikes, Marcia on one side, leafing through a magazine, Rhett in the middle, watching VH1, and Roy on the other side, sweating almost at once and trying not to huff and puff. Trying not to huff and puff interfered with his air supply. He huffed and puffed, glanced furtively at himself in the mirror from time to time, seeing how out of shape he was, making resolutions. Once Marcia's eyes met his in the mirror. She smiled at him. Because of the mirror—that was the only reason Roy could

think of—it was like a stranger smiling, a fit stranger in a leo-
tard and tank top, and very exciting. *Isn't this the craziest
thing? Like an affair, or something.*

In the weight room, Marcia did squats, not with a lot of
iron on her shoulders, but real squats with good form. When
had she learned that? And her form: good in both senses of
the word.

"Let's see those push-ups," Rhett said.

"What push-ups?" said Marcia.

"Dad said he could do twenty."

"Fifteen," Roy said.

"Twenty," Rhett said.

"All right," Roy said. "But you first."

Rhett got down on the floor, started doing push-ups.

"Back straight," Roy said, and: "You going to count that
one?"

Rhett did nine; seven real ones. "Now you."

Marcia lowered her bar back onto the rack. Roy said:
"Who's getting hungry?"

"He's chickening out, Mom. Don't let him chicken out."

Marcia raised her eyebrows at Roy, made a clucking sound
like a chicken asking a question. She was fun: what with
how she looked, and how things had been in bed, and how
he'd like to be there right now, he'd let that slip his mind, the
fun part.

He got down on the floor. Fifteen? Twenty? Who was
he kidding? Rhett stood over him. "One, two, three, back
straight, four, five, you going to count that one?"

Six, seven, what the hell had happened to him? Had there
really been a time he'd been able to do a hundred, win free
beer at parties? Hard to believe. At eleven, he'd had enough,
was about to stop, just flop down there on the mat and make
some light remark, although he didn't know what, when he
thought: How many could Barry do?

Roy did twenty-nine.

"Dad!" said Rhett.

"Let's feel that muscle," said Marcia, or something like

that, the words fuzzy with Roy feeling a little faint the way he did. But Marcia's hand squeezing his biceps—no doubt about that.

They sat in the whirlpool together, Marcia's foot touching Roy's once underwater, maybe by accident, then showered, changed, went to lunch. "I've never been this hungry in my life," Marcia said. She ordered barbecue, Rhett a burger and fries, Roy a tuna sandwich even though the barbecue looked pretty good. The three of them ate lunch in almost complete silence, their heads quite close together over the table. Rain ran down the windows of the café.

The waitress brought a newspaper from the bar. They opened it to the movie page. "Oh, let's see this," said Marcia, pointing to an ad. "Barry's friends with one of the producers."

That changed the mood a little bit.

"More of a business associate," Marcia said.

Barry's business associate's movie was about a nun given a month to live; she leaves the convent and winds up at a Club Med. Marcia laughed a lot. Rhett ate a jumbo popcorn and drank a jumbo Coke. Roy couldn't get into it, passed the time watching little things in the background of the scenes and wondering about Barry.

"Enjoy it?" Roy said, as they walked back to the car.

"Pretty cool," Rhett said. "Do a lot of nuns have tattoos like that?"

Roy parked in front of Marcia's house. Rhett got out, walked to the door without waiting for Marcia, as though leaving them alone on purpose. Marcia turned to Roy.

"Thanks for a very nice day."

"How about tomorrow?"

"Tomorrow what?"

"We could do something."

"Tomorrow's Sunday."

"So?"

"Don't, Roy."

"Don't what?"

"Let's just take our time, that's all."

"Take our time for what? Getting to know each other?"

"In a way," Marcia said. She laid her hand on his. Her skin was cold. "You're a good man, Roy. Even I can see that."

"But?"

"No buts."

In the rearview mirror, Roy saw the Mercedes coming up the street. "Was it the truth, Marcia? When you said you'd made a mistake about Barry."

"Oh, yes," said Marcia. "I made a mistake about Barry. A doozie."

That was that. What else was there to know? Roy couldn't imagine any other impediment he couldn't handle. He reached into his pocket. "Here," he said.

"What's this?"

"For you."

"These are beautiful."

"A kind of emerald."

"I know that, Roy. But I just couldn't."

"Why not?"

"I couldn't, that's all." She rolled the emeralds gently in her fingers.

"Just try it out for a few days. It can always go back."

"I couldn't."

The Mercedes turned into the driveway. Barry got out, glanced at them—he didn't look good, unshaven, shirttail hanging beneath the hem of his jacket—and hurried toward the house, carrying an armful of papers. Barry had a little trouble with the front door, dropped two or three sheets without knowing it. A rainy gust of wind whisked them away. The emeralds made a soft clicking sound.

"It can go back?" said Marcia as the door closed behind Barry.

"Why not?"

"In that case." She slipped the necklace in her purse.

Later that night, Rhett called Roy. "Can I get a dog?"

Roy laughed at that, laughed again when he was brushing his teeth, once more getting into bed. He slept like a baby.

SIX

It was still raining, or raining again, when Roy drove through the gates of the Girl Scout camp the next day. He parked in the lot beside a Porta Potti truck, put on a rain jacket, opened his umbrella, and walked toward a row of tree-sheltered cabins he could see in the distance. The cabins were padlocked, the windows boarded up. Roy kept going, beyond the cabins, up a path covered with pine needles, into deeper woods. He came to a three-pronged fork where signs on the trees pointed to NATURE WALK, COMPUTER LAB, and ARTS AND CRAFTS. Roy chose NATURE WALK.

The nature walk path led up a gradual slope lined with pines and waxy-leafed trees whose name Roy didn't know. The rain fell harder, making percussive sounds on the waxy leaves, still bright green and shiny new. Other than the rain, it was quiet. Roy slipped on a tree root, stepped in a puddle, got his foot wet. Had no one come? Had they canceled the event? Roy was slowing down, almost ready to turn back, when he heard a voice close by.

"No one's worth that kind of money."

Another voice: "Know what your problem is? You're living in the past."

"Bullshit."

"No bullshit. Sports is entertainment now, pure and simple. Drive in a hundred and thirty runs, you write your own ticket, just like the movies, that faggy little actor, what's his name."

Roy looked around, saw no one. "Anybody here?" he called.

Silence. Then came the sound of metal clanking on rock.

"Hey!"

"Not 'hey,' for fuck sake."

"Oh, yeah. Who goes there?"

Two men wearing uniforms like Gordo's came scrambling out from behind a boulder ten or fifteen feet off the path, both of them now calling, "Who goes there?" They saw Roy. One stuck a flask in an inside pocket. The other said, "Stand and identify yourself." A low-hanging branch knocked his hat off as he came closer.

"I am standing," Roy said.

They didn't seem to hear him. The one with the flask said, "Oops."

"What do you mean—oops?" said the hatless one.

"We forgot the guns."

"Muskets, for Christ sake. Or weapons. Never guns. Guns are cannon."

"Whatever. Shouldn't we get them?"

They looked back toward the rock. Roy saw that they'd built a shelter behind it—plastic trash bags stretched over muskets stuck in the ground, bayonet first.

"Probably."

"But then we'd have to put the whole damn thing back up again."

They turned to Roy, waiting under his umbrella. The hair of the hatless one was already soaked flat against his skull; the peak of the other one's hat—kepi, was that what Gordo had called it?—was directing a tiny waterfall onto the tip of his nose.

"I'm looking for Gord Coker," Roy said.

"Gordo?"

"Correct," said Roy.

"He's in camp."

"In a tent, nice and dry."

"Where is it?" Roy said.

"Lucky son of a bitch," said the one with the flask.

"Third on the right," said the other.

"Third is Jesse," said the one with the flask. "Gordo's one more down." He turned to Roy. "Fourth tent on the right."

"I meant the camp," Roy said.

"The camp?"

"I'm sure I can find the tent on my own."

"Huh?"

"After I get to the camp."

"You asking where the camp is?" said the hatless one.

"I am."

"Thataway, quarter mile or so."

"Thanks."

Roy started down the path. He heard one of them saying, "Isn't one of us supposed to accompany any stranger into camp?"

And the other: "Stranger? You heard him—he's here to see Gordo."

Pause. "We should have asked him to send someone back with those BLTs."

Roy passed a tree labeled SWEETGUM, another labeled AMERICAN SYCAMORE, and a third, resembling the waxy-leafed one, although he wasn't sure if it was the same species, labeled POST OAK. He came to a grassy clearing. There were about a dozen white tents in the clearing, arranged in two rows on either side of a black cannon. It was quiet and still: nothing to hear but rain on canvas, nothing stirring but the rebel flag on a pole above the first tent on the right. Roy paused outside.

"Anybody home?"

"Roy? That you?" The flap opened. Gordo appeared in his uniform, the butternut jacket, gray trousers, yellow suspenders, black half boots that conformed to no current fashion. He actually looked pretty good. "Come on in."

Roy folded his umbrella. Another uniformed man came up behind Gordo, peered out. "Where's the picket?" he said.

"What's that?" said Roy.

"Like a sentry," Gordo said.

"Supposed to be a picket escorting every visitor," said the other man. "Standing orders."

"They need BLTs," Roy said, ducking into the tent.

"Now you know why we lost the war," the man said; a man of about Roy's height, but thinner, slightly stooped, balding. He reminded Roy of an English teacher he'd had in high school.

"Roy," said Gordo, "Jesse Moses, second lieutenant, Seventh Tennessee. Jesse, Roy Hill I was telling you about. Roy Singleton Hill."

They shook hands. "Gordo's been telling me about you," said Jesse Moses. "Welcome to the Seventh Tennessee."

"I'm just visiting," Roy said.

"Glad to have you. I'll fetch the colonel." He threw a gray cape over his shoulders and left the tent.

Roy looked around, saw a rough wooden table, the kind of thing you might find at a flea market. A candle burned on the table, illuminating a map that looked yellowed with age in the dim light.

"There were Jews in the Civil War," Gordo said in a low voice. "Both sides."

"So?"

"So it's authentic."

"What is?"

"For Christ sake, Roy. Jesse Moses is Jewish. We've got a Jew for second lieutenant."

"But it's kosher."

Gordo gave him a look. "That's not a reenactment kind of word."

"What about *putz*?" Roy said.

The tent flap opened and Jesse Moses returned. He glanced at Roy, then Gordo, back to Roy, and seemed about to say something—*Who said putz?*, Roy was sure of it—when a short round man came in behind him. His uniform bore lots of gold braid and culminated in a green plume poking up from his broad-brimmed hat.

"Colonel," Jesse Moses said, "Roy Hill. Roy, this is our colonel, Earl Sippens."

"Earl Sippens?" Roy said, shaking his hand, a small hand and damp, but that might have been the rain. "Not the Suzuki guy?"

"Isuzu," said Earl.

"Isuzu," Roy said. "Sorry." Sippens Isuzu was one of the biggest car dealerships in Cobb County, regular sponsor of late-night movies.

"No biggie," said Earl. "I sold Suzukis at one time. Hell, I sold them all. Remember the DeLorean?"

"No."

"Course not—too goddamn young." Earl Sippens looked Roy up and down. "Roy Singleton Hill. I get a chill, now I really do. What was he—your great-great-grandpappy or one more greater than that?"

"I don't know," Roy said.

Earl didn't seem to hear that. "Roy Singleton Hill," he said, putting his hand on Roy's back and propelling him toward the table. "This calls for a drink."

They sat on overturned crates. "Ah," said Earl, glancing at the map, "Chickamauga."

"Jesse and I were just going over it," Gordo said, setting down tin cups, pouring from an earthenware jug.

"Chickamauga," said the colonel. "What might have been, eh, boys?"

"That's debatable," Jesse Moses said.

"How so?" said Earl, his eyes getting small real quick. Roy smelled whiskey, a strong smell. All the smells—damp wool of the uniforms, canvas, grass, melting candle wax, whiskey—were suddenly strong.

"If you're talking about Bragg's so-called failure to pursue," said Jesse Moses, the candle wavering for a moment, sending a brief shadow across his face, "remember there's a difference between winning the field and winning the battle."

"Maybe I'm not bright enough to see it," said Earl. "Bragg

chases them down the night of September twenty, smashes them up"—he set his tin cup on the map, hard enough to slop a little whiskey over the side—"then there's no Lookout Mountain come November. No Lookout Mountain means no march through Georgia, no Atlanta goin' up in flames. What we call a turning point, like fucking Little Roundtop, curse the name."

"That's debatable too," said Jesse Moses.

Earl's voice rose. "You saying we take Little Roundtop we still don't win that fight?"

Jesse nodded. "It was unwinnable. Lee should have decamped the night of the first."

Earl sat back, folded his arms across his chest. "And gone where, you don't mind my asking?"

"Where he ended up going anyway, back over the Blue Ridge—but before they'd jammed his tail between his legs," said Jesse.

"And how're you supposed to win a war like that, always runnin'?"

"Ask Ho Chi Minh," Jesse said.

"Don't start that shit."

Jesse gave Earl an unfriendly look. Earl gave one back. Then he blinked, turned to Roy. "Sorry, Roy, things get a little heated sometimes. The nature of war, you might say."

"No problem," Roy said; they'd lost him from the start.

"Wouldn't mind hearing your opinion," Earl said.

"About what?"

"Chickamauga," said Earl. "Meaning specifically Bragg's failure to pursue the Army of the Cumberland after Longstreet's breakthrough at the Brotherton Cabin."

"I know nothing about it," Roy said.

"No?" said Earl. He raised his cup; the others did the same, Roy too, to be polite. "Victory," said Earl, emptying his cup in one gulp. Gordo and Jesse did the same. Roy drank a lot less, not even half, but it went to his head anyway. "Refill, Private Coker, if you please," Earl said.

Gordo refilled the cups. Actually looked all right in his uniform, and what was more, seemed to move in a different way, almost with a swagger. Gordo caught Roy's glance, gave him a wink. Regional supervisor, area manager: Gordo thought the job was his. "Tennessee sipping whiskey, Roy, twelve years old," Gordo said. "Authentic."

"Except for the twelve-year-old part," said Jesse. "The boys drank rotgut."

"Beauregard as a for instance?" said Earl. "You saying Beauregard drank rotgut?"

"Beauregard was hardly one of the boys."

Earl and Jesse exchanged another unpleasant look. Roy wasn't sure what they were arguing about, was also confused by all the names—who was real and who was not, or rather who was living and who was dead.

Earl took out a thin cigar, slightly bent, bit off the end, lit a wooden match with a flick of his thumbnail. The smell of smoke drifted through the other smells, rich, concentrated, like a bonfire in a tobacco field, packed tight. Earl smiled at Roy, wisps of smoke trailing from the corners of his lips. "Strikes me as pretty funny," he said, "you not having an opinion on Chickamauga."

"Why's that?" said Roy.

"Because," Earl said, "right there"—he jabbed at the map—"was your grandpappy. Reed's Bridge, eighteen September."

"Not my grandfather," Roy said. "I told you—it was much more distant than that."

Earl drained his cup again. "Practically the first skirmish of the whole goddamn battle. Bet he had an opinion. Bet I could even tell you what it was."

Roy took another sip of whiskey, gazed down at the map—saw markings that made no sense to him, names he didn't know, like Thomas, Crittenden, Polk, Wheeler, blue rectangles here and there, mostly on the left, gray rectangles mostly on the right, a winding stream or river farther to the right. He didn't see anything that looked like a bridge. "What year are we talking about?"

Earl put down his cup. "You're asking what year was Chickamauga?"

"Yeah."

The uniformed men all looked at each other. "Eighteen sixty-three, Roy," said Gordo. "You must have learned that in school."

"With the quality of education in this state?" said Earl. "Don't count on nothin'." He spat out a shred of tobacco leaf.

Jesse took the jug, poured whiskey in Roy's cup. "Look, Roy," he said, leaning over the map. "Reed's Bridge." He pointed with his index finger: a long, delicate finger; Roy couldn't help thinking of all those Jewish pianists and violinists, stereotypical or not. "And right here," said Jesse, "where it says 'Forrest'? That's Nathan Bedford Forrest. Roy Singleton Hill—your ancestor—rode with him, that's clear from the muster rolls and from when he was mentioned in dispatches, which is how we know he must have been there, September eighteen, 1863."

"This is about history," Earl said. "We're historians. Historians in action."

"And 1863 is our year," Jesse said.

"What do you mean?" Roy said.

"It's always 1863 in the reenactment world," Jesse said. "By general agreement, North and South."

"Why?"

"That was the year," Earl said. "Been no year like it, before or since."

Or maybe he said *'fore or since*. Roy wasn't sure: not with the whiskey going to his head, and the smells, and the rain on the tent, and the hiss of dripping wax, and the creaking of the leather belts when Earl, Jesse, or Gordo shifted on the wooden crates; not with the flickering candlelight, and how it made that blue creek or river seem to move, just a little. All at once, Roy was out of air, but completely. He got up, mumbled something, stepped outside.

Still raining, but not as hard. Roy stood near the cannon, took deep breaths. He checked his watch, gave it a close look, in fact, much longer than normal. A commonplace, utilitarian watch of no great value: but digital. He felt a little better.

The rain stopped, the breeze died, but a mist thickened almost at once between the trees and down the line toward the most distant tents. A soldier—a reenactor, Roy reminded himself—appeared out of the mist, walking briskly forward, an object under his arm.

The man nodded as he went by Roy. The nod was curtailed, military, the man young and smooth-faced with two stripes on his sleeve and a single earring in one ear. He carried a long curved sword in its scabbard.

"Colonel?" he said, standing outside the tent. "Light's perfect."

Earl came out of the tent, took the sword. He had trouble buckling it on. The man helped him, spinning him around once like a top, which was roughly Earl's body shape, and getting all the belts—Earl was now wearing three—in order. The soldier wasn't tall—perhaps not even as tall as Earl—but lean, trim, the most soldierly looking reenactor Roy had seen so far.

"Met Roy yet?" Earl said. "Roy Singleton Hill, like I was mentioning at the meeting. Roy, shake hands with Corporal Bridges. Sorry, Mr. Bridges, what with you transferring in so recently, your Christian name momentarily escapes me."

"Lee," said the corporal, shaking Roy's hand. Lee's hand was small, smaller than Earl's, but dry, and the grip was strong.

Earl moved toward the cannon. A man dressed in jeans and a yellow slicker backed out of a tent, hunched over a camera on a tripod. Earl got ready in front of the cannon, one hand on the hilt of his sword, the other inside his shirt, like Napoleon.

"Nice," said the photographer.

Lee stood beside Roy, watching. "He does a digital thing to make his pictures come out just like Matthew Brady's," Lee said.

Roy was about to ask, *Who's that?* when Earl said: "How about getting Roy in the picture?"

Roy got in the picture, wearing Gordo's hat and jacket, standing so the cannon obscured the rest of him.

"Nice," said the photographer. "Now why don't we try just you two?"

"Me?" said Lee.

"And this gentleman," said the photographer, nodding at Roy.

"Don't want me there?" said Earl. "I could stand in the middle, like this."

"How about we try that next?"

Earl stepped out of the shot, Lee stepped in, posing with Roy behind the cannon.

"They often put their arms over each other's shoulders," the photographer said.

Roy put his arm over Lee's shoulder; Lee put his arm behind Roy's back. Roy felt Lee's hand, a small hand, on his spine.

"Yeah, just like that," said the photographer. "Nice. Very."

Roy gave Gordo back his hat and jacket. "Say hi to Brenda before you go?" Gordo said.

"Sure."

Roy followed Gordo to the fifth tent on the left—both sentries had got it wrong—followed Gordo inside.

"Get your ass in here this minute, Johnny Reb," Brenda said.

And then, from her position on some sort of low camp bed on the tent floor, she saw Roy. "Oh my God," she said, pulling the covers up over her breasts; the rough border of the gray wool blanket snagged for an instant on one nipple.

Things get pretty hot in those tents. Some kind of transformation takes place.

A strawberry-colored nipple. Her face was the same. "Ever heard of knocking?" she said.

"Sorry," Roy said.

"Not you, Roy. I'm talking to the oaf here."

"How do you knock on a tent?" Gordo said.

"I'll show myself out," Roy said, and stepped back through the opening, lowering the flap behind him. As he walked away, he realized that Brenda had looked good, probably better than he'd ever seen her. He'd never felt a twitch of desire for Brenda, until right now. He heard her laughter through the canvas.

Roy walked back down the nature trail, past the silent sentry post—he could see the trash bag shelter still in place—and into the parking lot. The sight of his car was jarring for some reason, the sight of the Porta Potti truck even more so. Roy was opening the car door when he heard a light, muffled drumming, looked back up the path, saw a horse in full gallop, coming his way. The horse, big and black, bore down right at him, closer and closer, the rider reining in just a few feet away.

"Easy, boy," he said. It was Lee. He handed the umbrella down to Roy. "You forgot this."

"Thanks."

Lee patted the horse's neck; the horse stood still. "Enjoy your visit?" Lee said.

"Yeah," Roy said. "Thanks."

"What did you think?"

"It was nice."

The horse snorted. Lee gazed down at Roy. "I mean truthfully," he said. "I'd like to know."

"What I really think?"

"No risk," Lee said. "I'm a big boy."

"It kind of reminded me of golf."

"Golf?"

"Harmless fun in funny clothes."

"That's a good line," Lee said. But he didn't laugh, didn't smile, showed no emotion of any kind. "Probably true given what you've seen. Being as it's only the soft-core version." Lee had the heaviest down-home accent Roy had heard in a long time.

"There's another kind?" Roy said.

Now Lee smiled, a quick smile, a flashing display of white teeth, small and even, quickly gone. And then he was gone too, wheeling the horse around in one easy motion without a word of command, and galloping back into the woods. The mist closed around him.

Roy drove out of the lot and got back on the freeway.

SEVEN

"**F**unny, the golf joke," Gordo said, coming into Roy's cubicle. "Everybody got a kick out of it."

"Even Earl?" Roy said.

"Especially. Don't sell old Earl short. The dealership? Built from nothing, and that's not the only iron he's got in the fire."

"No?"

"Fact is"—Gordo took a step closer, which brought him up against the desk, and lowered his voice—"if things weren't all of a sudden so promising for me around here, I might be looking to hook up with Earl in one enterprise or another."

"Enterprise," said Roy. "That sounds good."

"Want me to put in a word?"

"No."

Gordo seemed a little surprised that Roy didn't even think it over. "How come?"

"What do you mean?"

Gordo opened his mouth, closed it.

"What's the big secret?" Roy said.

"I'm probably out of line."

"Go on."

"The thing is, Roy, realistically speaking . . ."

"What?"

"I really shouldn't."

"Talk."

"It's just that sometimes you come to a dead end in life."

Their eyes met. Gordo had deep, dark circles under his; Roy wondered if his own were the same way.

"Know what I mean?" Gordo said.

"Not exactly."

There must have been something in Roy's tone, some edge that made Gordo hold up his hand and say, "Correction, not life. I'm talking about the job, that's all. Don't you ever ask yourself—Where is this job taking me? Not me, Roy, you. I'm in the process of lucking out, which just goes to show, because in terms of job performance, the truth is there's not all that much to choose between us."

Roy's turn to say something, but what? *No, Gordo, you do a much better job*. Couldn't say that, not with what was coming down. Roy settled for: "I'll be okay." Right away, he wished he'd kept his mouth shut. How would that little sentence strike Gordo in retrospect, the day they announced the job was Roy's?

"Course you'll be okay," Gordo said. "Didn't mean to horn in."

"You're not horning in."

Gordo leaned over, squeezed Roy's shoulder. "No offense?"

"None."

Gordo's face was close to Roy's. "You're a good buddy," he said, then thought of something and smothered a little laugh. "Poor Brenda."

"Why do you say that?"

"She's embarrassed."

"Nothing to be embarrassed about."

Gordo smiled, a confidential sort of smile. Roy smelled tooth decay. "You know what they don't tell you about life back then?" Gordo said.

"What?"

Gordo's eyes shifted. Curtis was walking by. Gordo straightened, said, "Thanks for the help," a little too loudly, slipped a manila envelope onto Roy's desk in what he must have considered a deft maneuver, and left the cubicle, knocking against the padded wall on his way out. Roy recalled how he'd moved in uniform, only the day before.

He opened the envelope. Inside were two black-and-white photographs and a two-page computer printout entitled "Roy Singleton Hill—A Biographical Sketch." The attached Post-it read: "Dug this up last night. Enjoy—J. Moses."

The first photograph: Roy and Earl posing by the cannon. Was this like a real Civil War photograph by Matthew whatever his name was? Not to Roy. He and Earl looked silly, that was all. But the second photograph, the one with Lee, was different. Roy and Lee stood side by side with their arms around each other, the way the photographer said the soldiers often posed. For some reason, this one wasn't silly, not the photograph as a whole, not Lee, and not Roy, even though he was wearing exactly what he'd worn in the first shot, snapped only a minute or two before.

Roy dug out a magnifying glass he had in the drawer, left over from when they dealt in printed labels. His own expression was the same in both pictures, that face he always wore in photographs, angled toward the camera like a cooperative subject, but uneasy. Roy was surprised to see that Earl looked fierce, his eyes hooded under the shadow of the huge brim of his hat, as though sending the signal—to Sherman? Grant?—that he was not to be messed with. Only Lee seemed unaware of the camera; his eyes gazed into the farthest distance, and as Roy examined them, he thought he detected something like battle weariness, as though Lee were a veteran of bloody campaigns that had changed him forever.

"What have you got there?" Curtis, in the cubicle. For a moment Roy thought Curtis might have been talking into his headset; but Curtis's eyes were on the pictures. Roy noticed for the first time the Confederate flag flying over a tent on the far side of the cannon.

"That you, Roy?" He tapped a pencil on one of the photographs.

"Not really."

Curtis looked down at him, his eyes narrowing. Curtis had

this sense of dignity, didn't like anyone jerking him around, even when sometimes they weren't. But Roy wasn't thinking about that: he was noticing the way Curtis's narrowed-eye expression resembled Earl's hooded eyes in the picture.

"Not the real you?" Curtis said.

"I was just visiting," Roy said.

"Like in Monopoly?"

"It was one of those reenactment camps. I guess you could say a kind of a game."

"And?" Curtis said.

Roy sensed he was being asked to say something negative about the reenactors, or the camp, or that stupid flag. He did think the whole thing was pretty stupid but he said nothing. He just wasn't going to do it.

"Kind of a game," Curtis said. "Did you know they've got World War Two reenactors now? Some of the participants dress up in black SS uniforms."

"That's weird."

"Is it?" Curtis said. His eyes shifted. He listened to something coming over his headset, pressed the button, said, "Malabar," clicked off. He focused on Roy. "Heard of slave reenactors?" he said.

"No."

"They're out there too."

"Doing what?"

"Playing the slave game. Would that be the term, Roy? Supposed to be a big contingent of slave reenactors going up to Chattanooga for some Lookout Mountain event. Never used to see the point of it myself."

"But now?"

"Now?" Curtis said, and seemed about to go on when another call came over the headset. He nodded at whatever was being said, started backing out of the cubicle, then remembered something, came back, and handed an audiocassette across the desk.

He'd been gone for ten seconds when Gordo looked over the wall. "What was that all about?"

"Did you know there were slave reenactors?"

"Don't start."

"Don't start what?"

"The war had nothing to do with slavery, Roy. Everyone knows that."

"Like who?"

"Historians. Ask any reenactor, North or South. Talk to Jesse. Or Lee. He's just as sharp, you get to know him."

"You're telling me that if there'd been no slavery, there still would have been a war?"

"Yeah."

"You're starting to scare me, Gordo."

"What the hell's that supposed to mean?"

Gordo's face, hanging over the partition, was flushed. "Got to get back to work," Roy said.

Gordo didn't move. "What's that tape Curtis gave you?"

Roy glanced at the label: *Managing in a Complex World: The Acclaimed Five-Step Program for Managers in the New Millennium, with Workbook, Internet Support and 24-Hour Hotline.*

"No idea."

"What's it say?"

There was nothing to do but hand Gordo the tape.

Gordo read the label. "Why'd he be giving you this?" The accent was on *you.*

"No idea," Roy said again, but maybe not as convincingly this time.

Roy popped the tape in the car player on the way home.

Why don't you like filling out the new weekly activity report, Jerry?

Well, Carol, it takes too much time, and who reads it anyway?

I read all the reports, Jerry, and so do the people at headquarters. How much time does it take?

Half an hour, Carol, and that's time I really can't spare if I'm going to be a productive member of the team.

In this interchange between Carol and Jerry, we see a common reaction to change, one you'll probably be faced with sooner or later in your managerial career. What are Carol's choices? The most common response is what we call the—

Roy's mind wandered from the little office drama. *His managerial career.* Curtis wanted him to know something about handling people, to be ready. The promotion was real, and was coming soon: the tape was tangible proof. Knowing for sure that the future would be better than the present: what a feeling! The next thing Roy knew, he was on the cell phone calling Marcia's home number.

"Hello?" she said; her voice subdued, even tentative, not like her.

"Doing anything special for supper?"

She perked up right away. That was a good feeling too. "Why, no, Roy."

"How about I'll get three steaks, throw them on the grill?"

"Three?"

"You, me, and Rhett."

Pause. "Right. Sounds good."

"Give me an hour," Roy said.

He stopped at the market on the way, bought three sirloin strips, a box of frozen French fries, a bottle of Chardonnay. He knew that Chardonnay didn't go with steak, but Chardonnay was what she'd wanted the last time.

"What's your best steak sauce?"

"This here Creole one. Can't hardly keep it in stock."

"I'll take two," Roy said.

Everything made sense. You worked all day, put good food on the table, sat down together, drank a little wine, the kid said something cute that made you smile at each other over his head, you relaxed, body and soul. Driving up to the house, he began to think about Marcia's return, her actual moving back in. Should he suggest it, or wait till she brought it up herself? Roy had a funny thought—what would Carol do?

Maybe better to think of her as "Carol." Carrying the grocery bag into the house, Roy decided that this was probably one of those problems that solves itself: step six of the five-step managerial program. He was almost laughing to himself when he went into the kitchen.

The answering machine was beeping. Roy let it beep while he put the wine in the icebox, turned on the oven for the fries, went out back and scraped the grill, rubbing it after with butter, a trick he'd learned from his mother. Then, putting the steaks on a plate and pouring on the Creole sauce, one whole bottle, he reached over and hit the playback button.

"Message for Mr. Hill. This is Mrs. Searle, social services up at Ocoee Regional. We've got your father in here quite sick, Mr. Hill, maybe not expected to last the night, according to the chief resident, and your name is on the next of kin form. Our number here is—"

She gave the number up in Tennessee. Roy called. Mrs. Searle repeated what she'd said.

"What's wrong with him?" Roy said.

"I believe it's his liver, sir."

Roy believed it too. He called Marcia, postponed dinner.

"What's wrong, Roy?"

"Something's come up." He didn't want to get into it, not with the way things were starting to go between them— maybe better than ever, that was his secret thought—and not with the weird scene his father had pulled the only time he and Marcia had met.

"Too bad," Marcia said.

"Yeah," Roy said. "Maybe we could—"

"Oops, I've got a beep," Marcia said. "Bye, Roy."

He put the steaks in the fridge, turned off the oven, got back in the car.

Roy drove north on 75.

It just seems like I'm taking all the risks and getting none of the rewards.

Believe me, Jerry, I'll do everything I can to make sure your efforts are appreciated. How would you like a special mention in next month's newsletter?

Jerry said something neutral but Roy could tell from his tone that he was starting to come around. The narrator came on and made some important points about managing, but Roy didn't catch them all because he was wondering about that next of kin thing. He and his father hadn't seen each other or spoken in ten years, and there was an even longer gap the time before, their relationship being mostly gaps. Maybe his father had simply written his name because it was the correct answer, him never remarrying, so far as Roy knew, and Roy being the only child. Otherwise—what? Some kind of deep-rooted guilt rising up in a dying man? Roy had seen things like that on TV but didn't know if they happened in real life.

He took the 411 exit, crossed the state line an hour later. Jerry caved in on the activity reports. Carol got him mentioned in the newsletter, page one. Jerry thanked her for everything she'd taught him. The narrator summarized what that was. There were seven points in all, subpoints really, since this all appeared to be part of the second step of the five-step program, but the narrator was still discussing the third subpoint—how to enlist the help of your biggest opponent—when Roy pulled into the visitors lot at Ocoee Regional.

"Patient's name?"

"Hill."

"That would be three twenty-seven. You can go on up."

"I can?"

Roy went up, walked along a wide hall, all harsh blue from the fluorescent strips overhead. Doors were open on both sides. Roy didn't like what he saw: a man reading from a Bible to a bald kid, an old toothless woman with her mouth wide open, a man with something hard to describe covering half his face. Roy began having problems with his air supply, felt in his pocket, wrapped his hand around the inhaler, held on.

The door to room three twenty-seven was closed. A transparent plastic bag full of dirty linen lay on the floor outside. Roy could see blood on the rolled-up sheets, lots of it. He glanced up and down the hall, looking for someone to ask a question he hadn't quite formulated, but there was no one. He turned the handle, pushed the door open.

A room for two, but an old shirtless guy had it to himself. The old shirtless guy had little stick arms, a hollow chest, a hard potbelly, a few long strands of rust-colored hair crisscrossing his bald head. He was spooning Jell-O into his mouth and watching Roy with pissed-off eyes. Pissed-off eyes: that was the giveaway.

"You don't look like you're dying," Roy said. That just came out. Sounded pretty bad, but he didn't wish for it back.

"I'm a fucking medical miracle is what they say." A blob of Jell-O—the green kind—quivered on his lower lip and dropped to the bedding. "Maybe if your ma had learned you some manners you'd know enough to hide your disappointment a touch better."

The deep-rooted guilt thing was out.

EIGHT

Roy's father finished his Jell-O. "Seeing as how you're here anyways," he said, "maybe you could be runnin' one or two little errands for me."

"Like what?"

"I could use a few things from out at the place."

"Where's that?"

"My place? That what you're asking?"

"Yeah."

"Don't know where my place is?"

"Why would I?"

"Why would you? You were born in that fuckin' house, for Christ sake." His father turned that pissed-off look full on him.

"And then?" Roy said.

They stared at each other for a moment or two before his father looked away, gazed out the window. Or possibly at the window itself: it was fully dark now and the glass reflected his TV program, cars going round and round a dirt oval. "Guess I fooled the shit out of them, anyways," he said, after a while.

"Who?"

"Goddamn doctors is who. Know what they thought?"

"No."

"I was a dead man less they stuck some new liver in me. Who's gonna argue with the old one now?"

Roy didn't argue.

"Know my number on the list?"

"What list?"

"Got to get on a list for every goddamn organ. I'm in the fucking thousands." He squinted at Roy. "Want to hear what's even more fucked up than that?"

Roy said nothing: he had an idea what was next.

"The liver they give you—it could be a nigger's."

As he had expected. But Roy hadn't heard the word in some time and it gave him a sick feeling in the gut, partly from the word itself, more from the fact of it coming from the lips of this man, his father. A nurse entered at that moment, didn't say, "All done with your supper, now, Mr. Hill?" or "Got a visitor, I see," or any other amiable remark Roy would have expected from the habitual cheeriness of her face. She just took the tray and left in silence. She'd heard, all right.

His father turned to him. Roy wondered whether he was embarrassed. "Any case," his father said, "it's not far."

"What's not far?"

"My place, of course. They don't listen where you come from? Key's under the mat. What're you drivin'?"

"An Altima."

"One of them little Jap shitboxes?"

Roy didn't answer.

"You're working, right? Got a job of some kind?"

Roy nodded.

"What as?"

"Shipping."

"Lumber yard, that nature?"

"I'm with Globax."

"Never heard of it."

"Used to be Chemerica."

"Never heard of that neither."

Roy offered no explanation.

His father noticed a tiny bit of Jell-O on his plastic spoon, licked it off. "How's the pay?"

"Not bad."

"What's that mean in dollars?"

"It means not bad."

Roy's father watched the cars racing on the inside of his window. "How's that wife of yours?" He might have said *yourn*; Roy wasn't sure.

"Good."

Roy's father raised his eyebrows. "Still together?"

"That's right."

"And the kid?"

"He's good too."

His father was toying with the plastic spoon, twisting it in his hands. "Why'd you go and give him a name like that for, anyways?"

And they were right back where they'd left off ten or eleven years ago. Roy and Marcia, at Marcia's insistence, had brought Rhett up to see his grandpappy. It was Marcia's first meeting with him too: Roy's father hadn't made it to the wedding. The get-together, at the Pizza Hut off exit eleven on 75, had lasted forty minutes, about twenty minutes too long.

"Why don't you give me directions and a list of things you want and I'll be going," Roy said.

"What's wrong with the name we already got?"

"Just write it down," Roy said, finding a pen and an old envelope in his pocket, laying them on the tray table. His father wrote on the envelope, handed it to Roy.

"You dint answer my question—what's wrong with the name we already got?"

Roy read the list: *breefs, 3 bags cheetoz, 1 bottel (over sink)*. He looked up at his father. "A boy needs a name of his own," he said.

"What's that supposed to mean?"

By the time his father had repeated the question, louder this time, Roy was out in the hall. A doctor was writing on a chart. Roy waited for him to finish, introduced himself, explained about the call on his answering machine. "Glad it's just a false alarm," Roy said.

"False alarm?"

"With the way he's sitting up, watching TV, eating."

"I rejigged his medication a bit," the doctor said. "He seems to be responding well."

"So was the problem with his liver or the previous medication?"

"I don't quite get what you're saying," the doctor said. A phone beeped in the pocket of his white coat. "Excuse me," he said, putting the phone to his ear. After a while, he said, "Is that the one with Johnny Depp?" Roy went out to the parking lot.

Roy followed the diagram on the envelope. East on 40 in light traffic, north on 315 in almost none, second right past "prair hall," and left on the first paved road, all by himself.

The road climbed a hill, rounded a bend. Potholes appeared, more and more frequent until they became the road itself. Roy's headlights picked out a tumbling black stream behind tall trees, an unlit house with a tarpaulin sagging from the roof, another house with a blue TV light glowing in the back. The climb grew steeper, the turns tighter; the road narrowed to a single lane. There were no houses now, just trees covering steep slopes on either side, and sometimes a clearing, one with a still, bear-shaped shadow in the middle. Roy flicked on the inside light, glanced down at the diagram. His father had marked an X at the end of the road, but there was no indication of distance. Roy kept going, higher and higher. It was far from silent, especially with the state of Roy's muffler, but he felt silence all around him, just the same. He tried the radio; nothing he wanted to hear came in clearly. Roy settled for his management tape.

It's only fair I get a raise, Carol.
Why is that, Jerry?
Because Tony's making ten percent more than me.
Jerry's right. Tony is making ten percent more. Carol
  knows Tony was approached by a headhunter
  promising a higher-paying job at a rival company. She
  raised his salary in order to keep him. She'd like to

*keep Jerry too, but Jerry is not as valuable to the
company and she doesn't believe he deserves a raise.
How can she deny Jerry and at the same time keep him
a happy and productive member of the team?*

Before Roy could learn the answer, his headlights shone on
a wooden gate and the road came to an abrupt end. Roy
stopped the car. STAY TO HELL OFF was spray-painted on the
worn, uneven slats of the gate; a strange gate with no fencing
on either side, nothing to prevent someone from simply
walking around it. Roy got out of the car, walked around the
gate, across a dirt yard. Metal things gleamed here and there
in the moonlight: a washer lying on its side, an engine block,
a TV with a smashed screen, hubcaps. Beyond stood the
house, a misshapen thing with a porch resting on cement
blocks, duct tape on the window of the front room, a crooked
chimney overhung by dark trees. Roy mounted the porch. It
creaked under his weight. An animal cried out, not far away.

Roy paused in front of the door. Born in this house, in this
fuckin' house: he waited for the door, its dark paint chipped
and peeling, to prod his memory, the way inanimate things
were supposed to do sometimes. He felt nothing, but that
might have been his fault: it occurred to him that maybe he
missed a lot when it came to the subtleties of life.

Key's under the mat. Roy bent down to somehow turn back
a corner of the mat without getting any of the filth on him. His
shoulder brushed the door. It swung open.

Roy went inside. He couldn't see a thing, but he smelled
many smells, none pleasant. He ran his hand along the walls
on either side of the door, felt a switch, flipped it. A light went
on over a sink, and a second one, hanging from the ceiling.
The room had kitchen things in it—sink, card table, two card
table chairs, icebox, stove; but there were living-room things
too—frayed couch, TV; and bathroom things—a seatless
toilet in one corner. Roy saw a spark, heard a little pop, and
the hanging light went out.

Briefs, Cheetos, bottle. He'd seen the bottle already—Old

Grand-Dad—on a shelf over the sink. There were two cup-boards under the counter. One was empty, the other so full of Cheetos that the packages cascaded out when he opened it. That left the briefs. Roy went into the next room, the soles of his shoes sticking once or twice to the floor.

A shadowy room. Roy got the feeling he wasn't alone, went icy on the back of his neck and between his shoulder blades. At the same time, something soft brushed his face. Roy snatched at it—a cord or string—and pulled. A light went on, a strange red light, as though for some fantasy bor-dello. But this was no bordello, just a small bedroom with a lopsided chest of drawers and a narrow unmade bed, littered with crumpled Cheetos packages, an empty bottle of Old Grand-Dad and—and what? Something dark on the pillow, something that gave a twitch, a twitch of a long tail. A rat, the biggest Roy had ever seen. He made some kind of noise, startled and scared. The rat leaped off the pillow, flew across the floor, disappeared through a hole in the wall.

When Roy got his breath back, he went to the chest and opened the top drawer. Didn't most people keep underwear in the top drawer? Not his father. His father kept a jar of Vase-line and a magazine called *Horny Black Bitches*. Roy tried the next drawer, found a pile of socks and underwear that in-cluded a three-pack of briefs from Wal-Mart, still wrapped. He picked it up, uncovering a cigar box underneath.

Roy told himself, Don't touch that box. What are you? The box is none of your business. But he didn't believe that last part.

Roy took out the box, slid open the top. There were three photographs inside. The first was a faded Polaroid of a young woman in a summer dress. She stood on some steps—might have been church steps, Roy couldn't tell—laughing at some-thing, maybe the way the wind was blowing her hair around. An attractive woman, with lean arms and shapely calves. It didn't hit him at first that she was his mother.

She was in the second picture too, a better-quality print, standing beside one of those test-your-strength hammer machines at a county fair. The man with her was wearing a sleeveless T-shirt and making a muscle. She was feeling it with her fingertips and going, "Oooh." His ears were identical to Rhett's. He didn't have that pissed-off look in his eyes, just a Budweiser in his free hand.

The third photo was clipped from a newspaper. "DeKalb Whiz Signs Intent Letter with U. Georgia." Roy had on his high school uniform and the funny haircut all the seniors had worn that year.

Roy stared at the picture, stared through it, trying to get the dates right. Senior year meant fourteen or fifteen years after he and his mother had left Tennessee, and nine or ten years before the visit with Rhett, the only time he'd been back. He closed the cigar box. What was he supposed to make of the contents? Roy didn't know. He shut the drawer.

And in closing the drawer, happened to glance out the back window. The yard sloped gradually uphill toward a low, massive shadow in the distance. Roy knew what it was even though he couldn't really make it out: a barn, one of those cantilevered barns found only in these parts. This half sighting did things to his memory that the house had not. Whatever those things were, whatever was stirring, hadn't risen to the surface before Roy saw a chink of light, the kind of narrow ray that might escape between cracks in old barn siding.

Roy left the house, started up the sloping backyard, more of a field, really, with stubbly vegetation and the shells of several cars. A strange sound came and went, a sound Roy couldn't identify until it had gone: the beating wings of some heavy bird flying over his head. He glanced up, saw no bird, just the moon, so big and clear, its stony nature apparent. He came to the barn. Yes, one of those east Tennessee barns, as he had thought, and yes, a chink between the weathered planks. Roy put his eye to it.

His gaze swept almost unseeing past many things in the shadows—a tilted tractor missing one wheel, a battered demolition derby car with *Sonny J* written on the driver's door, trailing flames, a set of drums, with *Sonny J* on the bass—and locked on the man in the center of the barn. The man, a big shirtless man with hair falling to his shoulders, had his back to Roy and was busy with something in front of him. At first, Roy couldn't tell what that something was; then the man raised his arm and Roy saw it was a deer, hanging by its hind feet from the rafters. The man's arm slashed down—only then did Roy see the knife—and the deer's white belly split apart, spilling gore. A surprising amount of gore; at least, the man was surprised: he said, "Goddamn," and spun around. Too late: Roy saw blood all over his thick chest, and a splotch or two on his face. At the same moment, the man's eyes went right to the chink in the wall. Roy jerked back, as though he was afraid, but what was there to be afraid of? His memory, down at the bottom in the earliest part, was already making connections. They were cousins. Roy walked around the barn to the big double doors, said, "Sonny?" and pulled them open. "Sonny Junior?"

Maybe not. "Who the hell are you?" said the man, the knife not quite still in his hand, as though it had a pulse of its own.

"Roy."

"Roy?" A moment or two, and then a smile spread across the man's face. "Son of a bitch." He came forward, almost trotting, shifted the knife—the blade must have been a foot long—to his left hand, offered the right to Roy. They shook hands, not the horizontal business handshake that Roy was used to, but the vertical kind he'd seen on the streets, a handshake in the arm-wrestling position. "Ain't this the living end?" Sonny Junior said, not letting go. "Talk about a blast from the past."

"How many years has it been?" Roy said.

"Don't want to know," said Sonny Junior, gazing down at Roy. Sonny Junior was about two inches taller, and in better shape than Roy had been on his best day. "Lookin' good, Roy. Lookin' real successful." His expression changed. "Uh-oh," he said. "You being here—did Uncle Roy . . . is Uncle Roy . . . gone?"

"He's made a recovery."

Sonny Junior shook his head. "Tough old bastard. Let me guess—he got you to come out here for booze."

"You know him pretty well."

"And Cheetos," Sonny Junior said. "The Cheetos you can get away with. The booze they're gonna confiscate unless you're real smart."

"I wasn't going to bring him the booze anyway."

Sonny Junior's eyebrows went up; there were scars over both of them. "Why the hell not?"

"It's his liver, Sonny."

"So?" There was a pause. Then Sonny Junior flashed that smile again, patted Roy on the back, said, "Hell, you're probably right, Roy. But there's nothing to keep us two from throwing one back now, is there?"

"I'm not much of a drinker."

"We're not gettin' wasted, Roy. It's just a how-d'you-do, is all."

Roy realized he was being rude. "A drink sounds good."

"Now you're talking," said Sonny Junior, laying his hand, a big, heavy hand, on Roy's back and guiding him into the barn. "Sorry if I was a little sharp there at first, Roy. I reckoned maybe you'd be one of them assholes from fish and game."

"How come?"

"How come, Roy? Ain't exactly hunting season, now is it?"

Roy hadn't thought of that.

"But the truth is I'm innocent as a newborn babe. This critter was the victim of an unfortunate road accident up near Turtletown. I just happened to be the first lucky motorist on the scene."

Roy found himself gazing at the big eyes of the deer; he had the crazy idea they were trying to tell him something.

"Do much huntin', Roy?"

"No." The truth was he'd never hunted in his life, never even fired a gun.

"Then this might interest you," Sonny Junior said. He reached deep in the carcass, rooted around, and tore out a fist-sized bloody gobbet that Roy couldn't make sense of at first, and then realized was a baby deer, tiny but perfectly formed. "Probably worth a few bucks," Sonny Junior said.

"How's that?"

"Up at the college. Genetic research." Sonny Junior held up the fetus, gazed at it for a moment, then dropped it in a trash barrel. "Vodka all right? I got vodka and maybe whiskey."

Roy saw a sleeping bag on a bare mattress in the can-tilevered section. "You live here?"

"From time to time," Sonny Junior said. "Need space for all my stuff. Want to see some of it?"

"Some of what?"

"My stuff, Roy."

"Sure."

Sonny Junior paused, bit his lip. "Shit, Roy."

"What?"

"Family. What's more important?" For a moment, Roy thought Sonny Junior was going to give him a hug. Instead, he opened a cooler, took out a bottle of vodka topped with one of those measuring spouts they use in bars, poured several measures into two paper cups, added water and a few spoonfuls of Tang powder. "Here's to family."

They touched paper cups. "What's our relationship, exactly, Sonny?"

Sonny Junior paused, drink halfway to his lips, looked sad. "Ordinary circumstances, we'd of growed up together, Roy. We're first cousins, you and me. Your daddy and my ma were brother and sister."

"Were?"

"She passed."

"Sorry."

"Long time ago," said Sonny Junior. "She had what Uncle Roy's got, but worse."

Roy didn't know whether he meant liver disease, a drinking problem, or both. "What about your father?"

"Big Sonny? He's gone too. Succumbed of an unlucky chain of events, down in Angola."

"The prison?"

"What else they got down there?"

Sonny Junior took Roy by the arm, led him across the floor. "This here's my last demolition derby car. Came second in it at the Waycross Fourth of July Invitational a few years back."

"Still racing?" Roy wasn't sure if *racing* was the term, but he couldn't think of another.

"No money in it, Roy, believe it or not. Now over here, these rockets is what's left from the fireworks stand I had up by Maryville. And this is my drum kit. We got a band plays once a week, once a month now, at a bar in Gatlinburg." He sat down on the stool, picked up the sticks, started into something thunderous. Sweat popped out on his skin almost at once, sweat that mixed with drying deer blood, forming pink droplets on his chest. A crash of cymbals; silence. Sonny Junior beamed. "Recognize that?"

"I'm not sure."

"The break from 'Friends in Low Places,' adapted a bit by myself."

Roy drew a blank.

" 'Friends in Low Places' by Garth Brooks, Roy. We play all his stuff. Had a singer sounded just like him, swear you couldn't tell the difference, but he quit. I sing a bit myself, tell you the truth, just my own material."

"You write songs?"

"I'll send you a demo. Not in the music business by any chance, are you, Roy?"

Roy explained what he did.

"Any money in it?"

"Not a lot."

"But steady work. You got a family, I recall."

"Yes."

"How I know is Uncle Roy goes on and on about the name you gave that boy."

"He does?"

"Talks about you a lot. Football. But mostly that name. What was it, again?"

"Rhett."

"Yeah, Rhett. Truth is, he don't like it."

"I know."

"Thinks it's a fag name."

Roy said nothing. He'd thought something along those lines at first, but Marcia had insisted: it was the boy name she'd dreamed of from the day she'd visited the Margaret Mitchell Museum on an eighth-grade trip. Now Roy's reaction to the name, the whole feeling it gave him, had changed completely: it was Rhett's name.

"What's he like?" said Sonny Junior.

"A good boy."

"He'd be my nephew."

"Cousin, I think."

"Like to meet him," said Sonny Junior. "Maybe pay back some for all the things Uncle Roy's done for me."

"He's done things for you?"

"Such as letting me hole—stay here, store all my shit." He reached for the bottle.

"No more for me, thanks," Roy said.

"Don't drink it, then—it's a free country," said Sonny Junior, filling Roy's cup anyway but dispensing with the mix this time. "Tell me about the football star thing."

"I wasn't a star. One year on special teams at Georgia, that was it."

"You got cut?"

"Just about. Had a concussion or two and the doctor wouldn't clear me to play. Ended up losing my scholarship."

"That sucks."

"Worked out okay," Roy said. A wife like Marcia, a son

like Rhett, a house in a neighborhood like Virginia-Highland, seventy-two seven, before bonuses: standing there in this barn, Roy knew he'd come a long way.

Sonny Junior was watching him over the rim of his paper cup. "You grew up kind of sizable, Roy."

Roy shrugged.

"Remember how we used to rassle a little in this here barn?"

"No."

"Long time ago, naturally. I was probably about four, you must've been three."

"I don't remember."

Sonny Junior nodded. "Place used to creep me out too—all this shit on the walls, hasn't changed a bit."

Roy glanced around, saw rusting farm tools hung on nails and hooks—hoes, rakes, scythes; something else he didn't recognize.

"Know what that is?" Sonny Junior said, picking up on it right away.

"No."

Sonny Junior rose, lifted whatever it was off the wall with a grunt, brought it back to Roy. "Ball and chain," he said. "Sixteen pound." He dropped it on the floor. It made a booming sound, cracked one of the old broad planks.

Roy thought at once of Angola and some connection to Sonny Senior, and so didn't get it. "Check this out," said Sonny Junior, sitting on the floor at Roy's feet, very supple for such a big man, and fitting the leg clamp around Roy's ankle. He closed the clamp. It had a long black key in it, a key Sonny Junior turned and withdrew. "Give it a try," he said.

Roy tried to walk. "Jesus," he said.

"Wicked," said Sonny Junior. "Only way is to pick the thing up and carry it."

Roy picked up the iron ball in both hands, took a step or two, the chain clanking between his feet. "I didn't know they still used these," he said.

"Huh?" said Sonny Junior, surprised enough to drop the

key. It bounced once or twice and disappeared under the demolition derby car. "No one still uses them, Roy. How humane would that be? This one surely goes back to the old days."

"What old days?" Roy said, his gaze on the shadows under the car. The ball was getting heavy. He put it down.

"Why, back to the original Roy, I guess," said Sonny Junior.

"The Civil War hero?"

"Don't know much about that part. But the original Roy owned this place, plus the old mill on the crick, a working proposition back then, and all the way up to the Mountain House."

"What's the Mountain House?"

"Just a ruin—all state forest back there now. But the point is, with the mill and owning all that land, he'd have slaves. Stands to reason, right?"

"I guess."

"So that's how he handled the bad ones," Sonny Junior said, nodding at the big black ball on the floor. "Hell of a thing." He drained his cup, poured more. "But you know what gets me, Roy, now we're talking about this?"

"What?"

"From here all the way up to the Mountain House—any idea how much land that is?"

"No."

"Square miles, Roy. Fuckin' square miles. We were rich, back then, lords of all we surveyed." He took another drink, still sweating a little from the drumming. "Who took it away from us, what I'd like to know," said Sonny Junior.

"I don't think it's a question of that."

Sonny's eyes narrowed. "What's it a question of?"

"It's just . . . events, that's all."

"Events? Listen to the way you talk." Sonny Junior gave him a long look. "You know you're inheriting what's left, don't you?"

"I doubt that."

Sonny Junior's voice rose, just a little. "I'm telling you what I know." Their eyes met; they held the gaze. Roy heard a quiet drip from where the deer was hanging.

"Got that key, Sonny?"

"Key?" said Sonny. "Oh, yeah." He crawled under the car, wriggled back out with the key, unlocked the leg clamp.

Roy stepped free. He glanced at his watch. "Better be getting back. Work tomorrow, and I've got to drop his stuff off at the hospital first."

"I'll handle that if you want," Sonny Junior said. "Going into town anyway."

"Take you up on that," said Roy. "Thanks."

"Family is family," said Sonny Junior. They shook hands again, that arm-wrestling handshake Sonny Junior liked. "Cousin Roy?"

"Yeah?"

"No good being strangers, is it?"

"No."

Roy left the barn, walked down past the house to his car, parked by the gate. He could hear the creek now, bubbling faintly in the night. As he put the key in the ignition, he noticed the stain on his hand: blood, deer blood, a handshake imprint. His palm felt hot. That rasslin' in the barn, when Sonny Junior was four and Roy was three? It started to come back to him now. On the way home, he tried listening to Carol and Jerry, but couldn't make any sense of them, not until he saw the glow of Atlanta.

NINE

Next morning. Gordo's turn to drive. He'd cut himself shaving again, a triple-bladed Mach-3 gash this time, under his chin.

"Name Pegram mean anything to you?" he said.

"Seventeenth floor?" said Roy.

"Correct," Gordo said, glancing at Roy. The car sagged across the lane. Someone honked. "How'd you know that?"

"One of those names that floats around the building," Roy said, a slippery reply that gave him a bad feeling in his gut.

"Nice way of putting it," Gordo said. "Those guys on the seventeenth floor—are they that much smarter than us, Roy?"

"What makes you think they're any smarter?"

"Can you read them, Roy? I can't read them."

"What do you mean—read them?"

"Don't play dumb with me, Roy."

They rode in silence, wedged between eighteen-wheelers. "Sorry," Gordo said after a while. "Thing is, I called Pegram at home last night. Ever call one of those guys at home?"

"No."

"Not a good idea, right? Never call them at home unless it's a big bang somewhere." Gordo made a big bang sound, but soft. "Don't you wish sometimes?"

Roy kept quiet.

The truck ahead of them took the next exit, opening a sudden view to the northwest, and there was the building, brass-coated in the distance, the Globax sign fully in place now, the word bigger and brighter than Chemerica had been.

"I wanted to know," Gordo said. "Is that so terrible? Course I'd had a couple pops, bad idea again, right? But I can't stand the way they make you hang, hanging all the time. Next thing my finger was on his number in the company directory. Guess what I heard in the background."

"Background?"

"At Pegram's house, while I was waiting for him to come to the phone."

"I don't know." Roy didn't want to know, just wanted to be at his desk, plugged into the monitor, but there was construction ahead and they'd come to a stop.

"Tinkling."

"Tinkling?"

"Or clinking. The sounds in one of those movies where rich people are eating supper? Like that. How was I supposed to know they were eating supper—it was after eight. Should have hung up right then."

"But you'd already said your name."

Gordo turned to him. "Going psychic on me, Roy?"

Traffic started moving but Gordo, eyes still on Roy, didn't notice. An angry cop waved him ahead.

"You know when everything's all set and then you get the feeling that something's going wrong?" Gordo said.

"No."

"No?"

"I don't get that feeling," Roy said. "The going wrong part always takes me by surprise."

Gordo laughed, then said, "Didn't mean to laugh. Meaning Marcia, of course."

"Yeah," Roy said, "although funnily enough . . ."

"Funnily enough what?"

Roy wished he hadn't started, didn't want to go on, didn't want to jinx anything. "Things are looking up a bit in that department."

"The new guy's not working out?"

"Maybe not."

"Give you some advice, Roy. Don't make it easy for her."

"Why?"

They wound down the ramp under the building, out of the sunlight. "You don't understand women too good, do you, Roy?"

The garage attendant stopped them, which he never did, and checked them off the list. He wasn't wearing his Braves cap; they'd given him a brass-colored uniform that looked uncomfortable and a police-style hat that said *Globax*.

Roy and Gordo got in the elevator at sublevel five. Gordo hit the button, took a deep breath. He didn't let it out till they stopped at sublevel one: Roy was watching.

"Thanks, good buddy," Gordo said as the doors slid open.

"For what?"

"Not asking any questions."

6:59. Roy sat down at his place in B27, Asia/Oceania, under the IRREGULARS banner. He logged on, saw what was ahead. First, he tackled the phosphates problem. That meant exchanging emails with Kumi in Lahore. Kumi had his own way—or her own way—with the language. "What does *dis-potentialities* mean?" Roy said.

He heard someone—P.J. or DeLoach—over the padded wall: "That fuckin' Kumi."

Roy thought: The promotion is great but I'll miss some things. Then he had another thought, an unusual, complicated thought for him: the very fact that he'd had that first thought, about missing some things, meant in some way that he was probably ready. What had Curtis said? *Bill doesn't think you're ready, but I do.* Was Curtis right? Was Roy growing in some way? Was he about to move to a new stage in life? Were things going to get easier? Was it already starting—Marcia coming back, the promotion? Was this what it was to be on a roll? If so, I'm going to make them happy, Marcia and Rhett, I swear.

Then he heard Gordo in the next cubicle: "Yes, sir, I'm on

my way." Gordo's head appeared over the wall, a smile spreading across his face. "Hey, Roy," he said.

"Hey," said Roy.

"You're a good buddy, man," he said, fixing the knot on his tie, a green one with yellow stripes. "Sorry for dumping all that paranoid shit on you before."

"Hey," said Roy again.

Gordo tapped the top of the wall a couple times, pumped his fist, a little half pump, and started across the floor, walking fast. Roy's gaze ran on ahead to the square dais with its raised glass-walled office, where Curtis and Mr. Pegram were waiting.

Gordo climbed the stairs, knocked on the door, which was kind of strange since Roy could see they were looking at Gordo and he was looking at them. Gordo went inside, started extending his arm for handshaking—Roy could sense Gordo's energy all the way from his cubicle—but no handshaking actually happened. Curtis's lips moved and the three of them sat down: Curtis in his chair, Mr. Pegram on the edge of the desk, Gordo in the chair on the other side, his back to Roy. Curtis's lips kept moving. Suddenly Gordo's head tilted up, than snapped in the direction of Mr. Pegram. Mr. Pegram's lips moved. Gordo half rose. Mr. Pegram's lips kept moving. Gordo raised both hands, palms out like a supplicant. Mr. Pegram held up one of his, palm up like a traffic cop. Gordo subsided in his chair.

Roy lowered his gaze. He heard P.J.'s half whisper: "What's going on?"

And DeLoach: "Didn't I fuckin' tell you?"

Roy checked his screen. Messages were piling up. Two from Kumi, the first only three lines long but incomprehensible, with routing codes Roy had never seen and the word *prioricity* underlined, the second an incomprehensible correction of the first. Roy opened messages from Cesar in Miami, the Osaka subsidiary, customers in Singapore, Bangkok, Santiago—how did that get there?—someone else in Lahore, not Kumi, the tariff office on the seventeenth floor:

all of them more or less routine, all suddenly as incomprehensible as the worst gibberish Kumi ever sent. Roy was thinking: *How can she deny Jerry and at the same time keep him a happy and productive member of the team?* He hadn't heard the answer.

Something made him take another look at the Miami message. Cesar sent email almost every day, but this one ended with: "How's everything up there?" Had Cesar ever asked a question like that before, ever written anything personal at all? Roy was thinking of examining past communications in the mailbox when another message popped up, this one from someone he didn't recognize—lbridges at an edu address. Roy didn't know lbridges, never got messages from any edus, began to get the strange feeling that his screen was spinning out of control; and then Gordo was back.

Gordo's face was red; bright red, as though lit from within. He turned it on P.J., DeLoach, and finally Roy, a glowing red thing in the vast muted space of pastels, beiges, and grays.

"What's wrong?" Roy said. Gordo glared at him, or maybe unseeingly right through. "Is it about the promotion?"

Gordo's glare intensified, became ferocious, and there was no doubt he saw Roy now. "Promotion?" he said, his voice rising. "They gave me the boot."

"The boot?"

"The boot, Roy, you dumb fucking cracker." His voice rose and rose. Roy thought Gordo might vault the partition and attack him. "Canned, fired, sacked."

"But—"

"Canned, fired, sacked." Gordo was shouting now; his triple-bladed cut opened up and blood dripped off his chin. "I'm the dumbest fucking cracker of them all." Gordo in his cubicle, kicking something: first, the partition went down, a whole L-shaped section, then another, and Roy saw that P.J.'s feet, under his desk two cubicles away but very close in distance, were clad in bedroom slippers. Then Gordo's monitor was in midair—it went right over Roy's head—and the mouse, trailing after like a kite tail, caught the IRREGULARS banner and tore it from the strip lights. A crash on the open floor beyond the cubicles—some of the strip lights going down too—loud in a place where crashes never happened, and then security guards moved in, two from the receiving end, more from the elevator bank. Gordo whipped around, saw them coming from both directions, said, "Just try it," screamed it at the top of his lungs, in fact, cords standing out white as bone under the stretched skin of his red neck, and reached in his pocket, as though for a gun, as though he thought he had a gun in there. But of course he didn't. Then Roy was on his feet, had his arm around Gordo, turned Gordo away from the guards, started walking him toward the elevators, at the same time saying something soothing, he didn't know what.

"Get the fuck off me," Gordo said, and tried to shrug Roy off. He kept trying until they came to the elevators, but Roy didn't let himself be shrugged off. Elevator doors opened, a lucky thing because the security guards were right behind, issuing commands Roy's brain didn't register. Doors opened and out came Hector from supplies. He had an armful of toner cartridges he could hardly see over, but what he could see alarmed him. Roy felt a hand on his back. He gave Gordo a little push, past Hector—but not quite cleanly—and onto the elevator, occupied by three or four women from maid service, their eyes widening. The doors closed.

Roy turned back to the room. There was toner all over the place. Curtis and Mr. Pegram watched from behind the glass wall, far away, their faces featureless smudges, one black, one white.

Roy worked late, all by himself on the floor, except for maintenance still rebuilding around him. He found the phosphates, lost them again, sorted through several new messages from Kumi, dated the next day. He received a long set of email protocols from the Globax office in New York. It included a warning about personal communications and a reminder that electronic traffic was monitored. He opened the edu message from lbridges.

> *Roy—interested in a little black powder shooting?*
> *Lee*

Bridges. Roy had forgotten the last name. He was wondering whether to reply, and if so what to say, since he wasn't sure he understood the message, when Curtis came in; walked through the opening, the wall still down.

"Working late?" Curtis said.

"Catching up to do," Roy said. Curtis pulled up a chair. Could he read the screen from where he was? Depended on his eyesight; *black powder shooting* looked huge from where Roy sat.

"Bill said to make sure you were properly thanked."

"For what?"

"For how you handled today's situation. It bodes well—his words."

Roy shrugged.

"We're going to wait forty-eight hours, let things blow over, before making the announcement."

"What announcement?"

Curtis glanced around; a new wall snapped up in Gordo's old space, no flag stickers on this one. Curtis lowered his voice. "The promotion, Roy. Your promotion. Sometimes I wonder if you're even interested."

Roy lowered his voice in imitation, making their conversation seem intense, as though they'd slipped into italics. "Of course I am."

Curtis nodded. "I know that. Wouldn't make sense otherwise." He gazed at Roy's screen, resumed a normal volume. "How about a drink? We could try that new place on Edgewood."

"Thanks, but another time."

"Or anywhere you like."

"I wanted to get home and give him a call," Roy said.

"Who?"

"Gordo."

Curtis's eyelid did its fluttering thing.

"It hasn't blown over for me yet," Roy said.

Curtis leaned forward. "He wasn't part of the Globax future."

Curtis gave Roy a chance to respond. Roy said nothing.

"Not to get too philosophical about it, Roy, but there are new forces on the loose. Whether you choose to recognize them or not won't change anything."

Roy knew Curtis was right about those forces: he could feel them, like some kind of accelerator in a NASA g-resistance test.

"Never fired anybody, have you, Roy?" Curtis said.

The maintenance guy heard that: he hoisted two trash barrels instead of one, and struggled off.

"No," Roy said.

"That's going to change."

"I know," Roy said, but he hadn't, not consciously, until that moment.

"The hiring makes up for it."

Roy hadn't thought about that either.

"New territory," Curtis said. "But you've got the experience, you've got the instincts. Remember, when in doubt—there's always the vision statement."

Roy's memory of the vision statement was vague. He recalled a few of the headings as they applied to his department: *on time, safety first, team*.

The maintenance guy returned, crumpled the IRREGULARS banner and tucked it under one arm, grabbed the stepladder with the other, said, "Look all right now, Mr. Curtis?"

"Better than new," said Curtis.

Roy called Gordo as soon as he got home. No answer; the machine didn't pick up.

Roy was restless that night. Forty-eight hours. Why hadn't Curtis said a day or two, a couple days, a little while? Forty-eight hours made it sound like something from a James Bond movie; this was only a job. Roy went downstairs, tried to work on Rhett's shelves, couldn't concentrate. He thought of reading the vision statement, but couldn't find a copy. He opened the fridge, not from hunger, just for something to do, and saw the steaks, still marinating in the Creole sauce. He checked the time; Marcia and Rhett would probably have eaten by now, but what was there to lose by calling?

Roy called.

"Hello?" said a woman; Roy didn't recognize the voice.

"Is Marcia there?"

"No."

"Rhett?"

"He's doing his homework."

"This is his father."

"Just a sec."

Rhett came on.

"Hi."

"Who was that?"

"Jenny."

"Who's Jenny?"

"The baby-sitter."

"Ma out somewhere?"

"That's why Jenny's here."

"Think she'll be back soon?"

"Who?"

"Mom. Your ma."

"She's in New York."

"New York?"

"She's going to bring me some souvenirs."

"Barry go with her?"

"He's here. Want to talk to him?"

"No. Is it for work or something like that?"

"He e-trades at night."

"I meant Mom. Your ma."

"I don't know."

"When's she coming back?"

"Tomorrow?"

"What did she . . . I mean, why all of a—"

"Dad?"

"Yes?"

"I'm watching *The Simpsons*."

Roy didn't answer right away; he was having air supply problems.

"Dad?"

"I'm here. Done your homework?"

"Most of it."

"Okay. Talk to you tomorrow."

"Bye."

"Love you."

But the last line was spoken to the dial tone.

TEN

A horseman with a smudged face bore down on Roy, saber flashing under the moon. Roy felt in his pocket for a gun, but of course he had no gun. Worse, he was wearing the ball and chain.

Roy reached for the phone. "Hello?" The bedside clock read three something; Roy's vision was blurry.

"Sorry if it's a little late," said Gordo. "I can't sleep."

"It's all right."

"I'm handling it pretty good, Roy."

"Yeah?"

"Except for the not sleeping part. Guess where I am?"

"Uh-oh."

Gordo laughed, a laugh that went on a little too long, wavering on the verge of something else. "At the camp," Gordo said.

"What camp?"

"Our camp, Roy. Seventh Tennessee. I'm on my cell."

"You're out there now?"

"On patrol."

"I thought the camp was only on weekends."

"Right. The tents aren't up."

"Are you alone?"

"I see the stars. I hear the rolling thunder."

"There's no thunder."

"It's from a song." Gordo sang it: " 'I see the stars. I hear the rolling thunder.' " His singing voice surprised Roy: Gordo did much more than get the notes right.

" 'How Great Thou Art,' " Roy said.

"You listen to gospel, Roy?"

"Not really." "How Great Thou Art" wasn't one of his favorites, didn't do to him what "Milky White Way" did, but he liked how the drummer made a booming sound whenever the rolling thunder part came along. Could Sonny Junior make a booming sound like that, on his drum kit in the barn? Roy had the crazy idea of getting Gordo and Sonny Junior together.

"Still there, Roy?"

Roy thought he heard crickets. "Aren't you a little cold?" he said.

"Got my cape."

"Cape?"

"Regulation cape. Part of the uniform, Roy."

"You're wearing your uniform?"

"And bucking for corporal."

Pause. Crickets for sure.

"Maybe there's no thunder," Gordo said, "but the stars part is true."

"Must be nice," Roy said.

"No sign of life at all, life as we know it," Gordo said. "The sky glows over in the east—I got that right, east?—but that doesn't have to be life as we know it. Could be a distant fire. Like . . . like a wooden town going up in flames."

Roy remembered the long path up from the parking lot and past the cabins to the tents in the forest. "Got a flashlight?" he said.

"Nope. Just my musket."

"Not loaded," Roy said.

"We just fire the powder, Roy, you know that. Although . . ."

"Although what?"

"Roy?"

"Yeah?"

"I'm about to tell you something very important."

Roy thought of the oxidized bullet from Kennesaw Mountain and got afraid. But what was there to fear from spent bullets?

"Are you listening?" Gordo said.

"Yes."

"This is the most un-fucked-up place I've ever been."

Gordo's laugh that had wavered on the edge of something else? The something else was happening now.

"Gordo?"

"I'm not upset."

"Does Brenda know where you are?"

"Let's not talk about her. I'm not exactly persona whatever it is. She was going to cut back to part-time, with the p-p-promotion and all."

Silence. Roy heard crickets, and another sound, a rumble.

"Hear that?" said Gordo. "Thunder."

Roy listened, heard nothing this time.

"Know what it sounds like to me?" Gordo said. "The long roll."

"The long roll?"

"What the drummer boy played, Roy—the call to battle." Pause. "I'm gonna hold the phone up to the sky."

Roy listened, thought he heard something.

"Well?" said Gordo.

"Most likely the overnight cargo planes coming into the long strip at Fulton County." Roy wished he'd said something else, anything but cargo planes.

Muffled sounds. A long silence, the dead kind when a palm covers the receiver. Then Gordo said, "I want you to do me a favor."

"What?"

"Find out if the call was what did it."

"What call?"

"Fuck, Roy, the call to Pegram's house. I told you the whole story."

"It wasn't a factor," Roy said, and thought, Oh, Christ.

"Huh?"

Roy sat up, switched on the light. "I meant—I don't see what difference the call could have made." Roy saw his face in the mirror over the dresser. The expression on it—calculating, tricky, dishonest—made him turn away.

"How come?" Gordo said.

"Unless you said something."

"I just asked him how are things coming along with the promotion."

"And?"

"Roy? How come you said it wasn't a factor, so sure and all?"

Roy looked at his face in the mirror again, tried to make it normal. "What was Pegram's answer?"

"He said they'd have something for me soon."

"That was it?"

"Pretty much."

"So? What harm could that have done?"

"You're confusing me, Roy. Harm got done, didn't it?"

If there was a moment to tell Gordo the truth, it was now. Roy knew that, knew Gordo needed to know right now, would never need to know this badly again. So Roy started to tell him; the words were unreeling in his mind. Then he thought he heard that distant thunder, coming in over the phone. "Better get in your car, Gordo," he said. "Go home."

"Why?"

"Because."

"Because? What kind of reason is that? How do you know the call wasn't a factor? What were the fucking factors if you're so smart?"

"Just go home, Gordo."

Roy heard another sound, the kind liquid makes coming from a bottle. "Why should I?" Gordo said. "I see the stars. I hear the rolling thunder." The *s*'s were starting to get like *sh*'s. The line went dead. Roy called back and was put into voice mail. He switched off the light, tried to go back to sleep, gave up trying, left the light off.

*What's the difference between the vision statement and
    the company plan, Carol?*
*An important question, Jerry. What comes to mind when
    you hear the word* vision?
Seeing?
And what is it we're trying to see?
The future?
Right, Jerry.

On the way to work a few hours later, Roy tried to get the
difference between the vision statement and the company
plan straight in his mind, rewinding passages of Curtis's tape
several times. It wouldn't take, not this particular morning.

6:59. Roy sat at his desk. B31, Gordo's old cubicle? There
was someone in it, someone new, tapping at the keys.

P.J., hurrying in a minute or two late, struggling with his
tie, saw too. "Fuck," he said, just mouthed the word, really.

Then came DeLoach's voice, over the wall. "Speak to him
last night?"

"Yeah," Roy said.

"How's he doin'?"

"What you'd expect."

"Fuck," said DeLoach.

But that was about it. There was turnover, guys came and
went, and nobody kept up with anybody after they were gone.
A quiet morning, though: Roy could hear the tap-tapping in
B31, lighter and faster than Gordo's.

On his coffee break—walk to the machine, walk back,
time for a quick personal call—Roy tried Gordo at home: no
answer, but the machine was back on. "Gordo?" he said.
"You all right?"

He went back and forth with Cesar in Miami over a container ship out of Mobile that Cesar thought was supposed to
stop in Pensacola. "Any news up there?" Cesar asked at the
end of his last message, when they'd finally straightened it
out. What was going on with Cesar? Was this about Gordo?
Gordo was just a name on the screen to Cesar. Roy was

thinking of emailing back, "What kind of news?" when his phone rang.

"This is Barry."

"Barry?"

"Yeah, Barry. Let's try to go a little quicker. Kid's fucked up again at the school and they want someone over there. Like you, Dad."

"What do you mean, fucked up? Is he all right?"

"Don't know the details. Got to run."

"Where's Marcia?"

A pause. Then an odd laugh, more like a little explosion of air, having nothing to do with amusement. Then click.

Roy called the school.

"We have a strict weapons policy," said Ms. Steinwasser.

"Weapons policy?" said Roy. "Did something happen to him?"

"In the sense you mean, no."

"What are you saying? Is he wounded? Did someone bring a gun into school?"

"Please calm down, Mr. Hill. Your son's not hurt. But the someone you're talking about was him."

"I don't understand you."

"Your son violated the weapons policy."

"That's not possible," Roy said. "Rhett's got no weapon." Unless, he thought, unless: Barry.

"Better come down here," said Ms. Steinwasser.

"But—" Roy checked his watch. Then he slammed down the phone, maybe not slammed, but put down hard, without saying good-bye. Not like him at all.

He crossed the floor, went up the stairs to the glassed-in office, took a deep breath; or tried to. Curtis was at his desk, writing on a legal pad. He waved Roy in with a smile.

"Things settling down?" he said.

"What I—"

"Got a second to look this over?" Curtis said, sliding a glossy magazine across his desk.

Roy picked it up: an office furniture catalog, open somewhere in the middle.

"Bottom of the right-hand page," Curtis said.

Roy checked the bottom of the right-hand page, saw office chairs: the Cremona, the Portman, the Benchley. He looked up at Curtis.

"Any of them strike your fancy?" Curtis said.

"I—"

"Because you get to choose your own chair, Roy, one of the perks of the new job."

No air. Roy's hand was in his pocket, squeezing the inhaler.

"Roy?"

"I want this job, Curtis, I can't tell you how bad, but—"

Curtis frowned. It made him look much younger, made it easy to picture him as a boy. "What I said yesterday— sometimes I wonder if you're even interested—is that what's bothering you?"

"No, I—"

"Because it was ill considered. I apologize. I'll tell you what I told Bill Pegram—you're a nice guy, Roy, and sometimes people mistake niceness for a lack of ambition." He paused to let that sink in, just the way preachers did when they came to a main point; a pause that went on and on, at least in Roy's mind. "We straight on this now?" Curtis said.

"I've got to leave, Curtis, this minute." An explosive little sentence that left Roy breathless.

"I beg your pardon?"

Roy fought for air. "My kid. I don't know what's happening. This is a temporary . . . things are actually looking . . . in a little while, everything'll be . . . but—"

Curtis sat back in his chair. Roy had a sudden moment of clarity: it was the Portman, he could tell from the little brass things on the leather arms.

"Another problem with your son?" Curtis said.

The complicated explanation Roy had been working on, the one with an optimistic promise at the end, got bottled up in his struggling throat. He nodded.

"We're off to an unusual kind of start here, aren't we, Roy?"

Roy nodded again.

"Why don't you take the rest of the day," Curtis said.

Roy turned to go.

"With someone covering, of course."

It was just like the last time, except now Rhett had a split lip instead of a black eye. "What's going on?" Roy said, hurrying across the nurse's office. "I thought you said he wasn't hurt."

"It's not as bad as it looks," said Ms. Steinwasser, "is it, Tanisha?"

"Not so bad, no," said the nurse, lowering an ice pack to Rhett's mouth. Rhett batted it away, a violent little act that Roy didn't like at all.

Roy knelt in front of him. "What happened to you?"

Rhett wouldn't meet Roy's eye, hung his head. The motion brought a quivering drop of blood to the edge of his lip.

Roy, still on one knee, turned to Ms. Steinwasser. "What the hell happened here?"

"Language," she said, "please."

Roy stood up.

"Your son," said Ms. Steinwasser, backing half a step, "threatened to shoot another student."

"I don't believe it."

"Nevertheless."

"Shoot him with what, for Christ sake?"

"I asked you nicely."

"Shoot him with what?"

"We'll get to that," said Ms. Steinwasser. "The fact that he had ammunition gave us every reason to take the threat seriously."

"Ammunition?" Roy said.

"Which he says you gave him."

"Never."

"He got it from somewhere."

"Got what? I don't know what you're talking about."

"This," said Ms. Steinwasser, holding up a whitish thing Roy thought was some sort of thimble at first, and then recognized: Gordo's Kennesaw Mountain bullet. *What was there to fear from spent bullets?*

"That's it?" Roy said. "That's what this is about? A souvenir?"

"Souvenir?"

"A relic," Roy said. "Spent. Harmless."

"I don't know about the harmless part," said Ms. Steinwasser, opening the door to an adjoining room. Another boy, the big, broad-faced boy—Cody, Roy remembered—was sitting on an examining table, holding a bandage over a cut on the side of his nose, or possibly the inner corner of his eye. She closed the door.

"But you'd need a musket," Roy said, "an antique, and there's no—"

Rhett looked up. "I threw it at him," he said. He sounded fierce and defiant. The drop of blood rolled down his chin; another took its place in the split of his lip.

"You threw it at him?" Roy said.

"He said I didn't have a real Civil War bullet, and even if I did it was geeky, and I threw it at him."

"This was after he hit you in the mouth?"

Rhett shook his head.

"Your son was the initiator," Ms. Steinwasser said.

"I thought that wasn't supposed to matter," Roy said. "And there's still nothing about a gun or anything like that."

"I told him I'd shoot him," Rhett said.

"With what?"

"He picks on me all the time."

"But shoot him with what?"

"He rubs my face in it."

"Shoot him with what?"

"I made up the gun part."

Roy faced Ms. Steinwasser, ready to make his argument about the nonexistence of a weapon.

Then Rhett added, "Lucky for him."

Roy just stood there.

"Have you read the parents handbook, Mr. Hill?" said Ms. Steinwasser.

"Parents handbook?"

"A copy is sent home with every student. The policy is very clear. No weapons of any kind. No knives. No guns." She held up the oxidized bullet. "No ammunition."

"But—"

"Must we bring the police into this?"

Rhett got a one-week suspension. Roy drove him to Marcia's in silence. Rhett took out his key, unlocked the door. No one home. Roy got some ice cubes, wrapped them in a dish towel. "Here."

They sat at the card table, much like the one at his father's, but clean. The piles—dirt in the backyard, mail on the table—had grown. Rhett held the dish towel to his lip, gazed at nothing. Roy watched him.

"You could have put his eye out," he said.

"You're just like all the others," Rhett said. "Taking his side."

"I'm not taking his side. You could have put his eye out."

"Good."

Roy made a decision, made it, he realized, on the basis of his vision, on how he saw the future, the way Carol said to do it: he would ask Marcia to move back in right away. Rhett could then return to his old school, never face the other boy again, get back on track. What better time? She'd understand.

"When's your ma coming home?"

"Who gives a shit?"

Roy laid his hand on the table. "Don't you speak like that about your mother."

Rhett muttered something into the dish towel.

"What was that?" Roy said. He reached across the table, pulled the towel away, not roughly, but he pulled it away. "What was that?"

"Those stupid lips of hers," Rhett said, almost inaudible.

"What do you mean?"

"Nothing."

"I don't understand."

Rhett looked up, met Roy's eye; yes, fierce, defiant. This was new. Roy had no idea how to handle it.

"You can go," Rhett said.

"I'm staying."

They sat. The bleeding stopped. Rhett left the room and didn't come back.

Roy heard a car, went to the front door, looked out: not Marcia in a taxi, but Barry in his Benz with the BARRY plate. Roy took out the inhaler, sprayed it down his throat.

ELEVEN

Barry came into the kitchen.

"Moving in?" he said.

"You know why I'm here," Roy said, standing by the table, wishing some sarcastic put-down had come to mind.

Barry dropped his briefcase, loosened his tie, shrugged off his suit jacket—there were sweat stains under both arms of his striped shirt—and hung it on a chair. "Bail the kid out already?"

"His name is Rhett."

"Super," said Barry, opening the fridge. Roy saw what he'd seen before—Absolut, yogurt, lemons—plus a few cartons of Chinese food. Barry removed one, sat at the table, began eating from it—round balls, possibly chicken, in a congealed orange sauce—with chopsticks. His soft, pudgy fingers handled the chopsticks with a skill that took Roy by surprise; he himself had tried chopsticks once or twice, out on a date in high school or college, but never actually learned to use them. Barry steered several of the little balls quickly into his mouth, suddenly looked up.

"You're with Globax, right?"

"Yeah."

"Anything unusual going on there?"

"Unusual?"

"Here, sit down. Something to eat?"

"No."

"You could throw it in the microwave."

"I'm not hungry."

"How about a drink?"

"A little early for me," Roy said.

"Yeah? Woulda taken you for a bit of a shooter."

"Shooter?"

"You know, guy who throws back a few, knows how to have a little fun."

"No one's stopping you."

"Drinking alone's not me. I'm a social animal."

Don't I know.

Barry plucked another chicken ball, started talking again before it reached his mouth. "You were some kind of football hero? Played for Tech?"

"Georgia," Roy said.

"What position?"

"Tight end."

"Yeah? You weren't on the small side?"

"That's the way it turned out."

"Played high school myself," Barry said. "Offensive tackle. Screwed up my knee or I would have gone a lot farther."

Roy said nothing. Barry popped the chicken ball in his mouth, reached for another.

"So now we have something in common, what's the story at Globax?" he said.

"Story?"

"Stock's been behaving strangely the past week, ten days."

"In what way?"

"Some big blocks changed hands, bing bang bing, in the millions—starting to make a move, right? So I took a position, and when I take a position I don't dick around. Then what happens? Poof, it all goes soft."

Roy didn't really know what he was talking about.

"Something's going on, I got it from several sources." He waited for Roy to tell him what it was.

"They changed the name from Chemerica," Roy said; he couldn't think of anything else.

Barry gazed at him. "Hard to get, huh?" He kept chewing,

but slower, more thoughtful. "Suppose I made it worth your while. Say some little nugget of information came your way, why couldn't we work out a mutually beneficial arrangement, you and I?"

"About what?"

"I don't blame you for being careful. Total discretion guaranteed, up front. I've got an offshore setup, if that eases your mind."

Roy missed the significance of that. "What kind of information?"

"Could be anything—anything that'll let me know what's going down. It's all about knowing the future today."

"That's what Carol says."

Barry stopped chewing. "Who's Carol?"

"No one you know."

"She wouldn't be on the financial side, by any chance?"

"Financial side?"

"At Globax. That would be sweet, a contact on the financial side."

Roy shook his head. They watched each other. Roy had no idea what Barry was thinking. He himself was having a thought he knew was arrogant and unworthy, but couldn't help: I can see why she's coming back to me.

"When do you expect Marcia?" he said.

Barry finished eating, pushed the carton aside, leaned back, clasped his hands behind his head; the sweat stains had spread. "Familiar with the term *POV*?"

"No."

"Point of view. I only know it from my Hollywood connections. Why I bring it up is I'm starting to see things from your POV."

"I don't know what you're talking about."

"Just that now she's diddling me," Barry said, "the way she diddled you."

That sent a jolt through Roy. Had Marcia told Barry that she and Roy had slept with each other again, that they were getting back together? Roy could think of no other explana-

tion, but why would she do that? A horrible possibility struck
Roy: to make Barry jealous. Why make someone jealous unless you were still interested? Roy ruled it out. The man
across the table wasn't jealous. Neither was he angry, bewildered, humiliated, crushed: none of the things Roy had been
when he'd found out about Barry. So Barry didn't know
Marcia was leaving him, at most had sensed something and
was fishing for information.

"Where are you from, Barry?"

"What's that got to do with anything?"

"Because where I come from we wouldn't be talking about
her like that."

"Yeah?" said Barry. "Where would a place like that be, exactly?" He went to the fridge, took out another carton.

"I'll just have a word with Rhett," Roy said.

"Be my guest."

Roy went upstairs. Rhett was playing a video game in
his bedroom, back to the door, tuft of hair sticking up on
his head.

"Why'nt you come on home with me for now?" Roy said.
"Till your ma gets back."

"I'm all set," Rhett said, not turning.

"What are you going to eat for supper? There's nothing in
the fridge."

"There's Chinese."

"It's old."

"I'm not hungry." Rhett hunched closer to the screen.

Roy watched him play the game. "Got to keep up with
your studies even when you're not there," he said. "Can't fall
behind."

No answer. On the screen, a pumped-up warrior ran down
a dark tunnel.

Roy drove home. He checked the messages, none, and the
mail, bills, then went downstairs and worked on the shelves
until they were done. He carried them up to Rhett's old
room—Rhett's room, period—set them up, tried a few books

here and there. He remembered Rhett's Pop Warner trophy—
every kid got one—and his Pop Warner highlight tape, found
them in the closet, put them on the top shelf. The setting sun,
reflecting off someone's windshield on the street, glowed on
the cheaply plated trophy figure, a hard-charging boy with a
football tucked under one arm. Roy stood there until the light
faded; probably only a moment or two.

Roy switched on the kitchen lights, sat down with a Coke,
a pencil, a blank sheet of paper. He wrote three headings: *House Projects*, *Budget (w/new salary)*, *Managerial
Skills*. Under *House Projects* he wrote *bathroom*. Marcia
had always hated the bathroom. Maybe start by ripping out
the linoleum, laying those tiles that looked like marble, then
hanging a bigger mirror, framed by little makeup lightbulbs, and—

The buzzer. Marcia didn't like that either, Roy remembered as he went to answer it. She wanted chimes. He opened
the front door.

Gordo. Gordo in muddy uniform, eyes blurry, propped up
by a boy—no, it was Lee, not in uniform, wearing a denim
jacket and jeans, which was probably why Roy didn't recognize him right away. Gordo swayed back on the stoop and
Lee, so much smaller, almost lost him. Roy grabbed Gordo's
arm. Gordo tilted forward, his eyes making an exaggerated
attempt to bring Roy into focus.

"Hi, good buddy," he said.

Roy pulled him inside. "You all right?" he said.

"I hear the rolling thunder."

Roy got him in the living room, laid him on the couch.

"Puke city," Gordo said.

Roy sat him up.

"Roy has a secret life," Gordo said. He turned green.

"I'll get some water," Lee said, going into the kitchen.

"What's my secret life?" Roy said.

"Listenin' to gospel. Don't you worry none. I'll take it to
my grave." Gordo's arm shot out abruptly, jerked Roy down
beside him on the couch. "Tell you something confidential,

good buddy." Roy smelled alcohol in several states, from raw to almost completely digested. "He's not gay."

"Who?" Roy asked.

A mistake, asking a question, because Gordo put his lips to Roy's ear to answer. His breath was hot, his lips wet. "Lee. Thought he was gay, but he's not. You think he was gay?"

"No," Roy said; but he remembered the feeling of Lee's hand on his back as they posed by the cannon.

"Could have taken advantage of me out there, couldn't he of?" Gordo said. "If he'd of been—"

Lee returned with a glass of water.

"Not thirsty," Gordo said.

"Drink," Lee said.

Gordo stopped shaking his head. "Is that an order, Corporal?"

"Yes."

Gordo drank, but the green tinge on his cheeks and upper lip didn't go away.

"Where's my canteen?" he said. He felt along his belt, patting frantically with both hands. "Lost my canteen." He started to cry.

"Canteen's in the car," Lee said. "All your gear's in your car, right outside."

"Think I care about that goddamn car?" He turned to Roy. "Know my plan for that piece of shit?"

"No," Roy said.

Gordo wiped away tears with the back of his sleeve, muddying his face. "Think of China," he said.

"China?"

"Boom," said Gordo.

"What does that mean?"

"If you don't know, who does? Big bang, good buddy."

"He wants to blow up his car?" Lee said.

Gordo put his lips to Roy's ear again. "Ammonium nitrate in the trunk, in the back, under the hood, everywhere. Sub-level five. Boom." The words buzzed through Roy's auditory tubes and into his brain.

He got up, moved away. "Better sleep it off, Gordo."

"I might lie down," said Gordo, lying down, "but you can forget about the sleeping part. Think I trust anybody now and forevermore?" His eyes closed. "Boom," he said, and then went silent.

Roy and Lee gazed down at him. He twitched once or twice. The corners of his lips curved down. Can you look unhappy, anxious, troubled with your eyes closed, and drunk? Gordo did.

"Hope you're not angry," Lee said.

"About what?"

"Bringing him here. He didn't want to go home. He wanted to be here."

"What about Brenda?"

"I called her."

"And?"

Lee glanced at Roy. Roy couldn't tell how old he was. From the face alone, the skin poreless, the features small and precise, Roy would have guessed about nineteen or twenty. But the eyes were at least ten years older than that, and so was the way he talked, the way he carried himself.

"She's upset. Didn't really want him home—"

"Until he sobered up." Roy finished the sentence for him. Not something he usually did, if ever, but he'd known what Lee was going to say and it had just popped out.

Their eyes met. "Which could be some time," Lee said.

Gordo twitched suddenly, as though he knew they were discussing him and didn't like it. They both gazed down at him.

"Lucky you were there," Roy said.

"Where?"

"At that camp of yours."

"I wasn't. Satchmo boards close by."

Satchmo? Roy didn't get it at first. Then images from the dream of the smudged-faced horseman came streaming back to him, as clear as when he'd dreamed them.

"They've got stables out there?" Roy said.

Lee nodded. "I saw Gordo's car in the lot on my way up."

Gordo groaned.

"So you need a drive back?" Roy said.

"It's not necessary."

"Going to saddle up instead?"

Lee smiled. "Would if I could."

They got in Gordo's Altima, just like Roy's but newer and smelling of booze. Lee drove, Roy sat in the passenger seat. He heard empty beer cans rattling in the back as they turned onto Virginia, headed for the highway.

"Hope we don't get stopped," he said.

"I never do."

But Roy didn't know why. Once they were up on the connector, Lee drove fast, weaving in and out of the passing lane, hitting eighty-five, ninety, more. The funny thing was it didn't feel like going fast. It felt just right, smooth, effortless, safe. Lee's hands—not big, but strong looking and finely shaped—held the wheel in proper ten-to-two position, relaxed; his eyes gazed straight ahead in that steady way of his, without concern. Roy even wondered if he was thinking of something else. They blew past a Corvette, hit ninety-five.

"You've done some driving," Roy said.

"A little."

"I meant the competitive kind."

Lee nodded, or made a slight motion that might have been a nod. "The guys are pretty jacked about you," he said.

"I don't understand."

"What with this connection. It's like you're history, walking and talking."

"Because I have the same name as this great-great whatever he was?"

"That," said Lee, "and the fact that he was in the regiment, and"—Lee shot him a quick glance; Roy's foot stomped a brake that wasn't there—"you look the part."

Roy remembered what Gordo had said, but also remembered the touch of Lee's hand again, felt a little uncomfortable. Lee's eyes were back on the road.

"What did you think of the bio?" he said.

"Bio?"

"I thought Jesse put together a bio."

"I haven't had a chance to read it yet," Roy said, not even sure where it was.

"Did you get my message about black powder shooting?"

"I haven't had much time lately."

"Work."

"Yeah."

"Poor Gordo."

Twenty, the perimeter, Bankhead: record time. As they crossed the river, Roy had an idea. "What about Earl?"

"What about him?" said Lee, suddenly decelerating. A few seconds later they cruised lawfully past a patrol car hidden by trees at the side of the road. Roy checked to see whether Gordo had installed a radar detector; he had not.

"I hear he's got a lot of things going. Maybe there'd be a job for Gordo."

"I wouldn't know about that," Lee said. "Or business in general." He sped up without a glance back in the mirror. Traffic was lighter now, the night darker. The needle touched one hundred. "There was heavy skirmishing right around here," Lee said.

"You're talking about the Civil War?"

Lee smiled; a quick flash lit by the dashboard gauges. "Is that a surprise?" he said. One of his hands left the wheel, made a broad arc. "Sherman razed all of this, down to the ground."

Roy looked out, saw the suburbs.

"Too bad he can't come back and do it again," Lee said, "now when it might do some good."

"What do you mean?"

"Just take a look," Lee said. "Couldn't be a better demonstration of what we lost."

"You really think of it as we?"

Lee turned up the road to the camp, slowed down. "The very fact you can ask that shows how total the conquest was."

"How so?"

"They've occupied your mind."

Roy laughed.

"What's funny?"

"You make it sound like one of those alien possession movies."

"That's a good way of putting it."

They pulled into the parking lot. The headlights swept over the empty pavement, shone on the lone vehicle, a motorcycle leaning on its stand near the beginning of the path. Lee stopped beside it.

"When I say occupied your mind, I'm not talking about your soul. That's a different issue."

"Are you a college professor, something like that?" Roy said.

"No."

"What do you do?"

"This," Lee said. "The regiment."

"I didn't know it was a paying job."

"It's not." Lee turned to him, shifting easily, even gracefully, on the seat. "This mind and soul dichotomy—I've done some thinking about it, in reference to Gordo."

"Yeah?" Roy hadn't dwelled much on either aspect of Gordo, not in any analytical way.

"It's the cause of all the problems he's having. He can't succeed at that place of yours—what's it called?"

"Globax."

"There we go," said Lee. "A Yankee thing. They've imposed their way of life on us, even fooled us into believing it's our way of life too. That's the mental part. But we can never do it properly, never really compete, never be happy. That's the soul part."

"The soul part?"

"Unconquered, unoccupied, waiting."

"So we're like the Bosnians?" said Roy, not buying it. Why would he? Seventy-two seven, before bonuses! If that wasn't competing, what was?

Lee didn't laugh at his little joke, didn't smile. "It's much worse than that. They're just Bosnians. Look who we were."

"Slave owners," Roy said.

Lee went still for a second or two. Then he reached out, touched the back of Roy's hand, lightly, briefly, almost not at all. "You have to get that out of your mind," he said. Then he got out of the car, mounted the bike, roared away, leaning low around the corner.

No helmet.

Roy opened the door to his house, smelled something sizzling. He went into the living room. Gordo was where he'd left him, but not alone. A big, long-haired man was bent over him, going through his pockets. Adrenaline shot through Roy's body. Maybe the big man felt it too. He wheeled around: Sonny Junior.

Big smile. "Hi, Roy." He held up Gordo's wallet. "Just IDing this dude in case he's some kind of perp."

"He's not a perp, Sonny. How did you get in?"

"Happened to have a key that fit. Lucky thing, what with the way this guy's responding. What's with him?"

"He's a Confederate reenactor."

"Got the blind drunk part down pretty good," Sonny Junior said, dropping the wallet on Gordo's chest. He came forward, gave Roy one of his arm-wrestling handshakes, pulled him into an embrace. "Cousin," he said. "Son of a bitch."

"How's my father?"

"Right. We should eat pretty quick. I saw you were having steak tonight so I threw them on the stove. Case you were hungry when you got home, you know?" Sonny Junior went into the kitchen, Roy following. Sonny Junior had the three steaks frying in a pan, the Creole sauce bubbling around them. He drew a knife from his pocket, cut a piece off one of the steaks, speared it, popped it in his mouth.

"Mmm," he said. "Where'd you get this sauce?"

"Why should we eat pretty quick?" Roy said.

Sonny Junior took down two plates—he seemed to know his way around already—put a steak on each, cut the third one in two, slid the slightly bigger portion on Roy's plate. He sat down at one end of the table, Marcia's place, actually. "Dig in," he said.

"You didn't answer my question, Sonny."

"This is so fuckin' good." Sonny Junior chewed on a big mouthful, talked around it. "Yeah, your question. It's about Uncle Roy. He's not doing too well."

"He's had a relapse?"

"A relapse, yeah. I didn't want you to think it was my fault, which was why I came down personally."

"Why would it be your fault?"

"Against my better judgment I brought him that ol' bottle from up over the sink. The one he wanted. Turned out he had some kind of reaction."

"How bad?"

"The worst kind. My heartfelt condolences, cuz."

TWELVE

"Sorry for your troubles," said Curtis from his car phone that night. Roy recognized voices in the background: Carol and Jerry. "Do what you have to."

"But what about the forty-eight hours?" Roy said.

"What forty-eight hours?"

"Till the announcement. About my . . ." Roy didn't want to say it.

"Since when have you been such a worrier, Roy?" Curtis said. "You can take this one to the bank. See you the day after tomorrow?"

"Seven sharp."

"We'll announce it then. Picked out that chair yet?"

The gravediggers were black, very dark-skinned, like pure Africans. They leaned against the bulldozer, waiting for the preacher to finish. The preacher was a very white, almost pigmentless man, old and emaciated, with wispy hair and a wispy voice. He spoke against a strong breeze, and only a few prayerful scraps reached the mourners facing him on the other side of the hole: Roy, Sonny Junior, and Rhett in the middle.

When it was over, they each threw in a shovelful of earth because that was what the preacher seemed to be motioning them to do. Roy remembered how his mother's coffin had looked, down in a hole like this, and the agony of that day. He didn't feel much of anything now. The preacher came around to their side, stepping carefully past the dirt pile at one end of the grave. The bulldozer bumped up the path, blade descending.

"This the grandson?" said the preacher, looking down at Rhett.

Rhett showed no reaction.

"Nice to meet you, boy," said the preacher, offering his hand.

"Shake hands," said Roy.

Rhett shook hands.

"Fine-looking boy," said the preacher. "How'd you come by the fat lip?"

Rhett looked blank.

"I was asking myself the same question," said Sonny Junior.

Rhett's mouth opened, closed, opened again. "Football," he said.

"Good game," said the preacher.

"Good autumn game," said Sonny Junior, stressing *autumn*.

The bulldozer operator revved the engine. The preacher glanced at it with annoyance. "Used to be a good game," he said. "Wonder if you folks have a moment. Like to show you something interesting, while you're up here."

They followed him across the cemetery, away from the chapel, toward wooded hills rising on the other side. A flock of crows swept down on them, shot into the trees, vanished. The gravestones grew smaller, simpler, more worn. Names repeated themselves: Searle, McTeague, Nevins, Teeter, Hill. The preacher came to the edge of the trees, kept going. Gravestones pushed up here and there through dead leaves and fallen branches; with just their rounded white tops showing, they might have been giant mushrooms. The preacher stopped before one of them, set near the base of a tall tree that blocked the sun.

With a groan, the preacher got down on one knee, cleared away brush, exposing about half of the stone's face. It had sunk a little into the ground, or the ground had risen up. The preacher dug at the earth with his hand.

"Give me some help here, boy," he said.

"Me?" said Rhett, looking at Roy.

Roy nodded. Rhett knelt by the preacher. They clawed the dirt away, moist brown earth, easily clawed.

"That's the spirit," said the preacher. He scraped a few clods off the stone with his fingernails. It read:

> *Roy Singleton Hill*
> *1831–1865*
> *Hero*

"You can read that, boy?" the preacher said.

"Uh-huh," said Rhett.

"Read it out loud."

"Roy Singleton Hill," said Rhett. "Eighteen thirty-one dash eighteen sixty-five. Hero."

"Dash?" said Sonny Junior.

"Very nice," said the preacher, ignoring Sonny Junior. "That's your great-great-great-grandfather what's laying there in his eternal peace."

"Why was he a hero?" Rhett said.

The preacher smiled at Rhett, revealing a mouthful of brown-edged teeth. "A bright youngster," he said, tousling Rhett's hair, leaving a few particles of earth behind. "He fought for his people," the preacher said. "Gave his last full measure. That's what makes a hero."

"So he'd be my what, exactly?" said Sonny Junior.

"Great-great-grandfather, of course," said the preacher, "same as his." He nodded at Roy. "A crying shame, you fellows not knowing that. Who are you, anyways, if you don't know your own past?"

"Never thought of that," said Sonny Junior. "True he owned a lot of land around here?"

"The very ground we're standing on," said the preacher. "All the way down to the crick. And back up"—he pointed into the woods—"past the old cart path, the copper works, on up to what they called the Mountain House."

"Jesus Christ," said Sonny Junior. The preacher's eyes, narrow to begin with, narrowed more. Sonny Junior gazed down at the gravestone. "Kind of makes you reverent," he said. A crow cawed, somewhere up the hill.

"Nothing more to see," said the preacher. "Just remember what they say about the past—whosoever forgets it is condemned to repeat it."

"Is that from the Bible?" said Sonny Junior.

"Might as well be," said the preacher. "Donation box is on the left side as you go in, hard by the door."

The distant crow cawed again. This time another crow responded, much closer, possibly in the very tree under which they stood.

Roy had an appointment with the attorney.

"How about I take Rhett back to the place?" said Sonny Junior. "We can meet up later."

"Rhett?" Roy said, figuring Rhett would want to stay with him.

"Okay with me," Rhett said.

The attorney had a one-room office in a strip mall off the Cleveland ring road. When Roy walked in, he was alone inside, smoking a pipe and working on a newspaper puzzle.

"My condolences," said the attorney, waving Roy into a chair. "Last time I saw you, you were this high. Your father and I went to high school together, or maybe you knew that already."

"No." The room was hazy with pipe smoke. Roy started having air supply problems.

"Course he was a popular kid—do you believe I still remember that powder-blue Chevy he had? Whitewalls. And a big old bull horn mounted on the hood. Not a loudspeaker—I mean a real horn from a bull. Whereas I was what they'd probably call a nerd nowadays, 'cept there was no word for it then. Like a lot of things."

He sucked on his pipe, waited for Roy to say something, maybe ask some questions about his father. When Roy did not, he picked up the will.

"All pretty straightforward," he said. "He really didn't have a whole lot at the end, enough to pay the funeral expenses, my fee, sundries. And the place, of course, but it's got a mortgage."

"I'm going to sell it anyway," Roy said.

The lawyer gazed into the glowing bowl of the pipe. "Mind a personal question?"

"Go on."

"You paid him a visit over at Ocoee Regional the other day."

"That's right."

"Anything unusual happen?"

"Like what?"

"I know he could be a mite cantankerous. Specially when he was hitting the bottle."

"He was all right."

"Would you say he was of sound mind when you saw him?"

"Sound mind?"

"Not crazy."

"He didn't seem crazy. I wasn't there long. I drove up to the place for a few things, ran into Sonny, and he took the stuff back."

The attorney nodded, his eyes shifting to the will. "Reason I asked is that's grounds for breaking a will, if you can prove unsound mind."

"Why would I want to do that?"

"Thing is," said the attorney, "next morning, morning after you paid that visit, he called me in to add a codicil."

"I don't know that word."

"Means like an amendment. Has the full force of any other clause, long as it's drawn up right, and it was." He handed Roy the will, open to the last page.

Roy read the codicil:

I replace clause 2(c) with the following:
(c) Title to the above-mentioned item shall pass to
my nephew Sonny Nevins, Jr.

"What's the above-mentioned item?" Roy said.

"Just a legalism saves me retyping if changes come up," said the attorney. "Refer back to two B."

Roy referred back to 2(b). The above-mentioned item was his father's place, the house and the barn at the end of the long dirt road. His eyes moved down the page to the original 2(c): *Title to the above-mentioned item shall pass to my son, Roy Singleton Hill.*

Roy looked up. The attorney was watching him through a cloud of pipe smoke. "Which is why I was wondering if anything unusual took place when you paid that last visit."

Wasn't the whole thing unusual, hardly seeing your own father all your life? What would be unusual after that? "Not really," Roy said.

"You didn't say anything might have pissed him off? He got pissed off kind of easy, maybe you didn't know."

Roy shook his head, but at the same time he was remembering: *Why'd you go and give him a name like that?* Couldn't be, could it?

"Thought of something?" said the attorney.

"We were estranged, I guess you'd say. That's all."

"Okey-doke," said the attorney. He opened a desk drawer, took out a key. "As for what you do got coming to you," he said, "check two D."

Roy read 2(d): *The old trunk under my bed, with contents, is for my son, Roy Singleton Hill. The key to the trunk will be delivered to him by my executor.*

The attorney handed Roy a key. "Any questions?"

"Just one," Roy said. "Does Sonny know about this?"

"Not from me. Wanted to talk to you first, see your reaction, in terms of the sound mind part."

"I get the idea you kind of want me to contest the will," Roy said.

"I could never take a position like that," the attorney said. "You're a family man, that's all. And Sonny's . . . Sonny."

But Roy knew he wouldn't do it. Didn't sit right with him, contesting a will. And whatever money was involved didn't matter—money wouldn't be a problem, not with the new job, and Marcia and him back under one roof. Roy rose.

"Best of luck," said the attorney. As Roy moved to the door, he added, "Don't suppose you can help me with *vreans*."

"Vreans?"

"Got to rearrange it into a word for the Jumble."

Roy had no idea. He'd never been good at puzzles.

Roy drove back to the place, Sonny's place now. He kept the windows open the whole way but the pipe smell was still with him when he parked at the end of the dirt road and walked past the washer, engine block, broken TV, hubcaps, and up to the house. No one was inside. Roy started across the field to the barn, was halfway there when he heard laughter. At first, he didn't realize it was Rhett laughing, a sound he hadn't heard for some time.

Roy went into the barn. Rhett and Sonny Junior were way at the back, in the shadowy part where a few shafts of light crisscrossed over their heads from the windows in the loft. Roy made his way around the demolition derby car, past the drums, close enough to see that Rhett and Sonny Junior were both stripped to the waist and wearing boxing gloves. Sonny Junior threw a slow looping left a foot over Rhett's head. Rhett stepped inside and bounced two quick left jabs and a right cross that surprised Roy with its strength off the ridges of Sonny Junior's abs. Sonny Junior said something, of which Roy caught only one word: "pisspot." Rhett laughed again, a real happy sound, unrestrained. While he was still laughing, Sonny Junior caught him a pretty good one upside the head, not a real punch with the force he was capable of, but real enough. Rhett blinked. Then his lower lip started to quiver, just the tiniest tremor, but Roy saw. Roy raised his hand—in fact, it came up by itself—but before he could say anything, Rhett lowered his head, stepped inside again, and hit Sonny Junior with another right cross, this one even better than the last, and a little higher up. Sonny Junior said something; Roy caught "sack of shit" and "peckerhead." Rhett laughed again, but kept his hands up this time. Then they were both laughing. Sonny Junior saw Roy, waved.

"Ding," he said, lowering his hands. Rhett lowered his hands too. Sonny Junior threw a savage punch, quick as the strike of some predator on top of the food chain, just past Rhett's ear. Rhett flinched after the fact. " 'Member to keep 'em up after the bell, case some asshole's lookin' to clock you by surprise," said Sonny Junior.

He came over to Roy. "A quick learner, my little nephew," he said.

"It's cousin," Roy said. "We discussed this."

"Same diff," said Sonny Junior. "He's a good kid, all I'm saying."

"Thanks," said Roy.

"No thanks necessary—rubs off on me too," said Sonny Junior. "How'd it go in town?"

Roy told him what had happened. As the story unfolded, Sonny Junior's forehead wrinkled, then his eyes got wider, finally he shook his head.

"That's bullshit," he said.

"What do you mean?"

"Place belongs to you, Roy. All I was hopin' would be you'd let me stay up here, take care of it, like."

"Did he let on at all, when you brought him the stuff?"

"Stuff?"

"Briefs, Cheetos, the bottle."

"Shit," said Sonny Junior, "I forgot the briefs."

"Did he let on?"

"I only saw him for a minute or two. All's he went on about was that business of the name."

"What name?"

Sonny Junior glanced back—Rhett was throwing punches

at one of those mote-filled rays of light—lowered his voice: "Rhett's name."

That was that.

"I'll give it back to you if you want," Sonny Junior said. "Say the word."

Roy said, "No. I would have sold it anyway."

"Yeah?"

"But you're going to live here."

"I just might," said Sonny Junior. He loosened the strings of his boxing glove with his teeth. "No hard feelings?"

"No hard feelings."

Sonny Junior pulled off the glove. They shook on it, arm-wrestling style.

Rhett approached.

"Uncle Sonny?" he said. "Can I try the drums?"

"Can you try the drums," said Sonny Junior. "Does the pope shit in the woods?"

Rhett laughed. Sonny Junior helped him off with his gloves, led him toward the drum kit.

Roy went up to the house, entered his father's bedroom, switched on the red light. No rat on the pillow this time, but everything else was the same, crumpled Cheetos packages and an empty bottle of Old Grand-Dad on the unmade bed, plus one or two balled-up tissues that Roy hadn't noticed before. The old trunk was underneath. Roy pulled it out, a leather-covered trunk, the leather dry and cracked, wood showing through it. The key fit. He opened the lid.

First came thick sheets of what Roy took to be wax paper, although they were hardly waxy anymore. Roy removed them carefully. Under the bottom sheet lay a gun. An old gun, much shorter than Gordo's reproduction musket; possibly a carbine, Roy thought, although he didn't know much about guns. There was a word carved in the wooden stock: *death*.

Under the gun was another sheet of wax paper, and under that a small leather-bound book, this leather also dry and cracked, with *RSH 1861–1865* burned on the front, possibly by some sort of branding iron. Roy opened it. The yellowed corner of the first page broke off in his hands, fluttered back down in the trunk. Roy turned the brittle pages. There was a lot of writing on the first few, very small and hard to read, then less and less. The last page had been torn out.

Roy knelt by the trunk, removed more wax paper, dug deeper. At the very bottom, he found a uniform, the gray faded almost white. It was a lot like Gordo's uniform, or Lee's or Earl's or any of the others, but real. Roy couldn't have said why. He ran his hand over the fabric of the jacket; wool, rough to the touch. The tip of his index finger caught in a frayed round hole on the left side of the chest. Roy started having air supply problems, maybe something from the wax paper. He went to the window, opened it, took a deep breath. Rhett and Sonny Junior were coming across the field, carrying fireworks.

Roy repacked the trunk, locked it, carried it out the front door to the car. As he put it inside, he heard a boom from the other side of the house, then another. The sound frightened the birds. They rose from their roosting places—bluejays and some small brown birds Roy didn't know the name of— and flapped around in a circle. Then a crow flew up, a big one, and chased them out of the sky.

Roy went around the house.

"Time to get going," he called.

Out in the field, Sonny Junior lit a match. He and Rhett jumped back. Another rocket went whistling high above, exploded in a green burst that would have looked pretty good at night.

Rhett and Sonny Junior came over, big smiles on their faces.

"Okay if I stay overnight? Uncle Sonny says it's okay with him."

"No," Roy said.

"But I can't go to school anyway."

Roy shook his head.

"Some other time, killer," said Sonny Junior. "You all'll be back here real soon."

Roy knew he'd never be there again.

Sonny Junior walked them to the car. Roy saw that Rhett had a box of firecrackers, let it go. Sonny Junior opened the passenger door for the boy. Something fell out. Sonny Junior picked it up.

"What's this?"

"Furniture catalog," Roy said. "I get to choose one of those chairs for my office."

Sonny Junior looked them over. "Take the Cremona," he said.

THIRTEEN

The phone woke Roy the next morning, before dawn.

"Roy?" said Marcia. "Where have you been?"

"Where have *I* been?"

"I must have called you five times yesterday. Have you got Rhett?"

"Of course I've got him. Didn't Barry tell you?"

"We're not speaking."

"You're not speaking?" It sounded like a line from some teenage movie.

"Don't take that tone with me, Roy."

"Rhett's been expelled for the week—"

"You're joking. I can't even go away for two days without—"

"And my father died." That part came out louder than Roy had intended. The silence that followed made it seem even more so.

"I'm sorry," Marcia said.

"It's all right. I took Rhett to the funeral."

He heard Marcia letting out her breath, a long slow sigh, and could almost feel the pressure she was under. It made him a little sorry for her. He would do his best to take that pressure off, very soon. She and Barry not speaking was a good thing—further confirmation that they were finished. Roy checked the clock, sat up, started getting out of bed. This, he thought, the day of his promotion, could be an even bigger day than that if he handled it right.

"Why was he expelled?" Marcia said.

"It was partly my fault."

"Your fault?"

"Why don't I bring him over?" Roy glanced down at the bed, saw his rumpled pillow, and the other one, unused. "We can talk."

"Now?"

"On my way to work." He thought: Her head on that pillow tonight. And then some silly stuff: Champagne! The Cremona! "I'll explain."

"Explain what?"

"What I have in mind."

Pause. "Are you all right, Roy?"

"Sure. Fine. Okay to stop in?"

Another long slow breath. "Okay."

"Wake up, Rhett."

"Don't want to."

"Got to. Your ma's back. I'm taking you over to her place before work."

"Don't want to."

"Can't stay here by yourself all day."

"Don't want to do that either."

"You want to go to school? That's good. This week'll be over before you know it."

"School? I'm not talking about school. Can't I go back up there for a few days?"

"Up where?"

"Up at Uncle Sonny's. He promised to let me drive the demolition derby car."

"No."

"Why not?"

"Get up, Rhett. There's not much time."

Roy showered, washed his hair, shaved with a new blade, dressed, carefully knotted the tie he considered his best, the one with the little blue diamonds, drove Rhett to Marcia's. The tuft of hair on Rhett's uncombed head stood up like a blunt feather.

Marcia answered the door. She didn't look good, not good for her: face puffy, hair in disarray, a streak of blue eye makeup across her cheekbone. For some reason, the change in her lips was obvious now; they resembled Rhett's, still swollen from his last schoolyard fight. She wore a T-shirt with a big apple on the front, just long enough to be decent. Not looking good for Marcia was still pretty good.

"Rhett," she said, reaching out, drawing him to her. He went stiff, but didn't stop her. Over Rhett's shoulder, she held out a hand to Roy. "Sorry about your father, Roy. How did he . . ."

"Liver," said Roy.

She nodded. Her hand was cold. "Coffee?" she said.

"If it's ready," Roy said. "Can't be late—big day today." He almost told her about the promotion, the salary, the bonus, might have spilled it all the next second, but somewhere in the house there was a thump, like a book falling, or a shoe. Marcia's eyes shifted.

He drank his coffee in the kitchen, standing up.

"Look what I brought you, Rhett," Marcia said.

"What is it?"

"Never seen one of these snow globes?" she said. "This here's Manhattan—that's the fancy part. Statue of Liberty, Empire State Building, I forget the name of this one, and Trump Tower. Turn it upside down to watch the snow."

Rhett turned it upside down, but lost interest before the snow had done falling.

"A good trip?" Roy said.

"All right."

"Did you like New York?" Roy had never been; neither, until now, had Marcia.

"I had to get away for a day or two."

Roy understood: Barry. "After work today, let's have that dinner," Roy said.

"What dinner?"

"From the other night. Why don't you come by around six?"

Marcia bit her lip. Roy didn't remember her doing that before; was it the start of a new habit that came with the implant, or injections, or whatever they were? "I'll try," she said.

"But—" But what did it depend on? Work, most likely, Roy decided: she'd have to make up for the missed time. "Doesn't have to be six," he said. "Whenever you can make it is fine."

"I said I'll try."

For the drive to work, Roy selected the tape that followed Jerry's promotion.

A promotion is one of life's big changes, Jerry, and
    business these days is about change. Any concerns?
I'm worried about the attitude of my old colleagues,
    Carol, the men and women on the floor.
That says a lot about you, Jerry, but don't overdo it.
    There may be some resentment at first, but it usually
    passes. After all, Jerry, everyone understands this is a
    business.

Were there snow globes of Atlanta? Would the Globax building be included if there were? It seemed especially tall today, its color a few shades darker than the brassy sky, the blue Globax sign a brilliant blue, and as he watched it, Roy realized they'd added a new feature: a sparkling image of the planet that somehow spun back and forth between the G and the X. Roy laughed out loud, it was so dazzling, the kind of effect that would get a building into the snow globes for sure. At that moment, it hit: a company this good, this important, believed in him, Roy Hill; a stamp of approval from the big time. He realized he was doing all right, even felt a bit of pride.

Roy turned into the garage. The attendant was in his booth, chewing on a sugar donut, the new bronze Globax hat tilted back on his head, his feet up on the counter. He looked up at Roy in surprise. Roy checked the clock: 6:55. On time, nothing to be surprised about. Then Roy figured it out: Curtis parked in the upper garage, S2, with the guys from the seventeenth floor. The attendant had already been told that Roy would be parking there too, as of today. This was his last day down in S5. He found a space right by the elevator, which never happened after 6:45. In fact, there were lots of spaces. His lucky day.

6:57. Roy got in the elevator, pressed S1. He rode up alone, watching his reflection on the inside of the bronze door. He thought he looked the same as always—except for the tie; the tie really was special, an anniversary present from Marcia, not the last anniversary, but the last one that they'd still been together. No one looking at his reflection could have seen how he felt inside, so ready.

The doors opened at S2, the executive parking level. No one got on, but Roy saw a man in a dark suit walking toward an SUV, one of the really big ones. The man started to unlock it, then suddenly bent forward and vomited all over the cement floor, his gleaming shoes, the cuffs of his pants. As he straightened back up, Roy got a good look at his face. It was Mr. Pegram. The elevator closed.

6:58. The doors opened. Roy got out. Left to receiving, right to shipping. Roy turned right, toward the cubicle grid, laid out like a vast silicon motherboard, with U.S.A. first, divided into sections A1, A2, B, C, D1, and D2; Canada and Caribbean; European Union (excluding U.K.); U.K.; Eastern Europe (excluding Russia); Russia; Mexico; Central/South America (excluding Mexico); on down to the end, Asia/ Oceania. The problem was the cubicles were gone. The cubicles, the desks, the chairs, the monitors, the phones, the framed family pictures, the Far Side cartoons, P.J.'s slippers: all gone. And the people. Roy must have made some kind of sound, because it came echoing back to him across the empty space, a startled little cry you might hear in the night woods.

Roy looked closely at his watch to make sure of what it said. 6:59. He turned back to the elevators. Surely in the next minute the shipping guys would come swarming out, and a team from maintenance to make everything right, install the new cubicles, computers, T-1 connections, phone system, whatever it was. Maybe they'd decided to redo everything in Globax colors, bronze and blue. But the next minute came and nothing happened.

What day was it?

He checked his watch: Wed. The right day.

You can take this one to the bank. See you the day after tomorrow?

Seven sharp.

He checked his watch: seven sharp.

Roy had a crazy idea. Someone had found out about his promotion yesterday, there'd been a riot, everyone had walked off the job. Ludicrous, but nothing else occurred to him. Then he noticed that he wasn't quite alone. Someone was standing in the glass office, very still. Roy couldn't make him out because for the first time in his memory the lights weren't on in the glass office. It rose like a dark island in the center of all that empty bright space.

Roy crossed the floor, climbed the stairs, went in. The glass office had been stripped of everything, but Curtis looked the same, dressed in a perfectly fitting dark suit, and wearing a tie, Roy saw, exactly like his, with the same blue diamonds.

"I knew I forgot something," Curtis said.

"What are you talking about? Where is everybody?"

One of Curtis's eyelids did that fluttering thing. "You being away. It slipped my mind." He noticed Roy's tie, went silent.

"What slipped your mind?"

"Informing you, Roy."

"Informing me what?"

"They let them all go," he said, making a panoramic gesture with his hand. "The whole department."

"I don't understand."

"Globax," said Curtis. "Fired every single shipper on the

floor. Plus receiving. Did it by email from New York at 4:25 yesterday afternoon. At 4:30 every screen went dark. When I came in this morning it was like this."

"Impossible," Roy said. "How can there be no more shipping?"

"Of course there's shipping, Roy, for God's sake. As of this minute it's all being done out of Miami, that's all."

Cesar must have heard rumors: Roy understood those emailed questions now. "P.J.?" he said. "DeLoach?"

"Every single one."

"Jesus."

"Yes."

Roy felt sick. "Survivor guilt," he said.

"I beg your pardon?"

"Now I know what it means."

Curtis looked puzzled; maybe he'd never heard the term. Roy had been to Miami twice, once for football, years later on a long weekend with Marcia. They'd had a good time. Miami would be all right, might even help them make a fresh start. He could handle it. This was a business, after all, and change was a big part of it, as Carol had just finished pointing out. He pulled himself together.

"When do we start?" he said.

"Start?" said Curtis.

"In Miami. When do we have to be there?"

"We?"

Roy got it. "You're staying here?"

Curtis nodded.

"For that Eastern Europe thing."

"That job's gone."

"Gone?"

"As part of the rightsizing."

"What rightsizing?"

"That's what this is all about, Roy. They even let Bill Pegram go this morning."

Roy felt a tiny nauseous uprising deep in his throat. "That's why you're staying?"

Curtis's eyelid fluttered.

"You got his job?"

Curtis's eyelid fluttered again, almost stayed closed this time.

Roy held out his hand. "Congratulations." Curtis's handshake was strangely weak; he'd have to do something about that, up on seventeen. "So when do I go?"

"Go where, Roy?"

"Why, Miami, of course."

"To do what?"

"My new job," Roy said. "Regional supervising, area managing." The titles made him laugh. "There's still shipping, Curtis, like you said. What's a global chemical company without shipping? There's no virtual chemicals yet." Roy surprised himself with that last observation; he got the feeling it might be the kind of remark that would land him on a seventeenth floor of his own someday.

"Almighty God, Roy. Don't you see?"

"See what?"

"You're not included."

Roy started to have trouble connecting the words in his mind. "Meaning?"

"They let you go too."

"Me?"

"I did everything I could. You're the one I fought for."

"I don't understand."

"How else can I put it?"

"Say it again."

"They let you go."

"Again."

"Please, Roy."

"Again."

Curtis said it again.

No air. No air at all. Roy barely got a word out. "But what about the area supervision, the regional . . ."

Curtis shook his head. "Miami's handling that. Cesar got the job."

Roy's hand was in his pocket, clutching the inhaler. It took a lot of strength not to pull it out.

"They did throw me one little bone," Curtis said. "There's an opening on the shipping floor up in New York. They said you could try for that."

Roy had a vision of smashing the glass office to smithereens, but all he did was say, "Fuck New York," and even that not forcefully, what with the lack of air.

"There's nothing personal, Roy. It's a business."

But there had to be something personal, because Curtis couldn't look him in the eye, couldn't get his gaze any higher than the knot on Roy's tie with the blue diamonds.

FOURTEEN

7:17. Roy drove out of the parking garage under the Globax building. The day was still young; a fresh springtime breeze was blowing the brassiness out of the sky, turning it blue. Carol and Jerry were talking about Jerry's promotion, and how to apply the vision statement in his new job.

In your memo, you asked me to develop a new
perspective, Carol. What did you mean by that?

Roy tore the tape out of the deck, rolled down the window, almost threw it out. But not quite. Throwing the tape away would be tantamount to ... what? Roy didn't know, didn't even know exactly what *tantamount* meant, only knew that whatever the statement was, he didn't want to make it.

But he wanted to do something. All that readiness inside him, all that eagerness, was still there. Not in its original form: what remained was the revved-up energy, like some animal force with the head cut off. What he wanted to do was make everything right immediately, to get to his desk, his new desk or his old desk, or some other one, to get back to work. How? His first thought was to turn around, to march up to the seventeenth floor, to say the right thing to the right person. But what was the right thing, who was the right person? He knew no one on the seventeenth floor, not even casually, now that Mr. Pegram was gone. And the decision hadn't even come from the seventeenth floor; it had come from New York, from headquarters, about which Roy knew nothing.

Miami? Rightsizing? What did it mean? Did it have anything to do with the name change? What had DeLoach said the very day CHEMERICA had come down and GLOBAX had gone up? Roy couldn't remember. All he remembered was his own reply: *it's just a name change*. He should have asked Curtis more questions. The reasons for what had happened were already slipping away from him, threatening to leave him stranded in some meaningless place. He couldn't live like that, like one of those people with a "Shit Happens" bumper sticker, or their unknowing counterparts with the "Grace Happens" reply. Roy's life had meaning, made sense. *You worked all day, put good food on the table, sat down together, drank a little wine, the kid said something that made you smile at each other over his head, you relaxed, body and soul.* That thought, coming back, made him squirm inside. Marcia was coming for dinner that night. He was going to tell her all about the promotion, the seventy-two seven, the bonus on top of that. Roy threw the tape out the window.

At that moment, the tape still in midair, he realized something important: under all this pressure, the worst pressure he had ever felt, he was thinking on a new level, deeper, smarter. Had his brain ever come up with connections like that shit-grace thing before? No. But now it was racing, and in this racing mode maybe reaching some potential that was always there. They were right to promote him. He could do the job.

Could have done the job. This firing had nothing to do with him. Maybe it made sense on one level—although Roy couldn't see how anything that put all those men out of work and left a big empty space in the building could make sense—but it didn't make sense in terms of him. He had the goods—some goods, at least—and someone somewhere would want him. He stopped at a red light, looked around, saw he was lost.

Not lost, because he'd lived in the city so long, but in the kind of neighborhood he normally would avoid, somewhere south of Abernathy. A big black guy came lurching toward him, the kind of black guy people would still be leery of if he were white, just not as much. Roy didn't roll up the window: he hated the way car windows went up in this kind of situation.

"Lose somethin', chief?" said the black guy, bending down, his face in the open window, a sweet alcohol smell already wafting in.

"No," Roy said.

"Then what's this?" said the black guy, holding up the tape.

"Nothing."

"Don't look like nothin'. Looks like music." He tried to bring the label into focus with his red and blurry eyes, failed. "I'm guessin' Perry Como, maybe, or Engelbert Humperdinck."

"It's not music."

"Then what is it?"

"Advice."

"Valuable advice?"

"I don't know."

The black guy stuck his head in, glanced around. "Don't know what's valuable?" he said.

"Everything has some value," Roy said.

"Who tol' you that, chief?"

"Listen to it," Roy said. "You decide."

"Sure will, on my shiny new sixty-three speaker Bose built-in system wit' the woofer under the floor, you just give me a little help on the down payment."

The light turned green. Roy had a few one-dollar bills in the ashtray, could have handed over one of those, but fell for another idea. He took out his wallet, found more ones, a five, and a ten. He gave the ten: a bet on the future.

"My lucky day," said the black guy. "Runnin' into Mr. Big at last." He shambled away without another word. Roy went home to work on his resume. The leftover energy dissipated. He emptied the inhaler on the way.

* * *

Roy wrote down his name: *Roy Hill*. The resume form asked for his middle name. He wrote: *Roy Singleton Hill*. And stopped right there. Maybe this wouldn't be necessary. He'd played high school football with the shipping manager at Georgia Chemical in Marietta. Roy reached for the phone, his hand trembling slightly in the light coming through the window, as though he'd suddenly developed Parkinson's or aged in a hurry.

"Don't tell me, Roy," said the shipping manager at Georgia Chemical, a ferocious five-foot-five, one-hundred-and-eighty-pound nose tackle who'd screamed his head off for sixty minutes every game, then lain inert on the locker room floor, "not you too?"

"What do you mean?"

"Your guys have been calling all morning, twenty or thirty of them by now. Just got off the phone with a real asshole. DeLoach, maybe? You know him?"

"And?"

"And I told him what I'll tell you, only I don't feel good telling you. There's no jobs here, Roy. We're hiring nobody. Fact is, although word's not out yet, we're licensing Globax's software next month, the V-trak, meaning better efficiency, meaning layoffs of our own. Otherwise I'd take you on in a minute."

Roy didn't know what to say. He just stood there with the phone to his ear. A crow flew past the window with something shiny in its talons.

"How's your boy?" said the shipping manager.

"Good."

"Playing football?"

"Pop Warner."

"I've got a daughter."

"I know."

"Looks just like me," said the shipping manager. "Same body type. Ain't that a hell of a thing?"

*   *   *

Roy got back to work on the resume. He filled it out, wrote
a list of possible employers in north Georgia, addressed envelopes, hit Kinko's and the post office. Then what? It was
barely noon on a working weekday. He could go home.
Home, where the pile of bills waited on the kitchen table, almost a living thing, stacked up against him. He could go to a
diner, a bar, the gym. He could curl up in a ball. He could look
in on Rhett.

He looked in on Rhett. Roy had his reasons, good—an
eleven-year-old shouldn't be home alone on a school day, or
home alone with someone like Barry—and not as good—
seeing Rhett might be a comfort, not to Rhett, but to Roy,
might calm him down. Was that using Rhett in some way, or
just the kind of thing that happened in good families? Roy
hadn't made up his mind about that by the time he pulled into
Marcia's driveway, and parked beside another car already
there, not Marcia's or Barry's, but a black Porsche with New
York plates; New York plates with MD before the numbers.
He pictured Barry and his doctor friend huddled over Barry's
screen upstairs, trading stocks. But the only car he saw
through the window of the closed garage door was Marcia's.

Roy went to the front door. Nothing was growing in any
of the planters; a Chinese menu lay in one of them. Roy
knocked, waited, knocked again. No one came. He thought of
Rhett inside, lying on his bed, hand between his knees, face
to the wall. He tried the door. Locked.

Roy walked around the house. The dirt pile in the backyard
was even higher than the last time. Roy glanced into the pit,
expecting to see sawed-off pipes or twisted cables. There was
nothing down there but a football.

He mounted the deck, put his face close to the sliding glass
door, looked in. He saw a big tile-floored room, empty except
for a sunken hot tub, bubbling away; and superimposed, his
own reflected eyes ringed in shadow. Would he have tried this
door too, if it hadn't been open a crack?

Roy widened the crack and went inside. Something red lay

at the bottom of the hot tub but Roy couldn't identify it until he'd found the switch and turned off the jets. The surface of the water hissed and went still. A bikini top took shape, the kind with very thin straps. There was a name for those straps but it didn't come to him. Roy followed the damp tracks that led from the hot tub across the tile floor, around a corner, down a hall, up the winding stairs. They'd dried out by the time he came to the third door in the upstairs hall.

The door was closed. This, Roy remembered, was the room with the big-screen TV, the desktop computer, and the king-size bed. The next room was Rhett's. Roy stood outside the third door. He knew it was the wrong door. His business was down the hall. He might even have kept going, had he not heard a sound inside, an indistinct sound, low and muffled, but resembling, at least to Roy's ear, the sound someone makes when they've tasted something good. Roy's hand went to the doorknob; one of those old-fashioned glass knobs—he could feel every facet. Then the door was open, silently open.

The big-screen TV, the desktop computer, the king-size bed: a naked man Roy had never seen sat on the edge. Marcia, wearing red bikini bottoms, was kneeling on the floor between his legs. It was like a scene from a pornographic movie except one of the performers was the mother of his son. The next moment it wasn't like a movie at all, not even like life. Life broke up. The laws of physics seemed to fail. Parts of the visual world vanished; other parts—Marcia's eyes seeing him, especially—appeared with a clarity he'd never experienced. Marcia's eyes seeing him, the naked man fumbling the sheets over his fleshy thighs, her new lips: all that much too sharply clear, like some photo lab trick, and then Roy was in the room, raw things surging through him, air supply problem gone, powered up with oxygen.

He took Marcia's arm—he was so hot her skin felt like ice—pulled her up.

"Hey," said the man with the sheet wrapped around him, or "What the hell," or something like that, or maybe he just thought it, and then he was flat on the bed, bouncing off the wall, actually, thumping it with his head, sagging back down, his fancy haircut all messed up.

"Grant," Marcia said, trying to go to him, but Roy wouldn't let her.

"With Rhett in the house," he said.

"He's not in the house."

But Roy didn't hear. "With Rhett in the house." Roy led her out of the room. Not led: it wasn't gentle like that. Out in the hall, he closed the door, let the whole house feel its closing, down to the foundation.

"He's not in the house."

Roy heard it that time, in the silence that followed the closing of the door, the whole house trembling.

"You sent Barry out with him?"

"Stop it, Roy."

"You sent Barry out with him so you could, so you could . . ." The words, *blow job* and others, stuck in his throat.

"Barry's in Houston," Marcia said, trying to tug free. "Rhett's at school."

"Lie to my face?" Roy said, his hand suddenly so strong it could squeeze right through her arm. "He's suspended."

"They let him back."

"What do you mean—they let him back?"

"I asked them."

"You asked them?"

"Let go of me."

He wouldn't let go.

"Don't spoil it, Roy."

"Don't spoil what?"

"How I think of you."

"Is that supposed to be funny?"

Marcia shook her head. "If you hadn't canceled dinner the other night . . ."

"What's that got to do with anything?"

"That's when Grant called."

"So?" But he started to remember, remember how he'd

canceled the steak dinner after hearing the message from the hospital, how Marcia had got a beep as they were saying good-bye.

"It might not have happened, Roy. But it did."

"What did?"

"We went to New York."

It came together in his mind. "He's your doctor?"

"Yes."

"The one who gave you the new lips?"

She nodded.

"And now he's putting them to use."

With her free hand, she hit him in the face, a raking blow. He didn't stop her. She started to cry, very ugly, with cawing sounds and snotty nose. "I have a right," she said.

"What right?"

"To be happy."

Roy didn't say, *We can be happy,* or *I can make you happy.* That belief was dying, dying, dead. He let go. She covered her breasts. The name came to him: spaghetti straps. "What were you doing with me, then?" he said.

"That's what I don't want you to spoil."

"I don't understand."

"What happened between us at the end, it made it like that movie where they always have Paris. We'll always have that other night, and that day at the gym."

"You think that makes sense?"

"Grant's fellowship is up next week. I'm going back with him to New York. I've never felt anything like this before."

"You keep saying that. Go."

"I'm taking Rhett."

"You're not."

"I am. I've already called my lawyer."

"I'll call mine."

"It won't do you any good. I have custody, and they look at what's best for the child. Rhett's going to be living in a four-story brownstone in Park Slope, with all the advantages. A good steady job like yours is not the same as a doctor's salary in the eyes of the court."

The bedroom door opened at that moment and Grant appeared in a shirt and boxer shorts. Overweight, like Barry, but much shorter, with monogrammed initials on his chest and a Porsche in the driveway. Roy thought, *good steady job,* and pushed him back in the room. Thump. And closed the door. Bang.

Roy looked down at Marcia, covering her breasts. A bruise was already rising to the surface of her upper arm. She was shaking. He was too. He turned and walked away.

Roy went home. Where else? He could go to a diner, a bar, the gym: all dismal. He went home, dismal too. He paced in one room, then another. He sat down. He remembered the night Marcia had slept with him, the night that began their brief affair, as she'd called it, and how Grant, Dr. Nordman, had phoned her cell. How fast he'd worked, or she, or the two of them together: she hadn't even known his first name that night. Roy got up, paced some more. Pacing was better than sitting.

Roy tried to think. He thought: I can bear losing my job. I can bear losing Marcia. But Rhett? No. Not because if he didn't have Rhett the past eleven years would add up to nothing, although that was true: but just because he had to be with him, his son.

He called Curtis.

"Hi, Roy. How are you do—"

"I want that New York job."

"There were no guarantees, Roy. The opportunity to apply is what's being offered."

"Good enough."

"I'll see what I can do."

"I'm going to fly up today."

"Fly where?"

"New York. To meet them."

"Meet who?"

"Whoever's doing the interview, for Christ sake."

"I don't even know if the job's still available."

"Find out." Roy was dimly aware that he'd said that much too loud.

Curtis spoke more softly, balancing it out. "I'll call you back," he said.

The phone rang within five minutes.

"They like the sound of you," Curtis said.

"Thanks, Curtis."

"You don't have to fly up. They can do a video interview."

"When?"

"Next Tuesday, one thirty." He heard Curtis take a deep breath. "Or today, at four forty-five. But that's pretty short notice, and everyone will understand if—"

"I'll be there." Roy checked his watch. Three fifty-two.

"Sure you wouldn't prefer Tuesday, Roy? Maybe take a little time to collect your—"

"I'm on my way," Roy said.

Roy parked in the visitors lot, checked in at the security desk in the lobby, received authorization from Curtis. He rode the elevator to the seventeenth floor, alone all the way. Curtis met him at the top.

"That's how you're dressing for the interview?" Curtis said.

Roy looked down at himself. He was still wearing the chinos he'd had on in the morning, but the collared shirt with buttons and the tie with the blue diamonds, his best one, was gone. He was wearing a faded and frayed T-shirt with *Georgia Football* on the front, a T-shirt he hadn't worn in years, had forgotten he owned. When had he put that on?

"Come into the bathroom," Curtis said.

Roy followed Curtis into a bathroom with a marble floor and marble sinks. Curtis took off his suit jacket, his tie with the blue diamonds, identical to Roy's, his silk shirt, finer than any shirt Roy had ever worn, with French cuffs and gold cuff links. "Here," Curtis said.

Roy put on Curtis's shirt. He could smell deodorant, and under that, the smell of Curtis. Did Curtis notice him smelling it? Maybe. The shirt was too tight across his shoulders and chest, and because of that he had trouble tying the tie. Curtis did it for him: a tie just like his, had to be a good omen. He'd never worn cuff links before; Curtis did that too. Roy put on the suit jacket, made of the softest material he'd ever felt, but as tight as the shirt, or tighter.

Curtis stepped back, looked him over. "That's more like it," he said. "Except for your face."

"My face?"

Curtis pointed to Roy's cheek. "What happened there?"

Roy checked the mirror, saw three parallel scratches on the side of his face, like red war paint. "Nothing," he said, going to the sink, dabbing with a damp paper towel.

Curtis, standing behind him in suit pants and a sleeveless undershirt, watching in the mirror, said, "Why don't we postpone this till Tuesday?"

Roy shook his head.

Curtis sat him down at one end of the long table in the conference room. A technician placed a microphone in front of him, said, "One, two, three, New York, can you hear me?"

"Yup," came the reply from speakers Roy couldn't see. An image flickered on a screen suspended from the ceiling: a conference table like this one, but darker and shinier. A camera hung from the screen; it swung around until the lens pointed at Roy. The red light blinked on.

"Video, New York?" said the technician.

"Gotcha," said the voice.

"Need me here?" the technician asked Curtis.

"Call you when it's over," Curtis said. The technician left the room. Curtis moved to the far end of the table, sat down. The camera on the other end tightened on the New York table, focused on a yellow legal pad, a red pen, a green soda can from a maker Roy had never heard of.

A man came into the shot, sat behind the legal pad. He had

a shiny bald head, a bushy mustache, purple bags under his eyes. He looked right at Roy.

"Name's Ferrucci," he said. "Assistant VP, tech personnel. We've got five minutes for this, tops. You're Roy Hill?"

"Yes."

"Speak up a little."

Roy wasn't used to the TV talking to him personally. He loosened the knot on his tie, undid the top button of the too-tight shirt. "Yes, I'm Roy Hill."

Ferrucci gazed at him. "We got an opening here you might be the man for. It's on the shipping floor in Jersey City, East Asia section, which sounds pretty close to what you've been doing already. Familiar with the V-trak program?"

"We're just starting to use it."

"Any problems?"

"None so far."

Ferrucci checked the legal pad. "Played football for Georgia Tech?"

"Georgia."

"Who was the coach?"

Roy told him.

"They say he was a real asshole."

"He treated me all right," Roy said.

Ferrucci nodded. "Willing to relocate, Roy?"

"Yes. Jersey City—is that anywhere near Park Slope?"

"Park Slope? What's that got to do with anything?"

"It's supposed to be a residential neighborhood."

"Not one you'll be able to afford. Pay on this job's the same as yours, plus two point five cost-of-living adjustment. Still interested?"

"Yes, sir."

"Your boss says you can do the job. Gonna need more than that. Gonna need hitting the ground running."

"I promise," Roy said. He glanced down the table. Curtis gave him a thumbs-up.

"What's that on your face?" Ferrucci said, squinting at him on the screen.

"Nothing."

"Tell you what we'll do, then," Ferrucci said. "If you can get up here by the—" He stopped, looked off camera, listened to something Roy couldn't make out. Someone handed him a sheet of paper. Ferrucci read it, the top of his shiny head glaring from the screen. When he looked up, he had a new expression on his face. The air began leaking from the room; Roy's lungs felt it right away.

"Know K. C. Chen?" Ferrucci said.

"The subagent in Shanghai?" Roy said. Without taking his eyes off Ferrucci's image, he was aware of Curtis's forehead wrinkling. He reached for his throat to loosen the tie, unfasten the button, found he'd already done that.

"Correct," said Ferrucci.

"I've worked with her."

"She a straight shooter?"

"I've never had any problems with her," Roy said.

"It's not mutual," said Ferrucci.

"I'm sorry?" Roy said. His hand was in his pocket, wrapped around the inhaler.

"She says you hung her out to dry"—his eyes went to the paper in his hand, then locked on Roy—"with three freight cars of ammonium nitrate. Three open goddamn cars, running loose through the rice paddies."

"But—" Roy couldn't get a breath. He fumbled with the blue diamond tie, struggled with it, tore it off. "But—" No air, no air at all. Roy jerked himself out of the jacket, ripped open the shirt, still couldn't breathe. Couldn't breathe, but could somehow smell his smell and Curtis's smell mixed together in the silk of the shirt. "Just a minute, I'll ex—" Then he had the inhaler to his mouth, sprayed it down his throat, took a deep breath. He was still taking it when Ferrucci spoke to someone off camera and the screen went black.

"Wait," Roy said. He picked up the microphone, rose so the camera had a better view of him, leaned his face right into it. "I can explain, Mr. Ferrucci. It's just a misunderstanding, nothing came of it, there was no harm—"

Curtis snatched the microphone from his hand. "Why didn't I know about this?"

Roy looked at Curtis, up at the black screen, back at Curtis. Was it over? It had to be some technical difficulty, maybe an electrical—

Curtis grabbed a handful of Roy's shirt—his own shirt—pulled him close. "Why didn't I know about this?"

Because you're just a dumb nigger.

But maybe there was a God: Roy didn't say it out loud.

He left without another word, bumping something, table, chair, on the way. A gold cuff link fell to the floor with a bright clinking sound.

Roy sat in his kitchen, frozen to a chair. Night fell but he didn't turn on any lights. He opened the bottle of Chardonnay, the only booze in the house. He drank some, didn't like it, drank more. What he wanted was Old Grand-Dad, and he'd never even tasted it. When the bottle was empty, he got up and went through his dark house and into his dark bedroom. He took off his Georgia Football T-shirt, his socks, shoes, chinos, boxers, lay on his bed, passed out. His mind went blank.

Roy thought he heard crying in the night. He sat up. That would be Rhett, down the hall. Poor kid. Roy got up. The moment his foot touched the cold floor, he remembered everything: Rhett, Marcia, job—gone.

Roy stood there, naked and still, for a long time. He became aware of a shadow in the corner of the room, a squat shape he couldn't identify, didn't remember being there. He went over, laid his hand on it. The old leather-bound trunk. He gazed down at it, and as he did, thought he heard crying again. Impossible: but crying, and close by. Roy opened the trunk. Everything went silent. He got on his knees, dug through the layers of thick wax paper, found the uniform, held it; heavy in his hands.

Roy put on the uniform. A complicated uniform, with

things he wasn't used to, like a button fly, suspenders: but he had no trouble with it, none at all, even in the darkness. The uniform fit him like a glove. His finger found the little hole in the jacket right away, poked through, felt his own beating heart.

FIFTEEN

Roy heard the phone ring, heard the click of the answering machine picking up. It didn't all come back to him, no coming back necessary. It was all there now, securely fixed inside, ready to be a part of him the instant he awoke. Securely fixed inside, but maybe not totally understood, because he could still think: Curtis, Marcia, Ferrucci, Cesar—someone calling to make things right!

It was Gordo.

"Rise and shine, good buddy. We got job huntin' to do. How about we start with bacon, eggs, and brewskis? Get back to me." Beep. Gordo: cheered by all the company he suddenly had.

Roy tried to sink back into sleep. He couldn't do it. Memories were waiting now, little shards of them, coming in waves. The clothing memories alone—blue-diamond tie, silk shirt with cuff links, Georgia Football T-shirt, red bikini top—were enough to drive sleep away all by themselves. But how he wanted it, the unconscious part, at least.

Roy got up, went into the bathroom, gave himself a shock. There he was in the mirror, fully dressed in his inherited uniform. He'd forgotten that part, the final act of a long day. He stared at his image, had a funny moment of not quite knowing it was him, as though he were looking in the mirror and seeing someone else. More than a moment, actually; he wasn't able to snap out of it, not completely. And the battle-weary look that Lee had worn in the photograph beside the cannon: the man in the mirror had it too.

The phone rang again. He heard a woman's voice coming over the answering machine, missed the first part of what she said, caught, "calling from Globax. You can reach—"

Roy hurried out of the bathroom, snatched up the phone.

"Roy Hill here," he said, unbuttoning the uniform jacket, shrugging off the suspenders.

"Oh, you're there." She introduced herself. "I'm with human resources," she said.

"Human resources?" Were they offering him a job in human resources? He didn't know anything about human resources. He knew shipping.

"All terminated employees are entitled to free career counseling. I'm booking appointments."

"For what?"

"A forty-five-minute career-counseling session, at Globax expense. We outsource it to several companies so you can actually choose the one you want. As luck would have it, two happen to be quite close to you." She named them. "I can book either one, your choice."

"Then what?" said Roy.

"Then if you decide to add extra sessions, Globax subsidizes the cost on a sliding scale depending on the number of sessions."

Not what he'd meant. He'd meant: How long till I get a new job?

"Still with me?" said the woman. "This sliding scale goes from fifty down to ten in even increments. Percent, is what I'm talking about, Ray, depending—"

"It's Roy," Roy said, and too loudly. "Roy Hill." He came very close to saying *Roy Singleton Hill.*

There was a pause. Roy could hear a stock market report from a TV in the woman's office. "Sorry, Roy," said the woman. "I'm just trying to inform you about the counseling opportunity, that's all. A lot of people have found the program very helpful."

"Helpful for what?"

"Why, resumes, retraining, interview skills, networking, job search—everything you could possibly want."

Roy had a vision of Mr. Pegram puking on his shoes.

"I'll let you in on a secret," said the woman, "based on twenty years' experience. A lot of people in the same boat as you end up in much better jobs. They look back at all this fuss and muss as the beginning of a positive period in their working careers."

Roy caught his image in the bedroom mirror, a full-length mirror beside the closet, in front of which he and Marcia had once—he throttled that memory right there. He saw that the uniform was back on properly, suspenders in place, jacket all buttoned up: when had he done that?

"So I can book you an appointment?" the woman said.

"What kind of appointment?"

"At one of these services." She named the two near him again.

Roy shrugged.

"Hello?" said the woman.

"Yeah?" said Roy.

"What about it?"

"I guess."

"Which one would you prefer?"

Roy took the first.

"All set," said the woman. He could hear the squeak of her felt pen making a check mark. "Three-fifteen this afternoon okay for you?"

"Why wouldn't it be?"

Squeak.

Roy took off the uniform, folded it away in the trunk between layers of the thick wax paper. He flossed and brushed his teeth, showered, shaved; groomed himself like any other office worker. What were you supposed to wear for career counseling? Roy dressed the way he did for the job, minus the tie. He went into the kitchen, opened the fridge, closed it again. Not hungry.

Roy boiled water in the kettle, poured it in a cup. He didn't make coffee or tea with it, just drank it as hot water, something he'd never done before, never even thought of doing.

The front door buzzer buzzed. Roy put down his cup, almost dropped it in his hurry, thinking, Some kind of good news, although he couldn't imagine what. But it wasn't good news, just Lee, in his denim jacket and jeans, motorcycle parked in the driveway.

"Thought you might be ready for some black powder shooting," Lee said.

"Not today." Roy didn't feel like talking to anybody, not if they weren't in a position to make things better.

"No?" Lee said. "From what Gordo told me, I thought today might be good."

"What did he tell you?"

"About Globax. Sorry, Roy. Not that I was surprised."

"Why not?" Roy said. "I'm good at my job."

"I'm sure you were. I'm talking about the mass firings. That's the nature of the beast."

"What beast?" Roy said.

"Put it this way, Roy—where's the headquarters for Globax?"

"New York. But it could be anywhere, and the work ended up in Miami."

"A model Southern city," Lee said. He held out a paper bag. "I brought you some muffins."

Roy stood there, not taking the bag. Not hungry.

"Baked them myself," Lee said.

Roy took the bag. "Cup of coffee or something?" he said.

"Sounds good."

Roy didn't think he'd made it sound good at all. He moved aside, let Lee in. Lee went by him with a light, springy step. He reminded Roy of a kid he'd played high school football with, one of those too-small but very fast kids who get to play safety or wide receiver. Roy's teams had always had big kids just as fast, so this one had been cut, but not before one preseason ninety-yard punt return Roy could still see in his mind.

"Instant okay?" Roy said.

"Sure."

But he was out of instant. All he had was a foil bag of beans he'd bought at Starbucks in preparation for Marcia coming home. He thought of returning it, getting his money back: an idea that filled him with self-disgust but also opened a window on a possible future and its meanness. He got busy with the grinder, the coffeemaker, filter basket.

"Who did these?" said Lee. He was standing by the fridge, looking at the artwork taped to the door.

"My son."

"They're pretty good."

"Yeah?"

"His number's fifty-six?"

"How did you know?"

"Fifty-six has a kind of prominent role in these pictures, Roy." Roy went over to look. "I like the way all the helmets are too big," Lee said. "Must be how it feels to him inside one. And see those eyes between the face mask bars?"

The eyes looked scared. Roy hadn't noticed before. "You think he has talent?"

"I'm not competent to judge," Lee said. "What's his name?"

"Rhett."

Lee turned to him quickly.

"It's his name," Roy said.

"A fine name," Lee said.

"My wife chose it. I like it too."

Lee looked at him for a moment, his gaze fixing on Roy's cheek. The scratches: Roy had forgotten that part too. "That makes three of us, then," Lee said.

Roy heard sounds from the coffeemaker. He turned away, filled two mugs. One was an Olympics souvenir; the other said *Globax*. He noticed that too late, after he was done pouring, took the Olympics mug for himself.

They sat at the kitchen table.

"This is a nice house," Lee said.

Roy watched the steam rising from his coffee, the way it bent in a little plume, then disappeared. A nice house, with a big first mortgage, a maxed-out home equity loan—the emeralds!—no savings, no paycheck.

"Muffin?" Lee said, reaching into the paper bag, taking out two: small light brown muffins with dark red berries poking out here and there.

With an effort, Roy took his eyes off the rising steam. The smell of the muffins reached him. "You baked these yourself?" he said; he himself had never baked muffins, doubted he knew another man who had.

Lee nodded.

Roy tasted one, just to be polite. Not hungry at all, even though he hadn't eaten since . . . when? He couldn't remember. But that feeling of not being hungry left him the moment he tasted the muffin. Had he ever tasted a muffin this good? Just sweet enough, just tart enough, light and firm at the same time, and the berry so close to being bitter, but not quite. He was ravenous by the time he finished it.

"There's one more," Lee said.

Roy shook his head. Lee took the third muffin from the bag, slid it across to Roy. He thought of the steaks and Sonny Junior.

"Split it?" Roy said.

"All yours," said Lee.

Lee watched him eat. "Picked the berries yesterday," he said.

"Berries this time of year?" Roy could hear his mother asking the same question, the same way.

"Mountain winterberries. There are still some around my place."

"Where's that?"

"Not far. We can do some shooting while we're there."

Roy finished the second muffin. It had a strange effect on

him: he was still ravenous, but now felt himself warming up inside. "I've got a gun," he said.

"What kind?" said Lee.

"I'm not sure."

"Where is it?"

Roy looked at Lee: he had a fine face, open and honest, as far as Roy could judge. Roy didn't want to get into the whole leather-bound trunk thing, but neither did he want to sit by himself in the house all day, waiting for his career counseling opportunity. "I wouldn't want this generally known," he said.

"You can trust me."

Roy took Lee into the bedroom.

The bedroom was dark, still smelled of sleep. Lee put on a pair of glasses, the kind with small lenses that Roy associated with European revolutionaries or hippies from the sixties. Lee didn't look at all like a hippie—he had short dark hair and was smooth shaven, almost like a boy who hadn't started shaving. His gaze went to the bed, one side unslept in, the other in disarray.

"What else did Gordo tell you?" Roy said.

"About what?"

"Anything."

"Just that they fired everybody. All he doesn't understand is why he was the first to go."

"Anything else?"

"Like what?"

Roy opened the leather-bound trunk. "My father died."

"I'm sorry."

Roy shrugged. "I got this."

"Can I look?"

Roy didn't see why not.

Lee bent over, started going through the trunk. "My God," he said, straightening up, the uniform jacket in his hands. He went to the window, examined the threads, then pressed the jacket to his face, breathed in deeply.

"There's more," Roy said.

Lee went back to the trunk, pulled out the gun, Roy Single-ton Hill's gun with *death* carved on the wooden stock. He ex-amined it from several angles, ran his fingers along the barrel, tested the hammer with his thumb.

"Is it a carbine?" Roy said.

"Oh, yes, one of the very best—a Sharps fifty-two-caliber breech-loading carbine made in eighteen fifty-nine, as it says right here." Lee raised the gun in an easy, economical move-ment and took aim at something across the room; a pillow at the head of the bed—Marcia's, actually.

"Will it still work?" Roy said.

"No reason why not. I can check it out for you, if you like."

"Course there'd be no bullets," Roy said.

"Bullets are easy to make." Lee handed Roy the gun, started folding the jacket, paused. He felt in the pockets, turned the jacket upside down, gave it a gentle shake. Bullets fell out, eight or ten, landed on the sheets where Roy had been sleeping. They were smaller than Gordo's bullet and not as completely oxidized, glinting dully here and there with lead. Lee cupped them in his hands, held them out for Roy like they were nuggets scooped from a stream.

"Let's do some shooting," he said.

Roy checked his watch. He didn't see why not.

Mountain winterberries, picked yesterday: Roy in his Al-tima, the Sharps breechloader in the backseat, following Lee on the motorcycle, assumed they were on their way to one of the expressways out of town. But Lee went under the con-nector, turned up Northside, entered Buckhead.

Buckhead, but not Marcia's Buckhead. This was the part Sunday drivers liked to tour, especially when they had visi-tors from out of town. The houses got bigger, but how much bigger was hard to tell because they were set farther and far-ther from the road. Lee rounded a bend, much too fast, Roy thought, disappeared from view. By the time Roy picked him up again, he was darting through gateposts a quarter of a mile ahead, leaning low.

Tall brick gateposts, Roy saw as he drove between them, joined by a brick arch. Two stone eagles stood side by side on top of the arch, one facing forward, one back. The lane Roy followed was brick as well, a long lane that took him past perfect lawns, blooming gardens, more lawn, a house that seemed low and massive, but was four stories tall in the central section, possibly with another half story above. Lee kept going, down a curving grade, past a pond with floating purple flowers, to a small brick house with purple shutters, a purple door, leaded windows, brass fittings.

"Welcome," Lee said, coming to Roy's car.

Roy got out. "This is your place?"

"This is my grandmother's place, Roy. I live in the guest house." Roy glanced toward the big house, mostly hidden by a grove of low trees. Roy could see shiny red berries clinging to the nearest branches. "Got the gun?" Lee said.

They went inside: books everywhere, on floor-to-ceiling shelves, on tables, chairs, the floor. On the spines and jackets Roy saw the same images—muskets, cannons, flags—read the same words—*blue, gray, Lincoln, Davis, Grant, Jackson, war.*

Lee took the gun into the kitchen, laid it on the table beside a vase of purple and yellow flowers; a fine crystal vase—Roy remembered Marcia admiring a similar one in a store window. "Know much about small arms?" Lee said.

"Nothing."

Lee knelt, peered down the barrel. "No rust at all—it must have been practically soaked in oil. Whale oil being what they used back then. First, you pull the hammer back to half-cocked. Then bring the lever down like this. Rotate the pin, pushing down this little button. And the whole breech block slides out just like so." Lee held up the breech block. "These are the vent holes—it's all about controlling rapidly expanding gas." He dug a toothpick into two tiny holes in the breech block. "Like it was cleaned yesterday." Lee put the gun back together, found linseed oil under the sink, rubbed it into the stock and grip. He went still. "Don't laugh at me if I tell you this."

"What?" Roy said.

"It feels like something coming alive in my hands."

Roy didn't laugh.

Lee laid the bullets on the table. "No cartridges," he said, "meaning these were probably picked up off the ground. I doubt cartridges would have fired anyway, after all this time. Instead—" He left the room, returned with a small plastic tube, a brass cylinder, and a red can with *Globax* on the label.

"Not wearing synthetics, are you, Roy? Static electricity can be a problem with this stuff."

"I know," Roy said.

Lee glanced at Roy, then at the label. He turned the can so the word was out of sight and held up the brass cylinder, as though distracting a child with something shiny.

"Adjustable powder measure," he said, twisting a screw in its base. "A fifty-two caliber takes sixty grains, but we'll shoot straighter with fifty." He poured powder into the plastic tube. "No plastic tubes back then, of course, but they do work well with these ring tails." He stuck one of the bullets in the top of the tube, opened the breech, jammed the tube right into the barrel, leaving the bullet and powder inside. "As for caps, musket ones will do." He stuck a tiny hemisphere of copper onto a nipple under the hammer, then closed the lever with a snap. The sound itself was satisfying.

They went behind the house. It was very quiet, not like being in the city at all. Ahead lay a long, narrow stretch of lawn, not much wider than a country lane, with a line of trees on one side and a high brick wall on the other. "There were riding trails in here when my grandmother was young," Lee said. He raised the gun, aimed at a low wooden fence—a riding jump, Roy saw—in a sunny patch a hundred yards or more down the grassy lane. Glass bottles glinted on top of the fence.

Lee lowered the gun. "You first," he said, handing it to Roy.

"I've never fired a gun," Roy said.

"Then this is even more special," Lee said. "Hold it like so." Roy held it like so. "Look through that V with your right eye." Roy looked through the V with his right eye. Coke bottles, seven of them. The middle one was framed in the V. "Pull the hammer back all the way, Roy. Now squeeze like you want just a little toothpaste, but all at once." Roy squeezed the way Lee said. He heard a bang, felt the kick of the gun, much stronger than he'd anticipated, strong enough to hurt, saw a puff of blue-gray smoke, smelled burned chemicals—nitrates, a smell he knew.

Lee put on his glasses. "My God," he said.

The middle Coke bottle was gone.

"Beginner's luck," Roy said.

Lee took the gun, reloaded it, handed it back to Roy. "Don't you want a turn?" Roy said.

"I'd rather watch y— I can wait."

Roy raised the gun, got the Coke bottle on the left end into the V, squeezed the way Lee had told him. Bang—another satisfying sound; kick—a kick he was more prepared for this time, a lively kick, he thought; puff: and the Coke bottle on the left end was gone.

"You lied to me," Lee said.

"About what?"

"Never firing a gun before."

"It's true."

Lee shook his head. "I can tell, just by the way you stand."

Roy looked down at his feet; he hadn't been aware of standing in any particular way. "I know nothing about guns," he said.

Lee looked at him, eyes sharp and intent behind the small lenses of his glasses. His gaze shifted again to Roy's cheek. "Whatever you say," Lee said. He reloaded the gun.

The scratches, her new lips, Dr. Nordman. His whole body started to shake. Roy knew he wouldn't hit another bottle. He tried to take aim at the next one on the left, trembling in the V, forgot everything Lee had told him, thought only about Dr.

Nordman sitting on the edge of the bed. How was anyone going to make that right? The next bottle on the left shattered, glass bits like sparks in the sunlight, although Roy wasn't aware of pulling the trigger.

Area managing. Shatter.

Regional supervising. Shatter.

Ferrucci. Shatter.

Rhett in New York.

One bottle left. Roy became aware of that, also became aware of a big problem, which was the tears pooling in his eyes, rolling down his face. The bottle went blurry in the V.

Rhett in New York: living in a fancy kind of building Roy couldn't visualize, in an expensive part of a city he'd never seen, growing up in a life he didn't know. There were forces out there. Some people knew how to use them: Curtis was probably one of those. Some people didn't: Marcia, most likely. And the rest were barely aware of the forces at all: that was him.

Rhett in New York.

Shatter: the glass bits making a strange golden explosion this time because of the wetness in his eyes. Lee looked away, said nothing. He walked slowly toward the riding fence, moving through the shade of the trees and into the patch of light, staring down at all the glittering in the grass.

Roy didn't remember his career counseling appointment until it was too late.

SIXTEEN

Roy turned over the sheet of paper on which he'd written the headings *House Projects*, *Budget (w/new salary)*, *Managerial Skills*. On the blank side, he wrote: *Bills*. Then he wrote: *$*. He sat there. The stack of mail on the table had an unsettling personality of its own.

Roy admitted something to himself: he wasn't good with money. Money had rhythms that he didn't get. Some people heard the beat: Barry, for example, watching money move on his screen, shorting Yahoo, all that. Barry, hunched over, ass hanging out of his briefs, felt the rhythm. Roy closed his eyes, tried to think of some moneymaking idea. Nothing came.

He needed a moneymaking idea. While he was admitting things, why not admit the truth about his finances since the divorce and the loss of Marcia's income? The house was all his now, but the equity was tapped out and the full mortgage payment was now all his too. Seventy-two seven, plus bonuses. He never wanted that number in his head again. It was the very next thing he thought of.

After that came the emerald necklace. Six grand on the home equity, two thousand on his credit cards, now maxed out. *It can go back?* He remembered her saying that. Didn't it mean she would be sending it over any day now? Roy looked out the window, saw a UPS truck coming slowly down the street. It went slowly by and slowly disappeared around the corner. Could he call her and ask for it? He turned the sheet back over. Under *House Projects*, he read *bathroom*, and under that *tiles*, *mirror*, *little lightbulbs*. He wrote: *Hello, M.,*

I was wondering about that necklace. He scratched that out and tried: *Now that things turned out the way they did.* And: *Maybe it slipped your mind but.* He couldn't do it.

Roy reached out toward the pile of bills. His hand hovered above the top one, moved to a manila envelope lying on the other side. Roy had forgotten all about it. He took out the two old-style photographs—he and Earl, he and Lee—and the computer printout: "Roy Singleton Hill—A Biographical Sketch." He removed the Post-it—"Dug this up last night. Enjoy—J. Moses"—and started reading.

> **From the Nathan Bedford Forrest Homepage: NBF called Roy Singleton Hill his "Angel of Death." Hill's forebears came to east Tennessee from North Carolina in the early 1800s, not later than 1813 when the marriage of Robert Hill to Elizabeth Singleton is recorded at the Church of the Savior in Ducktown, Tennessee. The Singletons owned land in what is now Cherokee National Forest, but they didn't become prosperous until Robert Hill's decision to build a lumber mill on a stream that passed through their property, sometime in the 1820s. RSH was born in December of 1831 or January of 1832, third of six children, four of whom survived to adulthood. Little is known of his early life or education (if any). He met NBF on a trip to Memphis in the mid-1850s, perhaps as a customer. RSH joined the 7th Tennessee Cavalry in February 1862, just before the retreat from Fort Donelson. He served in all Forrest's major campaigns and had a noted reputation as a horseman and marksman, being mentioned in dispatches after the battles of Spring Hill, Brice's Crossroads, and Chickamauga. His feat on the morning of the second day of Chickamauga, when he single-handedly took a Yankee battery before turning the cannon and firing it into the Union ranks, became legendary in CSA annals. He was also present at the capture of Fort**

Pillow, April 12, 1864, but his role, if any, in that controversial action is unknown. RSH married in the early 1850s and had one son, who may have died in infancy. RSH himself was killed at the end of the war or shortly after, possibly while defending the mill from an attack by renegade Yankee deserters and freed slaves.

Roy read it again. He knew little of Chickamauga, had never heard of Spring Hill, Brice's Crossroads, Fort Pillow. All he knew was that Roy Singleton Hill's only son couldn't have died in infancy, not with him sitting here reading this. He picked up the pen, the pen he'd used to write *Bills*, *$*, and those preambles to Marcia, crossed all that out, and in the empty space below began to draw. Roy hadn't drawn anything for a long time, not since grade school, probably around Rhett's age: he remembered Mrs. Hardaway standing by his desk, her finger following the line of some picture he had drawn. He could even remember the drawing—a football player, diving for a loose ball—and Mrs. Hardaway's finger—skin the color of coffee beans, her nail bright red. Mrs. Hardaway had had a funny laugh that got more and more high-pitched until it went inaudible and left her shaking silently; he'd liked Mrs. Hardaway.

The drawing he was making came into focus. Scribbles, really: they showed a uniformed man, his face still blank, gun butt raised high. There was a cannon in the background and the sketchy beginning of a body at his feet. A flag—the rebel flag—hung in the sky, suspended like a religious vision.

Night fell. His drawing, the bio, the stack of bills all faded away. Roy didn't turn on the lights. He didn't hear the key in the lock and the front door opening, didn't hear footsteps in the hall. A form materialized in the kitchen.

"I'm not going," Rhett said.

Roy snapped out of it: Rhett, appearing like this to remind him of what he should be doing instead of zoning out in the dark. He rose. "Son," he said. "Your ma—your mother bring you?"

"No."

"How did you get here then?" Roy switched on the lights.

"I'm not going." Rhett wore new clothes, or at least clothes Roy hadn't seen on him before, a polo shirt and khakis with cargo pockets; his hair was cut short and the unruly tuft of stick-up hair was gone.

"Not going where?" Roy said, peering out the window, failing to see Marcia's car, or the Porsche, or any car parked in front of the house.

"Fucking New York," Rhett said.

"Don't say fucking."

Rhett mimicked him. "Don't say fucking."

Roy turned from the window. "You can't talk to me like that," he said.

"Everybody else does."

That knocked the life out of Roy for a moment. Then it came rushing back, and he was rushing, had his hands on the polo shirt, had Rhett up off the floor, the boy's eyes widening. The buzzer went.

Roy froze with Rhett in the air, their gazes locked together, Rhett's eyes turning frightened, Roy with no idea what his were like. He lowered Rhett to the floor, not gently, not hard, just lowered him, and went to the front door, fighting for breath.

Gordo, with Jesse Moses and Earl Sippens standing slightly behind him: Jesse in a suit and carrying a briefcase as though he'd just come from work, Earl wearing a pink blazer and smoking a cigar, perhaps coming directly from work as well.

"Hey," said Gordo, "the man."

They were all looking at him funny, gawking the way the guys from shipping had gawked at Dan Marino one night when he'd walked into Sportz. "I'm kind of busy right now," Roy said. What were they gawking at—the way his body trembled, aftereffect of laying hands on his son?

"A crack shot, for Christ sake," Gordo said. "Who'd of guessed?"

"It's not true."

"Fuckin' dead-eye dick is what I hear," said Earl, pushing his way up onto the top step with Gordo. "Oops, there, son, sorry about that F-word, didn't see you."

Roy turned, saw Rhett watching from the kitchen door. Earl went past Roy, into the house.

"This your boy?" he said.

"Yes, but—"

"How's it goin', son? Earl Sippens." He grabbed Rhett's hand, pumped it up and down. "What's your name?"

"Rhett," said Rhett, but not clearly; Earl probably didn't catch it.

"Have one of these already?"

"No," Rhett said.

"Take it," said Earl, handing Rhett something Roy couldn't see.

"Thanks," said Rhett, pocketing it.

Earl poked his head in the kitchen. "Fine place you got here, Roy."

Roy turned back to the stoop, looked past Gordo, beaming in that way he did when he'd had a few but no more than a few, to Jesse.

"Maybe if we could just have a quick peek at the carbine," Jesse said.

Roy brought the gun into the living room.

"Sharps new model eighteen fifty-nine," Jesse said, "and brass mounted too. Know how many of these they made?"

"Hundred thousand?" said Earl.

"Not brass mounted," said Jesse. "Thirty-five hundred."

"Worth some shekels, then," said Earl.

Jesse paused, his long and finely shaped finger tracing the outline of those five letters on the stock. "But who would want to sell it?" he said.

"Missed me with that one," Earl said.

They clustered around the gun, passed it back and forth, aimed it out the window at the streetlight.

"Pretty cool, huh, Rhett?" Gordo said.

"It looks old," Rhett said.

"Course it's old," said Gordo. "Belonged to your great-great-whatever he was."

"One of the best marksmen in the South," said Jesse, "according to the documentation."

"And a talent passed on to your daddy, seems like," said Earl.

They all looked at Roy; Rhett followed their gazes, up to his father.

"Any pellet primers in that patch box, Roy?" Earl said.

Roy didn't understand the question.

"Lee used musket caps," Jesse said, opening a bit of filigreed brass in the stock that Roy had thought was just decoration. There was a little hollowed-out box underneath. Something fell from it, dropped on the floor.

Gordo picked it up.

"Pellet primer?" said Jesse. "Wonder if the compounds are intact."

But it wasn't a pellet primer, unless pellet primers looked like keys. Gordo held it on the palm of his hand, a brass key, small and simple, with a ring for a handle, a thin cylinder, two little teeth at the end.

Earl took it. "What's it open?" he said, squinting at it under the light.

No one had any ideas. Jesse put it back in the patch box, handed the gun to Roy.

"We've got an event this weekend," he said. "Up at Chickamauga."

"Be some Yankees there," Gordo said.

"Mostly from Pennsylvania," Jesse said, "but some all the way from New Jersey and Connecticut."

"Gonna have us a fun time," Gordo said.

"Shooting contests and the like," said Earl, "aside from

the battlefield reenactment. Sure be nice to show those Yan-kees a thing or two."

"We've talked this over, Earl and I," Jesse said. "You could tent with us. Not necessarily joining the regiment—"

"No obligation whatsoever," Earl said.

"—but getting a better perspective than the ordinary spec-tator," Jesse said.

"And having some fun," said Gordo.

"This weekend is out," Roy said.

"Maybe later then," Jesse said.

"When's Lookout Mountain?" Earl said.

"This is a busy time for me in general," Roy said.

From the way Earl and Jesse were looking at him, Roy knew they'd heard all about Globax.

"Help me with something for a second, Roy," said Gordo, drawing him into the kitchen. He closed the door. "Might do to reconsider about Chickamauga," he said. "Take your mind off things."

"What things?"

"Come on, Roy. I know what you're going through."

"Do you?"

"Even worse, in my case—I was headed for promotion."

"The fuck you were."

"Huh?"

"Forget it."

Gordo came closer, close enough for Roy to smell his boozy breath. "What's that mean, the fuck I was?"

Roy didn't say anything, probably wouldn't have, if Gordo hadn't repeated the question, a little louder, jabbing a finger at his chest this time, almost touching.

"The job was mine," Roy said.

Gordo's face got all confused. "You didn't get fired?"

"You stu—" Did he himself appear to Barry, say, the way Gordo appeared to him now—slow, dull, out of it? He toned himself down. "Yes, I got fired. But before that, you were Pe-gram's choice, I was Curtis's. Curtis won."

Gordo's face went through another stage or two of

confusion—Roy could feel him adding it all up—then returned to normal. "Curtis," he said.

"Don't start."

"Were you ever going to tell me, good buddy?"

"Probably not. What difference does it make now?"

Gordo thought that over. "If it does, I'm not smart enough to see it."

"Me neither."

They shook hands.

"Come this weekend," Gordo said.

"Marcia's taking Rhett to New York."

"With that Barry guy?"

"Someone else. To live."

Gordo didn't know what to say.

After they left, Roy called Marcia.

"You mean he's not in his room?" she said. "We—I just got home."

"Better come get him."

"But how did he get there?"

Roy hung up, turned to Rhett.

"Why did you have to do that?" Rhett said.

"Think about it."

"I'm not going."

Roy went over, put his hand on Rhett's shoulder. Rhett shrugged him off.

"There'll be opportunities I can't give you."

"Why not? You've got a good job."

Roy didn't say anything: how would the truth help Rhett?

"Grant's an asshole," Rhett said. "Not an asshole like Barry, another kind."

"How would you describe the difference?"

Rhett looked at him for a moment. Then he started laughing, loud unrestrained laughter of a kind Roy had never heard from him before. Roy caught a glimpse of what he might be like as a man.

*   *   *

A taxi pulled up outside, Marcia in the back. The driver honked.

"Where's her car?" Roy said.

"Sold," said Rhett. "There's a BMW waiting in New York."

The driver honked again. Marcia got out. They watched her come up the walk, listened to the buzzer.

"I'll see you before you go," Roy said.

"And then what?"

"It's two hours by plane," Roy said. "Back and forth is easy."

Rhett looked at the floor. Roy couldn't get used to him without that tuft of untamed hair. Children had a kind of power they lost in adolescence.

The buzzer again: she kept her finger on it this time. Roy went to the door, opened it.

Marcia had new things too, including a diamond ring. Roy came to a decision, at least about the jewelry angle.

"I hope you explained his behavior is unacceptable," Marcia said.

"I did not."

"Does that mean you think it's acceptable?"

"Rhett," Roy called over his shoulder. "Go on out to the car."

Rhett went out to the car. Marcia glared at him, but Rhett didn't see it. He wasn't looking at either of them.

"We've got to be civilized about this," Marcia said, "for his sake."

"What's the real reason?" said Roy.

"What kind of remark is that?"

Roy stepped outside, so they were standing on the same level, down on the stoop. "I'll have that necklace back," Roy said.

"What the hell are you talking about?"

But she knew: he could see it in her eyes. "Try a more civilized answer," he said.

Marcia bit her lip; that new habit, and the last thing to do her any good with him. "It's gone," she said.

"Gone?"

"I owed him a lot of money."

"Who? You owed who a lot of money?"

"Barry."

"You gave the necklace to Barry?"

"It's partly your fault. If you'd of just steered him right on Globax, but oh, no."

"Explain yourself." Rhett and the driver were watching from the taxi. Roy said it again, more quietly.

"He thought the company was a mess and you didn't set him straight when he asked you about it, so he ended up going short, with options this time, maximum exposure. All you had to do was tell him about the reorganization and he would have made the opposite play."

"I don't understand a word you're saying."

"For Christ sake, Roy, don't you even know what's going on at your own job? The stock's gone into orbit. Barry lost the house."

The house—this house, Roy's house—felt funny when he was back inside: like a football field an hour after the game, when everybody's gone. This house was lost too.

Roy took the key out of the patch box, tried it in the old trunk. But it was nothing like the key he already had, and didn't fit. He replaced the key, sat at the kitchen table with the gun across his legs.

Gordo called. "Earl likes you," he said.

Roy grunted.

"Remember I told you he had irons in the fire? He might have a job for me."

"What kind of job?"

"At one of the dealerships."

"You're going to sell cars, Gordo?"

"Course not. This would be in the service department."

"You're not a mechanic."

"Running the desk, Roy. He might take me on as a trainee for service manager."

"What's it pay?"

"I didn't like to ask right off the bat," Gordo said.

There was a long silence. Roy could hear the shopping channel on Gordo's end. He sat with the gun on his lap.

"Tell me about this Chickamauga thing," Roy said.

"That's my man," said Gordo. "Makes sense to get on Earl's good side."

But that wasn't it.

SEVENTEEN

Friday was his last day with Rhett. Roy knew he shouldn't be thinking of it that way. Not the last day: flights were cheap if you booked ahead and he'd have a new job soon, all that back and forth on cheap tickets, making those jokes people made about the peanuts in the little foil packs, plus Rhett would come back for two or three weeks in the summer, Marcia had already said so, all of this adding up to not such a bad picture from a certain perspective. And in a few years Rhett would be in college somewhere, hooked to neither parent in particular, spending vacations where he wanted, and that might be good too: another not so bad perspective. So it wasn't the last day or anything dramatic like that. It was just the last day when they'd all be living in Atlanta. The trick was finding those good perspectives and sticking to them. That was how to handle it, no question. But maybe not today, when for some reason Roy kept thinking about the night Rhett was conceived.

Rhett's last day, or the last day they'd all be living in Atlanta, wasn't a twenty-four-hour day, but ended at 5:45, departure time of the flight to La Guardia. Rhett was supposed to go to school until 10:30, something about saying good-bye and picking up his transcripts. The plan was for Roy to pick him up there and deliver him to the airport at 4:45. The hours in between were all theirs.

"Anything special you'd like to do?" Roy asked him on the phone.

"Like what?"

178

"I don't know. Something fun."

Pause. "Drive the car."

"What car?" Roy said, but even as he did, he understood what Rhett was getting at: he wanted a driving lesson from the old man. He was a little young, but why not? They could go to a parking lot at some mall and—

"Uncle Sonny's car," Rhett said.

Roy had gone wrong again. "Uncle Sonny's car?"

"The demolition derby car. He said I could."

Out of the question: that was Roy's first thought. But what kind of a day was it going to be, just the two of them already separating in their minds, Roy trying to be cheerful, Rhett doing God knows what, the end of the day casting its shadow back on the hours before? What kind of a day was that?

"I'll give him a call," Roy said.

Roy pulled up outside the school at 10:15, just in case Rhett was early. He looked out the window at the playing fields, the swing set, all the swings hanging still, the chains gleaming gold in the sunlight against a background of green spring. A beautiful day, no doubt about it. It had been raining hard on that drive down to New Orleans the weekend Marcia decided the time for conceiving Rhett had arrived, a long drive with the windshield fogging up, Marcia leaning on his shoulder, giving him bites from her burger, the two of them holding hands while the backsplash from the eighteen-wheelers came like a monsoon. Roy didn't want to think about it. He pressed play.

> *"I'm gonna tell my mother howdy, howdy, howdy,*
> *When I get home,*
> *Yes I'm gonna tell my mother howdy*
> *When I get home, well, well, well.*
> *I'm gonna shake my father's hand*
> *I will shake their hands that day*
> *That's where we walk, oh that Milky White Way*
> *Lord one of these days."*

He listened to it a few times, more like just having it there with him, he knew it so well, and then a side door of the school opened and out came a kid, a boy, Rhett. Roy checked his watch. Ten twenty-five: good thing he'd come early. Rhett ran down the sloping lawn, his backpack bouncing along behind him, in the middle of all that sunshine and springtime green. The boy was going to be all right. That was what mattered. Roy tried to make his mind snap a lasting picture of that moment. He didn't have the kind of mind that was good at things like that.

Rhett jumped in the car. Roy fought off the urge to pat him on the shoulder or, yes, give him a kiss, which was what he really wanted to do. "Glad to be out, huh?" he said.

"Out?" Rhett sucked on his knuckles; they were bleeding a little.

"Out of that school."

"It's not so bad," Rhett said. He glanced at the school. "Let's go."

"What happened there?" Roy said.

"Just a scrape," Rhett said. "Opening up my locker."

Roy started the car, drove off.

"Do we have to listen to that?" Rhett said.

Roy switched off "Milky White Way."

"Vroom vroom," said Sonny Junior, raising a Bud in welcome. He sat on the back of a flatbed truck with *Ducktown Salvage* on the door, the demolition derby car already down on the dirt track, an abandoned course near the South Carolina line. "Any trouble finding the place?"

"Some," said Roy.

"Did I say south on four forty-one?"

"It doesn't matter."

"Meant north. South coming from Tennessee."

Roy's watch felt heavy, ticking away the time.

Sonny Junior flipped the empty bottle over his shoulder, slipped down off the truck. "How's it goin', killer?" he said.

He wore a sleeveless T-shirt and his arms and shoulders were reddening in the sun.

"Pretty good," said Rhett.

"What happened to your hair?"

"Got cut."

"Lookin' good," said Sonny Junior.

"My mom made me. I'm moving to New York."

"That's what I hear," said Sonny Junior. "Ready for a spin?"

They got in the demolition derby car, yellow with red flames except for the deep dents where bare metal gleamed, Sonny Junior behind the wheel, Rhett beside him. Roy watched the car circle the track. On the first go-around, Sonny Junior talked and made gestures and Rhett nodded. On the second, Rhett was on Sonny Junior's lap, hands on the wheel, and they were both laughing. On the third, Sonny Junior was on the passenger side, his arm hanging out the window, and Rhett was driving. The car veered over to the side of the track, a little abruptly, and stopped near Roy. Sonny Junior hopped out. The car started rolling.

"Hey," Roy said, stepping forward.

Sonny Junior put a hand on Roy's arm. "Can't hurt himself, cousin. He knows not to go over twenty and I got him all strapped in—it's like a cage in there."

Roy watched Rhett drive off, just tall enough to see over the wheel. For a moment, he strained a bit against Sonny's hand, and Sonny strained back. Then Rhett came to the first turn, appeared to have no trouble with it, continued slowly around the oval, dead center in the track. Roy relaxed a little. Was he going to ruin this treat, act like an old woman on Rhett's last day, leave Rhett with that memory to fly off with?

Sonny Junior went over to the truck, opened another beer. "Cold one?" he said.

Roy shook his head, watched Rhett driving sedately up the backstretch.

"New York," Sonny Junior said.

"Correct."

"A lip doctor, what's that?"

"Some kind of plastic surgeon."

"You couldn't do anything about it?"

"Like what?"

Sonny Junior came over, put a beer in his hand. "I get you, Roy. If you could of done the kind of something that would of worked, it wouldn't of happened in the first place."

Roy turned to him. "Meaning?"

Sonny Junior raised his hands in surprise, reacting to some expression that must have been on Roy's face. "No offense, cuz. I'm just talking about a quick one upside the head— another one of those no-nos in this society we got goin'."

"That sort of happened," Roy said.

"You hit her?" said Sonny Junior. "Wouldn't have thought it of you, what with how smooth you are, Roy, in control."

Is that the way he appeared to Sonny Junior? "Not her," Roy said. "Him."

"The lip doctor? You popped him?"

Rhett came out of the number four turn, drove up the track their way at about ten miles an hour. He didn't look at them, just went by, both hands on the wheel, face glowing. He must have spotted some weeds growing up through the track, weeds with flowers on the end, because he swerved to run them over, crunch, under his left front wheel. Roy didn't answer.

"Popped him a good one, I hope," said Sonny Junior.

"What difference does it make?"

"Makes me feel better, anyway."

"You?"

"For what they done," said Sonny Junior. "Just when I'm gettin' to know him, takin' him away like this. What I'd fuckin' do to—" He went silent, tilted the bottle to his mouth. They watched Rhett rounding the number two turn; was that his arm hanging out the window? A skinny arm, but in its nonchalant pose an exact duplicate of Sonny Junior's. Sonny Junior patted Roy on the back. "So I know what you must be going through."

"What I'm going through?" said Roy.

"Yeah. Like the separation thing."

All at once, Roy found his eyes tearing up again, a crazy thing to happen in front of Sonny Junior. For cover, more than anything else, he took a drink from the bottle, unexpectedly found himself wanting more, drank more, chugging down the whole bottle in the end. His vision cleared.

"Wee-ooo," said Sonny Junior, his eyebrows—so fair they were almost invisible—rising in surprise. He chugged his beer too. "That's more like it, Roy. What's family all about anyways?" He hurled the empty bottle all the way across the track, smashing against the rusted stands on the other side. "This fuckin' society," he said.

Rhett was on the backstretch again, maybe going a little faster now. A strange question popped into Roy's mind and he said it aloud; this was his cousin, after all. "Was that the rebel yell, Sonny?"

"Huh?"

"That yell you just did."

"Wee-ooo. Like that?"

"Yeah."

"Hell if I know. Why, Roy? What's up?"

Roy looked at the sky, a deep blue sky that got deeper and deeper the longer he looked, like he could fall up into it and fall and fall forever. He tried that rebel yell.

Not too good. His air supply failed and the volume got nowhere near Sonny Junior's, besides which his voice cracked in the middle, the rest of it quavering off to nothing. That fucking night—*don't say fucking*—in the Hotel de whatever it was in the French Quarter where Rhett was conceived, and where afterward in the dim bathroom Roy had pissed in the bidet thing, not knowing any better: suddenly Roy's lungs folded up and he was out of air, but completely. He dug in his pockets; no inhaler. He glanced around, maybe a little wildly, drowning for air in all that blue sky.

" 'Nother frostie?" said Sonny Junior.

Everything started to fade, and in that fading, Roy heard

a roar and saw the demolition derby car, yellow with red flames, zooming down the backstretch, barreling into the number three turn, fishtailing, fishtailing, wider and wider, then starting to spin, spinning in clouds of dust, Rhett's face thumb-sized with a black O in the middle, and of course it rolled, the yellow red-flaming thing rolled and kept rolling, rolling across the infield right at Sonny Junior and him, flipping, flipping again, and once more before landing upright, and stopping just like that, quivering ten yards away.

Roy wasn't aware of his lungs reopening, of running across the infield, of ripping open the door, grappling with the harness, of nothing until he had Rhett out of the car and in his arms.

"Put me down," said Rhett, struggling free, dropping to the ground.

Roy just stood there, breathing. Sonny Junior came running up. "He okay?"

"I'm fine," said Rhett. He looked it, eyes wide, mouth open, not a mark on him. "That's the most fun I ever had in my whole life."

Sonny Junior took off his belt. "Want this, Roy?"

"For what?"

"The whippin' you're gonna give him—I told him no more than twenty miles an hour. Must have hit eighty."

"There's going to be no whipping. Let an eleven-year-old kid drive a car, whatever happens is on you."

"On me?" said Sonny Junior, turning to Roy, the belt in his hand. Roy had a memory of that barn up in Tennessee, Sonny's barn now but the way it was long ago, with those shafts of light crisscrossing over two little boys, way below, and blood on the straw.

"Correct," said Roy. "On you."

Roy and Sonny Junior faced each other.

"Sorry, Uncle Sonny," Rhett said. "Didn't mean to hurt your car."

Sonny Junior gazed down at the boy. He started to smile, a smile that got bigger and bigger. "Hell, boy, can't hurt a demolition derby car—it's already demolished, that's the whole deal." He started laughing. Then Rhett was laughing too, and finally Roy. Sonny Junior reached down, cuffed Rhett on the back of the head, not too hard. "Liked your hair better the old way, killer," he said. "Don't be forgettin' your uncle Sonny."

"Never," said Rhett.

Down below, Roy drove in an unending line of cars along the airport feeder. Up above, planes rose into the sky one after the other, higher and higher until they disappeared into that blue sky. It was like some automatic system, some immense machine—present-day life itself, was how Lee would see it, Roy knew that—all set up for taking Rhett away from him.

"We'll just make it," Roy said.

"I don't care," said Rhett. "You think I want to go?"

"Everything's going to be all right. Call home—call me anytime you like."

No reply.

"You know the number?"

"Yeah."

"What is it?"

Rhett said the number.

"You have to dial one and then the area code first. Do you know the area code?"

"No."

"Four-oh-four. Think you can remember, or want me to write it down?"

Rhett didn't answer. Roy glanced over and saw Rhett writing *404* on his hand in ink.

Marcia was where she'd said she'd be, standing on the curb by the American Airlines sign, checking her watch. No sign of Dr. Grant Nordman, probably waiting inside. Pulling over, Roy tried to think of the last words he should say to Rhett. *I love you,* probably, or maybe just *Love you.* Didn't want to burden the boy with too much emotion, but at the same time—

Everything happened quickly.

Rhett got out of the car before Roy had a chance to say anything.

Roy got out too, but a cop hurried over immediately: "Can't park here."

And Marcia was dressed like he'd never seen, could have been some high-society lady.

She said: "Okay, then," or something like that. And then to Rhett, "Why, you're filthy."

The cop repeated what he'd said, but Roy moved around the car anyway, up on the curb, turned Rhett around, gave him a kiss on the top of his head, a kiss meant for his forehead, the middle of his forehead, that was what he'd had in mind, but off-target in all the confusion.

Marcia took Rhett's hand. "The flight's on time." She looked at Roy. "I left the phone number and address on your machine."

Roy didn't know what she was talking about. Rhett stood beside her, eyes on Roy.

"Bye, son," Roy said.

Rhett nodded.

Marcia took him inside.

The cop said what he had to say one last time.

At home, Roy listened to Marcia's message on the machine, wrote down the New York address and phone number, stuck them on the fridge. There were two other messages, both from Ms. Steinwasser, asking him to call the school. Roy had just finished listening to them when the phone rang. Roy picked it up, thinking, Rhett, trying out one of those plane phones.

But it was some man he'd never heard of. "Are you aware of what happened at the school today? That little scumbag of yours ambushed my son. Cody's in bed right now—practically knocked unconscious."

"With what?" Roy said.

"What the hell kind of question is that? Your son walked up to my son and punched him right in the face."

"I'm sure you know there's been provocation," Roy said; at the same time remembering Rhett running out of the school five minutes early, his skinned knuckles, and the boxing lesson in the barn before that. All made sense, but much too late, maybe the only way things made sense to him.

"Now I see where it comes from," the man said. "It may interest you to know I've got an office full of lawyers just waiting to take a bite out of the likes of you."

"Are they licensed to practice in New York?" Roy said, and hung up.

Roy didn't have beer, didn't have anything to drink. Didn't want beer anyway, wanted Old Grand-Dad, so he went out and got some. Never even tasted Old Grand-Dad, but that was what he wanted. Drank a bit, then a little bit more. Much later, late at night, sitting in the darkened kitchen with the gun on his lap again, he decided to take another crack at the rebel yell. He rose, laid the gun on the table, took a deep breath—had no trouble taking it, for some reason, filling himself with air like never before—then yelled that rebel yell at the top of his lungs. At the top of his lungs, his throat free and open, all his strength turned into sound. His body went cold from it. The house shook from it. And after, in the silence, he pictured his little house from high above, a tiny square in an endless grid of tiny squares, the rebel yell escaping through the roof, rising into the night.

EIGHTEEN

Wearing the uniform with the little hole in the front and carrying the leather-bound chest on his shoulder, Roy climbed a slope on the east side of the battlefield at Chickamauga. With the sun just coming up, he walked in shadow, following a suggestion of a path through grass bent with dew. The soldiers of 1863 had fought over this very slope, a slope, as Jesse explained when Roy called for directions, not exactly within the military park itself, the Park Service almost always forbidding reenactments on hallowed ground, but on private land close by, rented for the weekend with money from registration fees. The wind blew in the trees, a cool wind for the time of year, but other than that there was no sound, just as it might have been, Roy thought, back then.

An obvious thought—he knew it at the time—but a few steps from the top of the rise, Roy heard a sharp snap, and looking up saw the Union flag flying straight out against the sky. From his angle he couldn't see any more, just the flag in unmarred blue, an empty sky as it might have been, back then. A little chill, perhaps from the cool wind, ran down his shoulders and back. Roy felt another one when he realized he'd thought of the Stars and Stripes as the Union flag.

Roy rose out of the shadow and into the pearly postdawn light, head, body, legs, in three steps. Thick woods lined the horizon, mist rising off the crowns of the trees. Closer lay a field with three or four rows of tents, the nearest tent, about ten yards away, flying the flag high above. Closer still stood a Porta Potti and next to it a man in blue, his fly unbuttoned, pissing in Roy's direction. He gazed at Roy—a bearded man with sergeant's stripes on his sleeve, as big as Sonny Junior but with a paunch, hanging freely at the moment—and said: "Little lost there, Reb?"

Flaps opened here and there, other men half-dressed in blue emerged, stretching, brushing their teeth. "I'm looking for the . . . other camp," Roy said.

"Thought so," said the man. "I can tell you're an ace already."

"I don't get you."

"At reenacting," said the man, shaking off. "Real rebs couldn't read maps neither, ninety percent of them being illiterate."

"Does it take being literate to know you piss on the inside of these things?" Roy said.

The man's cheeks reddened above his beard. He started buttoning up, had a little trouble, was forced to look down to do it. Uncircumcised, Roy noticed, and was thinking to himself, Another period touch? when a man—no, a large boy—came out of the nearest tent, a red-white-and-blue drum slung over his shoulder.

"Dad?" the boy said. "Where's the peanut butt—" He saw Roy and his eyes brightened. "You got a prisoner already?"

"Not yet," the man said. He gave Roy a look longer than Roy thought polite, as though committing some object to memory. "The battle don't start till three."

The other camp lay in a clearing in the woods, about half a mile beyond the Yankee tents. Roy encountered no pickets or sentries on the way, and no one was up when he arrived. He sat between two rows of tents on his leather chest, his face to the sun, or where the sun would be if not blocked by the trees. Once or twice it found a little gap between the branches and Roy felt the added warmth on his skin. He was almost at peace there for a moment. But only a moment: there were other things he should be doing. Roy didn't have the will to even list them in his head. The taste of Old Grand-Dad was still in his mouth.

Roy grew aware of snoring close by. A bird called, then another. This one made a different sound, harsher and more drawn out, not the kind of thing he usually noticed, if ever. He didn't know birdcalls, or the names of trees, wouldn't even have been sure of his orientation if the sun hadn't still been rising.

A low sound, almost inaudible, came from the tent directly behind him; a woman's sound. Then a man spoke, just a whisper, but it was so quiet in the clearing that Roy heard him. "Just this once," Gordo said.

"Not that," Brenda whispered back.

"But I might be dead by nightfall."

Brenda laughed, soft and muffled. Roy was already up and moving away when he heard her make another sound, not pleasure, but not quite pain either.

The flap of a tent bigger than the rest opened and Earl came out in full uniform, except for his sword and plumed hat, going at his ear with a toothpick. He laid eyes on Roy and beamed. "Am I still dreamin'?" he said. "Or is the battle good as won without me making a single command decision?" He tossed the toothpick away, patted Roy on the back. "That the uniform?"

"Yes."

"Up and down my spine, the chills," Earl said. "Way it fits you. Welcome to the regiment, Roy. And there's no need to call me sir when it's just us two having a private jaw like this." He called, "Hey, Lieutenant."

Jesse came out of the next tent, in his gray pants with the stripes down the leg, but still shirtless, a silver Star of David nestled in the hairs of his chest.

"Here's ol' Roy," Earl said. "Goin' to be our day, for sure."

"We knew that already," Jesse said, shaking hands with Roy, "this being Saturday."

"You duplicate the original results?" Roy said, remembering from his first visit to the regiment that Chickamauga was a qualified Southern victory.

"What would the point of that be, in the end?" Earl said. "This is just Lieutenant Moses funnin' on his superior officer." He smiled at Jesse as though he were having fun, except for his eyes, which got smaller.

Jesse ignored him. "South wins on Saturday, North on Sunday," he told Roy.

"In the reenactment world," Earl said.

"Or living history world, as some prefer," said Jesse.

They looked past Roy at each other, the expressions on their faces reminding him of things he'd seen at work. He didn't get that: they all earned the same money, which was zero. His mind was sinking back into Globax, set to go over things again and again, when a bird, dark and quick, shot up from the woods and caught his attention. Then came a light, brisk sound like the clattering of dry sticks, a sound that grew in volume, became drumming, and a little troop of men in blue came out of the woods, falling in step behind the drummer boy. The biggest one—the drummer boy's bearded father—carried the flag. Roy went still. They all did. The Yankees—Roy didn't know how else to think of them at that moment—looked so real.

"Fuckers are already up," Earl said, "and I haven't even had my goddamn breakfast." He raised the tent flap, paused with his eyes on Jesse. "That neck ornament, Lieutenant," he said.

"What about it?"

"Maybe on the farb side?" He turned to Roy. "*Farb* being our word for anachronisms."

"Believe it or not," Jesse said, "this ornament actually predates the war."

Earl frowned, appeared to be about to reply, but the Yankees were already nearing the outskirts of the camp. He ducked into his tent.

"By about two thousand years," Jesse said. Silence from the tent.

The Yankees halted in front of Roy and Jesse, the drummer boy ending with a little flourish, his father towering over him with the flag, the sun cresting the trees at that moment and glowing on his yellow stripes. Then came a command that Roy didn't catch; the soldiers went through a routine that ended with them all standing still, guns at their sides. An officer with thick muttonchop sideburns—had to be an officer, Roy thought, because he wore a holster on his belt and gold bars on his shoulders—stepped forward and saluted. Jesse saluted back, not as crisply. Roy stood beside him, feeling a little silly.

"Captain Peterschmidt of the Fifteenth New Jersey presents Colonel Finnegan's compliments and requests an audience with your commander," said the officer.

Jesse turned to the tent. Everyone followed his gaze. The canvas bulged at the side for a moment, something metal fell and rolled around on the ground inside, and Earl came out, plumed hat now in place but struggling with his sword. Captain Peterschmidt saluted again. Earl muttered something, gave up on the sword, thrust it at Roy, who almost dropped it, and saluted back, not even as crisply as Jesse, a motion that reminded Roy of President Reagan bidding good-bye as he got on a helicopter. Captain Peterschmidt presented Colonel Finnegan's compliments again.

"Where's Finnegan?" Earl said.

"The colonel sends his regrets," said Peterschmidt.

Pause. "You're a captain," Earl said.

"Correct, sir," said Peterschmidt.

"Normally," Earl said, "a colonel talks to a colonel."

"Unfortunately Colonel Finnegan couldn't make the trip, due to a last-minute closing."

"Closing?" Earl said.

"On a condo in North Bergen."

Earl looked wary, as though suspecting a Yankee trick.

"They had to move it up," Peterschmidt said. "The buyer was going to lose his rate lock."

Earl understood at once. "Fucking banks."

"Yes, sir," said Peterschmidt.

"And don't get me started on Alan Greenspan," Earl said. Was it Roy's imagination, or did Earl pronounce the *s* in his name as *sh*? Jesse's face was expressionless. "Do you know how much money the son of a bitch cost me personally last year?" Earl said.

"Captain Peterschmidt is here to discuss the battle," Jesse said, and Roy knew he'd heard it too.

Earl turned to him. "Then maybe you could bring us out a table and some coffee so's we can have our little parley like civilized men."

"Certainly," said Jesse, adding, "sir," after a beat or two. "Give me a hand, Roy?"

Roy moved to give the sword back to Earl. Earl looked at him as though they'd never met. "Yes, Private?" he said.

"Your sword, sir," Roy said, and almost laughed out loud because he'd come close to saying *my liege* instead of *sir*.

"Thank you, son," said Earl.

Roy followed Jesse into his tent. There were rough blankets on one side, an old table on the other. "Got your own tent?" Jesse said.

"No."

"You can bunk in here."

"Thanks." They each took an end of the table, facing each other; their eyes met. Roy lowered his voice. "How did Earl get to be colonel?"

"How do you think?"

"Showed up in his colonel uniform?" Roy said.

Jesse nodded. "They were sold out of general's."

They sat at the table, drank coffee perked over a pit fire, drank from tin cups everyone carried on his belt, and planned the battle—Captain Peterschmidt and the big sergeant, Earl, Jesse, and Roy, at Jesse's invitation. Roy said nothing, just drank his coffee and watched their faces, soon losing track of the conversation. The earthiness of the coffee, its heat, inside him and radiating through the cup, the little buzz it created:

coffee was suddenly important, a blessing, and he wondered whether this brew had been made with special beans or water or some Civil War method, because he'd never tasted better. That feeling of almost being at peace came over him again. The men around him all began to look natural in their uniforms, even Earl. The sun shone on his own uniform; it wasn't at all itchy, even though it looked like it would be, and warmed him like a blanket.

"That it, then?" Earl said, rubbing his hands together; Roy noticed a pale circle on his little finger, usually covered by his pinkie ring, no doubt too farb for the occasion. "Then let's get it on, like the brothers say," Earl said.

In the silence that followed, Roy saw the expression change on every face but Earl's, as though some invisible negative wave had passed over the field. Then everyone rose. There was more saluting. Captain Peterschmidt approached Roy.

"Can I ask you a question, Private?"

"Sure."

"Did you get that online?"

"Get what?"

"Your uniform. I haven't seen anything that good at any of the sutlers."

"No shit," said Earl. "That there's the original uniform worn by Roy's great-great—Roy's ancestor at this very battle. Roy Singleton Hill—rode with Forrest, the God's truth, completely documented." He took a loose bit of Roy's sleeve and rubbed it between his finger and thumb.

"Is that so?" said Peterschmidt. "Sergeant Vandam's great-great-grandfather fought here too. First Michigan Light Artillery."

The drummer boy looked up at his father. A muscle twitched in the sergeant's arm.

"First Michigan," Jesse said, putting his finger on the map. "Overrun by Liddell on the morning of the nineteenth, right about here."

"Overrun is one way of putting it," Sergeant Vandam said,

talking to Jesse but looking at Roy. "He took a bullet in the head."

"Sorry for your loss," Earl said.

Roy glanced around to see if anyone else found that a bit weird. No one seemed to. Earl and Peterschmidt shook hands.

"And come out fighting," Earl said, leaving the brothers out of it this time. "But safety first. I got a job to go to Monday mornin'."

"What is it you do, again?" Peterschmidt said.

Earl reached inside his jacket, handed Peterschmidt his card.

"My girlfriend drives one of these," Peterschmidt said.

"Can't beat it for the money," Earl said. "Seen the new convertible?"

"They've got a convertible?"

"Fact is, Captain, we do a shitload of out-of-state business. In case you're tempted to drive back over the Mason-Dixon line with the wind in your hair."

The regiment formed two companies in the woods, Company A led by Jesse, company B led by a lieutenant Roy hadn't met. Jesse placed Roy beside Gordo at the end of the line, just in front of the second sergeant.

"Any questions?" Jesse said.

"Maybe I should just watch," Roy said.

"Everyone gets a little nervous the first time."

But it wasn't that. "I don't know any of this stuff—the drilling, the formations, the saluting."

"Makes you just about perfect," Jesse said.

"How's that?"

"Drilling, formations, saluting—that's all Yankee shit," Jesse said.

"All's we know is how to fight," said the second sergeant, right behind Roy; his breath smelled of mints and tooth decay.

Jesse stepped outside the column. Everyone turned to him.

Roy noticed for the first time the lack of uniformity even though they were all in uniform: everyone's jacket a slightly different tone, no two hats the same.

"Safety check," Jesse said.

"Listen up," said the second sergeant.

"Absolutely no live ammunition of any kind on your person or in your weapons," Jesse said. "Only appropriate period weapons are permitted, with the exception of bayonets. No bayonets of any kind allowed—a thrust with the bare muzzle counts as bayoneting. Those with muzzleloaders are to leave their ramrods in place at all times. Anyone seen ramming will be sent from the field at once. No discharging of arms within thirty feet of an enem—"

Boom.

They all turned toward the sound. "What the hell was that?" said the second sergeant.

"Had to be Earl on number one," said Jesse.

"But it's way too early," the second sergeant said.

"And weren't the Yankees supposed to fire first?" said Gordo.

A voice drifted down from the branches high above: "The asshole couldn't wait." Roy looked up, saw someone descending, a lithe, butternut-clad figure who seemed barely in contact with the tree as he came down, dropping free much too soon but landing lightly on his feet, one hand securing the brass telescope that poked from his pocket. It was Lee, his cheeks and forehead blackened with charcoal. "We're never going to get there on—"

Boom: farther away this time, had to be the Yankees, and then an answering boom, but not Earl—this one was higher pitched, at least to Roy's ear. Then another distant boom, then two at once, and more.

"Might just as well bag the whole goddamn event," said the second sergeant.

"Shut up, Dibrell," Jesse said, with a harshness that surprised Roy, as though something important was at stake. Dibrell shut up. "In two lines at the double quick," Jesse said.

"March." He took off toward the sound of the fighting. The rest of them followed, trying to maintain two even lines as they ran through the trees but failing, spreading farther and farther apart.

"This is how we lost," Dibrell said, panting somewhere behind Roy.

"Shut up, Dibrell," said Lee, running easily a few yards ahead, not looking back.

Dibrell shut up, even though he outranked Lee; Roy checked the double stripe on Lee's sleeve to make sure. Dibrell's panting got a little louder. Roy himself wasn't panting, not even slightly, was running easily too, kind of strange because he'd stopped running years before on account of the air supply problem. Also strange was the inhaler in his pocket—not its presence, he always carried the inhaler—but that it was bothering him a little instead of giving comfort. He ran faster, caught up to Lee. Lee gave him a quick sideways grin and went into a gear Roy didn't have.

They dodged through the last trees, came out on the field. "Into ranks," Jesse shouted. "Form the company." Lee took a spot beside him. Everyone else started lining up in two rows to Lee's left, except for Gordo, who went the other way and Roy who hesitated in between. Jesse grabbed Gordo, spun him into place. Roy followed, stood beside Gordo. In the distance, he saw the Yankee battery, three black cannon drawn up in front of their tents. One flashed. The boom came a second or two later. The Yankee infantry, drummer boy in the center, was already halfway across the field, marching in a line, firing their muskets in unison, stopping to reload, marching again. Lining the field on both sides were hundreds of spectators, sitting on lawn chairs and blankets, aiming at the Yankees with their cameras. Directly in front of Roy, ten yards from the trees, lay their own battery, two cannon, the nearest of which was manned by Earl and the two sentries from the Girl Scout camp. Earl's face was black with soot and his plume had come loose, dangling from his hat at a droopy angle.

"Thanks for showing up," he said, yanking at the halyard. The sentries covered their ears. The cannon didn't fire.

Jesse didn't even look at him. He said: "Company— forward march." The men marched off across the field toward the blue formation marching at them. Roy, on the end with Gordo at one elbow and Sergeant Dibrell behind, heard Earl yelling, "Why the fuck won't this bitch fire?"

"Was it my turn to put in the powder?" said one of the sentries.

Another boom from the Yankee guns smothered Earl's reply. The blue lines halted and fired, front and second ranks simultaneously, puffs of smoke blooming from the mouths of their muskets.

"Where's our drummer boy?" Gordo said.

"Little League," said Dibrell.

Roy laughed. Did his laughter go on a bit too long? He made up his mind right then to drive back home as soon as he decently could.

"Company—halt," said Jesse. They halted.

"Firing by files, from the left," Jesse said.

"That's you, Roy," said Dibrell.

"Ready." Roy raised his carbine, looked through the V-shaped sight, swept it along the blue line.

"Aim." Sergeant Vandam came into the V. Roy steadied on his bearded face.

"Fire." A strange thing happened to Roy's vision at that moment. It sharpened, not just a little but acutely, as sometimes happens when a drop of water from the shower slides across your eyeball. He could see that Vandam was talking, could see his teeth, even the tip of his tongue, pink in the sunlight. He fixed on that little pink flap and squeezed the way Lee had told him. The gun kicked, but not as hard as it had firing real bullets. Vandam kept coming. Despite everything, Roy was a little surprised.

"Company—forward, reload." Roy pulled the lever, half cocked the hammer, bit open his cartridge, stuck it in the breech, set a new percussion cap in place, kept going; a complicated series of maneuvers performed without a slip, without even a thought.

The wind had died down now and clouds of smoke hung in the air, smelling of burned powder. The blue line was less than a hundred yards away now, the two lines closing fast, but without any special effort, at least that Roy felt, as though he were walking on one of those moving ramps at the airport. The drum beat faster, the boy missing with his sticks now and then, sending a sharp cracking sound off the metal rim.

"Company—halt." Roy halted, had his gun up before the next command.

"Firing by company," said Jesse. "Ready."

"All together, now, Roy," said Dibrell.

But he'd already guessed, was ready for someone's musket poking over his right shoulder from the back row.

"Aim." Roy got Vandam in the V.

"They should start falling now, according to plan," Jesse said. "If you're clearly hit, don't be an asshole. We want to get invited back."

The hyperclear vision returned. Roy could see that Vandam was taking aim right at him, his off eye shut tight. Roy's gun, the Sharps carbine with *death* on the stock, moved in a little arc. That was the way it seemed to Roy: he didn't move it. The barrel swung, as though under its own control, or the control of someone else. It swung, and fixed on another target: the boy.

"Fire."

Roy squeezed that little toothpaste squeeze. The drummer boy kept coming and so did Vandam, his eyes on Roy, but another Yankee staggered, doubled up, shrieked in pain, staggered some more, spun around, went down on one knee, raised his hands, held them there like Christ on the cross, slowly pivoted so the crowd on the other side of the field got a frontal view too, and slowly, slowly subsided in the grass.

Applause.

"Company—charge bayonets."

The two lines ran at each other, ran at full speed—Lee and

Jesse leading the rebels, but Roy closing fast—reached the firing limit. A Yankee aimed right at Gordo, pulled the trigger. Bang.

"Missed me," said Gordo.

Peterschmidt shot at Gordo with his pistol, inside the limit now.

"Saved by my belt buckle," said Gordo.

"Lie fucking down," Lee said.

Gordo lay down.

The two lines came together.

"Hand to hand, now. No injuries."

Someone tried a rebel yell, nothing like Roy's, just a yell. A man in blue grunted, pitched forward, lay on the ground crying, "Surgeon, surgeon." Peterschmidt pointed his pistol at Lee. Jesse dove at Peterschmidt, tackled him gently. Lee raised his gun, brought the butt down lightly on the ground, a foot from Peterschmidt's head. Peterschmidt said, "Nice job," and went still. A man in blue screamed, "Mother of God, I'm hit." A man in gray fell beside Roy and moaned, "Tell my wife that I'll always . . ." He bit down and red liquid came drooling between his lips. Gordo said: "Just a flesh wound." Vandam rose up, swinging his gun by the barrel at Roy. Roy was quicker, stepped inside, jabbed the muzzle of the Sharps into Vandam's gut, as though it had a bayonet, but barely touching him.

"You're dead," Roy said, and as he did, the memory of play fighting in the barn long ago with Sonny Junior awakened in his mind, ready to come alive in form and color.

"No bayonets on a carbine, you dumb reb," said Vandam, and the butt of his gun cracked Roy just above the ear.

NINETEEN

"**T**his here's for taking off arms and legs, amputations and the like," said a Southern voice.

"Got an edge to it, I'll grant you that," said a Northern voice.

"Sharper the edge, sooner it's over," said the Southerner.

Roy opened his eyes. It was dark, a gas lantern hanging from the shadows above shedding flickering, smoky light on the walls of a tent and two men, one in blue, one in gray, standing with their backs to him. Roy's vision wasn't good, everything fuzzy as though some knob needed adjusting, but he could make out the yellow serpents on their sleeves, and the shiny instrument they were examining under the lantern. The shininess hurt his eyes. He closed them.

"Any anesthetics in the kit?" said the Northerner.

"Chloroform, long as it lasts," said the Southerner. "Whiskey after that, less'n someone's got into it."

Roy opened his eyes. "There's nothing wrong with my arms and legs," he said.

They turned to him.

"So put that thing away."

"I think he's awake," said the Northerner.

"Are you awake?" said the Southerner.

Roy sat up. That made the pain in his eyes spread through his head but he stayed sitting up, even considered standing.

"Whoa, there," said the Northerner. "What's his name, again?"

"Roy," said the Southerner. "He's a new recruit."

"Why don't you just lie back down, Roy," said the Northerner.

"I'm fine like this," Roy said.

"The major wants to examine you," said the Southerner. He patted Roy gently on the shoulder. "Heard a lot about you, Roy. I'm the surgeon with the Twelfth Georgia—everybody calls me Doc."

"You haven't put that thing away, Doc," Roy said.

The lantern shone yellow on the pointed teeth of the instrument. Doc laid it in a wooden box at his feet, giving Roy a quick glimpse of other sharp things inside. "I was just showing the major some of my things, Roy—he's a doctor with the Second Connecticut."

"Lie back down, son," said the major. "This won't take a moment."

"No need," Roy said, standing up instead, but the lantern light got unsteady right away, and Roy sat back down, maybe with some help from Doc.

"Easy, Roy," he said. "You got dinged pretty good there."

Roy raised his hand, felt the bandages around his head. His first thought was a weird one: Sonny Junior. Then he smelled piss. Then it started coming back to him.

"Might have a slight concussion," said Doc.

"You a doctor?" Roy said.

"How do you mean?" said Doc.

"How do I mean? I mean a real doctor."

"Real in the sense of . . . ?"

"What you do for a living—that sense."

"When I'm not with the regiment?"

Roy nodded. It hurt.

"I'm currently between jobs," Doc said. "But I used to be a bartender at the downtown Ritz."

"So what makes you think I have a concussion?"

"The major said so."

Roy turned to the major. "You're the maître d'?" he said.

The major laughed. No way he was the maître d'. Younger than Doc, who was kind of distinguished looking, with those

wings of silvery swept-back hair long-ago movie stars had,
the major was scruffy; unshaven, with acne scars and a black-
head on the tip of his nose. "I'm a neurologist at Columbia-
Presbyterian," he said.

"Where's that?"

"New York."

Roy sensed some kind of conspiracy. "You know Dr.
Nordman?"

"Who's he?"

"Grant Nordman. Another doctor from New York."

The major shook his head. "There are thousands of doctors in New York."

"This one beat you to the punch," Roy said.

"I'm sorry?" said the major.

"Never mind," Roy said. But that wasn't strong enough,
and besides, his eyes hurt and his head hurt. He revised it to:
"Never fucking mind." He gave the major a look.

"Maybe you should lie back down for a minute or two," the
major said.

"How stupid do you think I am?" Roy said.

"I don't think you're stupid at all," the major said.

"Then why would I trust a Yankee doctor?"

The major and Doc exchanged a glance. "Think he's still
in character?" said the major, lowering his voice.

"Because of the blow to his head?" said Doc, lowering his
even more.

"Exactly."

"Wouldn't that be something?" said Doc. "Like a whole
movie, right there."

"I think it's been done," the major said. They gazed down
at Roy. "Ever play football?" the major asked Roy in a normal
voice.

"Tight end," said Roy. "I had a touchdown against LSU
but they called it back."

"LSU?" said Doc. "Who did you—"

"Ever get your bell rung?" said the major.

"Yeah."

"How many times?"

"One or two."

"Three or four, maybe?"

"I refuse to answer any more questions," Roy said.

He lay back. The lantern began to swing slightly. Or maybe not: maybe it was just the shadows of Doc and the major sliding back and forth on the canvas walls. Or maybe something else. Roy closed his eyes. He saw black clouds in an orange sky. Smoke and fire. Atlanta.

Silence, except for the faint sound of the burning wick, like shredding cloth, far away. Then an owl hooted, very near. When had he last heard an owl? Roy couldn't remember—possibly never, except on TV. He listened hard, hoping to hear it again. That effort, of listening hard, led him to imagine some connection between the owl and him, as if they were in this together, and the owl knew it too. He felt one of those strange new moments of almost being at peace coming over him.

"He'll be all right," said the major. "Time for the pig roast."

"Dinty Moore for us," Doc said. "More authentic."

"Dinty Moore?"

"Authentic looking anyway."

"Like that lantern's authentic?" the major said.

"They had lamp oil," said Doc.

"Not in the field. Much too heavy for the sutlers to cart in. But they did have pigs."

"Maybe you," Doc said. "We were starving."

The wick made its shredding sound.

When the major spoke again, his tone was gentler. "Sorry about Vandam," he said. "He pulled a stunt like this last summer at Antietam."

"What's his problem?"

"He and a few of the hard-core guys overdo it sometimes. They spend the winters getting all worked up at a bar he's got in Hoboken."

"What's that like?"

"Hoboken? Kind of happening now, in parts."

"I wonder if he's hiring," Doc said.

The owl hooted, a long, drawn-out sound that ended in a coo. Roy thought he heard owl breath after that. Then silence.

He felt something cool on his forehead. He pictured a hand, a cool hand: his mother's when he was home sick.

"Roy? Are you awake?"

A woman's voice: Marcia? Oh, that would be nice. But it wasn't Marcia, wasn't a woman he knew.

"No," Roy said.

"I thought I heard you singing," she said. "Something about the Milky Way."

"Not me," Roy said, and opened his eyes. He realized at once that he'd been dreaming this whole exchange, because no one had a hand on his forehead, and there was no woman in the tent, just Lee, sitting on a stool beside him, lantern light glowing in his eyes.

"Are you in pain?" Lee said.

"I'm fine."

"We all feel bad."

"Accidents happen."

The shape of Lee's nose changed for a moment, the nostrils widening, the bridge sharpening: he looked almost fierce. "That's what I was thinking." Lee drew something shiny from his belt; for a moment, his vision still fuzzy, Roy took it for one of Doc's instruments, and not the fat-bladed knife it was.

"No bayonets on a carbine?" Roy said.

"Course not," said Lee. "Carbines are for cavalry."

"Now I know."

Lee laid a sharpening stone in his lap. "Earl's writing a strongly worded letter," he said, "but I'm with you."

"You are?"

"Accidents happen." Lee worked the edges of the knife over the stone, back and forth.

Roy didn't get what Lee was driving at, just watched: the

stone, the knife, Lee's small, symmetrical hand—all without defects, all performing perfectly, pressure, speed, and angle perfect. He could almost feel the sharpness of the blade against the ball of his own thumb.

"You're going to miss the barbecue," Roy said.

"Barbecue? That was hours ago, Roy. It's two in the morning."

Roy looked around. "Where's Jesse?"

"Asleep. This is the medical tent."

"Why aren't you asleep too?"

"Couldn't."

"How come?"

Lee rose, slid the knife in his belt. "Want anything before I go?"

"Where are you going?"

"You must be thirsty."

He was. Lee handed him a canteen. Roy drank. Good water: cool, with just the right amount of dustiness, flint, and metal in the taste. Was this the water of 1863, how water was before everything got fucked up? Roy didn't ask, didn't want to hear that it was Poland Spring or whatever was in the convenience store cooler on the drive up from the city. By the time he'd slaked his thirst and was done thinking all those thoughts, Lee was gone. The tent flap made a few wavy motions, went still.

Roy got up. He was a little wobbly, his vision fuzzy, the air in the tent smoky from the lantern. This was a moment for air supply problems, and Roy got ready for them. But nothing happened. He raised the flap and went outside.

A full moon shone down on the camp. Then two moons, which Roy worked down to a moon and a half and finally back to one. The tents stretched in silver rows toward the woods, like a nighttime convoy under sail. There wasn't a sound, and nothing stirred except a shadow beyond the farthest tent, almost in the woods. Roy followed.

The shadow merged with the trees and Roy lost it almost at once. He kept going; not only going, but going fast, soon among the trees himself. That was strange—he was no tracker, no woodsman, plus his head hurt and he wasn't seeing well—but he sped along through the forest as though on a path he'd been taking all his life. Not only that, but speeding along in silence. He listened for sounds of himself, heard none—not his feet on the twigs, needles, and leaves of the forest floor, not the swishing of his woolen uniform, not his breathing. He did hear a tiny crunch, like a hard clod of earth disintegrating beneath a heel, somewhere ahead, and caught a figure in a little pool of moonlight between trees, almost flowing, then disappearing in darkness. Lee, for sure: the size, the way he moved, and the silver flash of the fat-bladed knife on his belt.

Roy was flowing too, no doubt about it, an easy mover, all of a sudden, in the night. He knew, absolutely knew, that the owl, his owl, was hovering over him, just above the trees, and he also knew that his owl was the descendant of the owls of 1863, owls that had gazed down with their huge eyes on Roy Singleton Hill. He was ready, despite a little bit of dizziness in his head, a little bit of fuzziness around the edges of his vision, for anything.

Ready, for example, for that campfire in a tiny clearing in the middle distance. He didn't creep up on it, just walked to the edge of the trees, invisible. Two men sat by the fire, both with blankets over their shoulders, but Roy could see that one wore blue, the other gray. The man in gray drank from a silver flask. The man in blue said, "Fifteen two, fifteen four, and a pair is six."

"You're the luckiest son of a bitch I ever met," said the man in gray, a little drunk—Roy could hear it. The man in gray a little drunk, while the man in blue sounded sober: it pissed him off.

Roy could also hear popping sounds from the fire and a much fainter crackle that he took to be incinerating pine needles, heard too the shuffling of cards as he circled the clearing and entered enemy territory; and yes, heard the beating of heavy wings, high above. He got the idea that this was the way Roy Singleton Hill had heard, so clearly, so precisely, and felt a bit chilly. But it was a chilly night, had to be: why else would the pickets have covered themselves with blankets?

Roy came out of the woods. Ahead lay the Yankee camp, a second convoy in the moonlight, bigger by a row or two than his own. Roy passed right by the tents, within feet of them, the light so strong he could read the words stitched on a regimental flag: *Wilderness, Antietam, Stone's River, Chancellorsville, Bull Run, Gettysburg, Chickamauga.* He was awake and in their sleeping camp. It was thrilling: had he ever been thrilled like this in his life? Had Roy Singleton Hill? Many times, for sure: many, many, riding with Forrest on nights just like this. A little breeze sprang up and the flag came to life, brushing against his arm. Roy moved on.

He picked up that silver flash from the far end of camp, saw Lee gliding toward the outermost tent. Moon, tent, guy ropes, knife—all silver, all connected in a way that made sense, so he knew what was going to happen before it did, very unusual, maybe unique, for him. Lee stepped up to the nearest guy rope of the outermost tent, slashed it through in a single motion, then scrambled around the tent very fast, slashing, slashing. The tent subsided, sank to the ground, revealing the Porta Potti eight or ten yards beyond. A voice rose from inside the fallen tent, a boy's voice, disoriented, scared. Lee paused, perhaps surprised, his back to the Porta Potti. And out from behind the Porta Potti stepped Sergeant Vandam in his underwear, the moon shining on his round white belly, his navel like a crater.

Roy knew just what to do: raise his gun and shoot Sergeant Vandam; the instructions, he realized, his instructions, were carved into the wood of the stock. But he hadn't brought his gun, and there were no bullets, just blank cartridges. Roy did the next best thing, did it without thinking: he clapped his hands, just once, like a gunshot but softer.

That got their attention: first Vandam, whose eyes were on him right away, then Lee, not quite as quick, who looked first at Roy, then spun around and saw Vandam. Vandam was already moving, but Roy had seen the way Lee could run and knew Vandam would never catch him. At that moment, the boy's voice came from inside the collapsed tent again: "Dad! Dad!" And Lee, half turning, about to take that first running step in Roy's direction, froze instead.

Froze: because this was all pretend, all make-believe, and Lee hadn't known there'd be a boy in that tent. It was just a prank. Roy understood what was going on in Lee's mind, and also learned something about Lee: he didn't quite have it.

Vandam hit Lee from behind—airborne, fully laid out, his shoulder ramming the middle of Lee's spine. Lee bent backward, doubling in the wrong direction like a contortionist, his butternut jacket ripping open in front from the force of the blow. The knife spun in the moonlight. Lee went down hard, Vandam on top of him. By that time, Roy was right there, although he had no recollection of how. He spoke, a rough, raw voice that wasn't his: "Let him go." But actually: "Le' 'im go," closer to backwoods than he'd ever spoken.

"I'll get to you," Vandam said, barely glancing at him, and drew back his fist a foot above Lee's ear. Roy grabbed Vandam's wrist, hauled him off. Just that easy, the way an actor handles a suitcase from the prop department. Vandam didn't like it. He aimed the punch he'd prepared for Lee at Roy instead, a punch that landed in Roy's middle, made him feel sick. But it could have been worse, could have been to the head, and Roy was landing one of his own at the same time, the first punch he'd thrown since childhood.

Vandam's nose made a crunching sound, or maybe Roy just felt the crunch in his hand. Then came blood, black in the moonlight, and Vandam staggered back.

"Enemy in camp," he called. "Enemy in camp."

Roy snatched Lee off the ground, flung him over his shoulder, took off for the woods. A man with muttonchop sideburns—Captain Peterschmidt—stepped out of a tent, in Roy's path.

"What the hell's going on?" he said, fumbling a set of earphones off his head.

"Isn't this on the schedule?" Roy said, and went right by him, past the tents, across the open field, into the trees, stronger than he'd ever been, dizziness gone, head pain gone, vision restored to its new hyperclarity.

"I'm okay," Lee said when they were safely in the woods, his lips close to Roy's ear. "You can put me down."

"Sure?"

"Sure."

Roy put Lee down. The crowns of the trees blocked the moonlight. There was no sound of anyone following them, no sound at all but the very soft one of fingertip ridges on rough wool. Roy knew what that had to be: Lee buttoning up his jacket. That brought back to Roy's mind an image he'd seen for only an instant, an image his mind might not have registered, what with all the commotion. What had he seen when Vandam's tackle from behind had popped open Lee's jacket? Only a moonlit glimpse, but the memory was clear in Roy's mind, he had it now: breasts; soft, pale, unmistakable.

Was Lee waiting for him to say something? He said nothing. There was no more talk. Roy and Lee walked in single file through the woods, Roy leading. They rounded the campfire, now dying, the two pickets asleep side by side, wrapped in their blankets, just touching. Roy heard the beating of heavy wings overhead.

TWENTY

The first thing Roy did when he got home Sunday morning—the commanders on both sides sending all the offenders out of camp for violating USV safety regulations—was check the machine for messages from Rhett. Four-oh-four: Rhett had written the area code on his hand. But there were no messages, none from Rhett, none from anyone else. After that, Roy sat at the kitchen table. For company he had the stack of bills he couldn't pay, a critical mass ticking silently away, getting ready to blow up house, car, all his material things. He also had the sheet of paper with *House Projects* on one side and *Bills* and *$* on the other. After a while, he crumpled it up and tossed it in the trash. He noticed a Popsicle stick in there, down at the bottom. Roy didn't eat Popsicles; Rhett did. Roy reached in, took out the Popsicle stick. There were teeth marks on the end, not big. Roy put the stick in a coffee mug on the shelf.

He took off his uniform, folded it, laid it on the bed, went into the shower. He didn't shave. Why bother? He opened his closet, the closet he'd shared with Marcia, now three-quarters empty, looked for something to wear. Nothing appealed; not that Roy wanted something new, more fashionable—he'd never been like that—but these clothes, the cotton shirts from the Gap, the khakis from some catalog, the jeans from another, didn't quite seem like his. In some way, they weren't even clothes, more like costumes from a play, a drab one he wouldn't want to see. Roy took a few aspirin for his headache, pulled the shades, and got into bed.

He dreamed he was reading the war diary of Roy Singleton Hill, the cracked leather one with *1861–1865* burned into the cover. There was no writing in it, not even the dates, only red fingerprints, the whorls and ridges sharp and defined, page after page.

Roy woke up in his darkened room. The first thing on his mind was the missed career counseling session. The thought was accompanied by a little spasm of anxiety that got him up and out of bed. He raised the shades to let light into the room, to get him started on making plans. But no light came in—it was night, as dark outside as in. What night? It took him a minute or so to straighten the time out in his mind.

Roy gazed out at the houses, the street, the traffic. All those people, watching TV, talking on their cell phones, doing the things everybody did—he was losing his feel for them. For example, the term *career counseling*: why didn't it make them sick, the way it was making him?

No answer to that one. Then came another question: Anything left in the Old Grand-Dad bottle? There was. Roy poured himself some, then made the mistake of letting his gaze wander to the fridge, more specifically to Rhett's football paintings taped on the door. Number fifty-six in his big helmet: the next thing Roy knew, he was up in Rhett's room, making an even bigger mistake.

Rhett's room, with the new shelves, still smelling slightly of varnish, and the Pop Warner trophy with the hard-charging plated figure on top. Roy left it there. He wasn't after the trophy, just the highlight tape lying next to it. He went downstairs, stuck it in the VCR.

Music: the theme from *Rocky*.

The Renegades, at home, wearing their red jerseys and green pants. Number fifty-six, at outside linebacker, takes two steps to his right, falls down, and the ball carrier falls over him. Fifty-six, on the sideline, listens to the coach, who stands over him, hand on his shoulder pads, then turns and runs at full speed into the huddle.

The Renegades, on the road, in their white jerseys with the

green pants. Fifty-six, after a twenty-five-yard run, helps chase down the opposing running back, is second or third on the tackle. The running back, getting up, says something to fifty-six that fifty-six doesn't like. Roy can tell by the way fifty-six goes still for a moment before joining the defensive huddle; he hadn't noticed that the only other time he'd seen the tape, a few weeks after the season.

The Renegades, at home against a team in brown and gold. The brown-and-golds have the ball on their own six- or seven-yard line. Some mix-up between the center and the guard and then the quarterback fumbles the snap. Fifty-six, at outside linebacker, although he's lined up wrong, pinched in too close to the middle—in fact, Roy remembered thinking *Get outside, get outside, they're going to burn you* because he'd seen the guard starting to pull—grabs the ball on one hop. More accurately, it jumps right into his arms. There's a pause, a pause that feels very long, none of the players reacting, including fifty-six. Then—another thing Roy hadn't caught before—comes a voice from the sideline, very faint: "Run." Fifty-six comes to life, runs into the end zone, runs right through it actually, as though not quite sure where he is, almost collides with a woman walking by with a hot dog, then slowly turns just in time to be mobbed by his celebrating teammates. They all fall down. The camera makes a wild sideways and up move toward the scoreboard, briefly catching Roy on the sidelines. The theme from *Rocky* comes to its climax, the screen goes blank.

Roy rewound the tape to that shot of his own face, froze it there. There was absolutely no expression on his face, which couldn't be right—he remembered what he'd been feeling inside. He remembered that, although he didn't remember shouting *Run* even though that was his own voice on the tape. His voice beyond doubt, despite the thing he had about parents who shouted instructions to their kids on the field. Roy turned off the sound, watched the tape again, from the start.

And again. Once more. And once more after that. The best part was the moment fifty-six, football in both hands like something precious, begins to turn at the back of the end zone. The woman with the hot dog is off balance, the hot dog raised high, a blob of relish flying away, and the sun penetrates the shade of fifty-six's oversize helmet enough to reveal the beginning of a smile. *I picked up that fumble.* Roy froze the smile right there, went closer to the screen to check it out. The smile turned into an arrangement of pixels.

Later, the Old Grand-Dad gone, Roy went back to bed. Sleep wouldn't come, not close. No sleep, but a dream began anyway, the dream of red fingerprints in a diary, page after page. Roy didn't like that, sleepless dreaming. That wasn't him. He got up, went into the kitchen, drank water. The wonderful water he'd drunk from a canteen at Chickamauga, almost like a food, the water of 1863? This wasn't like that at all. He opened the trunk, rooted around for the diary, opened it.

The diary was damaged, the leather cracked and flaking, the stitched binding loose in places. Now that he looked closely, Roy saw that a number of pages in the front seemed to have come loose and fallen out in their entirety; at the back, the last page had been torn out, leaving a narrow blank margin still attached to the binding. The paper itself was brittle and yellow, the ink faded to brown. The writing began in midsentence on the first remaining page.

Zeke says but I larnt him difernt. Rainin an no foder
fer Thunder went foragin.
3 days latter
home on ferlow rainin
23 januree
las day on Ferlo rainin. takin Zeke bac fer boddyman
sed godbis an wen up to th montan Hows fer godbis up
thar. filld up canteens from the crik.
14 febwaree
fitin in the mornin shot too mebbe 3. Zeke very hapy
with my ol red shirt.
2 days latter

surendin of ft. Donelson but Forest took us crost the
rivver at nit Zeke wen asculcin but I larnt him
difernt
3 martch
rainin an no foder fer—

The phone rang. Rhett, at this hour, whatever that was?
Roy snatched it up.

"Cuz?" said Sonny Junior. "Too late to be phonin'?"

"I'm up."

"Me too," said Sonny.

"Funny you should call now," Roy said, thinking of the
Mountain House.

"Funny? I been calling you all weekend."

"There's no message on the machine."

"I don't leave messages."

"Why not?"

"Don't think much of putting my voice on machines.
Hanging out there when I'm not around, you get what I'm
saying, Roy?"

Roy, who'd left hundreds, maybe thousands of messages
on machines and in voice mails, was surprised to find he sort
of did. "Never thought much about it," he said.

"You been drinkin', Roy?"

"No."

"I sure as shit have. How's my little nephew?"

"He's gone to New York, Sonny. You knew that."

"I knew that. Just wondering whether you heard anything."

"No. Sonny?"

"Yeah?"

"I've got a beep."

"Maybe that's him."

Roy took the other call. Not Rhett: he could tell by the in-
take of breath.

"Roy?" It was Lee. "Did I wake you?"

"I'm on another call."

"Should I hold?"

"I'll call you."

He went back to Sonny, heard a little gurgling sound, like someone was taking a drink.

"That him?" said Sonny.

"No."

"Who at this hour?"

"Just someone I know."

"She got a name?"

Roy didn't answer.

"Aren't you the quick little worker bee?" said Sonny.

"You're way off track."

"Whatever you say." Then came another gurgling sound. "Roy?"

"Yeah?"

"How come it's funny me calling now?" Sonny's tone changed. "Someone been talking about me, is that it?"

"I was just thinking about the Mountain House when the phone rang, that's all."

"Huh?"

"What's it like?"

"The Mountain House? Is that what you're askin'?"

"Yeah."

"A fallin' down ruin. I haven't been up there in years."

"Describe it a little."

"I just did. Fallin' down ruin." Another gurgling sound. "Tell you what, Roy. Why don't you come out and I'll take you up there?"

"When?"

"Now's all right. I got a little opening in my schedule."

"Between what and what?" Roy said.

Pause. Then Sonny Junior laughed, a big laugh that made the phone vibrate in Roy's ear. "Family," he said. "What it's all about."

Roy changed the greeting on his phone: "If it's you, Rhett, I'm up at Cousin Sonny's in Tennessee." He gave him the number. Playing it over, Roy found he'd said *uncle* instead of *cousin*. He didn't bother to fix it.

Traffic was as light as it ever got. Roy rode through the nighttime sprawl, his uniform folded beside him on the seat, the carbine in the trunk. *Sherman razed all of this, down to the ground.* And what else had Lee said? *The soul part— unconquered, unoccupied, waiting.* The meaning of that eluded him. He pressed play.

> *"I'm gonna tell my mother howdy*
> *When I get home*
> *I'm gonna shake my father's hand*
> *I will shake their hands that day*
> *When we walk that Milky White Way*
> *One of these days."*

It was so loud and Roy was so caught up in it, he and his mother walking on stars, that he almost missed the fact that he was running on empty. He filled up at an all-night place near the state line. The pump rejected his credit card, so he had to go in and pay cash. The clerk couldn't speak English. Roy did something he'd never done, bought a bumper sticker off the rack by the register. This one was the battle flag, not very big, no writing on it. He stuck it on the middle of his back bumper and drove off. In his rearview mirror he saw the clerk watching through the glass. He himself started looking at passing things—cell phone antennas, Super 8 motel signs, golden arches—the way they'd appear framed in that little V on the barrel of the Sharps fifty-two he had in the trunk.

TWENTY-ONE

"Looks like you lost some weight there, cuz."

"I don't think so."

"Gonna have a six-pack like mine sooner 'n you know it." Sonny Junior tapped the hard ridges of his abdomen; muscles popped up in his chest. "Girls'll be swarmin' all over you, they aren't already."

They stood in a patch of sunlight partway up the mountain, shirts off and tied around their waists an hour or two before on the long climb from where the last dirt lane petered out. There was no path, just trees, rocks, underbrush, the sound of running water and these occasional sunny openings, some of them, like this one, with a view.

"And you're not even huffin' and puffin' yet," said Sonny Junior, "which is pretty strange for a city boy."

It was true. Not only no huffing and puffing, but Roy had the odd sensation that his lungs had plenty in reserve. He felt the weight of the inhaler in his pocket, couldn't remember the last time he'd used it.

"Some view, huh?" said Sonny Junior.

"Yeah."

"A real—what's the word I'm looking for?"

"No idea."

"Starts with *p*," Sonny Junior said. He took out a flask, drank from it, passed it to Roy.

"Vodka and Tang?" Roy said.

Sonny Junior gave him a look. "You havin' fun on me, cuz?"

"Nope."

"This here's the good stuff."

Roy took it, drank: the good stuff. "Panorama," he said.

Sonny Junior's eyes widened. Then he clapped Roy on the back, hard enough to move him off his feet a bit. "Got the looks and the brains both, don't you, Roy? Panorama. Son of a bitch." He surveyed the view, all green and gold under a sky so densely blue it seemed to be made of something material. "You can see seven states from here," he said.

Roy scanned the distant vistas.

"Two or three, anyways," Sonny said. "You know what ticks me off, Roy? This view was ours."

"Views don't belong to anybody."

"Fuck they don't. Ever been to Malibu?"

"No."

"Every good view on the planet is bought and paid for. What I want to know is who took ours away?"

"That doesn't make sense, Sonny."

"Why not?"

"Whatever happened was . . . a long time ago."

"So?"

Roy didn't answer.

"I'm right and you know it," Sonny said. A lone bird, hawk or eagle, rose up and up on a thermal, shrank to almost nothing. Sonny took another draw from the flask, passed it to Roy.

Roy drank. "This Old Grand-Dad?"

"From the bottle I inadvertently brought Uncle Roy there at the end, him not having a chance to finish it for obvious reasons. Want another hit?"

Roy didn't.

They climbed on, back in dense woods for a while, then up a steep section with fewer trees but wildflowers everywhere, red and white. The steep section rose to a towering ridge, all covered with moss, seeping water. They made their way around it, on hands and knees a couple of times, and at the head of the ridge stepped across a narrow stream that came bubbling out of a hole in the rocks a few feet above. Sonny Junior bent down, drank from cupped hands.

"Is that a good idea?" Roy said, remembering a scary article about microbes or parasites or something.

"Huh?" said Sonny.

Roy dipped his hand in the stream. How fast the water ran through his fingers, icy and energetic. He cupped his hands and drank. It stunned him: the best water he'd ever tasted, even better than the water from Chickamauga. Tasting was the wrong word. Tasting meant the taster was the master and the tasted was a thing. This water was the master: the best water he'd ever put inside himself, cleansing, purifying proof that all those eco-people were right about the earth being a living thing.

"This here's the source of the crick," said Sonny Junior.

"What crick?"

"Why, ours, Roy, that used to be ours, the crick what run the mill, way down below."

"Does it have a name?"

"Course it has a name," Sonny said. "Every crick has a name. This is the Crystal."

"Crystal?"

"What's so strange about that?"

"I camped by a creek with that name years ago." With Marcia, but Roy left that out. "It couldn't be the same one."

"Course it could. This here bitty thing goes all the way into the Tennessee River."

Remember that time up in Tennessee? What was the name of that crick? Crystal: Marcia naked, sitting on a log, leaning back a little, legs spread a little, bare feet in wildflowers, her eyes right on him as he came out from his swim. How they could have done what they'd done in the next twenty minutes, half hour, and then ended up like this, Roy didn't understand.

They circled the ridge, found themselves in an up-sloping meadow with knee-high grass and more flowers, red and white. The meadow rose sharply at the end, then leveled out

abruptly onto a broad plateau. Not far back on the plateau
stood a dark-green grove of what looked like fruit trees, and
in the green shadows Roy caught dappled glimpses of stone
walls, a door frame, a wagon wheel.

"Not much to see," Sonny said as they got closer.

Not much to see: stone walls, but crumbling, and the roof
gone; door and window frames, but no doors and windows; a
wagon wheel but no wagon. Roy went through the front door,
smelled dampness and rot, looked out at Sonny Junior watching him through the doorway.

"Like I told you, a fallin' down ruin."

"What do you think they used it for?"

"Who?" said Sonny Junior.

"Roy Singleton Hill. I know he came up here."

Sonny stared at him. "You're gettin' one of them psychic
feelings?"

"He talks about it."

"Uh-oh," said Sonny. "You're startin' to scare me."

"There's nothing psychic about this," Roy said, but even as
he did, he recollected that crying sound he'd heard just before he opened the leather-bound chest for the first time. He
took the diary from his pocket, stepped outside, opened it so
Sonny could see.

Sonny ran his eyes down the page, his lips moving once or
twice. "A fuckin' illiterate," he said. He turned the page; half
of it flaked away, drifted down like a leaf.

"Easy," said Roy.

Sonny's gaze came up in a measured way, settled on Roy.
"What's that, cuz?"

"It's old, Sonny. Delicate."

"Don't trust me with it, Roy?" Sonny handed back the
diary.

Roy didn't take it. "What's up, Sonny?" he said.

"Don't trust me because you're thinking I screwed you out
of your inheritance," said Sonny.

"What are you talking about?"

"What am I talking about?" A bee darted down between

them; Sonny smacked it out of the air with the back of his free hand. "Uncle Roy's goddamn place and you thinking I jewed you out of it, is what."

"Don't talk like that."

"It's not what you think?"

"It's not what I think, but I meant don't say 'jewed.' "

"Not keeping up with you there, Roy."

"You didn't screw me out of the place, leave it at that," Roy said.

"He did it all on his own."

"I believe you."

"I went in there with the bottle and those Cheetos. Forgot the briefs, did I mention that? Right away he was poppin' off with all this negative shit about you."

"Such as?"

"I already told you. About you never being much of a son to him, what with the naming of little Rhett and all. I didn't say a word, Roy, I swear—just kept my mouth shut and handed over the bottle when he was good and done."

"Thanks," Roy said.

"So you're not pissed?"

"I got my inheritance," Roy said.

Sonny Junior gave him a long look. "You mean that in some kind of deep way, right?"

Roy smiled, held up his hand. They had one of those arm-wrestling handshakes.

"You're deep, Roy, that's what I'm realizin'," said Sonny Junior when they were still locked in it.

"That's a first," said Roy.

The sun shone suddenly through a rocky space where a window had once been, lighting up a complex spiderweb, first making it visible, then making it gold. "Only thing on God's earth that spooks me," said Sonny Junior.

"Spiders?"

"I ain't going in there."

*   *   *

They sat under a blossoming apple tree beside the Mountain House, their backs to the trunk, and checked out the diary.

"He was our what, again?" said Sonny Junior.

"Great-great-grandfather."

"Meaning my ma and Uncle Roy's father's father?"

"One more."

Sonny laughed. "What a pain in the ass." He ran his eyes over a page or two. "All's he talks about is the rain. And the thunder."

"Thunder's his horse." Roy turned the pages. He came to 18 September 1863.

"Can't even read that," Sonny said.

" 'Zeke done cut me with the razor.' I think that's *razor*," Roy said. " 'No time for larning him different. We found Yankees at Reed's Bridge, showed 'em by God.' "

"What's that all about?" said Sonny.

"Reed's Bridge is the start of the battle of Chickamauga, where he took a battery by himself."

"How do you know that?"

"The next day, I think it was." Roy read the next day's entry. " 'In the woods all day and hot. No water.' " He scanned the next few lines, looking for words like *battery* or *cannons*. *Got me three mebbe for. One of em spoken wen I lent don but I coont here cownt of noyz. Took his Water offn im. Bad bad thirst all day.*

"Anything about the battery?" Sonny Junior said.

"I'm not sure."

He read on: *20 sep fitin on Lafayet rd. Thunder all cuvrd in Blod but warnt hisn. Yankees runin and Forest angry as Hell. no Water.*

"I don't get any of it," said Sonny Junior.

"Forrest was their commander. He wanted to pursue the Yankees after Chickamauga but Bragg ruled against it. We ended up losing Chattanooga. That gave Sherman control of the railroads, setting up the march to the sea."

Sonny Junior turned to him in surprise. "How do you know?"

"I've been spending time with a regiment."

"What regiment?"

"Roy Singleton Hill's regiment—the Seventh Tennessee Cavalry."

Pause. "Like in your imagination or something?"

"It's a re-formed unit for reenactors."

"Play fighting kind of shit?"

"That's one way of putting it."

"Or just plain drinking, like that buddy of yours?"

Roy closed the diary.

"I piss you off, Roy?"

Roy stood up, looked down at Sonny. "Ever think how things would be if we'd won?"

"If we'd won what?"

"The war. What do you think we've been talking about?"

"The Civil War?"

Roy's voice rose a little. "What other war is there for us?"

Sonny Junior gave him that surprised look again. Roy was a bit surprised too. "You are deep, Roy. What's a thinker like you doin' in a family like this?"

Roy almost laughed out loud at the absurdity of that label. Sonny held up his hand. Roy took it, pulled him to his feet, felt Sonny Junior's strength. Sonny must have bumped the tree a little standing up, because the next moment a cloud of blossoms drifted down, wafting around them, nestling in Sonny's long hair, and in Roy's, still close to Globax length.

"We're like a couple of goddamn flower children," Sonny said.

"That's a good one," said Roy.

Sonny Junior flicked the blossoms out of his hair as though they were gnats. "I reckon I get what you're driving at," he said. He waved his hand over the view of the seven states, or two, or whatever it was. "This would still be ours, right?"

Not what Roy had meant.

                    *   *   *

Sonny Junior took him to a bar halfway between Duck-town and Roy's father's old place. There were a couple of pickups and motorcycles outside; inside, a jukebox, a knotty pine bar, the men leaning on it looking like they could be friends with Sonny, and two women at a round table with wooden kegs for chairs.

Roy and Sonny went to the bar. "Two beers, two Old Grand-Dads," said Sonny. "On ice, Roy?"

"Sure."

They stood at the bar, drinking Old Grand-Dad and beer. One or two of the men at the bar glanced at Sonny; they knew him, all right, but maybe not as friends.

"Got anything to eat?" Sonny said.

"Cheetos," said the bartender.

"Cheetos, Roy?" said Sonny.

"Not for me."

Sonny got himself a pack of Cheetos. He was chewing on a handful, orange powder dusting his lips, when one of the women came up behind them.

"Where you been keeping yourself, Sonny?"

Roy and Sonny turned to her. She wore a halter top re-vealing the upper half of a tattoo that promised to swell into something elaborate farther down.

"Where you can't find me," Sonny told her.

"That's not very nice, Sonny," she said.

"Don't know what got into me," said Sonny, washing down the Cheetos with beer. The woman was no longer paying at-tention: her eyes were on Roy.

"Gonna introduce me to your friend?" she said.

"No one's stoppin' you doin' it yourself," said Sonny.

"Hi," the woman said to Roy, "I'm Tyla."

"Roy," said Roy.

"I like that name. Where you from, Roy?"

"Atlanta."

"The big city." She glanced back to the table where the other woman, also in a halter top, also with a tattoo, was watching. Some little eyebrow signal passed between them.

"How about joining us for a drink?" Tyla said. "We got a big ol' pitcher of Bud we could never finish by ourselves."

"Five bucks says you could," said Sonny.

Roy and Sonny joined the women at their table. On the way over, Sonny spoke in Roy's ear: "Feel like gettin' laid tonight, cuz?"

Roy shook his head.

"You're too deep for me, Roy," Sonny said, watching Roy as they sat down.

"Deep how?" said Tyla, pouring beer. "Roy, say hi to Tonya; Tonya, Roy."

"Don't see no ring on your finger, Roy," said Tonya.

"Deep meaning he's got a brain in his head, unlike some," said Sonny. "Roy here's my first cousin."

"You never mentioned no first cousin, Sonny," said Tyla.

Sonny paused, glass halfway to his lips. "You questioning my veracity?" he said.

"Not so's I know," said Tyla. "You never mentioned him is all. I can see you're cousins with my own eyes."

"You can?" said Sonny.

"Which one's better looking, Ton?" said Tyla.

"They're both pretty good-lookin'," said Tonya. "But we all know Sonny Junior, and this one's"—she patted Roy's knee—"an unknown quantity."

Tyla laughed, spraying just a little beer. "Unknown quantity—no such animal in a man."

Tonya kept her hand on Roy's knee, under the table; gave him a little squeeze, in fact. This was not the first knee she'd squeezed: there was something expert in her touch, sending a message that she already knew more than he did about his every bodily urge. He considered moving his knee away, but did nothing. "Got any tattoos on you, Roy?" she said.

"No."

"I do."

"If you say so."

"If I say so? You blind or somethin'? Can't you see this?" She thrust her breast at him.

"I can just make it out," Roy said.

"And that's only the half of it," said Tonya.

"Give him a peek at the rest," said Tyla.

"Want a peek, Roy?" said Tonya.

"Don't go to a lot of trouble on my . . ."

Tonya, one hand on Roy's knee, leaned toward him. He felt her weight. At that moment he thought of the emeralds, green like her tattoo, and everything started to go sour. But then her breasts rose up out of the halter top, and a little scene of a man and a woman—possibly two women—began to take shape. "Can you see right down to the bottom, Roy?" said Tonya, leaning forward more, her hand sliding up Roy's thigh to support herself, her breast just inches from his nose. "That's the best part."

"It is," he said, and heard the thickness in his voice. He foresaw a night with Old Grand-Dad and this woman's flesh and no need to think a moment past that; a wild night with a stranger, the kind of night he'd never actually had, except maybe that once camping on Crystal Creek, and that was not a stranger but his wife-to-be.

"Don't be shy," said Tonya. "It's art. Feast your eyes."

Roy probably would have, suddenly seeing a night like this, or maybe many of them, as a way to get past the emeralds, past Marcia, past everything once and for all, to fuck his brains out, an expression he now understood, but at that moment the door opened and in walked Lee. Lee saw Roy right away, took in everything, went still.

TWENTY-TWO

"**D**oes this look like a gay bar?" said Sonny Junior, not loud, but it didn't have to be loud for everyone to hear in a little place like that.

"Easy, Sonny," Roy said. His voice didn't sound quite right. There was a strange undertone, almost a buzz, the threatening kind. Roy didn't think: Must be the booze doing that; or stress; or booze on top of stress. It was much deeper than that: The gene is in me.

The room was quiet, the men at the bar watching. Tyla's and Tonya's eyes were open wide in alarm; their eyelashes were coated thick with makeup, their eyebrows plucked almost all away. Sonny Junior said, "Anything you say, cuz."

Roy rose and went over to Lee.

"I'm interrupting something," Lee said.

"Probably a good thing," said Roy.

"I saw your car outside," Lee said.

"Just passing by?"

Lee reddened. "I called your place again, heard the message on the machine, and came up here."

"So it must be important," Roy said, "whatever's on your mind."

"I wanted to thank you, that's all."

"For what?"

"The other night."

"Comrades in arms," Roy said. "No thanks necessary." He glanced around, saw everyone watching. "Come meet my cousin."

228

Roy took Lee over to the table, got an extra glass, introduced everybody. Lee nodded to the women, shook hands with Sonny. Sonny didn't squeeze hard, Roy was watching, but all he saw was orange Cheetos powder spreading from Sonny's fingers to Lee's. Lee sat down between Roy and Tonya. Someone poured. Someone poured some more.

"Is that your bike outside?" said Tyla.

"Yes," said Lee.

"Looks like a nice bike."

"Thanks."

"What kind is it?"

"Harley Sportster."

"Oh yeah?" said Tonya, swinging around toward Lee. "Eight eighty-three or twelve hundred?"

"Twelve hundred."

"Take me for a ride?" said Tonya.

"Sometime."

"I like that name—Lee," said Tonya. "Where you from?"

"Atlanta."

"That how you know Roy?"

"We're in the same regiment."

"Regiment? Wouldn't'a taken you for military," said Tonya.

"Civil War regiment," Lee said.

"That sounds cool," said Tonya. "Got any tattoos on you, Lee?"

"No."

"I do." She stuck her breast out at Lee.

Lee did something Roy wouldn't have expected then, extending a finger, touching Tonya's breast, tracing the beginning of the tattoo design, carefully, as though carrying out scientific fieldwork. Tonya's mouth opened and stayed open, revealing crooked teeth with one or two gaps.

"Did it hurt?" Lee said, looking up at Tonya's face.

Tonya licked her lips. "Did it hurt?" Another pitcher of beer appeared, and two fresh glasses of Old Grand-Dad. "No guy's ever asked me that before. Nah, it didn't hurt—I was so loaded I couldn't feel a thing." Tonya's gaze rested on Lee's face. "Know something? You're the best-looking one of the bunch."

"I second that emotion," said Tyla, raising her glass, downing half of it.

"Isn't he a mite scrawny for two big babes like you?" said Sonny.

"Scrawny?" said Tyla.

"Big difference between scrawny and lean," said Tonya.

Sonny smiled at Lee across the table. "How tall are you, little buddy?"

"Five feet four inches," said Lee.

"What do you weigh?"

"One hundred twenty-five pounds."

"I've taken shits bigger'n that," said Sonny.

It was quiet in the bar, and Lee spoke quietly. "That just makes you an especially big asshole."

Sonny Junior went rigid: Roy could feel it, as though some powerful current had been switched on in the room. Then Sonny was up and on the move, brushing past Roy, keg chair topping backward. But not quite past Roy: Roy was up too, in his path. "Easy, Sonny," Roy said.

Sonny grabbed Roy, lifted him right off the floor. "Three times now you've told me that," Sonny said.

Roy looked in Sonny's eyes—Sonny had pale eyes with red flecks in the blue—knew Sonny'd had him helpless like this once before, long ago in the barn. Eyes don't change. As the memory stirred Roy went off, but inside, capped down tight; so tight that his voice sounded close to normal when he spoke: "I've got the gene too."

"Huh?" said Sonny.

Roy drove his elbow down into Sonny's shoulder, right where it meets the neck. Sonny made some bellowing noise, let him go. Then Tonya or Tyla spilled her beer, glass shattered, the bartender straightened behind the bar, a ball bat in his hands. Sonny tilted his head back a little, the angle somehow murderous. Did Roy look the same? He knew it was possible. What wasn't, now?

Lee stepped between them.

"That's enough."

Roy and Sonny looked down at Lee. Sonny was the first to find it amusing. As he started to laugh, Lee put a hand on each of their chests and pushed them apart. Sonny took a few exaggerated steps backward.

"No offense, tough guy," said Sonny.

"None taken," said Lee.

"I just didn't like the way you copped a feel of Tyla's tit back then."

"It was Tonya's tit," Lee said.

"I didn't mind, Sonny, honest," said Tonya.

"That's not the way we cop a feel around these parts," Sonny said.

Lee gazed up at him. "My apologies."

"It was a nice way of copping a feel," Tonya said. "Why doesn't anybody understand me?"

Lee dropped a few bills on the table, took Roy by the arm, walked him outside.

The moon was up, not quite full. And two moons, again, which Roy had to work down to one and a half, and one.

"That's the second time you've rescued me," Lee said. "I've decided I don't like it."

"It won't happen again," Roy said; and knew at that moment that despite the copping of feels and the breaking up of fights, his eyes hadn't deceived him at Chickamauga: no man would have said that.

"Did I mention we've got a little group inside the regiment?" Lee said. "More hard-core?"

"Something about it," Roy said.

"Interested?"

"What's it about?"

"Tacticals. Behind the lines kind of stuff. Basically live in 1863."

"When the water was good," Roy said.

Lee looked up at him. "Was it, Roy?"

"I can prove it," Roy said.

Two cars with New Jersey plates turned into the lot as Roy and Lee pulled out.

Roy drove up to where the last dirt lane petered out, Lee following on the bike. Lee kicked down the stand, glanced inside the Altima, saw the uniform.

"Why not put that on, Roy?"

Roy nodded.

"Mine's in the saddlebag," Lee said.

A cloud shaped like a slender bird slid over the moon. They changed into their uniforms in darkness.

"Got your weapon?" Lee said.

"In the trunk."

"Bring it."

Roy heard a muffled clink, knew it was the sound of bullets, heavy bullets, dropping into Lee's cartridge pouch. Then the moon came out and there was Lee, the most natural sight in the world, in full uniform with an Enfield muzzleloader like Gordo's, much longer than Roy's carbine, held over one shoulder in marching position, a mule collar supply roll over the other. Roy got the carbine out of the trunk and started up the mountain. Behind him, Lee moved so quietly Roy had to glance back in the moonlit patches—the sunny patches of daytime—to see if they were still together. They were every time.

The ridge appeared, a black bulge in the night that seemed to be falling slowly toward them. Roy heard water bubbling up above, the source of Crystal Creek, climbed toward it. The ridge stopped falling, now backed away, retreating with every step. This sudden elasticity of the physical world could have been unsettling, but wasn't, might even have led to air supply problems, but didn't. Roy kept going, almost as quickly as he had by day, breathing evenly. He listened for the sound of Lee breathing, heard nothing. They were good. This was the way to move behind enemy lines, to enter their camp by night, spike the guns, run off the horses, blow up the powder. He rounded the head of the ridge; the moonlight caught the water pouring from the rocks—the sound was frothing water but the sight was diamonds spraying from the earth.

They knelt by the stream and drank. Then something strange happened: without a word, and as one, they dipped their faces in the water. Pure, cold, savage water: it went right through Roy's skin, into his blood, readied him for anything. He opened his eyes underwater, watched the diamonds flowing by. He turned his head and saw Lee's eyes open too— silver ovals black at the core.

They climbed around the ridge, up through the sloping meadow, the moon bright enough to bring out colors now, the silver-green of the tall grass, gray-green of the flower stalks, charcoal-gray of the white petals, beet-red of the red ones. Only the distant trees remained black, and even they flashed silver in their crowns when a breeze passed by. Lee came up beside him. Roy smelled fresh sweat and hot wool, in no way unpleasant.

To the top of the meadow, into the apple trees on the plateau, and didn't the moon, lower now, shine through that same rough stone rectangle that had once been a window, turning the complex spiderweb silver? The web trembled slightly, like a tiny trampoline under a tiny athlete. Roy heard Lee take a deep breath.

"The Mountain House of Roy Singleton Hill," he said.

Lee went inside, looked around, then leaned the Enfield against the wall, took off the mule collar roll, laid it on the ground.

"Hungry?"

"A little."

Lee reached in the roll, handed Roy a small, dense square.

"What's this?"

"Hardtack."

Roy bit into it. "Is it food?"

"You can live on it indefinitely."

"I like your muffins better."

They stood in the Mountain House, moonlight on the

metal of their weapons and buckles, the spiderweb, Lee's eyes. "The muffins aren't authentic," Lee said.

Lee bent down, spread the roll on the ground: a wool blanket with hardtack inside, a canteen, a candle, and a few smaller things Roy couldn't identify.

"The blanket's authentic," Lee said, "but not as authentic as no blanket at all."

Lee pushed the hardtack, the canteen, the candle, the other things to the side, lay down on the blanket, gazing up at Roy.

"We're sleeping here?" Roy said.

"Got a better idea?"

Roy shook his head. "But I don't have a blanket of my own."

"That's authentic too."

Roy sat down on Lee's blanket. He smelled wool, fresh sweat, and mint. The air was rich with mint. He filled his lungs with it, glanced over at Lee. Lee's eyes were closed. Roy lay down on the far side of the blanket.

The moon sank below the treetops, and in a way that made no sense the air got colder, as though there was some kind of celestial confusion. Stars popped out all over the sky, more than Roy had ever seen, and not just white, but blue, red, yellow. This was reality, Roy realized, all those stars were present all the time, blazed away all the time, didn't go anywhere. The daytime part was false.

Lying on his back, watching that distant reality, Roy cooled down from the climb. For a while he felt just right. But his sweat soaked into the wool uniform, kept him from drying off completely, and he started to shiver. Had Roy Singleton Hill shivered too, in this uniform, on this mountain, in 1863? Roy doubted only the shivering part.

"Is there a blanket for on top?" he said, not sure Lee was awake.

"Almost never happened," Lee said, from closer than he thought. "They spooned on cold nights."

"Spooned?" said Roy.

"Roll over," Lee said.

Roy rolled on his side. From there he could see the spider-web, no longer moonlit, just a faint pattern in the night, still trembling. He felt Lee slide in against him, adapting to his shape, front to back.

"Nothing more authentic than this," Lee said, voice close to Roy's ear. Roy shivered, maybe because of the cold, maybe because of the voice in his ear. He smelled Lee's breath, the same minty smell of the night, shivered more.

"You're cold," Lee said.

Roy felt a hand, a small hand, touch his side, move around to his chest, press him gently. What he had to go on—that one female remark about not wanting to be rescued, plus the image he'd glimpsed after Sergeant Vandam's tackle had popped the buttons of Lee's jacket—didn't seem very substantial at the moment. Remarks were open to interpretation and he'd never been better than average at that sort of thing, usually worse; and a nighttime image could be mistaken, or nothing more than wishful thinking.

Roy rolled back over. Lee was watching him, mouth slightly open, small even teeth lit by the stars. Roy slipped his hand under the high waistband of Lee's pants, forced it down below, eliminated all doubt.

"Authentic," Lee said.

Roy shifted his hand up, under Lee's jacket.

"If it's Tyla's and Tonya's tits that heated you up," Lee said, "then these are going to be a disappointment."

"You don't know me," Roy said.

He kissed her mouth. They moved together, half in, half out of their rough wool uniforms. Whatever he'd imagined happening with Tonya, or that real time with Marcia farther down Crystal Creek? They didn't compare. The daytime part was false.

TWENTY-THREE

Roy smelled smoke, thought the Mountain House was on fire and everyone in it would die. He opened his eyes: daytime, and alone; in uniform, lying on his side on the blanket, a lone spoon in a drawer. On Lee's half of the blanket lay the two guns, side by side.

Roy got up, followed the burning smell out the back of the house, found a small fire pit dug in the ground, with a rusted grill over it and wood burning underneath. Not far away stood another ruin he hadn't noticed before, this one made of faded barnwood slats, most of them gone. Roy went closer, called, "Lee." No response. He peered inside, saw weeds sprouting through a dirt floor, and what he thought at first was a blackened basketball, then realized was the ball part, flaked and rusted, of a ball and chain.

Roy went back through the Mountain House, past the apple grove, to the edge of the plateau. He saw Lee, or at least someone in a rebel uniform, at the distant end of the sloping meadow, waving flowers marking the route like a sailboat's wake. Not long after, the figure, tiny now, disappeared over the top of the ridge. Roy started down across the meadow. An electric-blue dragonfly buzzed up from under his feet and got lost in the sky.

Roy went through the meadow, cut across the face of the ridge, came to the hole in the rocks where the creek poured out. He scanned the mountain for signs of movement, saw nothing through the trees. Something splashed in the creek, not far away. Roy walked over, looked down, saw a small fish making no headway against the current. He began following the creek.

It led him around the side of the mountain, away from the ridge. He soon heard a sound like the wind, faint at first, then louder, although the air was still. Roy struggled through a thicket, came out on a rocky shelf: a cliff, actually, with the creek falling off it, straight down.

Roy stood at the top. He'd never stood at the top of a waterfall, didn't know whether everyone who did had to fight the urge he was fighting now. Down below lay a pool, frothy under the waterfall, placid at the other end where it narrowed, the creek continuing down the mountain. Flat rocks lined the narrow opening, and on one of them lay Lee, in uniform with sleeves rolled up, hands in the water, motionless.

Roy watched. He was beginning to think that Lee was day-dreaming, meditating, perhaps even asleep, when there was a sudden movement and Lee sprang up, a fish in his hands. In her hands. A big brown fish: it wriggled frantically for a second or two and then went still. The look on Lee's face when that happened scared Roy a little. He started back up to the Mountain House.

Trout: with clear brown eyes, fins and tail still pink at the edges, no sign of injury. Lee cooked it whole over the fire pit.

"Where'd you find the grill?" Roy said.

"Out back," Lee said, nodding toward the remains of the barnwood shack.

"Where the slaves lived," Roy said.

Lee, squatting by the fire, gazed at Roy sitting cross-legged on the other side, heat shimmering in the air between them. "Slavery was just about universal throughout human history."

"So?"

"So you've got to decide if you're going to let that ruin everything."

"What do you mean by everything?"

Lee took out a knife, sliced up the trout, put some pieces on a broad leaf and brought them to Roy. "Us, for starters."

"Us?"

She knelt in front of him, trout steaming on the leaf. "Do you care about me at all, Roy?"

"Yes."

"I'm in love with you," Lee said. Her face glowed, perhaps from the heat of the fire.

Was this the moment he had to make some similar statement? Roy knew something big was happening between them but wasn't ready to call it love. "I don't know what Gordo's told you, but I've just been through—"

She cut him off. "None of that matters."

"None of what?"

"I don't need to know about your situation. Don't need to, don't want to."

"What's that mean, my situation?"

"Your present life, Roy." Lee rose. "Eat up."

Roy ate. The glistening flesh of the fish, its saltiness, its heat—he'd never tasted anything like this. Saying grace, a habit his mother had fallen out of when he was still very young: all at once, he understood where the idea came from; answer to a question he'd never even considered.

"You like?" Lee said.

"Yes."

She took something from the pocket of her butternut jacket, held it up. "Know what this is?"

"A bird feather."

"Quail feather, specifically. I found it on the ridge. Saw deer tracks too. And the creek's full of trout. Throw in a few chickens and you could live here forever."

A crazy idea: the list of objections so long it was pointless even to itemize them. Roy had a crack at itemizing anyway. First there was Rhett, of course. And next? And after that? Nothing jumped out at him.

"We've been searching for a place like this," Lee said.

"Who?"

"The progressive element in the regiment, I've been telling you about. Hope I'm not being too forward, Roy, but would it be all right with you if a few of them came up for a look?"

"What's that got to do with me?"

"It just feels right, Roy, asking you."

This line of talk put Roy in mind of Sonny Junior and their lost lands, but he didn't think it was a good time for mentioning Sonny, so he ate the trout in silence, washed it down with creek water Lee had brought back in her canteen. A bumblebee the size of one of those fifty-eight-caliber rounds flew by, not very fast. Then another, even slower, and a yellow butterfly, slower than that.

"Sleepy?" Lee said.

"Now that you mention it." But he wasn't.

They lay on the blanket.

"Does Jesse know?" Roy said.

"Know what?"

"Or any of the others—about you?"

"Of course not," Lee said. "How authentic would that be?"

"I don't understand."

"Women fought in disguise—horrible word—but no one ever knew until they got them to the surgeon's tent or the burial pit. Therefore telling people isn't authentic."

"What about me?"

"You," said Lee.

She put her arms around him, kissed his mouth. He'd always loved Marcia's kisses, but this was different: he got the feeling that Lee was giving every little bit of herself in this kiss, like there was no before and after. Made him want to do the same back, but still, with the sun up and him being sober, Roy knew he had no right to expect anything like last night. But it was like last night, or better; and therefore if not a right, what? A privilege? He thought about that after, sweat running off him, eyes closed, the day hot pink through his eyelids.

"You must have happened sometimes," she said.

"So I'm authentic too?"

"Oh, yes," Lee said. He felt her lips on his cheek, the side of his neck, against his ear. "That's the whole point."

Roy cooled off. Heat must have been shimmering up from their bodies. He thought he could hear the waterfall.

When Roy awoke, Lee was sitting in one of the window spaces, reading the diary. "Fell out of your pocket," she said. "Hope you don't mind."

Roy didn't mind. "Who's Zeke?" he said.

"His body man—doesn't he say that somewhere?" Lee turned the pages.

"Is that like a bodyguard?"

Lee looked at him over the diary. "Not exactly."

"Then what?"

"More like a personal servant."

"A paid servant?"

"No."

Roy went over, read: *takin Zeke bac fer boddyman sed godbis an wen up to th montan Hows fer godbis up thar.*

"The standard of literacy is pretty typical of the period," Lee said.

Roy didn't care about that. *Zeke wen asculcin but I larnt him difernt.*

He could feel Lee's eyes tracking along with his. This time she had nothing to say. Roy walked out the back of the Mountain House, past the fire pit, still smoking, and into the slave quarters. He had a careful look around, saw what he'd already seen, the rusted iron ball lying in the weeds that overgrew the dirt floor; the plant world reclaiming everything, but maybe not fast enough.

A crow cawed, rose up out of the woods behind the slave quarters, hunched over, wings beating furiously. Roy went outside, crossed to the back of the plateau where the mountain began rising again, found what might have been a trail, might have been a chance series of openings between the trees, started up. The air was still and warm, full of insect sounds. Roy was sweating and a little thirsty by the time the ground leveled and he stepped into a clearing the size of a baseball infield.

Roy thought of it as a clearing because there were no trees, but chest-high plants grew everywhere. A man with his back to Roy was hard at work chopping them down with a machete and stuffing them into a plastic trash bag. His tightly curled hair gleamed with sweat and his T-shirt, with a picture of Bob Marley on the back, was soaked through. He was singing a song under his breath, but Roy was close enough to catch it.

"Yes I'm gonna walk that Milky White Way
Oh Lord, some of these days."

Roy stopped breathing. The man must have sensed that, because he immediately stopped singing and spun around. He saw Roy, dropped the machete, raised his hands high.

"Don' shoot."

Roy hadn't realized he was carrying the gun, didn't even remember picking it up off the blanket. He almost said, *Don't worry, it's not real,* but of course that wasn't true. "Why would I do a thing like that?" he said.

"Seen you DEA types get testy after one of these long climbs," the man said. He looked more like Chuck Berry than Bob Marley, although he was lighter skinned than either. "I would too, hot day like this'n, specially with the money they're payin' you."

"I'm not a DEA type."

"FBI? BATF?" The man squinted a little at him; Roy was still in the shade. "Can't say as I recognize the outfit."

"You're safe with me," Roy said.

"I'm not feelin' safe, some reason," the man said.

"Put your hands down."

The man lowered his hands, but slowly, and kept them

open toward Roy. "Couldn't be a hunter, this not bein' huntin' season," he said. " 'Less you're not against bendin' a rule or two, the kind that don't make no sense, anyways. Which case, you and me have somethin' in common."

Roy moved into the clearing, glanced around, fingered a leaf of one of the plants. "How long's all this been growing here?"

"Since 't Adam and Eve. It's nature."

"I meant organized like this. A plot."

"Ain't no plot," said the man, his voice rising and turning a little querulous. "Thought you wasn't law enforcement."

"I'm not."

The man still looked worried. "Don't suppose you could be provin' that somehow."

"By flashing a badge that says 'not the police'?" Roy said.

The man laughed, revealing a mouthful of stained teeth. "There's the trouble with this ... hobby," he said, glancing around the clearing. "Sometimes you get to thinkin' not quite right. It's a relaxin' hobby, don't get me wrong, but the thinkin' part can lose its straightness, you know what I mean."

"Yes," Roy said.

"Name's Ezekiel, by the way." He held out his hand.

Roy shook it. "Roy."

"Happy to know you, Roy. Truth is, I'm feelin' relief you turn out to be whoever you turn out to be, what with this not even really bein' harvest time yet, and the crop off to such a promisin' start."

"Your secret's safe with me."

"Sweet," said Ezekiel. "Sweet, sweet music to my ear." He took out a cigar-size joint. "Hate to toot our own horn, but we make a fine produc' here in eas' Tennessee. You from around these parts, Roy?"

Roy shook his head. "Atlanta."

"Sure would love to go there one day. See much of Ted Turner?"

"No," Roy said. "You're from around here?"

"Time immemorial," Ezekiel said. He struck a wooden match with his thumbnail, lit the joint; a ball of smoke rose up like the first phrase in a tribal signal. Ezekiel took a big drag, passed the joint to Roy.

Roy had tried marijuana in high school, once or twice in college, not since. None of that was on his mind. His only thought was: Is it authentic? Why wouldn't it be? Why wouldn't there have been clearings like this, if not in the time of Adam and Eve, at least in 1863? He took a big drag and felt good right away, big and strong, at one with his uniform, comfortable in his double skin. Then he grew aware of the wooden stock of the gun in his hand, yes, a living thing, as Lee had said, the feel of it another comfort all by itself. He wanted to be shooting things with it, distant things, flying things, hiding things.

"Quality produc', Roy?" said Ezekiel.

Roy looked at Ezekiel and all at once could not get past the otherness. Their gazes slid past each other, focused elsewhere.

But Roy heard, heard after the sound was gone, the way the *y* in his name came out when Ezekiel spoke it, almost like pure air, a breeze, the same as when his mother said it, or Curtis. Curtis: whom he'd almost called a dumb nigger. And so what about that *almost*? He'd had the thought, which was what counted, and worse, was fighting a sick desire to say the word out loud, right now. He handed back the joint.

"You say something, Roy?"

"No."

"Didn't catch it, anyways. See them birds up there?"

Roy looked up, saw a V-shaped formation of birds high above.

"Means rain by midnight," Ezekiel said.

"Doesn't feel like rain," Roy said.

Ezekiel laughed, a laugh that got wheezy at the end. "Feel like rain," he said. "That's a good one. Like we're rubbin' up skin to skin with the weather." He took another drag, passed the joint to Roy. Roy took one too.

"You married, Roy?"

"I was."

"Me too. Was and was and was. You understand women, Roy?"

"I don't even understand the question."

Ezekiel laughed, wheezed, laughed some more. "Made my day, runnin' into you like this," he said, patting Roy on the back. "Never did get your last name, Roy. Should be on a last name basis, now we's becoming friends."

"Hill," said Roy.

"Same as me," said Ezekiel.

"Same as you?"

"Course, a common name," said Ezekiel. "Now say it was Schwarzenegger, wouldn't that be weird?"

Roy didn't answer.

"Seein' as Schwarzenegger ain't exactly a common name. That's the joke. Course you got to explain a joke, it's not funny." He glanced at his wrist; there was no watch on it. "No escapin' work ethics, is there, Roy?" He picked up the machete. "Don' suppose you'd be wantin' to make a bulk purchase at a surprisin' discount?"

Roy shook his head.

"Then I guess it's *hasta la vista*," Ezekiel said. "Careful on the way down, now. On the way down's where ninety point nine percent of accidents happen."

Clouds came, first small and fluffy, then big and dark. Lee buckled her belt, straightened her hair, picked up her gun, looked more like a man. They started down the mountain. It was raining as they crossed the creek, raining harder as they descended though the thick woods, the path now sometimes a stream. There was nothing to hear but the rain and the squishing of their boots.

"This is what it was like," Lee said.

"Not so bad," said Roy.

After that it really poured. An hour or so later, they stopped by a boulder twice their size to drink from the canteen. As

Lee passed it to him, Roy took her wrist, thinking of pulling her closer for a kiss, thinking if not now, when? When would the next one be? At that moment they heard a squishing sound like the ones they'd been making, and Sonny Junior came around the boulder, almost at a jogging pace. Roy jumped a little; so did Lee, or maybe that was just the force she used to jerk her hand free.

"Hey," said Sonny Junior, his eyes going from Roy to Lee, back to Roy. "You scared me." He didn't look scared. "Saw your car, Roy, and thought I'd spring this surprise. How do I look?"

Sonny did a little pirouette, which could have made a man his size look silly, but didn't. He was in full Confederate uniform, with sergeant stripes on the sleeve.

"What's this all about?" Roy said.

"That's what I'm gonna find out," Sonny said. "I'm signing up."

"Where'd you get the rig?" Lee said.

Sonny smiled down at her. "Hopin' we can be friends, little guy," he said. "Specially now that I outrank you. Bought it off a buddy of mine who's goin' away for a spell and won't be needin' it."

"It looks all right," Lee said, "except for the weapon."

"The AK?" said Sonny. "Hell, I know that. My buddy's bringing his musket around tomorrow. But meanwhile I didn't want to come up here with nothin'. What kind of soldierin' would that be?"

"We have to clear all new recruits with the commander," Lee said, "but I'm sure there won't be a problem. Welcome to the Seventh Tennessee Cavalry."

"Much obliged," said Sonny, rain dripping off his slouch hat. "The fireworks, the snake show, even the demolition derby—all nothin' compared to this. I know that already."

"You had a snake show?" Roy said.

"Did I leave that out?"

They walked down together. Sonny Junior had bagged a

deer on the way in. They found it strung up on a branch, dripping blood that the rain pinkened and washed away.

"I'm totally psyched," Sonny Junior said. "This time we're gonna win."

TWENTY-FOUR

Back home, Roy couldn't sleep when he was in bed, couldn't sit still when he was up, couldn't drink the water from the tap, couldn't eat the food from the cupboard. And home was a misnomer.

He walked from room to room in his underwear, didn't shave, didn't shower. The mail that came all had messages on the envelopes like *final notice*, *immediate reply required*, and *do not ignore*. Roy tossed it all into a trash bag, swept the mail from the kitchen table into it too, flung the bag into the alley out back. That left the kitchen table nice and clear, except for the diary, the Old Grand-Dad bottle, and the Old Grand-Dad bottle that came next.

The air? He couldn't breathe it. He used his inhaler, first a little, then a lot. After a few days, he went to the drugstore to get more. The clerk came back with his credit card.

"Sorry, sir. Better call Visa."

"Keep it," Roy said, and walked out.

He made calls: to Lee, and got no answer; to Gordo, and got the machine; to Rhett, and got some woman with an accent.

"They gone," she said.

"Gone? Rhett's gone?"

"Bermuda cruise," she said. "Back soon."

Bermuda cruise. Roy couldn't get the phrase to make sense in his mind. He said something, something that probably didn't make sense either.

"I can put you to his voice mail," the woman said.

"Whose voice mail?"

Beep. "Hi, this is Rhett Hill. Can't take your call right now, but if you leave a message I'll get back to you." Beep.

Roy opened his mouth to leave a message. The message was: *I miss you.* He didn't say it, didn't say anything. He did call back a few minutes later, maybe just one minute, to get into the voice mail again. Not that he said anything this time either; he wanted to hear Rhett's voice. It wasn't for the way he sounded so grown-up all of a sudden—that was a negative, if anything. It was to hear him say: "Rhett Hill."

Roy almost did it again.

He walked around the house, the bottle of Old Grand-Dad dangling from his hand. He opened some drawers, found a sewing kit, a hair dryer, the wedding album. She'd left it behind. But why not? Made more sense to wonder why she'd left the sewing kit and the hair dryer. Roy turned a page or two of the wedding album, stared at a few pictures, opened the nearest window, threw it out. What was it, day or night?

Night.

Night was a good time for watching the Pop Warner tape, over and over. Fifty-six did all the things he did: ran into the huddle at full speed, helped chase down the ball carrier, picked up the fumble, took it in for six, felt joy. The man on the sideline watched with no expression on his face. He did shout, "Run," that one time, but the camera wasn't on him then so there was no telling how he looked. Stupid, probably—the man knowing better than most that the players couldn't hear a thing outside the game.

Over and over.

Then it was day. How long did Bermuda cruises last? No harm in seeing if Rhett was back. Roy picked up the phone, dialed the number unsuccessfully several times before realizing that the line was dead. He tried the other phones in the house: all dead too. On his cell phone, he called the phone company and reported service problems. Then he used it to try Rhett. No one answered this time. A recorded voice told him to press one for Grant, two for Marcia, three for Rhett.

He pressed three, or maybe not, because the next voice he heard was Marcia's:

"You've reached Marcia. Please leave a message."

Nothing unusual about that, except for the way she pronounced her name. Now it had three syllables instead of two—Mar-see-ah—and sounded European, or like something from MTV or maybe Hollywood, Roy couldn't think what.

"Where are you?" he said; and angrily, when he hadn't meant to leave a message at all. Maybe not angrily, he hoped not angrily, called once more to check. But of course he didn't hear his own voice, couldn't hear messages in someone else's voice mail, that wasn't the way it worked. He'd got all mixed up about voice mail there for a second. He paced around the basement—what was he doing down there?—trying to get the elements of voice mail straight in his mind. There was voice mail, voice recognition, email, e-commerce, digital, analog, broadband, viruses, spam, and the little bulging trash barrel in the bottom corner of the screen. They were all the same, just a bunch of electrons, organized by a bunch of electron organizers who knew all the things he didn't. Roy was sick of electrons. That was the good thing about Old Grand-Dad, no electrons. He drank some to make sure; only a test. No doubt about it: they'd stripped the electrons away, probably the secret to the entire distillation process, right there.

He calmed down a little, now that he'd reached this understanding, was getting a grip on the basic forces way down deep. While he was calming down and figuring out the physics of his difficulties, if any, the cell phone buzzed, still in his hand for some reason.

"Rhett?" he said.

But it was someone from the phone company, answering his call about the service problem. "Your line has been disconnected due to lack of payment."

So what? He had his cell phone. The joke was on them. A technological solution existed for every technological problem. He'd learned that along the way, where exactly he couldn't remember. Had Jerry said that? Or Carol? He kind of missed them, wondered if they ended up getting married, maybe on the last tape. That brought the wedding album to mind, out the window. And in that wedding album would be pictures of his mother. He needed them, hardly having any, his ma being the type who didn't like having her picture taken and always said, "Oh, no, not me." She also said: "Will you look at that sky, Roy—blue as your eyes and not a cloud in it!" But he'd never taken her advice, never really looked at the sky until Chickamauga.

Roy went to the nearest window, checked the sky: hazy brown, like some storm was blowing in off a desert. Roy had never been to the desert, had no desire to. He liked it lush— was just realizing that about himself now. Meanwhile, was this the window where he'd jettisoned the wedding album? Roy opened it and climbed out.

Bad planning.

He climbed back in, got Old Grand-Dad, climbed out again.

Roy was in the little yard in front of his house. He walked across it a few times, saw that the grass needed cutting, weeding, liming, fertilizing, didn't see the wedding album. That walking back and forth had made him thirsty. A sip of Old Grand-Dad took care of that. A jogger went by, gave him a look and then another, speeded up. The speeded-up part might have been his imagination, but the trash cans lined up on the sidewalk were real, everyone's trash but his. Pickup day: he had a problem. Didn't have to be good at filling in the blanks—and Roy knew he wasn't—to piece together what had happened: wedding album out the window, scooped up by some passerby, dropped in a plastic barrel.

But which one?

Made sense to start with the nearest, didn't it? Perfect sense. Roy went to the nearest trash barrel, pried off the round plastic top, checked inside. Empty cans of dog food, sections of the *Journal-Constitution*, crushed milk cartons;

Roy pushed all that aside, dug down beneath kitchen-size white plastic bags—no sense looking inside those, no one would have packed the wedding album away like that—down and down to a level that was sticky and moist. Roy withdrew his hand: red, red, red. But not blood: one quick taste proved that. Ketchup. He caught a glimpse of bent paper plates, french fries, partial hamburgers, the meat coated in congealed white fat. Below the paper plates lay the promising white corner of something. Roy picked up the trash barrel, dumped it out. There was a little explosion, but that was just a passing car running over an empty economy-size bottle of Coke that was rolling around out there for some reason. The promising white corner? Must have been that Sharper Image catalog, now coming to pieces out in the street.

Roy moved on to the next barrel. And wouldn't you know it? Right on top, first thing he saw: the wedding album. He glanced around, saw that others had witnessed this little triumph, shook his head at the irony of it all, sharing a rueful moment with his neighbors, although he didn't actually recognize anybody, before crossing the yard and climbing back in through the window.

Roy looked through the wedding album. He didn't see his ma anywhere. For a minute or two he reasoned along the lines of her camera shyness. Then he remembered something key: his ma had died a few months before the wedding. How had he forgotten a fact like that? He smashed the bottle of Old Grand-Dad against the wall. Luck was with him: he had another, although how that had come about wasn't clear.

No pictures of his ma, but plenty of Marcia, smiling from every page. Roy crumpled up some newspapers, tossed them in the fireplace, piled on some logs, or maybe not logs but pieces of broken furniture he happened to have lying around, built a roaring fire. He flipped the wedding album in on top. The flames crackled and rose higher. Roy watched it burn, felt the heat, thought: Atlanta.

Not the time of year for fires, of course, made the room much too hot. Roy went down to the basement, much cooler there. Must have been the temperature change that did it, causing an air supply problem. Roy took the inhaler from his pocket, squeezed it into his mouth. Empty. Hadn't he got some new ones? He sorted through drugstore memories, got nowhere, winged the empty inhaler across the room, not hard, just winging, but it hit one of the street-level windows. Smash. Tinkle.

The basement had indoor-outdoor carpeting, the color of a putting green. Roy lay down on it for a rest. He started dreaming right away. He was at the top of the waterfall; Lee was down below on the rock, fishing with her hands the way she did. She leaped up suddenly with her catch, not a brown fish this time, but a brown human head. Then came a horrified little shout, and Roy woke up, covered in sweat.

Something was digging into his leg. Another inhaler? He took it out. The cell phone.

Almost before he knew it he was calling Lee.

"I'm at home," he said.

"Yes?"

Roy hadn't worked out anything to say. "I wondered whether you'd like to come over." Silence. "Or go out for coffee or something."

"Outside 1863?" Lee said.

"I'm sorry?"

"Seeing each other not in the context of 1863, is that what you mean?"

"I guess so," said Roy.

"I don't think that's a good idea right now," Lee said.

"Why not?"

"I think you know."

"I don't," Roy said. He followed that with something that shamed him as he said it, something he would probably have never uttered if that dream hadn't shaken him up: "I thought you loved me."

"I do."

Roy waited for her to elaborate. She said nothing. He waited. Was she waiting too? What for? He clicked off.

The phone buzzed right away. She was going to clear this up. But it was Gordo, not Lee.

"Hey, Roy, been trying to reach you. Did you know your home phone's out of order?"

"Must be some mistake."

"Roy? Are you all right?"

"As rain."

"You don't sound too good."

"Battery's getting low."

Pause. "Guess where I'm calling from, Roy?"

"Chickamauga."

"Why would I be there now? I'm at Sippens Isuzu."

"Trading in the Altima?"

"No, Roy, although I might, sooner rather than later—be getting a good deal now. I've started on the service desk."

"You're not making much sense, Gordo."

"The job I was telling you about—Earl's hired me."

"He's one lousy goddamned leader," Roy said.

"Are you kidding?" said Gordo. "Sippens Enterprises made an after-tax profit of three million dollars last year—Earl showed me the books."

"Who gives a shit?" said Roy. "I'm talking about in the field."

Pause. "You all right, Roy?"

"What did I say the last time you asked?"

"Right as rain, something of that nature."

"I'm saying it again."

Roy heard Gordo take a deep breath; maybe he was having air supply problems too. "The thing is, Roy, I have it on pretty good authority that if you gave Earl a call he might be amenable to doing something for you too."

"Lost me."

"Call Earl," Gordo said. "He'll give you a job on the service desk."

"And who would I be servicing?"

"Who would you be servicing? I don't get you, Roy.

The customers, the ones who bring their cars in for— Roy? What's that?"

"What's what?"

"Sounds like it's coming from your end."

"I don't hear anything."

"An alarm maybe."

Roy heard it now. He went upstairs. A high-pitched sound. Roy followed it into the living room, which was on fire.

"Roy? Roy? Everything okay?"

Or some other annoyance. Roy tossed the cell phone into the conflagration. Burn, he thought, burn until there's nothing left but ashes, and out of the rubble would rise . . . what? Roy couldn't find a good answer to that question. Then came a little vision from the future: Rhett's face as he listened to the story of how the house he'd grown up in burned down.

The next thing Roy knew he had the garden hose pulled in through the window and trained on the fire, nozzle turned to maximum pressure. That got the flames angry; they swelled up, assuming individual personalities. Roy got angry too. He strode in among them, attacking the most belligerent first, shooting them down with water until they all flickered and died away. Smoke boiled up, filled the room. Roy ripped out the smoke detectors to stop the hideous noise, closed all the doors and windows, went into the bathroom.

He gulped water from the tap, splashed some on his face, glimpsed some disgusting loser on the shiny silver faucet. Could it be? Roy straightened, looked in the mirror, took in the shocking sight: a disgrace to the uniform, the heritage, the memory.

Roy stripped off his smoky, filthy underwear, had a long hot shower, shaved, had another shower, longer and hotter, then dried himself, combed his hair, shook on some powder, checked the mirror again. Better, but a long way from right. He put on the uniform: much closer. The disgusting loser was gone; the face, so weird before, was hardening into something he could live with. Roy left the bathroom—already moving in that free and easy way he had

in his uniform—and smelled smoke in the hall. The intellec-
tual part of him knew it was all that remained of the fire, now
out. The soul part, to use Lee's expression, recognized the
smoke of his personal Atlanta, burned to the ground. He'd
smelled this fire ahead of time, up at the Mountain House.
Roy stuck his finger in the little hole in the jacket, worried at
the threads. What else had she said about the soul part? *Unconquered, unoccupied, waiting.*

Someone was knocking at the door. Roy went to answer,
preparing remarks about something left in the oven. He was
feeling better now, better with every heartbeat.

"Nothing to worry about," he began as he opened the door.
It was Curtis.

Curtis in the early morning, or possibly early evening. Roy
couldn't help staring, staring at that suit, that tie, that shirt,
all so perfect, like a princely costume from an exciting era
he couldn't quite place. Curtis was staring at him too. Roy
straightened his kepi.

"Maybe this isn't a good time," Curtis said.

"For what?"

"I've been trying to reach you, Roy."

"Phone problems," Roy said. "Very bad."

"I couldn't get you on email, either."

"Nope."

"Are you all right, Roy? Looks like you lost some weight."

"Fatty tissue," Roy said. He was going to add something
about fighting trim, but reconsidered.

"I can't help wondering about what you're wearing," Curtis said.

"Mutual," said Roy.

"Can I come in?" Curtis said. "I'd like to talk."

Roy was on the point of saying no, citing oven problems,
when he happened to notice all the trash on his lawn. It confused him. "Why not?" Roy said. "You're a good talker." He
motioned Curtis inside.

Curtis didn't move. His eyelid fluttered, the way it sometimes did. "What do you mean by that?"

"I always liked hearing you talk," Roy said. It was true. Curtis made sense, and when he got rolling he sounded like a preacher. Roy wondered whether he knew "Milky White Way."

"A bit messy," Roy said as Curtis followed him inside. "Lacking a woman's touch."

"Everywhere's like that nowadays," Curtis said, "women or not."

Roy understood perfectly. "That's a Yankee thing," he said.

"I'm sorry?"

"Nothing."

They sat down at the kitchen table. Curtis sniffed the air.

"Overcooking problem," Roy said.

"The reason I wanted to talk to you," Curtis said, "one of the reasons, is I got a report that you haven't taken advantage of the career counseling program."

"You know about something like that?"

"I make it my business to."

"That's a kindness," Roy said, adopting for the first time in his life one of his ma's pet phrases. "But there's no need to worry about me."

"You've landed on your feet, then?" Curtis said.

"All set."

"What as, Roy, if you don't mind my asking?"

Roy sniffed the air. He too smelled smoke. "Be right back," he said. He went down the hall, opened the living room doors, looked in. The smoke didn't seem quite so thick now, but little fires flickered here and there, harmless. Roy stamped them out and went back to the kitchen. Curtis was looking through the diary of Roy Singleton Hill.

Roy didn't like that. Roy plural.

"That's the war diary of my ancestor, Roy Singleton Hill," Roy said. "The writing is typical of the period."

"Probably better than mine," Curtis said.

"Yours?" Roy didn't get that at all: Curtis was known for the quality of his memos.

"My ancestors' writing," Curtis said. "They were . . . on the scene too."

"One of those facts of life," Roy said.

"Definitely."

They stared at each other across the table. Roy realized that if the conversation went a certain way they could come to blows. He knew himself now, knew the Roy inside: Curtis wouldn't stand a chance. Too bad because Roy liked him, always had. But why was Curtis pushing him like this?

"Are you a reenactor now, Roy?" Curtis's eyelid fluttered. "Like Gordo?"

"No." He didn't like the way Curtis said Gordo's name.

"There are slave reenactors."

"You mentioned that."

"Big contingent going up to Chattanooga for the Lookout Mountain event."

"And that," said Roy. "You thinking of joining them?"

"I hadn't seen the necessity."

"What necessity?" Roy said.

"Of making sure the blanks get filled in." Curtis turned to the end of the diary. "Did you notice how the last page is torn out?"

"Looks that way."

"Did you do it, Roy?"

"This is my inheritance," Roy said. "Why would I damage it?"

"Maybe you didn't like what was written there," Curtis said. "Have you read these final entries?"

"Scanned them," Roy said.

"Scanned them?"

"Looked them over."

Curtis nodded. "It's history, a diary like this."

"A part of it."

"Living history—isn't that what reenactors say they're up to?"

"Don't know about that."

"Do you know about Fort Pillow?"

"I've heard of it."

"What have you heard?"

"What's written in there. It was a Union fort on the Mississippi."

Curtis read: " 'Twelve April, 1864, Fort Pillow. Best day of this . . .' " Curtis struggled to make out a word. " '. . . conflict so far. Forrest asks for unconditional'—I think that's what it says—'surrender but they refuse.' " Curtis read that part in his normal, educated voice. But as he went on, he began sounding more and more like a dumb cracker. " 'And thems tauntin' us from over the walls. So's we charge down from the east and Thunder takes a ball in the neck. I got my finger on the blood vessel and keeps ridin' until Thunder goes down. We comin' in over the walls shootin' and hollerin'. Now theys thinkin' twicet bout not surrenderin' but we has our orders from Forrest and they was to—' " Curtis looked up. "Which is where the diary ends."

"Correct."

"What happened after that?"

"They took the fort. I don't know the details." Roy found himself gazing at Curtis's dark hand on the last remaining page of the diary. "Do you?"

"I'm not an expert," Curtis said. He closed the book. "And I didn't come to talk about this."

"You came about career counseling," Roy said. "And I told you—I'm all set."

"There's one other thing, some potential good news that I'm not really authorized to discuss."

"Then don't."

"Concerning new developments at Globax."

Roy shrugged.

"I understand your being bitter, Roy, but it won't help to—"

"I'm not bitter. Quite the opposite."

Curtis put the diary on the table. "The plan is to spin off a few of the less profitable divisions in the next few months, perhaps involving employee ownership, but you can't breathe a word."

Spin-offs, Globax—these were nonsense words to Roy, scarcely words at all. "No problem," he said. He just wanted Curtis to leave.

Curtis was looking at him, as though trying to convey some message. Whatever it was didn't arrive. He pushed the diary away.

"Thanks for stopping by," Roy said.

Curtis rose. A moment for handshaking came and went. Roy walked Curtis to the door, Curtis sniffing a couple of times on the way. "Stay in touch," Curtis said.

"Bye," said Roy. He noticed it was night again, or still.

Roy went into the living room, stamped out the fires. After that, knowing he must be tired, he lay down on his bed, that bed made for two. He thought about calling Lee again, now that he was in uniform, but did not. He wasn't going to beg, was all through with begging or anything close. Did Roy Singleton Hill beg? No. Roy Singleton Hill yelled that rebel yell, fired the Sharps carbine, used his finger to plug the bullet hole in his horse while he rode on and on, attacking all the time.

So he wouldn't beg, or anything close. That would be a disgrace to the uniform. This basic understanding settled him down a bit, but failed to bring sleep, no matter how tired he must have been. He tried putting on "Milky White Way," but the player in the bedroom wouldn't work. None of the players were working; in fact, there was no electricity in general. Roy packed up his Confederate kit—gun, diary, canteen—went into the tiny backyard, lay down under the stars.

Except there were no stars, and nothing that resembled the night sky in any way. The city made noises all around him, Yankee noises. The air above seethed with them. Plus those brown heads waited down below. Roy knew what Lee would say: *They occupied your dreams*.

Roy got up. He went out to the street, put his Confederate

things in the trunk of the Altima, drove away. A tiny flame burned in the rearview mirror. Later there were distant sirens. Roy didn't have to listen to them or any other bothersome sounds. "Milky White Way" still worked fine in the car.

TWENTY-FIVE

Roy came up through the high meadow, the Sharps carbine with *death* on the stock over one shoulder, word carved there by Roy Singleton Hill, and thus part of his inheritance, although the exact message was still unclear. Roy also wore the mule collar with everything he needed rolled up inside. From a long way off, but very clearly, his eyes working the way they worked when sighting through the V, he saw something new. Red background, blue bars, white stars: the flag now flew above the apple trees around the Mountain House.

Wasn't a flag a signal, a code? This flag spoke to him and he understood every syllable: *Unconquered, unoccupied, waiting.* The sight of it fluttering in the breeze puffed Roy up inside his uniform. He felt strong, stronger than on his strongest day and much stronger than normal men, his lungs powerful, bathing every cell in his body with oxygen, clean and pure. He breathed that unspoiled air, felt the lovely wildflowers brush against his legs. Tennessee wildflowers: no need to pick these flowers, to take possession of them—weren't they already his in every way that counted? He'd been born not far from here, had owned this land, this very corner of Tennessee, now lost; lost in a narrow sense because of Bragg's failure to pursue after Chickamauga, lost in a broader sense because of broader things he probably wasn't smart enough to understand. Lost, no doubt about that, but here he was anyway, still in uniform, still armed, still marching toward that flag, that flag still flying.

Three tents now stood on the flat ground between the

Mountain House and the slave quarters. Over to one side, at the edge of the plateau where the downward slope resumed, Lee and Jesse were digging a trench, Jesse with his shirt off, that silver Star of David glistening on his chest, Lee buttoned up to the neck. They both looked up, both gazed at Roy. Lee gave him a nod, maybe even more distant than it had to be, went back to digging. Roy heard her little grunt—*his* little grunt, he corrected himself. It would have to be that way in camp, must have been that way then if no one knew until it came time for the dead and wounded. Jesse jumped out of the trench, hurried over, shook hands.

"I want to thank you, Roy."

"What for?"

"Offering your place like this. We're digging the latrines down there, right where the original ones must have been, judging by how thick the vegetation grows. Hope that's all right."

Roy took a quick glance at his hand, slightly soiled from the handshake. "It's not really my place," he said.

"Yours and Sonny's," Jesse said.

"Sonny's here?"

"Gone down for a few things. He'll be back soon."

Roy glanced at the meadow. The wildflowers all bent suddenly in the same direction, blown by a gust that didn't reach the plateau. "What kind of things?" Roy said.

"Sonny didn't specify," Jesse said. "He's going to be a big help, your cousin."

"At what?"

"All the things we can do now, Roy. We're taking this to a whole new level and you're a big part of it."

"It's not my land," Roy said. "Not Sonny's neither." Did he say that: *Not Sonny's neither?* Couldn't have, wasn't the way he talked. Did he even know anyone who talked like that?

"As far as I'm concerned," Jesse was saying, "personally and as the ranking officer of this subgroup, it is your land."

Roy looked up at the mountaintop, rising behind the slave

quarters. He didn't argue, didn't say anything. He didn't know how it would come out, him or this other voice.

"We've got the men," Jesse said, rubbing his hands together in a way that reminded Roy of primitive people starting fires. "We've got the site. All we need now is a name."

"A name?"

"Can't call ourselves a subgroup," Jesse said. "They didn't talk like that."

"How about the Irregulars?" Roy said.

"They talked like that."

The name: Irregulars.

The site: Mountain House.

The soldiers (no civilians allowed in a hard-core camp): Jesse, lieutenant in command. Sergeant Dibrell, ranking noncommissioned officer. Lee, the corporal. And three privates, Roy, Sonny, and Gordo; Gordo with the chance to try it for the long weekend, Brenda helping with the new baby at her sister's. Gordo mentioning *weekend* was how Roy found out what day it was.

Latrines dug, supplies stored under a shelter they'd built in a corner of the Mountain House, the Irregulars sat outside in the shade of a tree now past blooming, all but Sonny, still absent with leave. They drank the creek water from their canteens and gnawed on Slim Jims, which substituted for beef jerky.

"These are disgusting," said Gordo. "I'll be farting all night."

"An authentic touch," said Lee.

Gordo, looking right at Lee, let loose a big fart. Lee's face reddened, but so slightly you had to be watching closely to see it. Roy was, and wanted to smack Gordo. He liked Gordo, they were friends, but Gordo wasn't going to make it. Funny thought: make it through what?

"Food was bad," Jesse was saying. "We don't complain. What I thought we'd try, after it cools down some, is an assault on a higher position. If you've done any reading, you know they avoided these if possible, both sides. But assaults on higher positions happened—Little Roundtop being an obvious example, Lookout Mountain another. The commanders usually sent the men up with arms at right shoulder shift, ball loaded but musket uncapped. Any idea why?" Jesse looked around. Roy realized he could listen to Jesse talk all day. He had a thought, maybe not nice: If we'd had more Jews we'd have won.

"You a teacher, Jesse?" Gordo said.

"I'm a lieutenant in the CSA," Jesse said. "And your membership here is probationary."

"Hell," said Gordo, "I'm a founding member of the Irregulars. Tell him, Roy."

Roy said nothing. Joking around was for winners, not losers. Losers had to fight back and that was all. Not only that but it was the duty of the not-so-smart ones to listen to what the smart ones had to say. The odd thing was, even though he was one of the not-so-smart ones, he had the answer to Jesse's question. Roy's answer was based on a mental image, the kind of mental image he usually called a memory, impossible in this case, because what memories could he have of assaulting higher positions? In this nonmemory, he was toiling up a slope with hundreds of other men. Must have been imagining it, of course, although Roy knew he didn't have much of an imagination, had never imagined any scene at all, and this one was so clear.

"Too slow," he said.

"What's that, Roy?" said Jesse.

They were all watching him. Roy didn't like it—he'd never been the type to raise his hand in class. "Can't stop to shoot," he said.

"Why not?" Jesse said.

The answer was obvious to Roy, down on that slope with hundreds of other men. What could be more obvious than bullets buzzing by like bees, and how hands shake and fingers fumble trying to reload. "No time," he said, hearing his voice change a little, slowing, broadening into that voice of someone else, not too different from his own. "They're firing down and you're firing up. Got to get there first."

Jesse nodded. "Pretty much it," he said. "Firing uphill you're more likely to hit your own men in the back than anything else. Better to keep moving quick, fight on even terms." He looked around again. "Any questions?"

Roy had the only one. "Why are we waiting till it cools down?"

They started up the mountain on a little ribbon of packed earth that led from the back of the slave quarters and soon disappeared in thickening undergrowth. Jesse went first, hacking with the blunt edges of his bayonet, Lee right behind him, then Gordo, Roy, and Dibrell last. The climb steepened almost right away, sometimes forcing them to their hands and knees, not easy with their weapons and gear. Roy heard Gordo's labored breathing ahead of him, Dibrell's, with a wheeze to it, behind. His own was silent. The space between Lee and Gordo grew until Lee was out of sight. Gordo leaned against a tree, pink blotches on his cheeks. Roy went past him, heard him say, "Are we having fun yet?"

And Dibrell reply: "I kind of wish I'd asked my PO about this."

"PO?" said Gordo.

"Parole officer," said Dibrell. "Need his permission to leave the state. Maybe he'd of said no."

Roy came to a rocky shelf, caught his first sight of the summit, maybe two hundred feet above. Jesse and Lee were sitting on the edge of the shelf, dangling their feet in space. Roy sat beside them. He could see all the way to Lookout Mountain on the horizon—the big bend in the Tennessee River a faint gleam—even make out the tall buildings of downtown Chattanooga on the horizon; the only thing wrong with the view.

"What happened at Lookout Mountain?" Roy said.

"The Battle Above the Clouds," said Jesse. "You've never seen pictures of the Yankees posing on that promontory up top?"

"Don't want to," Roy said.

When Dibrell and Gordo finally arrived, Jesse said, "From here, we split up. I'll take Dibrell and Gordo up this side, you two find a way round the back. Always want to look more numerous than you are, Roy—one of Forrest's favorite tricks."

Roy was on his feet. "Let's go."

But Gordo and Dibrell wanted to sit down too, dangle their legs, start complaining about the heat, the bugs, the briars. Jesse let them. Roy didn't understand that. It wasn't the way to beat Yankees.

Lee and Roy started a minute or two ahead of the others, Lee first, Roy following. They made their way around to the other side of the mountain, crouched into the slope, sometimes pulling themselves along on roots and branches.

"What did Dibrell do?" Roy said.

"No talking."

They climbed the rest of the way in silence. Just before the top, they went flat, wriggled on their bellies to the trunk of a fallen tree. Ahead lay the summit, a small clearing circled by forest. A small clearing, but not empty: in the middle stood an array of instruments surrounded by a barbed-wire-topped fence. A sign on the fence read: NO TRESPASSING. U.S. NATIONAL WEATHER SERVICE. VIOLATORS WILL BE PROSECUTED.

Lee frowned, looked more mannish frowning, but Roy's heart was beating faster and he wasn't really thinking about that, wasn't really thinking. He propped the carbine on the tree trunk, cocked the hammer, checked to see that he was capped. He was. The instrument at the top, just above a small satellite dish, was one of those spinning things with cups on the end, Roy couldn't think of the name. He raised his weapon, looked through the V, waited for one of those cups to come around, saw it with that hyperclarity, even the perforations inside, squeezed.

The crack of the gun, the flash, the kick, the smell of the smoke: all thrilling. And just as thrilling was what happened next. The spinning cup blew to bits. Sparks cracked at the end of the mechanical arm where it had been. Little sparks, but suddenly there was a huge one, like a thick rope of lightning, arcing all the way down to a box at the base of the array. Then came a flash and a boom, and a big ball of fire shot into the sky, blinding Roy.

When his vision returned he saw the instruments all blackened and twisted, flames licking here and there, and three men in gray on the other side of the clearing, openmouthed. Except for the occasional sound of metal popping, it was quiet, the birds and insects all silenced, nothing stirring in the woods.

"Did someone fire a live round over there?" Jesse called across the clearing.

"Is that wrong?" said Roy.

He started to get up, and as he did felt Lee's hand on his crotch, giving him a squeeze, furtive, gentle, hidden from sight by the tree trunk. He glanced at her: face scratched by brambles, blackened by the explosion, something powerful in her eyes, the eyes of a woman beyond a doubt—how did the others miss that?—this powerful something perhaps not love, maybe closer to adoration.

"What are we going to do?" Dibrell said.

"About what?" said Gordo, a big smile spreading across his face. Roy knew why: he'd gotten his big bang at last.

"For fuck sake," said Dibrell. "Open your eyes."

"It was a lightning strike," Jesse said. "We deny everything."

"Why would anyone find out in the first place?" Lee said. "We're way up here."

That made Roy smile too.

Jesse began walking back and forth across the clearing, head down.

"What are you doing?" Gordo said.

"Can't deny anything if they find a bullet."

Jesse was one of the smart ones that the nonsmart ones should listen to, no doubt about that. At the same time, Roy didn't care at all about finding the bullet. You fired bullets in battle, didn't hunt around for them after. He helped search for it anyway out of duty—they all did except Lee, who lay on the log, eyes closed—and found nothing.

"Probably melted," Gordo said. "No one else will find it either."

"What about DNA?" Dibrell said. "We must of left DNA all over the place. That's how they got me the last time."

"For what?" said Gordo.

Dibrell shook his head. "Just a crazy chain of events."

"Never heard of that crime," said Gordo, still with that grin on his face.

Dibrell moved in front of him. "What's that sposta mean?"

Jesse stepped between them. "Soldiers," he said. "Form the squad."

Nobody moved. Roy saw they weren't going to do it. They were hot, tired, angry, confused; even Gordo, no longer smiling. Plus they weren't soldiers, a strange observation for Roy to have, but he knew it was true. Dibrell had the makings of a soldier but was too fucked-up inside. Gordo would never be a soldier: he was a mama's boy and Brenda was mama. Roy even thought he understood the anal sex thing, all part of Gordo's childishness.

Roy said: "Yes, sir," and took his place near Jesse, stood motionless with his gun across his chest. He didn't say anything, but that voice inside him, the one with the broad accent and no self-doubt, was talking: *Form the goddamn squad.*

They formed the squad.

Down below the land went hazy blue and slowly darkened, but the sun still shone on the Mountain House. The Irregulars sat outside their tents, eating Slim Jims and hardtack. Gordo sent a flask around, and so did Dibrell, but whatever they had wasn't Old Grand-Dad. Roy took a sip of each and no more.

He didn't want it. Even food wasn't a necessity. The water from the creek was all he needed. Hazy darkening blue rose up the mountain, but without any hurry. Watching evening come and breathing were enough for Roy. Not that he was tired, although he could see the others were. He himself felt as strong as he had in the morning, maybe stronger. Time stretched, sagged, formed the shape of a bowl, accommodated itself to him. A short life span didn't mean life was short; a long life span didn't mean it was long. Roy liked 1863. He took wonderful deep breaths of its air.

The hazy blue had crept halfway up the meadow when Roy heard something. He rose, gazed down from the edge of the plateau.

"What is it, Roy?" Lee said.

"That sound."

"I don't hear anything."

"Listen."

None of them heard it.

"The cops?" Dibrell said. Gordo tucked his flask in his back pocket, like that would make a difference.

"Can't you hear it?" Roy said.

"What? Hear what?" Except for Lee they were all looking at him funny, like he was losing it, or maybe already had. Lee wasn't looking at him at all; she was getting her gun ready.

Was he losing it? "That," he said. "Drumming."

"Drumming?"

But Lee said: "Yes."

Rat-a-tat-tat, rat-a-tat-tat, soft and steady, from somewhere down in the gloom. The sound grew louder, sharper. Lee stepped behind a tree, musket trained down on the meadow. Rat-a-tat-tat, rat-a-tat-tat, and out of the deep blue haze and into the soft angled light of the setting sun marched Sonny Junior in his uniform, a long gun over his shoulder. A drummer boy, also in gray, marched beside him. Rat-a-tat-tat, rat-a-tat-tat: crisp and steady. The drummer boy's slouch hat was a little too big, drooped some over his forehead, which was maybe why Roy didn't recognize him until he and Sonny had almost reached the top of the meadow. Should have been the other way around, that too-big hat, should have been a clue reminding him of the too-big helmet on number fifty-six.

TWENTY-SIX

"**D**id I do wrong?" said Sonny Junior.

The fire glowed bright in his eyes, more dully on the buckles and bayonets of the Irregulars. They sat around the fire under a sky more starry than black, Roy on one side of Rhett, Sonny on the other. The question—like all the details that had come tumbling out of Rhett's mouth, and Sonny's—didn't really penetrate. All that penetrated was that first, and only, embrace with Rhett, who was actually sitting a little closer to Sonny right now.

And the details? That part reminded Roy of his last year of high school Spanish, the year when English wasn't spoken in class and he'd had to make guesses, island-hopping over fuzzy seas. Roy made his guesses: guessing that Rhett hated the new husband, his school, the tutors for English and math after school; hated Bermuda, or the cruise to Bermuda, where hated ties were worn at dinner, even by eleven-year-olds; hated Park Slope, New York, the kids and the way they talked; hated his mother. Then came a fuzzy patch with a call to Roy, where Sonny's number had been left on the machine; a call to Sonny's; and after that: action.

The action Sonny took: a bus ticket? a plane ticket? Sonny went and got him? The stories they told didn't quite match. And on the crucial issue of whether Marcia had been told anything, and if so, what, Roy found out that Rhett had left a note, or Sonny had talked to her, or some other not very credible connection had been made. Roy didn't care: the meaning of crucial was changing. Even under the old meaning, what harm could there be? It was only for the weekend, or a little longer.

"You did right," Roy said.

Sonny Junior grinned, patted Rhett on the back. Rhett, staring into the fire, didn't seem to notice.

"More to eat?" Lee said.

Rhett nodded.

"Hardtack or Slim Jim?"

"Slim Jim."

Lee passed him one. They all watched him eat it, even Gordo and Dibrell, both half-drunk. The boy, in his uniform, leaning back on his drum, his skin smooth and golden in the firelight: they couldn't take their eyes off him.

"He's a natural," Sonny Junior said. "Learned practically all the drum calls on the way up."

"You know the drum calls, Sonny?" Roy said.

"Guy in the store showed me—basic stuff."

"What do I owe you for the gear?"

"Don't insult me, cuz."

A flask went around again. Gordo, Dibrell, and Sonny drank; the others did not.

"I mean it," Roy said.

"Me too," said Sonny, taking a second hit, then another.

"Hey, new guy," said Dibrell. "Save some of that for your superiors."

Sonny gazed at Dibrell on the other side of the fire. He took one more swallow, longer than the others. "Superiors?" he said. "Way I count, you and me got the same number of stripes on our arm." He flipped the flask through the flames to Dibrell, who made no attempt to catch it.

"You going to straighten him out, Lieutenant?" Dibrell said.

"It's not a question of straightening out," Jesse said. "There's no way Sonny could know that changes in rank are voted on by the full regiment, and all recruits enter as privates, barring the odd exception."

"I'm a private?" said Sonny Junior.

"Like Roy and Gordo," Jesse said.

"And the little guy here?"

"Lee's a corporal."

"And I'm a private?"

"For the time being."

"That sucks."

"War means sacrifice," Jesse said. His jacket was unbuttoned and the Star of David had worked free and now hung on the outside, picking up the fire's glow. It caught Sonny's eye. Roy saw he was about to say something, but at that moment Rhett slumped sideways, in Roy's direction, fast asleep. Roy caught him, picked him up, carried him into the Mountain House.

An owl hooted, somewhere above. Roy laid Rhett on his blanket, covered him up with an extra blanket someone had brought, watched him sleep for a while. The owl hooted again, a long oo-oo-ooo that mixed in with the rat-a-tat-tat drumming that was going on in Roy's mind, making a kind of song. Roy took off his hat, belt, brogans, lay down beside his son. The sound of voices came from the fire, but Roy couldn't make out the words. After a while he couldn't hear the sounds either. Rhett sighed in his sleep.

"Everything's all right," Roy said.

Rhett turned over. His hand brushed Roy's shoulder, went still, gave it one little press, as though testing something. He was quiet after that.

Lying on his back, Roy saw the Milky Way. Something slid along it, blotting out stars in bird-shaped patterns that kept changing, wings going up and down. The song in his mind took up the beat. The words and melody leaked in from "Milky White Way." Everything came together. The song was about a journey through time to put things right. That explained why it was so happy. Made perfect sense. He was happy too.

Roy heard feet running in the night. He may have been no more than a private, but he knew at once what was happening:

Yankees come to take his son away. Hadn't they already made off with his wife? He felt Rhett still beside him as he opened his eyes. A dark form loomed over him. They weren't getting Rhett. Roy kicked out, heard a grunt of pain, rolled, came up with the carbine in his hands.

A man lay on the ground. "Don' shoot," he said. An unarmed man, not a Yankee, not in uniform at all, but Ezekiel, in his Bob Marley T-shirt and jeans.

Roy lowered the gun, felt the murderous urge within him subside, but slowly, as though there'd been a contest of wills inside his own head.

"I keep on havin' to tell you not to shoot me," Ezekiel said, "like one of them dreams happens over and over."

"No one's going to shoot anybody," Roy said, his voice low. "What are you doing here?"

"You hurt my knee."

"What do you expect, breaking into someone's house in the middle of the night?"

"You calling this a house? You calling this breaking in when there's hardly no walls?"

"Yes."

"An' how's it your house? You said you was from Atlanta, hung with Ted Turner."

Roy didn't reply.

Ezekiel got up with another little grunt of pain.

"Quiet," Roy said.

"Your roots is up here, ain't they? What I thought from the very start."

Roy nodded: he was home, no denying that.

"You and me needs to talk," Ezekiel said.

"About what?"

"Oral traditions," Ezekiel said.

"Some other time."

"Has to be now," Ezekiel said. "Forces is on the move."

Rhett made a high-pitched little sound in his sleep, almost a whimper.

"What forces?" Roy said, lowering his voice still more.

Ezekiel glanced down at Rhett, spoke softly too. "In the mountain. Who's more in touch with the forces in the mountain than me, smokin' it every day in my own lungs, tastin' it on my own tongue?"

"I don't understand."

"About me tastin' the mountain?"

"I get that part."

"You do?"

"I don't understand what you want to talk about."

"Your name and my name," said Ezekiel. "Roy and Zeke. Must be the starting place."

"Zeke?"

"To all my friends. An' I got lots of friends, Roy, what with my hobby and such."

Ezekiel took Roy by the arm, led him out the back of the Mountain House. Roy didn't want to leave Rhett, and Ezekiel's grip was light, easily resistible, but Roy didn't resist. They stepped between the sagging slats of the slave quarters, went inside.

"Make yourself at home," Ezekiel said, sitting on the floor. Roy sat too. Ezekiel lit a candle, twisted it into the hard-packed earth. The candle illuminated a box lying next to it, a casket, leather-bound and shaped like Roy's inherited chest, but tiny, almost pocket-size.

"Roy Hill and Zeke Hill," said Zeke, "if you see the direction ahead."

"What's in the box?" Roy said.

"Family ashes, brother," Ezekiel said.

"Are you stoned?"

"Needless to ask. Care to partake of a small sample, on the house?"

"No."

"I'll join you in that," said Ezekiel. "Partakin' of nothin'." He glanced down at the casket. "Roy and Zeke. Know where we's sittin', this very moment in time?"

"The old slave quarters."

Ezekiel nodded. "Slave quarter to the Mountain House,

where the ol' massah—you know that word, massah?—like to come on up Sundays, spend some social time, accordin' to the oral traditions. With me so far, or you gonna object to oral traditions bein' history?"

"I'm not," Roy said.

"Then how about if I told you these family ashes was the earthly remains of my great-great-grandfather Roy Singleton Hill?"

"I'd say you're full of shit."

Ezekiel didn't seem to hear that. "Roy Singleton Hill, Confederate hero, best of the good ol' boys," he said. "His earthly remains passed on down in my family—my side of the family—from one generation to the next."

"Maybe you passed on the box," Roy said. "But what makes you think his ashes are inside?"

"Oral traditions," Ezekiel said. "What you already agreed was history. Got to pay more attention, Roy. Forces is on the move."

"I'm not saying there's no ashes," Roy said. "Just that they're not his."

Ezekiel shook his head. "You people in denial," he said.

"What people is that?"

"The kind of people that denies." Ezekiel extended his bare arm toward Roy, inches above the candle flame. "You see this?"

"The heart with the arrow?"

"Not the tattoo, man. I'm talkin' about the color of my skin."

"What about it?"

"How would you—what's the word we needin' here? describe—describe my skin?"

"Describe it?" said Roy. "Human skin."

Ezekiel's eyes met his. "You a good man," he said. "You jus' be careful now not to let the goodness get in the way of seein' right."

"You're losing me."

"Last thing I want," said Ezekiel. "What I'm tryin' to get across—does this look to you in your eyes like black skin?"

"Well," said Roy, "you're black."

"I'm black, but this ain't the color black. Ever go to kindergarten, Roy? Ever be mixin' up the paints? How would you come to a color like this, startin' with pure Dahomey black?"

Roy thought of Mrs. Hardaway tracing his schoolboy drawing with her coffee-bean-colored finger, polished red at the end, didn't answer.

Ezekiel shook his head. "You in bad denial, man. Mix in the white—any kindergarten kid tell you that."

"I'm not denying it," Roy said. "I'm saying his ashes aren't in there."

"That's the arrogance part goes hand in hand with the denial."

"If I showed you where he was buried," Roy said, "would that be arrogant too?"

A quiet night in the cemetery, the mountain rising dark on one side, the silhouette of the cross over the chapel on the other. Ezekiel drove his pickup along the cart path the hearses used, past all the gravestones, growing smaller and more worn, to the woods at the foot of the mountain.

"Stop," Roy said.

Ezekiel stopped. His headlights shone on the stone:

Roy Singleton Hill
1831–1865
Hero

Ezekiel went still.

"You've never seen this?" Roy said.

"How would I ever be doin' that? We in the white grave-yard, man."

They got out of the pickup, walked to the stone. Ezekiel knelt, ran his fingertips over the sunken lettering.

"I see a stone," he said. "I read the writing. Don' mean he's down there."

"Now who's in denial?" Roy said.

"Not me, man. The history of conspiracy is on our side."

Roy missed that one. "Why would you want him anyway?" he said.

"Want him?"

"If he slept with women who had no choice?"

"Funny way of sayin' rape," Ezekiel said. "I don' want him, Roy. It's just the fact—him and the slave women, all my ancestors." Ezekiel went to the pickup, came back with a long-handled spade.

"Why would I let you do this?" Roy said.

Ezekiel paused, gazed at Roy, the two of them standing over the gravestone. "You a good man," Ezekiel said. He pushed on the stone, grunted, toppled it over. The stone fell with a thump and the earth trembled, very slightly. Roy felt it in the soles of his feet.

Ezekiel drove the spade into the middle of the bare blackened rectangle where the stone had stood. It sank in easily, came up easily with a clump of earth that Zeke flung to the side. He dug for a while, fast in the beginning, then slower, the digging and flinging growing more labored, sweat dripping off his chin. Ezekiel got down only two or three feet, hard to tell because the sides kept caving in on him, before he leaned on the spade and said: "Satisfied?"

"Satisfied?" said Roy, looking down at him. Dust from the grave boiled in the headlight beams. An image took shape in Roy's mind, a crazy one, of Ezekiel lying in the hole he'd just dug.

"That he ain't here," said Ezekiel.

"Keep digging," Roy said.

Ezekiel shook his head. "Gotta accept things the way they is, Roy."

Roy stepped down into the hole, gripped the spade. Ezekiel didn't let go right away. In that moment, Roy and Ezekiel holding on to the long wooden handle, the headlights shining on their two hands, yellowing them both—more than yellowing, really, almost gilding—Roy thought he noticed an odd similarity in their size and shape, Zeke's hand and his. Zeke was staring at their hands too; he let go, climbed out of the hole.

Roy was prepared to dig all night, but he struck something on the very first plunge of the spade, something that gave with a soft splintering sound. Roy reached down in the darkness, felt through rotting wood that came apart like thick wet paper, touched a solid form, round and hard. He got a grip on it, sticking his fingers into two convenient holes like on a bowling ball, raised a human skull into the swirling light.

Ezekiel took a quick step back, almost fell. "What kind of trick you tryin' to pull?" he said.

His gaze wasn't on Roy when he asked that; it was on the skull. So was Roy's. He took his fingers out of the eye sockets—that didn't seem right—laid the skull on the piled earth beside the grave. Did any sign of a man's character cling to his remains? Would even a saint's skull seem anything less than threatening? Probably not; so the menace rising off this one—Roy could feel it—didn't mean anything.

"Somebody else, maybe?" Ezekiel said.

"Like who?" Roy said.

Ezekiel thought that over. "Then what's in my box, handed down from one generation to the next?"

"Your real great-great-grandfather," Roy said.

Ezekiel was silent for a moment or two. "Truth is," he said, "I never looked with my own eyes."

"What are you saying?"

"I never opened the box."

"Then how do you know there are ashes inside?"

"Oral traditions," Ezekiel said.

"Why not open it now?"

"No key," Ezekiel said. "Wouldn't be right to break in with violence, would it?"

Roy didn't say anything.

"You disagree about the violence part?" Ezekiel said.

But it wasn't that. Roy walked back to Ezekiel's truck. The little casket lay on the center console, Roy's gun on the shelf behind the seats. He opened the filigreed patch box in the butt of the gun, took out the brass key. Much too big to fit in the keyhole of Ezekiel's little casket, nothing to worry about on that score.

But the key did fit, fit perfectly, slid in like the box got opened every day. Roy glanced over at Ezekiel, still by the open grave, maybe working up the nerve to actually pick up the skull. Roy turned the key, felt the lock give, snapped open the lid.

No ashes, nothing in the box but a single brittle sheet of paper, the left edge torn and jagged. Roy recognized the writing on the page, stuffed it in his pocket, closed the box.

"What you got there?" said Ezekiel, suddenly beside the truck.

"Your box." Roy handed it to Ezekiel.

"Any harm in breaking in with violence now?" Ezekiel said. "Yes or no?"

"No."

Ezekiel put the box on the hood of the truck, struck the lid with the edge of his hand. It split apart, popped open. There was nothing inside.

Ezekiel stared into the box for a long time. He even picked it up, turned it upside down, shook it. Nothing fell out.

"I don't get this kind of joke," Ezekiel said. His eyes were damp, maybe on account of all the dust they'd raised.

They reburied the remains of Roy Singleton Hill and stood the gravestone back in its place, left everything just as they'd found it.

Roy Singleton Hill
1831–1865
Hero

TWENTY-SEVEN

Ezekiel knew an old logging trail up the back side of the mountain that would leave Roy with a shorter climb to the Mountain House. The old logging trail—just wide enough for the pickup, the forest scratching away at the paintwork like fingernails all the last part—ended in a small clearing. Ezekiel's headlights swept past three cars already parked there, two with New Jersey plates, one from Connecticut.

"Tourists," said Ezekiel, "come to hike up an' down the beautiful state of Tennessee, keepin' the economy strong."

He offered Roy his hand; an arm-wrestling-style shake, exactly like Sonny Junior's. That was one thing. Then their hands, Ezekiel's and Roy's, so similar—that was another. "Still a lot of mystery in my mind," Ezekiel said, "but that could be sidewash from my hobby. You been straight up with me, Roy. Many thanks. You always got a friend on this here mountain."

Roy felt Ezekiel's headlights on his back as he walked across the clearing, up into the woods, trees closing around him. Ahead, his shadow—head, body, arms, legs, gun—got longer and longer, and finally glided off into darkness, Roy following. In darkness, in the woods at night and invisible: but Roy felt Ezekiel's headlights on his back for a long, long time.

Roy climbed the back side of the mountain, as steep or steeper than the front, the trees as thick or thicker, but he knew the way, knew it without having to think or even pay much attention. He knew when he'd be having to go down on all fours to keep his feet from losing their grip, knew when he'd be coming to an open spot and seeing the stars, knew when the slope would level out and bring him into Ezekiel's marijuana patch. He even knew that his owl was flying overhead, long before he heard the beating of its heavy wings, like carpet thumping, high above. It was only for the weekend, or a little longer. Everything was going to be all right. Apple trees grew on the mountain, fat brown fish swam in the creek, deer roamed the forest; there was hardtack, Slim Jims, the water itself, heavenly: a person— especially a strong person, and now he was that, stronger than he'd ever been, even stronger than he'd have been if everything in his life had been golden all the way—could live here forever.

The owl hooted. "Don't have to do that," Roy said. "I know you're there." It hooted again, louder, sounding a little displeased, even angry, maybe at not being included in Roy's mental list of the mountain's bounty. But of course the owl, descendant of the owls of 1863, was included. Roy looked up, tried to find its outline against the night sky. But even with his new hyperclear vision, he couldn't, and besides, the night sky was gone all of a sudden and with it the stars and the Milky Way. Through the leaves above, still black, Roy saw that the sky was no color at all, just a faint canopy of untinted light, but growing more intense, as though someone was slowly turning up a dial. He listened for the owl, its beating wings, its call, and heard nothing.

Roy made his way through Ezekiel's marijuana patch, took his first steps down the slope that led to the back of the plateau. "Milky White Way" started up in his head. He was happy, so happy, except for one nagging thing. What was it? The brittle page in his pocket, last page of the diary of Roy Singleton Hill. Enough light for reading now, no excuse not to; or he could just rip it up and scatter the shreds unread, without an excuse, to silence that nagging. Roy paused on the wooded hill over the plateau, his hand in his pocket, finger-tips rubbing the old paper, feeling for some premonition. At that moment, while he was trying to come to a decision, something lying by the side of the trail, partially hidden by a tree root, caught his eye.

Roy went over, picked it up: a kepi, one of the common styles of Civil War soldier hats, the same style he wore, but with the silver horn on top denoting infantry. Otherwise the same in every way, except this one was blue.

Roy tried to get things straight in his mind: was there a battle here, up on his mountain? Did the Yankees pass this way on the retreat from Chickamauga to Chattanooga? Or had Sherman later come marching through from the other direction? Did it have anything to do with the copper pits, not far away, source of the percussion caps for practically the whole South? Were the copper pits in danger? He would do his duty.

Roy put the inside of the hat to his face. He smelled sweat; sweat and the strawberry aroma of Aussie Mega Shampoo, familiar because he used it himself. He got confused.

Roy walked down the path, the blue kepi in his hand, rounded a bend and came to an opening in the trees. A beautiful sight unfolded in the east, must have been east because the horizon was a band of fire, the dome of the sky turning mother-of-pearl as he watched. Down below lay the beautiful state of Tennessee, just as Ezekiel had said, soft as Eden. A pink mist was rising from the upper meadow, flowing over onto the plateau, several hundred feet below him. The mist blurred the ruination of the Mountain House, made it rosy, made everything right. Roy gazed down on the sleeping camp, the tents still and pink-edged, the flag drooped comfortably on its pole, and came close to tears. This was earthly glory, the end of a journey through time to make things right. *Stop here.* Time stopped, stopped at this red-banded sunrise on a day in the spring of 1863. Roy knew it for a fact. He felt no need to breathe. Poised on the trail above the plateau, his gun at his side, Roy felt inner peace at last. There was no need for the clock to tick one more second.

The moment Roy had that thought, time started up again. First came movement down in the slave quarters, hard for Roy to make out because the treetops blocked his view. But human movement, he was sure of that, and blue: he was sure of the blue part too. Roy flung the blue kepi aside and set off down the slope, each step quicker and more careless than the one before, as he thought, so late and stupid: License plates, kepi, blue. The woods blocked his view at every turn.

But sounds got through, muffled, urgent, rising off the plateau. Running, grunting, crashing: now Roy was running too, and might have been making all the sounds himself. He was wondering about that, wondering how much was imagining, how much of what he thought of as his life he had imagined, back and back to two little boys in that cantilevered barn, when he slipped on a tree root. Roy fell hard on his back, slid, tumbled down a steep rise, cracked his head, rolled to a stop under a cloud of rising dust. As it cleared slowly in the still air, he found himself on a ledge fifty or sixty feet above the plateau. The peaceful scene below was gone, replaced by something close to its opposite, hard for a civilian to take in.

But Roy wasn't a civilian, and it all came together in his mind in a crisp and military way: an attack by a superior force on a sleeping camp. Roy counted ten figures in blue—didn't have to count, the number coming automatically—some active in the Mountain House, the rest running crouched toward the tents. Then metal flashed in the hands of some of them, and the tents all started collapsing, forms struggling under the canvas. The Yankees laughed, the sound rising almost undetectable up to Roy, but their laughing posture very clear. He hated that laughing. It stopped abruptly; the postures all stiffened. Roy followed the Yankees' gaze to a lone gray-clad figure popping free from a pile of canvas, springing to his feet, long hair wild and whipping in the first rays of the sun: Sonny Junior.

Some of the Yankees raised their hands as though in explanation, which Roy didn't get at all, this being war. Sonny Junior didn't wait to hear. The next moment, he had something in his hand too, not metal, not a knife or bayonet, but a long wooden pole—a tent pole. He swung it, faster than Roy would have thought possible, and a Yankee went down. Then another, on the backhand side, still falling when Sonny lowered the pole, jabbed it into someone's gut—cry of pain rising clear up to Roy, like it came from right beside him— and wheeled to get at someone else. That wheeling was why Sonny didn't see a big man—bearded, sergeant's stripes, Vandam—coming from behind. Vandam raised his musket like a club, cracked it down on Sonny's head, just as he'd done to Roy. But Sonny didn't go down. He staggered a little, recovered, started to turn, the tent pole still in his grip. Vandam hit him again, same place.

That dropped Sonny, but only to his knees. Somehow he still had the pole, somehow was thrusting it at Vandam. Vandam stepped back—Roy caught the flash of his teeth in the middle of all that beard—stepped back, but right into the path of another reb diving at his legs like—like a linebacker. Vandam fell. The second reb was on him right away. Vandam threw him off easily—the second reb was very small—and was starting to rise when Sonny Junior, still on his knees, caught him a good one under the ribs. Vandam fell again. Sonny rose, rose slowly, blood all over, but rose and stood over Vandam, raising the pole like a pile driver. A Yankee captain—Peterschmidt, with the muttonchop whiskers—ran up from behind, brought the butt of his pistol down on Sonny's head, and a second time, real quick, as Sonny subsided. Roy was so sure that Peterschmidt wouldn't do something like that that he missed what came next.

Something to do with another small reb, just a little bigger than the first. A blue circle was closing around them, blocking them from Roy's view. Roy scrambled up, searched frantically for his carbine, found it wedged against a tree trunk a few yards higher up. He hurried back down the outcrop, opening the breech, checking to see if he was loaded—yes—closing up, raising the gun, looking through that V at the scene down below.

Down below and far away. Roy had no idea of the gun's range. In the V, he saw the blue circle part and Peterschmidt advance on the littlest reb, now lying on the ground, curled into a ball. The second reb got in between them, tried to push Peterschmidt away. Another Yankee knocked him—her, Roy knew that—to the ground.

Now. If it could be done, Roy could do it. He was deadly, that was certain. He got Peterschmidt's head in the center of the V, saw him clear, could even make out the cigar in his mouth, right down to the glowing end. The cigar enraged Roy. He drew a bead on Peterschmidt's near-side eye, started to squeeze.

"Now do you see why we keep a force in reserve?" said someone behind him.

Roy whirled. Two Yankees stood above him on the slope, a lieutenant with a pistol and a private with a musket, both pointed at him.

"Yes, sir," said the private. "Very wise."

"Throw down your gun," said the lieutenant. "We're taking you prisoner."

Roy had had enough.

"Fixin' to die?" he said.

"That's very good," said the lieutenant.

Roy didn't need to hear that: he knew it was good—that was how they talked, his father, his grandfather, his great-grandfather, his great-great-grandfather; and him.

"In terms of authenticity?" said the private.

"Did you say something, soldier?" said the lieutenant.

"Sir. In terms of authenticity, sir, what he said being very good."

"More like it," said the lieutenant. "Yes, this reb is particularly authentic. So he must know that the right response here is to throw down that gun. Meaning just lay it down gently—I know what these things cost."

"Out of my way," Roy said.

"What you forget," said the lieutenant, "is that you've got one shot to our two. That's what makes the decision easy, weapons dictating tactics."

"Even easy enough for a dumb reb," said the private, adding, "sir."

A cry rose up from the plateau, very faint, but Roy knew whose it was. "Last chance," he said.

"Is this a hearing problem?" the lieutenant said. "Or ADD?"

Roy shot him between the eyes.

No doubt about it: Roy was deadly and how could he miss from that range? The lieutenant said, "Ow," as the paper wad smacked his forehead with a noise like a book sharply closed.

Paper wad? Ow? What was this? It took Roy a moment or two to realize he'd fired a blank. But how? He knew he'd had a live round in that chamber. Roy flipped open his cartridge pouch: blanks, all blanks, where live rounds had been before. He'd been betrayed. The war was lost.

"Jesus Christ," the lieutenant was saying. He felt his forehead—red welt already rising—said, "Ow," again.

"Could of taken out his eye," said the private. "Don't you know the rules?"

"And I'm a photography teacher, you asshole," said the lieutenant, turning on Roy, "which your lawyer won't be happy about, not one damn bit."

These Yankees were all red-faced and furious, but about what Roy wasn't sure. It didn't matter: whack, whack, and they were both on the ground, Roy racing down the slope to the plateau.

And yes, the rebel yell, so huge it could have been the voice of the mountain itself.

TWENTY-EIGHT

Roy had a gun but no bullets, no bayonet neither—
neither, there was his ancestor thinking now, right with him in
his head. No bayonet because his weapon, ancestral instructions carved on the stock, was a carbine; he knew that now,
wouldn't let the cause down through ignorance again. No
shooting or stabbing possible, but Roy did have his strong
body, even stronger with these fresh new springs of ferocity
rising up within him, and he had the knowledge, so late ar-
riving, of what he was born, if not bred, to be: a fighting man.

He came down off the slope, tore down it really, his speed
almost sickening although strangely silent, all nature covering for him, and into the apple trees in back of the plateau,
trees planted by his ancestor for the comfort of his descending line, their nourishment, even their concealment, if necessary. The clear dawn light made the tiny new apples gleam
like hard painted decorations, bright red. The color encour-
aged him.

Roy ran through the slave quarters, into the Mountain
House. Through the hole in the wall where the front door had
stood, Roy caught sight of the Yankees beyond the collapsed
tents, standing over the Confederates, Confederates on their
knees. On their knees!

No one saw Roy. That meant he had not only his raw
strength, but the element of surprise as well, an element he
hadn't considered much in his life, knew only from the receiving end. This was going to be much better. He burst out of
the Mountain House, his gun gripped by the barrel, *death* on

its stock, so ready, so able, never more so, felt a sudden sharp pain across one shin, and went spinning through the air. Then came a tumbling glimpse of two Yankees crouched behind him, holding a thin line across the doorway, and the ground rose fast to meet him, like the beginning of some explosion from deep down, one of Ezekiel's mountain forces on the move. Roy tried to get his hands out front, protect his head, but couldn't, what with trying to protect the gun too. Then he was seeing two moons again. Before he could work them back down to one, or none since it was daylight, blue bodies were swarming over him.

Roy made them pay, one with his elbow, another with his fist, and then he was on his feet, swinging his weapon so hard it whistled in the air like a whip. The Yankees all backed off, eyes widening—Vandam too, his nose swollen and discolored from Chickamauga—as Roy stood on the threshold of the Mountain House.

"Get off my land," he said. His voice echoed off the mountain. At least, he thought it did, and was listening so intently to the echo, like another one of those forces on the loose, the mountain and he speaking as one, that he almost missed softer sounds behind him. He started to turn, heard a bad noise inside his skull.

They sat outside the Mountain House, blue and gray together, except blue sat in the shade of the apple trees and gray in the sun; a hot white sun, the first real hot one of the year, directly overhead. Roy was very thirsty, conscious at first only of that and the sun sucking him dry, his body the water supply for a demanding master; then, after a while, conscious of blue and gray together, outside the Mountain House. He was wondering whether the war was over when he noticed that everyone in gray was tied up, arms behind the back, him included.

Roy looked around. Things came into focus: the stubborn little tuft of hair, already growing back on Rhett's head; a drying-up trickle of blood running from one of Sonny's ears down his neck; Lee's jacket, the top two or three buttons dangerously open; a variety of expressions on the faces of the Irregulars, all of which Roy had seen before at halftime in football locker rooms whenever they were getting their asses whipped. He knew that was where he had seen these looks, but that world was distant, as though he'd come across it only in books. This was the real thing, when you started to realize you might lose not a game, but everything, when the enemy wasn't the Gators or the Yellowjackets, but Sherman and Grant. When that happened, some realized and quit, like Dibrell; some got bewildered, like Gordo; some kept calculating odds and strategies, like Jesse; some couldn't be read, like Lee; some didn't bother to realize and wouldn't quit, like Sonny Junior; some did realize and wouldn't quit, like himself.

Captain Peterschmidt came forward, crossing the line between shadow and sun. His muttonchops had a rusty tinge in the light. "Chickamauga was a fluke," he said, hand on his sword. "Guess you rebs know that by now." Was he talking about Lee's successful tent attack and Roy's subsequent rescue, or Longstreet's breakthrough at the Brotherton cabin? Made no difference to Roy: either way, this Yankee was saying they couldn't fight, and that was a damned lie. Roy tested the rope binding his wrists, a thick, bristly rope, the knots tight, and got nowhere.

"Under the rules of warfare, you are all prisoners of the United States," Peterschmidt said. "Don't be alarmed. There are no Andersonvilles where we come from."

"And no Fort Pillows either," said a Yankee corporal.

"Maybe there should be," said the Yankee lieutenant Roy had tangled with up the slope, his eyes, the one that was open, anyway, on Roy. The private beside him, with a bloody cloth around his head, started to nod, winced, and stopped.

"And since transportation of prisoners would be difficult in this case," Peterschmidt said, "it's our intention to take only one, as insurance for your future good conduct."

Jesse got to his feet, not easily, his hands behind his back.

"Who said anything about standing up?" said Vandam, coming up beside Peterschmidt.

Jesse ignored him. "I'm the ranking officer."

"Speak," said Peterschmidt.

"What good conduct are you talking about?" said Jesse.

Peterschmidt and Vandam towered over Jesse. "What's your name, Lieutenant?" Peterschmidt said.

"Lieutenant Jesse Moses, CSA," Jesse said. "We met at Chickamauga."

"This is different from Chickamauga," Peterschmidt said. "You've ruined it by your usual indiscipline."

"What are you talking about?"

"When we found out about your presence here we thought it was a positive development," Peterschmidt said. "We've been hoping for something like this for a long time. But you go too far."

"You started it."

"You did."

From where he sat, Roy could hear them pretty well, but he had trouble following, getting stuck on *when we found out about your presence*. He stopped right there. How did they find out? Someone must have told them, a spy or a traitor. Then Roy remembered: *forces on the move*. Why hadn't he thought of military forces first thing? And like a fool he'd felt those headlights on his back, when all along Ezekiel had been working for the enemy; a spy then, and not a traitor, although Roy felt betrayed.

"It was you," Peterschmidt was saying.

"You," said Jesse.

They glared at each other in the hot sun, patches of sweat spreading in the armpits of their uniforms. Roy thought he could hear the waterfall.

"But now it's over," Peterschmidt said. "And to make sure our campaign ends without any more of this, we'll take one prisoner with us, ensuring your good conduct, prisoner to be released at the conclusion tomorrow night."

"That won't be necessary," Jesse said. "You have my word."

Sonny Junior raised his bloody head. "Fuck you," he said, looking at no one in particular.

"Sergeant Vandam," said Peterschmidt. "Choose a likely prisoner."

Choose me, you son of a bitch. That voice deep inside Roy: it had some plan already.

Vandam walked down the Confederate line, all of them sitting in the sun by the Mountain House, hands tied behind their backs. He looked at Gordo, who tried to meet his gaze but blinked, then Dibrell, who didn't even try; went by Rhett without looking at him; paused at Lee.

"Here's a pretty little reb," Vandam said. He looked more closely, his eyes wandering down the opening at the top of the jacket. The expression on his face changed. He bent down, reached his hand in that opening, explored around. Something in Roy went boiling red; in another part of himself, the temperature was much lower. The cool part recorded the simple fact that Vandam was dead, as of that moment.

"Vandam," said Peterschmidt. "What the hell are you doing?"

"He's got—"

"There'll be no robbery of prisoners."

"But—"

"I gave you an order."

"Sir."

Vandam moved on to Sonny. Roy had one glimpse of Lee's face—distorted by whatever was going on inside—before Vandam blocked his view.

"This here's the one caused most of the trouble," Vandam said, standing over Sonny.

"We don't want him."

"No, sir. But can I clean him up a little?"

"If you're quick about it."

"I'll be quick." Vandam's voice was low and throaty, like a dog getting aroused about something. He took a knife off his belt, got hold of Sonny's long hair, jerked it all back, hacked it off with one stroke.

Sonny made a roaring sound, tried to bull his way up. Roy didn't really see what happened to Sonny after that because he was up too, butting at Vandam like an animal. Then there was blue everywhere and he was back down. Blue turned to red. Roy stared up at Vandam through a red haze.

Vandam was watching him, seemed to watch him for a long time. Roy could see Vandam making the prisoner decision in his eyes, knew he was going to get his way, that he would be the one; a decision Vandam would regret. Vandam gave him a little smile, turned, and said: "We'll take the kid."

"The kid?" Peterschmidt said.

Roy wasn't sure he'd heard right until he noticed everyone looking at Rhett. Rhett's eyes were on only one person, his father. He was trying not to speak, trying to keep something inside, but he couldn't.

"Dad," he said.

Roy strained against the rope, useless.

A mocking voice rose from the Yankees in the shade: "Da-ad." It was the other boy, Vandam's son.

Rhett's head whipped around. The boys' gazes locked on each other. Vandam's son got up, came out of the shade, stopped a few feet from Rhett.

"Da-ad."

"Captain Peterschmidt," Jesse said, "control this boy."

"I take no orders from you," Peterschmidt said.

"Your drummer boy's our prisoner," said Vandam.

Gordo spoke up. "Ever heard of kidnapping?"

Vandam gave Gordo a kick on the sole of his boot, very light. "No one mentioned kidnapping," he said. "We're taking a prisoner, as we got every right to do."

Roy knew he was right; he just wanted it to be him, and Rhett last of all. Gordo hung his head. Vandam gave him another kick, even lighter.

Peterschmidt licked his lips. He glanced at Gordo, then Rhett, motioned for Vandam. They moved away together,

Peterschmidt saying something that made Vandam scowl at first but smile by the time he finished. They came back.

"We'll offer you an alternative, Lieutenant," Peterschmidt said.

"To what?" said Jesse.

"To taking the boy prisoner, taking anyone prisoner," said Peterschmidt. "Instead we'll settle this once and for all, agreeing to abide by the result whatever it is and cease all hostilities after."

"Settle how?" said Jesse.

"In unarmed hand-to-hand combat between champions from each side."

"I'll take any three of you," Sonny Junior said.

"And since there's no point in anyone getting hurt, now that the campaign is nearly over," Peterschmidt said, "we'll elect the drummer boys as champions."

"Out of the question," Jesse said.

"Then you force us back to the prisoner alternative," said Peterschmidt.

"Let the boy fight," Sonny Junior said. "He'll beat him good for us."

"Something like this happened," Peterschmidt said.

Jesse, about to repeat what he'd said, paused. "Spotsylvania Courthouse," he said. "But it wasn't drummer boys."

"Close enough," Peterschmidt said.

Jesse was silent. Roy thought he heard the beating of heavy wings. Jesse turned to him. "What about it?"

There were three possible answers: *no; it's up to Rhett; yes.* Roy said, "Yes."

"Yes?" said Jesse.

"You heard right, rabbi," Sonny said.

"Shut up, Sonny," Roy said.

"I'll deal with you later," Jesse said.

"How?" said Sonny.

Jesse ignored him. "We agree," he said to Peterschmidt.

"And you'll abide by the result, as an officer and a gentleman?"

"Yes."

"Aren't you forgetting something?" Lee said.

Everyone looked puzzled.

"You haven't asked the boy," Lee said.

Rhett stood up. "I'll fight," he said, eyes on Roy.

A Yankee cut the rope binding Rhett's wrists. A strange moment for the memory that came then to Roy: the hospital bracelet around one of those wrists, the day Rhett was born.

They stood in a circle on the plateau, blue with their backs to the sun, gray, hands still bound behind their backs, with the sun in their eyes. The two boys, stripped to the waist, faced each other inside the circle. Roy forgot about his thirst and the pain in his head, was barely aware of the faces, sweating and intense, of the watching soldiers, had eyes only for the two boys. He saw things he didn't like, some of them things he maybe should have seen before: how Vandam's boy was a head taller than his, perhaps an inch or two more than that; how Vandam's boy had a thick neck, thick wrists, muscles under his baby fat; how he might even have been a little older, certainly more developed, with hair under his arms and a few sprigs already showing on his chest. Rhett looked scrawny, as though he'd actually lost weight since moving up north, what with his ribs showing, and those knuckle-shaped bones in his shoulders more prominent than before. Vandam's son's hands were already curled into fists; Rhett's hung stiffly at his sides, shaking slightly. All he had going for him was that wild tuft of hair sticking straight up.

"Get this over with, Griff," Vandam said.

His son nodded and swung his fist, a long, slow, looping punch that Rhett had plenty of time to block or sidestep or lean away from, but he did none of those things, didn't move at all, not even raising one of those shaking hands. The blow caught him flush on the side of the head, made a sound like a fastball smacking into a catcher's mitt.

"Yeah," Vandam said, and so did someone else.

Rhett still didn't move. Vandam's son took a step forward,

upper teeth showing now, and hit Rhett again, same way, same spot. Smack.

"Yeah," Vandam said again, louder now, and there were other voices: "Go get 'im, Griff. Get 'im again."

Griff got him again, a little higher up this time, no way to tell if he was trying to hit the same spot or not. This one, or the cumulative effect, split Rhett's cheek open, but not too bad. Not too bad, Roy told himself; maybe said it out loud, hard to tell with all the other voices rising.

"Yeah."

"Again."

"Get 'im."

"Again."

And Lee looking white, and Jesse looking sick, and Sonny: "Remember what I told you, for fuck sake."

Roy glanced at Sonny. What struck him wasn't so much the blood trickling from Sonny's ear, or his split lip, or the muscles and veins popping up all over the place, but the way his hair being chopped off made the facial resemblance to Roy's father suddenly obvious. He took that for a good thing, that they were practically brothers, all in this together, and therefore Rhett would come through. He had to.

Remember what Sonny told you, for fuck sake. Meant that to be a silent thought, but maybe it got out, and if it did this wasn't like football where the players couldn't hear, because Rhett looked his way, an expression in his eyes that Roy found hard to bear, and while he was looking his way, got popped again, in the mouth this time, bang on.

Rhett staggered.

"Oh, yeah."

"Smack in the fuckin' face."

"You got 'im now."

"Again, again."

Rhett's lip was split now too. He spat, and out came a little white tooth, might have been a baby tooth, Roy thought. It made him mad. He took a step forward and shouted: "Fight, boy. Fight like a son of a bitch."

But Rhett did nothing. Vandam's son, Griff, threw another one of those heavy slow rights, and Rhett just let it hit him, side of the face again, split that split a little wider. Blood poured freely now, and Rhett's legs went wobbly. He fell, almost melted, in the dust, lying at Sonny's feet.

"Atta boy, Griff."

"In the fuckin' face."

Sonny dropped to his knees, leaned over Rhett, spoke to him. Roy couldn't hear much of what he was saying, caught only "sack of shit" and "piss pot," but he saw, everyone saw, what Sonny did next: he licked the blood off the split in Rhett's face. What else could he do, hands tied behind his back?

Rhett got up. He spat out another tooth, this one trailing a pink plume in the dusty air. Then he looked up at the bigger boy and said: "I'm gonna kill you."

"Yeah?" said Griff, and he hit him again, same place, must have been his natural angle or something, opening the split wider than ever. "Yeah?" he said, higher-pitched this time, his mouth in a frozen grin but his eyes savage, and did it one more time.

"Again."

"In the fuckin'—"

Rhett stepped inside and bounced a quick left jab off Griff's nose, every muscle in his little arm showing. Griff leaned back, surprised. Rhett seemed to inflate; everything about him changed, his stance, his bearing, but most of all his eyes, suddenly fearless—and frightening in a way that Griff's, no matter how savage, were not, Rhett's being so much colder. He had the gene.

"You gonna let him do that to you, boy?" said Vandam. "Split his fuckin' face in two."

Griff bent his knees, drew back his fist, grunted, threw another of those looping right hands, this one the heaviest of all. But it didn't land. Rhett ducked, moved in, tilted Griff's face back with another left jab and then did something whether on purpose or not, Roy couldn't tell: with his right fist, Rhett punched Griff on his exposed neck, square on the Adam's apple.

Griff went down writhing, clutched his throat.

"Yeah."

"Got 'im, Rhett, you got 'im."

And Sonny said: "Now finish him off."

Rhett fell on Griff, punching, punching, punching. Red welts popped up all over Griff's face, red blood soaked into blue and gray, Griff cried out something about breathing or not breathing, Roy didn't care. He was just screaming, they all were, all the Irregulars, all the Confederates, screaming over their fighting hero.

Then Peterschmidt, Vandam, other Yankees were in the circle, not a circle now, too crowded, pulling Rhett off, Rhett, still punching as Vandam lifted him in the air. One of his punches caught Vandam in the gut. Vandam made a little oof sound. Then he hit Rhett in the head, very hard. Rhett fell to the ground, lay still.

Roy went wild after that. They all did, blue and gray, both sides kicking, spitting, butting, kneeing, the Yankees using their fists and rifle butts too. Wild: like snakes, bears, hyenas, but more dangerous; and they made wild sounds, wordless but human. One by one the Confederates, hands still tied behind their backs, went down, only Roy and Sonny standing; Lee down, jacket off, hands pawing at her, the noise rising louder and louder, now no longer completely human, beyond endurance, and then a helicopter shot up over the ridge.

Roy didn't even know what it was at first, could make no sense of the writing on its side: *National Weather Service*. The machine threw up a blinding cloud of dust, soared on up the mountain. Roy couldn't see a thing. He felt a glancing blow on the back of his head, not much, but that was all it took.

Adept little fingers were working at his wrists. Roy opened his eyes, saw an apple lying in the grass, a foot or so away. A tiny, perfect red apple; as he watched, an ugly bug crept around from the other side, like a destroyer coming over the horizon.

Lee untied him. Roy got up. The Yankees were gone and so was Rhett.

Lee, all buttoned up now, but the collar not high quite enough to hide the bruise on her neck, said: "They took him anyway."

"Said we cheated," Dibrell said.

They were all—Roy, Sonny, Lee, Jesse, Gordo, Dibrell—beaten and bloody.

"It's my fault, Roy," Gordo said. "Them finding us up here."

"No, it's not," Roy said; what connection could there be between Gordo and Ezekiel?

"It is," Gordo said, starting to cry. Combat fatigue, Roy thought—nothing to be ashamed of. "I told Earl we'd be up here," Gordo said, "asking for the extra time off and all."

"So?" said Roy. "What's Earl got to do with it?"

"Peterschmidt bought a car off him," Gordo said, wiping his eyes. "An LX, with the comfort and convenience package, loaded. Earl must of told him."

Roy didn't quite get it, but he felt those headlights on his back again.

Machine noise came drifting down from the mountaintop.

"Let's go," Jesse said.

Roy shouldered his gun.

TWENTY-NINE

By the time night fell, the Irregulars were safe in Sonny Junior's barn, patching themselves up. Roy had a bad, bad feeling that he wouldn't see his son again. He also had a feeling that he would never return to the Mountain House.

They drank water, not the heavenly water from the creek, but rusty water from the pump in the yard. They ate hardtack, the Slim Jims all gone. The sun set, but left an orange glow on the windowpanes; inside, two or three candles spread golden holes in the murk, not quite reaching the tilted tractor, Sonny's drum kit, the demolition derby car. High up on the walls, ember-colored tints showed here and there on a scythe, a rake, the ball and chain.

Dibrell took off his uniform, torn and bloody, put on jeans and a T-shirt.

"What the hell are you doing?" said Sonny.

"I'm out of here," said Dibrell.

"Say again?" said Roy.

"Can't be here when the cops come," Dibrell said. "You know my situation."

"But not the crime that got you into it," Gordo said; he had purpling rings around both eyes, one puffier than the other.

"All a misunderstanding," said Dibrell, "meaning they could misunderstand again, easy."

"What makes you think the cops are coming?" Lee said.

"The lieutenant says we're gonna call them."

"I said we'd discuss it," Jesse said.

They all looked at Jesse. His face wasn't too bad but his left shoulder seemed to be hanging lower than the right; he hunched forward on a stool, pushing up on his left elbow with his free hand.

"Discuss what?" said Sonny Junior.

"Calling the cops to get Rhett back," Jesse said.

"Are you out of your mind?" Sonny said. He turned on Dibrell. "Put that uniform back on."

Dibrell shook his head, inched toward the big barn doors.

Roy rose. He was all right, seeing just one of whatever there was supposed to be one of, even though everything trembled at the edges. Roy had never been a leader, hadn't really known what it was a leader did. Now he put his hand on Dibrell's biceps. "You can go," he said. "But your uniform stays here."

Dibrell shook himself free, or tried to. "You're out of line, Private."

Roy gave Dibrell's muscle a little squeeze, just to show him what was what. "One or the other," Roy said.

Dibrell looked to Jesse. Jesse said nothing. "That uniform cost me three hundred bucks," Dibrell said.

Roy released Dibrell. "Doesn't make it yours," he said.

Dibrell was a big man, almost Sonny's size. He deflated under Roy's gaze, turned and walked out of the barn, leaving the uniform behind.

"Cops," Sonny Junior said.

"We'll talk about it, that's all," said Jesse.

"No harm in talking," Gordo said. "Don't guess there'd be such a thing as an ice pack around here?"

"What do you mean, no harm in talking?" said Sonny.

Gordo licked his lips a couple times. "How are we supposed to find him by ourselves?"

Sonny frowned, didn't answer.

"Good question," said Jesse.

"Is it?" Roy said.

"I don't get you," said Jesse.

"I think you do, Lieutenant," Roy said.

Lee came over, stood behind him, put her hands on his shoulders. They all saw, but only Gordo raised his eyebrows, meaning Sonny and Jesse knew.

"Go on," Jesse said.

"The Yankees are on a campaign, said so themselves," Roy said. "Only one campaign it can be."

"What's that?" said Jesse.

"The Chickamauga campaign," Roy said. "All we need to know is what happens next."

"After the battle of Chickamauga?" Jesse said.

Roy nodded. That brought a bit of pain, a bit of dizziness, but he was learning big things, and very fast. Learning to lead, that was one. Learning that the battle of Chickamauga was the turning point of his life, 1863 the most important year, those were others. *Been no year like it, before or since.* Who had told him that? Earl? Earl. He glanced at Jesse. Was it possible they'd have been better off under Earl's command?

"Bragg failed to pursue, as you know," said Jesse. "And quite possibly the right decision considering his losses. The Yankees retreated to Chattanooga, ended up taking Lookout Mountain in the Battle Above the Clouds. Sherman used Chattanooga as his base for the march to the sea."

"So Bragg was wrong," Roy said.

"It's more complicated than that," said Jesse.

"Don't know what all this bullshit's about," said Sonny, " 'cept it seems like they got Rhett up on Lookout Mountain. That it, cuz?"

"Yeah," Roy said. "I'm just wondering if the lieutenant was going to tell us, if we hadn't figured it out for ourselves."

"Isn't there a big event going on up there?" Gordo said.

"Just one more reason to bring in the authorities," Jesse said.

"What did you say?" Roy said.

"Because of the reenactment, Lookout Mountain now being a suburb of Chattanooga, for God's sake, we should bring in the police."

"No," Roy said. "That word."

Lee's hand tightened on his shoulder.

"Authorities?" said Jesse.

"Don't like that word," Roy said.

"Fuckin' right," said Sonny.

"So are you in or out?" Roy said.

"That's not a question you can ask the ranking officer," Jesse said.

"Irregulars do things a little different," Roy said. "I'll ask one last time."

Jesse's gaze went from Roy to Sonny, past Gordo, settled on Lee. "What do you think, Corporal?" he said.

Lee looked him in the eye. "Are we men or not?" she said.

Silence. Then Sonny laughed. "The little guy, girl, whatever the hell she is, got more balls than the rest of us put together."

They all started laughing after that. It made them hurt, but they laughed anyway.

"So it's settled then," Roy said.

No one said it wasn't.

The windows went from the orange to black, the scythe, rake, ball and chain high up on the wall lost their ember-colored highlights, vanished from sight, the candles guttered and went out. The Irregulars bedded down for the night: Sonny Junior on the seat of the demolition derby car, Jesse and Gordo on straw behind the drum kit, Roy and Lee on the bare mattress back in the cantilevered section.

They heard Jesse groan, later a higher-pitched sound, almost like a child whimpering in the night, must have been

Gordo, after that Sonny's snoring, and finally silence. Roy whispered in Lee's ear.

"You all right?"

"Don't worry about me."

They weren't touching. Then they were, Lee making the first move. They held each other. Roy didn't want more than that. Lee did. That didn't make him feel any different, not at first. She was starting to do something about that, and Roy could see it all going very shabby, when one of her fingers snagged in the little hole on the left side of his jacket. Everything changed. What if he died in the Battle Above the Clouds, what if he lost Rhett up there too? Those apple trees, blossoming year after year for generations, the water flowing from the spring, almost holy: Roy went deep inside her, as deep as he could, maybe even a bit brutally.

"That was the best," she said after, in a low voice, but not whispering. For some reason he liked that not-whispering part most of all.

They breathed together, softer and softer. Roy listened for the beating of heavy wings, didn't hear them. She could name him, the baby, anything she liked.

Roy opened his eyes. Still night, the night before the battle. Bragg's failure to pursue: they wouldn't make that mistake again. Roy had arrived at his destination on the journey through time, had found the exact moment when he could make things right at last, undo the mistake of Chickamauga. Forces were on the loose, as Ezekiel had said. And not only Ezekiel: Roy suddenly remembered Curtis using that very phrase, after they fired Gordo. Did black people sense those forces first? If so, why?

Roy couldn't get back to sleep. He thought of all the rebels who had lain awake the night before the battle, thought: Help me, father. That didn't mean his biological father, or any sort of supernatural one, but his real father, the hero with many greats before his name, Roy Singleton Hill. Lying on the bare mattress in the cantilevered part of Sonny's barn, Lee's hand limp on his side, Roy remembered the diary page. He felt in his pocket: still there.

Roy got up. He slipped out of the cantilevered section, a shadow as quiet as all the others in the barn. The big doors hung slightly open, framing a narrow column of stars. Roy went outside.

It was cool, almost cold. The sudden temperature drop surprised him; so did the flickering yellow light he took at first for a firefly from the far side of the well. Roy walked around it, found Jesse sitting with his back to the rough stone wellhead, a candle stub burning in the ground. Roy sat beside him.

"Couldn't sleep," Jesse said.

"Shoulder?"

"I'm fine."

"Won't affect your shooting none?" Roy said.

"Not for firing blanks."

Roy smiled. "Was it you took away my bullets?" he said. "I had one in the chamber, a few more in my pouch."

"It was me."

"Why?"

"You're asking why I don't want you firing live rounds?"

"You hadn't done that, we'd have won up there, and I'd still have Rhett."

"Can't be sure."

"We can," Roy said. "I'm deadly."

"I know that, Roy. I'm sorry for that part, about Rhett."

"Don't worry yourself. Things'll be different tomorrow."

"They will?"

"Lee's got bullets—unless you took them too."

"I didn't," Jesse said. "Wasn't aware." He glanced at the barn, a massive shadow in the night, opened his mouth to say more, stopped himself.

"Then we'll be fine," Roy said. "You're a good officer."

"We'll see."

They sat by the well, the night quiet, the sky full of stars.

Roy tried to find the Milky Way, failed. After a while, he took the diary page from his pocket. "What went on at Fort Pillow?"

"Why do you ask?"

Roy pictured Curtis's dark hand on the last page in the diary: *Now theys thinkin twicet bout not surrenderin but we has our orders from Forrest and they was to—* "Just tell me," Roy said.

"It's not so easy," Jesse said. "Forrest took the fort. There were about six hundred Union troops inside, half of them black. It was a slaughter, but so were a lot of battles. There's controversy whether killing continued after the surrender, controversy whether the black soldiers were singled out. The evidence is inconclusive. Does it matter?"

Roy held the paper close to the candle.

kill the last God damn one of em. Was what Forrest says. Theys runnin down the bluff in thur uniforms, throwin down thar guns hands in the air, fallin on thar knees. Too late. We stood em back up and shot em back down. I shot some swimmin away in the rivr too, one at a rainge of for hunnert yard, mebbe more, the nigger in his uniferm. An Zeke I had to shoot Zeke too for desertin in batle.

There was more, but Roy didn't read it. He held the paper over Jesse's candle. It browned, curled, blazed up, burned away. Roy ground the ashes under his heel.

"What's that all about?" Jesse said.

"You were right," Roy said, getting up. "It doesn't matter."

He went back into the barn, lay down beside Lee. He kept telling himself it didn't matter. But it had mattered to someone, maybe some black Hill, mattered enough to pass that casket down the generations. Maybe Ezekiel was right all along: maybe the casket had held the ashes of Roy Singleton Hill. And that line from the bio Jesse had sent him, about his one son. What was the wording? *Who may have died in infancy.* Something like that. Roy wondered where the line between the white Hills and the black Hills was drawn.

"Milky White Way" started up in his mind at last, took him down, his last thought of sons dying in infancy.

THIRTY

Sonny Junior shook him awake just before dawn. The visual world was starting to materialize, but Roy knew who it was just from the strength.

"Got a problem, cuz."

Roy sat up. Sonny stood by the mattress. He had hold of Jesse by his bad arm.

"Caught him down at his car, Roy, going for the phone."

"Can't have you firing real rounds," Jesse said.

"Real rounds, hell," said Sonny. "I'm takin' the AK."

Lee stirred in her sleep. Roy rose. "Let him go," he said. Sonny released Jesse's arm. They went into the main part of the barn, stood near a window. The light was getting stronger now, but Roy couldn't even make out the house; the temperature drop had brought fog, as thick as any Roy had seen.

"Who were you calling, Jesse?" he said.

"Chattanooga police."

"Did you get through?"

Jesse shook his head.

"You lying to me now?"

"Why would I? If anything, I'd lie the other way to stop you."

Roy thought that over. Was it a trick? He wasn't clever enough to know, never would be. It didn't mean he couldn't lead.

Roy called Lee over.

"How many rounds have we got?"

"Three."

"Don't forget the AK," said Sonny. "Plus I got a shitload of other guns, comes to that."

"Corporal," Roy said, "get your weapon and take the lieutenant outside. Keep an eye on him. Sonny and I have to talk."

"Why should I keep an eye on him?" said Lee.

"The lieutenant is going on leave."

Lee took Jesse outside. Roy and Sonny stood by the window. "Gonna have to shoot him, Roy?"

"Where's his phone?"

"Taken care of."

Roy gazed at his cousin. His lip was puffy, but healing already, the blood around his ear all dried up and scaly: he didn't look too bad, even somewhat rested. The chopped-off hair effect was going to take getting used to, the way it made Sonny resemble a huge version of his father. Roy wondered whether his father's eyes had looked like that, red flecks in the blue.

"The AK stays behind," Roy said.

The red flecks seemed to get brighter, like they had some separate connection to a source of power. "You tellin' me what to do now, cuz?"

Sonny seemed to come a little closer, although he might not have moved at all. Behind him, a strange pattern of knots on the barnwood wall came into focus, like a sun with two moons. The sight didn't bring everything back, but enough. It had happened by this window, two little boys rassling, but Sonny bigger and much stronger, holding him down while Roy screamed to get up. There was also something about a corn cob, lost to memory. Didn't matter: he wasn't afraid of Sonny, wasn't afraid of anyone now.

"You'll do what I say or you don't come," Roy said.

Their eyes met. Roy knew how Sonny would go for him, right for the throat, also knew how he would counter, how he'd lay Sonny out. He had no fear at all. At that moment, something came into view from above: a black spider descending on its thread, a delicate black spider, quite small, coming between them. Sonny jumped back with a little cry.

"Jesus Christ," he said. "I can't stand when that happens."

Roy took the spider in his hand, opened the window, let it out. He turned back to Sonny; the red flecks were almost gone.

"There's always the Glock with the pump action—" Sonny began.

"None of it," Roy said. "We got there, Sonny. Now we have to do it right."

"Got where?" said Sonny.

"Where we want to be."

Sonny nodded. "Makes sense. Mighty happy to have a cousin deep as you, Roy. I feel a little bad about taking the farm and all. It wasn't quite as clear-cut as maybe I made it out to be, tellin' you before, the Cheetos and all."

"I couldn't care less," Roy said.

They went outside. Sonny looked around. "Where's Gordo?"

No Gordo. They found his uniform near the drum kit, neatly folded.

"So we shoot the lieutenant and hit the road?" Sonny said.

"Very funny," said Roy.

They left Jesse sitting comfortably in the barn, as comfortable as he could be with his shoulder the way it was and his leg attached to the ball and chain, a spike driven through one of the links deep into the floor. He had a big pail of water in reach and all the hardtack that was left.

"See you tonight," Roy said.

Jesse said nothing, gave Roy a look that Roy told himself had no effect at all.

They hit the road in Sonny's pickup, rolling through a narrow tunnel of fog, seeing almost nothing. Down on the highway to Chattanooga, they did catch a glimpse of two cars coming the other way, Tennessee State Police first, Georgia State Police right behind. A woman's face in the back of the second car seemed familiar to Roy. After a few miles, he realized it was Marcia.

*   *   *

Signs at Lookout Mountain read BATTLE ABOVE THE CLOUDS, pointed blue one way, gray the other, but you had to be close to see them on account of the fog, everything off the road—houses, garages, cars in the driveways—invisible. Soldiers were on the march, hundreds of them, maybe thousands, blue and gray, slipping in and out of the mist as the Irregulars drove up. They parked in a Confederate lot partway up the mountain, finding a space between two tailgate parties. Lee portioned out the ammunition, one round each. Roy loaded his carbine.

They got out of the car. A general with a lot of gold on his hat glanced up from his wicker picnic hamper.

"You guys look great," he said. "Who are you with?"

"We're irregulars," Roy said.

"The Irregulars," said Sonny. "I'm the sergeant."

"I see that," said the general. "Great, just great. You hardcores really show us how it's done. Be honored to have you march with us. We're shaping up over at the Craven House, assault on the summit scheduled for eleven, special NPS dispensation."

"They're on the summit already?" Lee said.

"The Park Service?" said the general.

"The Yankees," said Lee.

"Oh, right, the Yankees. I see where you're coming from. We're doing things a little in reverse, Corporal, a kind of what-if-there'd-been-a-rebel-counterattack scenario."

"Exactly right," said Roy.

"You can say that again," said the general. "With this fog and all—who could ask for more?" It thickened even as he spoke, dissolving the general's image. A cork popped in the mist.

The rebel brigades trod in double file along the path that wound up Lookout Mountain from the Craven House. A huge force, but Roy could see only a few soldiers in front and behind, all the rest hidden in the fog. Perhaps that was why he took no comfort in their numbers, even felt strangely alone.

Roy heard labored breathing all around him, but it was an easy climb for him, ambling along inside a cloud, the carbine almost weightless on his shoulder. Feeling those letters carved into the stock made him impatient, made him want to run up to the summit full speed, which he knew he could have done almost effortlessly, what with how strong he'd become.

A hiker with a fanny pack stepped out from behind a tree, said, "Cheese," and snapped their picture. Lee, marching at Roy's side, turned away.

"Go shoot us some bluebellies, now," said the hiker.

Sonny Junior, just in front, turned for a longer look at her bare legs.

The rebels rounded a switchback bend, climbed a long diagonal, crisscrossing higher up the wooded slope. The fog turned golden all around them, like childhood heaven. Then from up ahead came the crack of a musket, and another.

"Yankee snipers," someone yelled.

Not far up the line, a rebel grunted and fell, rolling to the side of the trail. "I'm hit," he moaned, "I'm hit. Tell my darling wife . . ."

Roy spotted one of the snipers, somehow knew where to find him right away: a green-clad figure on a low tree branch, almost lost in the golden haze. He pointed him out to Sonny. Sonny raised his musket, took aim.

"For God's sake," Roy said, jerking the barrel down.

"Huh?" said Sonny.

"Not now," Roy said.

Sonny nodded, shouldered his weapon.

"You don't want him, I do," said someone behind them. Then came a musket blast, and the sniper cried out, slid carefully down out of the tree, and lay still.

The gray column marched past the dying rebel, beyond the writhing stage now and preparing to meet his maker.

"Croak now and you'll miss all the fun up top," someone told him.

His eyes opened. "Maybe you're right."

"Then I'm not hit either," called the sniper, sitting up in the woods.

More musket fire up ahead now, at first sporadic, then almost steady. The fog grew more golden, the men marched faster and faster, at the double-quick now, although Roy hadn't heard a command, just did what all around him were doing, and suddenly he stepped into sunshine, dazzled above the clouds. Roy could no longer hold himself back, started running in daylight so bright it hurt his eyes. He crested the summit, Sonny on one side, Lee on the other. The Yankees had beaten the shit out of him just yesterday, and look at him now. Rebel yells rose all around. The long roll started playing, didn't stop.

The Union army waited on the battlefield: a strange battlefield, more like a park, with gravel walkways, benches, information plaques, even a tall monument in the center. None of that added up for Roy, but there was no time to figure it out. The Yankees were ready, a vast blue army in perfect order, ranks square, muskets all pointed at the same angle, a single blue machine of countless parts. The rebel army didn't look like that. The men straggled breathlessly up from the trail in twos and threes, glancing around in the sudden glare, distracted by things Roy hadn't seen until he followed their gazes: spectators sitting on bleachers lining the field, photographers in cherry pickers high above, pushcarts selling ice cream, hot dogs, tacos.

Roy saw all that now, but it didn't really penetrate. He found a place in the front line, scanned the Yankee ranks, could easily distinguish individual faces, recognized none.

Help me, father.

The Confederates formed ranks. The musket firing, somewhere down the slope, died out. The drumming ceased. The armies faced each other in silence. Generals rode up and down, waving their splendid hats, the horses' hooves the only sound, an earthly heartbeat. Then Roy heard a voice.

"Massah."

He looked down the line, saw a man, woman, and child approaching. Barefoot, all of them, and in tatters. The man carried a pole over his shoulders, two big tin buckets on either end, heavy enough to bend the pole, bend the man. The woman bore another bucket on her head. The child, not much more than a toddler, held a tin dipper.

"Thirsty, massah?"

They came closer, doling out water every ten yards or so, the man lowering the buckets to the ground, the child handing over the dipper, the man struggling to get the weight back up without spilling after the soldiers had drunk. Roy realized he was thirsty. He reached back for his canteen. Not there. He thought back, remembered last having it in the Mountain House, filled to the brim with water from the creek. Would he never taste that water again? His thirst rose very fast, as though some dam for holding back dryness had burst inside him.

"Water, massah?"

Now they were directly in front of him, the man and woman sweating under their burdens, the child's eyes wide with fear.

Afraid of me? I wouldn't hurt you.

The man's gaze met Roy's. "Water, massah? For your thirst?"

The torn clothes, the meekness, the weariness, the abjection: Roy almost didn't recognize him. It was Curtis. Roy shook his head, even violently. Curtis's eyelid fluttered. They both looked away. The slaves moved on.

A gun boomed, off to Roy's left. The generals—there were four in gray, and a few more than that on the other side—raised their swords.

"Ready."

"What's the scenario?" said someone in the ranks. "I got stuck in traffic."

Sonny Junior glanced at Roy. "What the fuck kind of army is this?"

"Language, please," said someone else. "This is a family event."

"Aim."

The generals brought down their swords, not quite in unison, but each with a nice flourish. The front rows fired. Some shouted command was lost in the deafening crash. The two armies started marching on each other, reloading, firing, reloading, and firing again. The Irregulars held their guns in the aim position, advancing with the others but not shooting. Some men fell around them, died spectacularly; others were immortal. Smoke hung in the still air, grew thicker and thicker. The smell went right to Roy's brain, the drug for him.

A wave of rebels flowed in from Roy's right, some maneuver he didn't understand. It drove him to the left, toward the cannon that had fired to start the battle, a cannon now surrounded by Yankees. Beyond it, Roy could see the green H flag flying over the infirmary tents. Between the tents, he glimpsed a tall figure, a very tall figure, dressed in a black frock coat and wearing a stovepipe hat. The tall figure was leaning down and possibly speaking to a much smaller figure standing before him. This small figure wore gray.

Roy broke ranks and ran, tried to run, toward that small figure, but his way was blocked by a column of his own men marching across his path. Roy pushed through them, elbowing, maybe knocking one or two of them down. Someone swore at him. A musket went off near his ear. A red-faced sergeant with a shaving cut on his chin appeared, screamed at him, the cords standing out on his neck, but Roy didn't hear a word, not even a sound from his mouth. He shoved the sergeant aside, kept going.

The Yankees around the cannon saw him coming, raised their muskets, fired a volley. Roy charged. A Yankee officer pointed a pistol at him, fired.

"Hey, hero, you're dead."

Roy ran on. More Yankees came up, took aim.

"Cease fire. He's inside the limit."

Roy went past them.

"You're the kind that ruins it for all the others."

Past the cannon, Lee suddenly beside him now, and Sonny pulling ahead, his face savage; bowling through a slow-motion mob of blue and gray in gentle hand-to-hand combat; into a cloud of musket fire and out; past the infirmary tents; and there on a promontory stood a sort of stockade, little more than knee high. Yankees were herding Confederates inside, unarmed rebels with their hands held high. The tall man in the stovepipe hat spoke to the prisoners, offered his hand to each one. He turned to say something to the people sitting on lawn chairs just outside the stockade, and there, right behind him, was Rhett. Rhett saw Roy coming, ran to the fence, a fence he could easily leap but did not.

"Help me, Dad." He was just a little boy.

Vandam stepped out of a mass of blue uniforms, grabbed Rhett, pulled him back, yelled something to his men. The Irregulars kept coming, sprinting now. Peterschmidt and the rest of his squad stepped over the fence, raised their muskets, aimed, fired. Noise and a big puff of smoke, of course, but nothing happened—except what was that? A bloody chunk, torn from Sonny's shoulder? And where was Lee? No longer at Roy's side, but lying on the ground, a red stain spreading down one leg of her butternut trousers.

"These guys are good."

"How do they do that, the blood part?"

Roy's little boy, and Roy had put him where he was. The gene took over. Roy was almost unaware of what happened next, of slowing down, not quite stopping, but slowing down enough to hold the carbine steady, see Peterschmidt hyper-clear in the V, even notice a small mole on his upper lip, and then squeeze the trigger.

The wonderful gun bucked against his shoulder. A red hole appeared in Peterschmidt's forehead. Peterschmidt's eyes went blank, just like that. His men gazed at him as he fell, then dropped their weapons as one, turned, and ran.

Applause.

Roy crashed through the fence, Sonny right behind him,

making a wild growling noise in his throat. The whole stockade came down. Vandam was backing out the other side, onto the promontory. He held Rhett with one hand, had a pistol in the other. Vandam's son, drum around his neck, said, "Don't hurt me."

The man in the stovepipe hat stepped in their way.

"Maybe you guys should tone it down a little. You're scaring the kids."

Sonny looked up at him, blinked a couple of times. Then understanding dawned on his face. He raised his musket, aimed point-blank at the man in the stovepipe hat.

"What are you doing?" Roy said.

"Gonna win it this time, cuz," said Sonny.

Roy knocked the musket aside just as it went off. The explosion almost smothered the sound of Vandam's pistol, so that at first Roy thought Sonny fell for no reason. But then he saw that Sonny had a red hole in his forehead too.

Roy dropped his empty weapon, went for Vandam. Vandam aimed the pistol at him, but Roy knew there hadn't been time to reload. Vandam pulled the trigger anyway, and the pistol surprised Roy by going off. Pistol, not a rifle: of course, they had six-shooters, he knew that. Knew it for sure because of the sharp pain in his chest.

Roy dove at Vandam as he fired again, the bullet passing so close to Roy that he felt its tiny breeze on his cheek. Roy, Vandam, Rhett, fell together, rolling on the hard rock of the promontory. Roy got hold of Vandam's arm, the one he had around Rhett, bent it back and back until Vandam cried out and let the boy go.

Roy and Vandam kept rolling, locked together, each with a hand on the pistol jammed between them, trying to pull it free. Roy hung on, but Vandam was powerful and Roy's great strength was suddenly gone. With one last twist, Vandam wrenched the pistol out of Roy's grasp. Roy didn't even have enough left to hold on to him, to keep him too close to point the gun. Vandam rolled free, started to rise, the pistol coming up. Started to rise, but one of his feet was already over the edge of the promontory, and Vandam stepped down on air. He tipped and fell backward off Lookout Mountain; falling, falling, turning gold, then vanishing in the cloud.

Roy sat up, tried to. He put his hand to his chest. Blood was coming through the hole in his jacket, the hole he'd inherited. Blood, but not pouring, or even flowing, more like seeping.

"Water, Roy?"

Roy looked up, saw Curtis in his rags, holding out the tin dipper.

Roy drank. "Thank you."

Curtis nodded.

Roy stood up. Curtis helped him off with his jacket, the two of them moving as one. Roy dropped the jacket over the edge. It disappeared too, in that golden mist.

Roy gathered Rhett to him, held him close.

"Honest Abe thought I was pretending," Rhett said. "He gave me some candy."

Roy patted his back. The muscles along Rhett's spine relaxed. Roy felt another one of those moments of perfect peace, but this one was in the now.

In the now came flashing lights and police cars, one after another. Uniformed men of the present age, with automatic weapons and flak jackets, ran onto the promontory, Marcia and Jesse, his arm in a sling, in their midst.

"I fought good up at the Mountain House, didn't I, Dad?" Rhett said, his mouth against Roy's chest, the question vibrating through Roy's body.

Roy looked down, saw his own blood, just a little of it, reddening that tuft of hair. "You fought good and I'm proud of you," he said. "Everything's going to be fine."

THIRTY-ONE

Maybe Roy had no business making that last remark, but for once he got lucky.

First, it was pure luck that he didn't die before he even had a chance to utter it. For some reason, perhaps Roy turning at the last moment, the bullet entered his chest at a sharp angle, shattering a rib, the pieces of which had to come out, but failing to reach anything vital. He spent a week in the hospital.

Then he was lucky he didn't go to jail. The Sons of the Confederacy raised enough money to hire the best lawyers, but Roy turned them down, went with a public defender. In the end, prosecutors in two states couldn't see their way past the kidnapping and self-defense issues. No bullet was ever found up at the National Weather Service station, and its destruction was put down to a lightning strike. Roy pleaded guilty to one count of disturbing the peace, a misdemeanor, and paid a $250 fine, money he didn't have at the time; the bank had already taken the blackened remains of his house in Atlanta. Lee, not long out of the hospital, lent him the money.

Dibrell served three months for a parole violation, specifically for leaving the state without the permission of his officer. His original conviction had been for shoplifting, although how that related to his fear of DNA evidence wasn't clear. Roy found all that out in an awkward phone conversation with Gordo, their last.

The investigation of the weather station fire did uncover

Ezekiel's marijuana patch, which was razed to the ground. Ezekiel got fifteen years.

Sonny Junior left no will. As his closest living relative, Roy inherited the old farm with that cantilevered barn of the kind still found in east Tennessee. He sold it to a New York publishing executive and her husband who were getting into fly-fishing. Roy used what remained after paying off the mortgage to hire a good lawyer for Ezekiel's appeal. Partly because he didn't like the contrast between fifteen years for marijuana cultivation and a $250 fine for killing two men. But mostly because he and Ezekiel were family, and family was what mattered: Sonny Junior had been right about that.

Globax spun off several small divisions, as Curtis had foretold. Curtis became CEO of one of them, a small company with an office in New Jersey and a patent for a device Roy didn't understand, but would be shipped by the millions if everything went right. Curtis offered Roy a job as head of shipping, paying more than twice what Roy had ever earned. It meant moving to New Jersey.

Roy took Lee on long walks to help with her rehab. On hot days, she wore a dress. They didn't talk much, perhaps didn't have a whole lot to say. Once they came upon a Confederate graveyard. Little battle flags flew here and there; Roy didn't feel a thing.

"I'm not pregnant," Lee told him.

Roy didn't say anything, didn't know where this was going.

"I actually can't get pregnant, Roy, meaning it's not possible." They were holding hands. She let go. "Are you going to take that job?"

"I want you to come with me," Roy said.

"To New Jersey?"

"We don't have to live in New Jersey. New York and Connecticut are close by."

"I'll think about it."

Roy ended up going alone. Marcia had seen to it that Roy lost all but supervised visitation rights. That was good enough for now. On the very first one, Marcia happened to mention how good Roy looked. The supervision part began to drop away in practice.

In the fall, Rhett signed up for Pop Warner and Roy volunteered as an assistant coach. Rhett was growing now, getting bigger and stronger. He played without fear, with no regard for his body, led the team in tackles and made the all-stars.

After the games, they always went to a barbecue place Roy had found. The head cheerleader started coming along, Roy surprised at first that Rhett didn't discourage her, which just showed that he still had a long way to go when it came to understanding things quick. She thought Rhett's little tuft of hair was dorky. It was gone the next time Roy saw him.

Lee came for a visit, stayed three extra days. "I need to get used to you," she said.

"What do you mean?"

"You. This present you."

"It's the only one," Roy said.

She booked another visit for Thanksgiving. By that time, Roy had already gotten his first raise. It was a good company, with a friendly atmosphere, flexible hours, and a generous health plan. Roy's inhalers were free.

*Please turn the page for a sneak preview of
the newest thriller by Peter Abrahams:*

THE TUTOR

Coming in hardcover in July 2002 from
The Ballantine Publishing Group.

ONE

Linda Marx Gardner awoke from a dream and felt her husband's erection against her hip. Not nudging it, not demanding; just there. Earlier in her marriage, or maybe more accurately very early, on predawn mornings like this, the bedroom dim and shadowy, Linda would have taken hold of Scott and started something. Those predawn somethings, their bodies still loose and heavy with sleep, would usually turn out pretty good, sometimes better than that.

Linda got out of bed. In her dream she'd been frantically erasing words from sheets of pink paper, but the words themselves were all forgotten. As she went into the bathroom, Scott made a little sound in his sleep, one of those soft grunts that indicate agreement. She had a funny thought, not like her at all: was he erasing something too?

Then she was in the shower, her appointment book opening up in her mind, time blocks dense with her neat writing. There was going to be an overrun on the Skyway account, most of it from the photography screw-up, but not all. Linda tried to figure out where the rest of it came from, letting go of everything but work so completely that she jumped as she caught sight of Scott through the steamy glass, his naked back to her as he stood before the toilet.

She called to him: "Can you wake Brandon?"

Scott said something she didn't catch because of the shower's noise, almost a roar—when they'd renovated instead of moving up from West Mill to Old Mill, they'd used nothing but the best, in this case the 10-Jet Tower from Kohler's Body

Spa collection—and when she looked again he wasn't there. The water, hot and pounding, felt so good she could have stayed there all day. Linda turned off the shower at once.

She got out, reaching for a towel with one hand, flushing the toilet with the other. Scott always forgot, or didn't bother, or something. Her watch, on the granite sink top—black granite streaked with midnight blue, the nicest feature in the whole house—told her she was running two or three minutes late, nothing to be all tense about. She took a deep breath.

"Bran? Bran? Bran? Bran?"

Over and over. The word penetrated Brandon's dreams, twisted them out of shape, finally woke him.

"Brandon? You awake, buddy? It's late."

Brandon came awake enough to know he had the covers pulled way up, know that he was totally warm, totally fuzzy, totally unable to get up or maybe even move at all. He got one eye open, not much, just enough to peer at his father through gummy lashes. His father: towel wrapped around his waist, shaving cream on his face, razor dripping in his hand.

"I'm really not—"

"Forget it, Brandon. You're going to school."

"I feel like shit."

"You're going. And watch your language."

Brandon didn't say anything.

"Show a little life. Sit up or something. Don't make me come back here."

"All right, all right," Brandon said, but the only thing moving was that one eyelid, closing back down.

"And this room is really getting out of hand."

Brandon, almost asleep, barely caught that last bit. The inner fuzziness repaired itself quickly, knitting up the little hole poked through by his father and then some.

A cut-glass prism dangled in the window of the bedroom across the hall from Brandon, a window that always caught the first light. As Brandon sank back into deep sleep, the sun blinked up through the bare tree limbs out back, sending a ray through the prism. A tiny rainbow instantly printed itself on the calendar hanging on the opposite wall, and not only that, but precisely on a special square, the one with the birthday cake drawn inside, eleven flame-tipped candles burning on top. That rainbow, quivering slightly on her upcoming birthday, was the first thing Ruby saw when she opened her eyes.

She held her breath. This was proof of God's existence. That was her first thought. She'd barely begun to deal with it, and its backpack—that's how some thoughts were, they carried backpacks—that God took a personal interest in her, Aruba Nicole Marx Gardner, before her mind got going with the facts: sun, east window, prism, a rainbow that had to land somewhere, coincidence. That was the way Sherlock Holmes would see it, and she respected Sherlock Holmes more than anyone on earth. Didn't love him—Dr. Watson was the lovable one—but respected him.

Still, coincidence could be tricky. Take that time she'd been eating a baloney sandwich and reading a story about a frog, she must have been four, when she'd suddenly puked all over the place, including on Brandon beside her in the backseat, frog and baloney getting all mixed up in some way. That was how she saw it, and hadn't touched baloney since. But she could hear Sherlock Holmes: "A long car trip and a winding road? One could produce the same result with peanut butter and a penguin." Elementary, my dear Ruby.

The rainbow moved on, sliding off her birthday, off the calendar, ballooning along the wall, warping around the corner of her open closet, vanishing in the shadows within. The spinning earth did that, stuck the rainbow in her closet. There would be lots of backpacks to that thought, but Ruby didn't get to them. Some commotion kicked up down the hall, only the sharp notes getting though her door, like when one earphone conks out.

"Scott? Didn't I ask you to get Brandon up?"

Muffle, muffle.

"Well he isn't, as usual, and it's five after seven. Brandon, get up now."

Muffle.

Then came sounds of movement, and Bran yelled, "Fuck. Don't fuckin' do that," in that deep new voice of his, ragged at the edges, that vibrated the walls, and Ruby knew that Mom had ripped the covers off him, which always worked.

The sounds that followed—Bran getting up, banging around in his room, crossing the hall to the bathroom they shared, turning on the shower—faded as Ruby took *The Complete Sherlock Holmes* off her bedside table and found her place: "The Speckled Band." Just from the title, she knew she was going to like it.

Speckled. A word she'd never spoken. She tried it out loud for the first time. "Speckled. Speckled." Her stuffed animals watched in silence from their perches on bookshelves. A strange word, with a kind of power, if that made sense, and maybe not power completely for the good. *Freckled* was on the good side, *heckled* a bit nasty, *speckled* different in some way she didn't know. The garage door opened under her room and her dad's old Triumph rumbled out, sounds that were far, far away.

> *I had no keener pleasure than in following Holmes in his professional investigations, and in admiring the rapid deductions, as swift as intuitions, and yet always founded on a logical basis, with which he unravelled the problems which were submitted to him.*

Yes, that was it, what was so special about him. As Ruby read, her room went still, began to lose its physical properties, became less solid. The bachelor lodgings at 221-B Baker Street went the other way. Ruby could almost hear the crackle of the fire Mrs. Hudson had had the good sense to light, could almost—

"Ruby! Ruby! Ruby, for God's sake!"

"What?"

"I called you six times." Mom, probably dressed for work, probably standing at the top of the stairs, that impatient look on her face, when the up-and-down line between her eyebrows appeared. "Are you up?"

"Yeah."

"Don't forget tennis after school, sweetheart." Just from the change of tone, Ruby knew the up-and-down line had smoothed itself out. "See you tonight." Mom's voice trailed away as she went down the stairs.

"Bye, Mom."

Maybe not loud enough, because there was no reply. Then Mom was backing out of the garage, lurching just a bit as usual, tires squeaking on the cement floor. The garage door closed—a long whine ending in a thump—and the sound of the Jeep Grand Cherokee, smoother than the Triumph and much less interesting, faded and faded to nothing. Sherlock Holmes deduced from seven spatters of mud that the terrified young lady in his sitting room had had a rough ride in a dogcart. A car honked on the street—Brandon's ride. The terrified young lady was going mad from fear.

Linda was dictating a memo about the Skyway account into her digital organizer when her cell rang. Deborah, her sister-in-law, married to Scott's brother, Tom—Linda always caught her breath for a moment when Deborah called. She was excited about something. Linda could hear it just in the way she said, "Hi."

"Hi."

"Are you at work yet?"

"Stuck in traffic."

"Me too." Pause, but not a long one. "Did you get Brandon's results?"

"What results?"

"The SAT."

"I thought they weren't coming till next week."

"That's if you wait for the mail," Deborah said. "There's a

number to call as of seven this morning. You just need a credit card and patience—it took me twenty minutes to get through."

Linda's dashboard clock read 7:32.

"So you got Sam's results?" she said. Sam, Brandon's first cousin, same age.

"Fifteen forty." The volume of Deborah's voice went way up, almost an explosion, like some spike caused by a change in atmospheric conditions. Linda held the phone away from her ear.

"Is that good?"

"Have you forgotten? It's out of sixteen hundred, Linda. Sam's in the ninety-ninth percentile."

Somehow she had forgotten; now it all came back. "That's great," Linda said, stop-and-go on the exit ramp. The homeless guy who worked this spot stared through her window, rattling his Dunkin' Donuts cup. It all came back, including her own score, and she added, "Wow."

"Thanks," said Deborah. "We kind of expected something good because of his PSAT—they track pretty closely—but still. Some kids do get sixteen hundred, of course, but we probably won't have him retake it. With his tennis and community ser—" She stopped herself. "Anyway, here's the number. Good luck."

Linda tried the number. Busy, and it stayed busy until she was about to enter the parking garage under the building, a cellular dead zone. That was when she got through. Linda pulled over to the side, her foot on the brake, the car in gear. Someone honked. Linda followed the automated menu on the other end, her heart suddenly racing. She needed Brandon's social security number, which she had in her organizer, and a Visa or MasterCard number and expiration date, which she had in her head. It cost thirteen dollars. There was a pause, a long one, during which she found she'd actually broken into a sweat, and then the digital voice uttered Brandon's numbers: "Verbal—five hundred ten. Math—five hundred eighty."

Linda clicked off and, as soon as she had done so, began to

doubt she'd heard right. Five hundred ten? Five hundred eighty? That would be what—1090 on the SAT? Impossible. Brandon was a good student, almost always got A's and B's. Those digital voices were sometimes hard to understand— they tended not to emphasize the syllables a normal human being would. Maybe it had been 610 and 680. That would be 1290, the exact score she'd had years before. She didn't think of herself as smarter than Brandon. It must have been 1290.

Linda tried the number again. Busy. The clock now read eight on the button. She was going to be late. No one up there cared about five minutes or even ten, but Linda had never been late, not in the three years she'd been on the job. She let up on the brake, eased the car back into the long-term check-in lane, hit redial. And connected. As she entered the garage, she went through the social security and credit card routine again, paying another thirteen dollars, waited for the long pause. While what? While some computer matched the social security number with the credit card number and activated a voice program. How long could it take? She stuck her parking card in the slot, jammed it in, really, and went through the raised gate as the digital voice said: "Verbal—"

And lost contact, now in the dead zone.

On the elevator, Linda tried once more. The building was seven stories, her office on six. Linda got through to the PSAT number as she passed three, repeated the social security and credit card numbers as she was getting out, paying thirteen dollars yet again, listened to the long pause as she walked down the corridor. She opened the office door and saw to her surprise that everyone was gathered around the conference table for a meeting. They all turned to look at her. The digital voice spoke once more: "Five hundred ten. Five hundred eighty." This time she caught the percentile too: "Seventy-fifth."

Brandon got into Dewey's car.

"Hey."

"How's it goin'?"

"I feel like shit."

"Tell me about it."

Dewey, the first of Brandon's friends to get his license, had a joint going, which sometimes happened on the ride home but never in the morning. He passed it to Brandon. Brandon didn't want to go to school fucked up, didn't want to go to school at all, but shit. He didn't take it any further than that, just hit off the joint, passed it back.

"Could use some gas money," Dewey said.

Brandon handed Dewey three ones.

"Am I driving a lawnmower and I don't know it?"

Brandon handed over two more, noticing that the fuel gauge read full. But so what? Dewey pulled away from the curb, squealing the tires just a bit. He switched on a CD, some rap about "fuck you, good as new, all we do, then it's through" that Brandon hadn't heard before. Not too bad.

"School sucks," Dewey said.

"Yeah."

"I'm thinking about dropping out."

"You mean before senior year?"

"I mean like now."

"But what about baseball?" Dewey had been captain of the freshman team and had started a few games for the varsity last spring.

"I'm not going to be eligible anyway," Dewey said. "I'm flunking two courses."

"Still time to get them up."

Dewey took a big hit off the joint, breathed out slow. "Right," he said.

Fuck you, good as new, all we do, then it's through.

Not too bad? It was great.

"Who's this?"

"You don't know who this is? Unka Death."

At that moment, Brandon remembered he had an English test third period, counting for 20 percent of the term grade. *Macbeth.* Hadn't studied for it, had fallen asleep after the first few lines, some weird shit with witches that was meant to be symbolic or ironic or some other term he'd have to define, probably getting points taken off even though he knew damned well what they meant.

"Got an idea," Dewey said. "Let's go to the city."

"What city?"

"New York, for fuck sake. I know this bar in the Village where they don't card anybody."

Almost two hours away. Brandon had been to New York maybe a dozen times, but always with his family. "I've only got, like, ten bucks on me."

"It's cool. I've got a credit card."

"You do?"

"On my mom's account. For emergencies."

Dewey started to laugh. Then Brandon was laughing too. Emergencies: he got it. They drove right past the school. Buses were pulling in and the student lot was filling up. Brandon saw people he knew. Dewey beeped the horn. Brandon thought, *Aw shit,* as they went by. Dewey passed him the joint.

"All yours," he said, ramping up the volume on Unka Death.

The house was quiet. Ruby loved having it to herself. The terrified lady told Holmes: *You may advise me how to walk amid the dangers which encompass me.* Ruby checked the time, stuck in a bookmark, the one with Dilbert's boss—it had finally hit her that the boss's pointy hair was meant to make you think of the devil, she was so slow sometimes—and got up. Out the window, she saw a cardinal at the feeder, poking its red head inside. It suddenly turned toward her window, then rose and shot off into the town forest behind the house.

Ruby brushed her teeth with the Sonicare toothbrush until the inside of her mouth tingled, then smiled into the mirror. Not a real smile with the eyes joining in; this was just an examination of teeth. Dr. Gottlieb said she was going to need braces. How crooked were her teeth anyway? She studied them from several angles. Some days they looked pretty straight. Today she saw a complete jumble.

Brandon hadn't flushed the toilet, also hadn't aimed very well. Careful where she put her feet, Ruby flushed it for him and got in the shower.

She chose the Aussie extra-gentle shampoo with the kangaroo on the front because she liked the combination of shampoo and kangaroo, Helene Curtis Salon Selectives conditioner because it said *completely drenched*, whatever that meant, and Fa body wash because it smelled like kiwi. Clean, dry, smelling great, she wrapped her hair in a towel and got dressed—khakis from the Gap, a long-sleeved T-shirt with a silver star on the front, black clogs with thick soles to make her taller—and went down to the kitchen. Zippy awoke at once, sprang up from under the table, bounded toward her, tail wagging.

"Down, Zippy."

But of course he wouldn't go down, did just the opposite, raising himself higher, resting his front paws on her shoulders.

"Down."

He poked his muzzle in her face, gave her a big wet lick on the nose.

"Up," she said, just as an experiment. Zippy dropped to all fours at once, snagging her T-shirt as he did. Two of the little arms of the silver star now hung loose.

"Zippy. Bad boy."

He wagged his tail.

His water bowl was empty. Ruby filled it. He ignored the bowl, but as soon as her back was turned she heard him slurping noisily.

Ruby made her breakfast—scrambled eggs, toast, and orange juice. No milk; she only drank milk when forced. Next to her bedroom, the kitchen was her favorite room in the house, the copper pots on the wall, the fruit bowl, now empty but sometimes full of all kinds of fruit, the wooden spoons, the spice rack, the big fridge humming in the corner—she needed both hands to open the door—the walls a lovely light yellow, perfect for the eating of eggs.

Ruby's seat at the table was in the actual sticking-out part of the breakfast nook, with windows on three sides. She ate her yellow eggs in a pool of yellow sunlight, leafing through *The All-American Girls Book of Braiding*, trying to think of the right name for those star arms, totally content.

Maybe her teeth weren't so great, but her hair, that was another story. Thick, glossy brown, full of all kinds of tints—it had a personality of its own. Ruby chose the Thumbelina Braid because the look reminded her of Dilbert's boss. She made two high pigtails, divided each into three strands, braided the strands, coiled them into buns, stuck them in place with bobby pins.

"How do I look, Zippy?"

He poked his head over the tabletop and snatched her last piece of toast, the one with the butter melted in perfectly.

"Zippy!"

He growled at her. She gave him the cold look. Zippy made himself smaller and slunk away, like the coward he was.

Ruby put on her blue jacket with the yellow trim and walked him out back and into the town forest, taking the short-cut to the pond. The banks of the pond were muddy. She let him off the leash.

"Run, Zippy. Make spatters."

He lifted his leg and peed on a tree.

Were dog spatters different from horse spatters, or was the important difference the one between a dogcart and a horse cart, which would probably stand higher?

"Run, Zippy."

He didn't want to run. She tossed him a stick, which he gazed at. She tossed another one into the pond. It disappeared without a splash, which was kind of strange.

"Go get it, Zippy."

But he wouldn't. She didn't blame him. The water, a blue so pale it was almost white, looked cold. She took him home. He lifted his leg at least a dozen times.

"Poo, Zippy, poo." He finally did, maybe stepping in it just a little.

Ruby loaded the dishwasher, her own dishes and the ones already in the sink, slung on her backpack and left by the front door, making sure it was locked. The school bus pulled up. She got on.

"Hi, beautiful," said the driver.

"Hi, Mr. V."

There was only one seat left, beside Winston. He was picking his nose.

"Don't eat it, Winston," she said.

But he did.

The bus rolled away. All of a sudden and for no reason, she remembered her book of Bible stories, sent by Gram to make up for the fact that Mom and Dad didn't go to church. Specifically, she remembered the story of Lot's wife, who wasn't supposed to look back. She had the strong feeling that it was very important not to look back right now. But she couldn't stop herself. The urge grew and grew in the muscles of her neck. Ruby looked back.

Nothing happened, of course. She didn't turn into a pillar of salt, and the house wasn't going up in flames. It stayed just the way it always was, not the biggest or fanciest house on the block, but square and solid, white with black shutters, the only color the red brick chimney, maybe a little too . . . what was the word? *Imposing;* too imposing for the rest of the house. She'd overheard her aunt Deborah say that the Thanksgiving before last.

Winston tore a Snickers in two. "Want some?" he said.

Ruby gave him a close look to see if this was some kind of joke. But no, he'd made no connection between the nose picking and his dirty fingernails on the candy bar. He was just sharing.

"Maybe Amanda wants some," Ruby said.

Amanda leaned over, with her goddamn pierced ears—Ruby had to wait another year. "Maybe Amanda wants some what?" Amanda said.

And what was that? She was wearing lipstick?

"Snickers," Ruby said, all of a sudden feeling the power

of those devilish horns on her head. "You like Snickers, don't you?"

"Oh, my favorite," said Amanda.

Winston handed her the thing. Ruby watched till she'd popped it in her mouth.

"Mmmm," said Amanda.

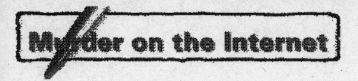

Murder on the Internet

Subscribe to the
MURDER ON THE INTERNET
e-newsletter—and receive all these
fabulous online features directly in
your e-mail inbox:

☠Previews of upcoming books for the
next four months

☠In-depth interviews with mystery authors
and publishing insiders

☠Calendars of signings and readings for
Ballantine mystery authors

☠Profiles of mystery authors

☠Mystery quizzes and contests

Two easy ways to subscribe to:
Go to **www.ballantinebooks.com/mystery**
or send a blank e-mail to
join-mystery@list.randomhouse.com.

Murder on the Internet—
the mystery e-newsletter brought to you
by Ballantine Books